A CORNISH INHERITANCE

Helen Fox and her bon viveur husband Harry are the toast of the Bristol set, in the years immediately following the Great War; popular, successful, and blessed with three charming, though wilful, children. Harry's family own Fox Bay, a hotel and private beach on the South Devon coast. Harry and Helen often bring large groups of friends down to stay, and their reputation for entertaining becomes legendary. But in 1920 their world is shattered. Following a disastrous investment in a shipping company, an investment suggested by his best friend, and unable to regain his lost wealth and social standing, Harry falls into a decline which soon spells tragedy and financial ruin for his family. Their future, and that of the family hotel, is set to become extremely complicated.

A CORNISH INHERITANCE

Helen Fox and her bon vivant husband Harry are the toast of the Bristol set, in the years immediately following the Great War: popular, successful, and blessed with three charming, though wilful, children. Harry's family own Fox Bay, a hotel and private beach on the South Devon coast. Harry and Helen often bring large groups of friends down to stay, and their reputation for entertaining becomes legendary. But in 1920 their world is shattered. Following a disastrous investment in a shipping company, an investment suggested by his best friend, and unable to regain his lost wealth and social standing, Harry falls into a decline which soon spells tragedy, and financial ruin for his family. Their future, and that of the family hotel, is set to become extremely complicated.

TERRI NIXON

---◆---

A CORNISH INHERITANCE

Complete and Unabridged

MAGNA
Leicester

First published in Great Britain in 2019 by
Piatkus
an imprint of Little, Brown Book Group
London

First Ulverscroft Edition
published 2021
by arrangement with
Little, Brown Book Group
London

*A catalogue record for this book is available
from the British Library.*

ISBN 978–0–7505–4882–3

This book is dedicated to my great-niece, Nala Rae Lang, born at just 29 weeks earlier this year. A true little fighter already, destined to take on the world and win!

Vulpes latebram suam defendit
(the fox defends his lair)

Fox Family Motto

PART ONE

1

Bristol
March 1920

The noise, the smells, the crowd . . . it was Harry's world, not hers. Engines revved and coughed, oil and smoke drifted through the air, and Helen peered through the crowd of racers at the trackside, trying to find him. But almost all of them had obscured half their faces with helmets and goggles, and just when she began to think he wasn't racing after all, and relief was creeping through her, she saw him wheeling his motorcycle out onto the track. If he hadn't raised a hand in greeting, she'd never have known him; it was an eerie feeling not to immediately recognise your own husband.

'I expect he's glad you came to one of these at last.' Jeanette Duval had appeared, unnoticed, at her shoulder. 'Adam likes it when I'm here, likes to have someone to coo and squeal over him when he comes back in.'

'I'm not really the cooing and squealing type,' Helen pointed out, her eyes still following the riders as they manoeuvred their motorcycles to the start line.

'Oh, you'll turn into one. They're so heroic.'

'They're idiots.'

'What's bitten you today?'

Helen tore her gaze away and looked down at Jeanette, glowing and over-excited in the chilly

3

spring air, and almost told her. But just because Adam was Harry's best friend, it did not follow that his fiancée must be hers, and in any case, it was too late to say anything now; there was too much noise. Instead she watched, her heart in her mouth, as the last riders to arrive kicked life into the monsters beneath them, and let their engines warm up.

For a moment the air was thick with the rising roar and an almost unbearable tension, then the flag dropped, and they took off, fighting to get ahead of one another and slide into a better position. Helen's skin seemed to shrink on her bones as she watched them, and she wished she'd remained in blissful ignorance, waiting at home with the children and not listening to the horror stories people were so happy to share. A single magpie swooped by, and Helen automatically saluted it. *Good afternoon, Mr Magpie, hope your wife is doing well . . .*

There were cheers from the crowd as individual favourites edged ahead, and Helen picked out Harry quite easily at first, by the Fox family emblem on the petrol tank. If she stared very hard she could keep up with where he sat in the race, but it made her eyes hurt and she soon gave up. Jeanette knew exactly where Adam was, however, and kept up a running commentary; Helen heard it only as a hum among the rest of the crowd and the noise of the motorcycles.

Gradually the worry began to subside, and she let her mind wander, but it never strayed from the man on the track, the man who was life and breath to her even now. Harry Fox, her first and deepest love; adoring and adored father of her three children; liar.

Even as the word flitted through her mind a gasp went up from the crowd, and then a cry, and as Helen dragged her eyes across the field she saw a rider fighting to keep his machine from spinning off into the barriers. Her breath caught, but the rider eventually won and, with wheels sliding and his booted foot pushing hard at the ground, he righted himself and re-joined the pack. There was no emblem on that tank, but the thought that it could so easily have been Harry was like a dash of icy water on her brow, and she felt the cold March wind blow harder. Why must he do this?

The field thinned out, as various machines coughed their last and their riders wheeled them off the track, hands raised in gloomy acknowledgement of the mingled cheers and jeers. Harry was still out there, and according to Jeanette he and Adam were jostling for second position, along with two others. She didn't care. She wanted it to be over, so they could go home and talk. Really, properly talk, about what they were to do now and how to explain to the children—

A roar, and a sudden, violent surge of the crowd took her completely by surprise, and she was carried forward several steps before she heard Jeanette's hoarse scream. 'Harry!'

Helen's disbelieving eyes found the thick, oily-black cloud on the far side of the track. Bright flame flickered in its depths before flaring and engulfing everything, but not before it showed her, horribly clearly, the still figure sprawled on the track.

Burleigh Mansions, Bristol
New Year's Eve 1919

Four, so far. Out of perhaps one hundred and fifty. But four was enough.

Helen pretended to fuss with her brooch until she felt safely alone in the crowd once more, then she raised her eyes and scanned the heaving room. Once again, the Foxes had delivered the party of the year – or this time, she supposed, the party of the decade. No matter how many events were put on tonight, the cream of the Bristol set was always going to be here at Burleigh, wafting around, congratulating one another, and themselves, on being the toast of the town. Not the biggest party, perhaps, but certainly the most lavish. All three of the townhouse's storeys were lit with twinkling lights, and, with the exception of her children's rooms on the top floor, were filled with music, laughter, and clinking glasses.

Harry caught her eye and raised an eyebrow; always concerned about her, even after nearly twenty years of marriage and of parties like this. She raised her glass to him, and he grinned and disappeared again, and, ever the conscientious hostess, Helen looked around to see if there was anyone she had not yet greeted. Jeanette Duval had arrived, and was hanging onto her handsome beau's arm as if she were terrified he was going to abandon her. She was probably right. Helen made her way over, and Jeanette turned as she approached.

Five.

Helen faltered. Five people, all friends to one degree or another, and each one looking at her with that same expression. Was it sympathy? Condescension? Genuine pity? Whatever the look was, it slid off Jeanette's face as soon as it had landed there, and she held out her small, bejewelled hand.

'Helen! Darling, come and rescue me.' She drew Helen into the group, and her blond male companion sketched a little bow.

'You're looking lovely tonight, Mrs Fox.'

'Mrs Fox!' Helen laughed. 'And how long have we known one another, *Mr* Coleridge?'

'I believe it's approximately thirty-three years, four months and . . .' he squinted into the distance, 'one and a half weeks.'

'He's joking,' Helen said quickly, seeing Jeanette's frown. Then, unable to help it, she added, 'It's two weeks, not one and a half.'

Jeanette smiled again, but it was thin and a bit strained, and Helen gave Adam a reproving look. He merely shrugged, but she noticed he brushed Jeanette's hand with his thumb, and the woman's features relaxed into a more natural smile. Thank goodness he had *some* manners, or Jeanette would have been the perfect wallflower tonight.

The small group picked up its conversation again, and Helen followed it for a few minutes, but it was all to do with new investments, and shipping, and she found herself instead concentrating on those odd looks she'd been getting. She wanted to broach the subject with Jeanette, but it was hard in this lively atmosphere.

'How's Harry?' Jeanette asked, finally letting go

7

of Adam's arm and leading Helen off in search of another drink.

'As you see him,' Helen said, pointing. Her husband was, predictably enough, surrounded by the biggest, noisiest crowd in the huge room; the glamorous centre of attraction. Helen felt the usual surge of pride in Harry, and in the two of them as a couple, but few of their friends and acquaintances believed that, when she'd fallen for him, she'd had no idea he was one of *those* Foxes, the wealthy family who owned the majestic Fox Bay Hotel down on the Cornish coast. And the beach below it, as he'd told her casually, on the train down for their first visit.

'Quite the host, as always,' Jeanette said, handing Helen a fresh glass. 'This champagne is very good.' She drank it more quickly than she ought to, given its fine pedigree, and Helen saw her eyes flicking around the room as she did so.

'Jeanette, do you know anything about why people are looking at me—'

'When's Harry racing again?'

Helen blinked. 'Not until the middle of the month. I assumed Adam was joining him?'

'Oh, I don't know, maybe.' Jeanette's laugh was brittle. 'He's so busy with his get-rich-quick schemes.'

'*Get* rich?' Helen shook her head. 'He's one of the wealthiest men in the South West.'

'Saving Harry of course.'

'Who's saving Harry?' He had appeared from behind Helen and slipped his arms around her waist.

'Oh, you're well beyond saving.' She leaned

8

against him, loving the warmth of him at her back, and put her hands over his, holding him closer.

He grinned down at her. 'Doesn't mean you can't try.' He nuzzled her neck, sending a flush of heat through her, and his voice dropped to a whisper. 'How does later tonight sound?'

She couldn't help laughing, and her spirits lifted once more. He could always do that to her, even after all this time. '*If* you're a very good boy,' she murmured, aware of Jeanette's eyes on them. As Harry withdrew, he patted her bottom discreetly, and winked.

With champagne fizzing in her blood, and the promise of a night of closeness and love, the party seemed to come to life for her again. Helen and Jeanette went their separate ways and Helen mingled with her guests, accepting compliments and returning them, swapping new year's resolutions and plans, but her thoughts contentedly resting on what would happen when the house was hers and Harry's again.

Six. The woman looked hurriedly away, but her expression exactly mirrored the other pitying, knowing looks, and Helen had had more than enough. She started across the room to demand an explanation, but a crash stopped her in her tracks, and she turned to see her son Benjamin, sixteen years old and attending his first society party, on his knees beside a suspiciously empty table. The snow-white lacy cloth was clamped between his hands, and he was laughing so hard he hadn't realised everyone within earshot had stopped talking to stare at him. Surrounded by broken crockery and spilled food, he dragged in

9

another breath and let it out on a hoot of laughter.

'You'd better get him off to bed, Helen,' one of her companions murmured.

'His father will have some tough words for him in the morning,' another said. 'Poor lad.'

'Poor lad?' Helen thrust her glass at them. 'I'll give him *poor lad*!'

On any other day she'd have seen the funny side, but tonight she felt only embarrassment and exasperation. Someone had helped Benjamin to stand, and Helen seized the boy's elbow. 'Come on, you little reprobate!' She turned to seek Harry's help, and as she found him her heart did a slow roll in her chest. The crowd around him had finally dispersed, and now only Jeanette stood looking earnestly up at him, her hand on his arm, her face wearing a beseeching expression. Helen suddenly felt quite sick; how hadn't she seen this coming? She looked around for Adam instead, but he was nowhere to be seen; no wonder Jeanette had taken her chance.

She turned away and put her arm around Benjamin's back, letting him lean on her as she led him towards the stairs. How many people knew? For a moment she didn't even know which was worse: that Harry was clearly being unfaithful, that it was with Jeanette, or that word was getting out and people felt sorry for her. But that moment was brief. Of course she knew. *Oh, Harry, not you ...*

With Benjamin safely deposited, fully clothed, on his bed, Helen went into her own room. Downstairs, over a hundred people were waiting to see in the new year with the famous Foxes; the perfect couple, the ones everyone turned to for advice when their own marriages were failing. *H and H, the Heavenly Twins*, Harry had laughingly dubbed them. Helen swallowed a tiny sound of mingled despair and humiliation, and checked her make-up in the mirror. She would *not* make a scene, not tonight.

Her dark hair, once described by a childhood friend as too curly, hadn't become any smoother with age, so she'd long since given up trying to tame it; Harry liked it, so why bother? She dragged a brush through it, then wiped a finger beneath her eyes to remove smudges and picked up her cake mascara to re-apply, but stopped as she saw her hand was shaking too hard. How could she compete with someone like Jeanette, the smooth-skinned, big-eyed, hand-span-waisted socialite? Helen was no great beauty, and no one but Harry had ever pretended she was, not even her mother. She was too short to wear the most fashionable clothes with any real confidence, and her figure was not the stick-thin outline those clothes demanded, but her slightly rounded face and childlike dimples would ensure she looked younger than her years as she grew older. And her sherry-coloured eyes were usually shining with good humour, which drew even the most fashion-conscious people to her long enough to find out that she had her share of intelligence and wit.

She also had dignity, and that's what she must show now; tomorrow would take care of itself. A quick re-tie of the yellow ribbon around that too-curly hair, a straightening of her shoulders, and she was as good as new. On the outside, at least.

Downstairs her hostess smile returned, but

11

although she neatly avoided coming anywhere near the treacherous Jeanette, she couldn't avoid Harry. He appeared at her side just before midnight, his hand warm on her hip, and it took every ounce of strength she possessed not to pull away and demand the truth. But at the same time as she resisted this urge, he smiled, and the smile was so familiar and sweet that she found herself questioning her own conclusions; was she mis-reading things? His hazel eyes picked up the glitter of the fairy lights strung across the walls, and those same lights played across his face, making him appear magical and beyond reproach.

'Sweetheart,' he murmured against her temple, 'you're not forgetting our appointment later, are you?'

She felt his hand tighten on her, and his lips pressed against her skin, and the longing came flooding back. Surely he couldn't be so convincing if his heart lay elsewhere? But then that was Harry Fox, wasn't it? A charmer. He could make you believe anything.

'No, I haven't forgotten.'

'Are you all right?' He tilted her face up to his. 'You look tired.'

'I am, a bit,' she said. 'Perhaps later we — '

'Ten!' The first shout of the countdown had begun, and Harry's hand curled around Helen's as they joined in. On the stroke of midnight, while other people shrieked and hugged one another, waving drinks in the air and joining hands for *Auld Lang Syne*, Harry took Helen in his arms and bent his head to press his forehead against hers. It was an affectionate, even a loving, gesture,

12

but one that cemented her certainty that his passion had led him elsewhere.

While Harry was seeing off the last of the revellers downstairs, Helen removed her party dress and draped it carefully over the back of a chair. She wiped her face clean of make-up, listening to the banging of doors all over the house as guests retrieved their coats and bellowed goodnight, and happy new year. Happy? Not for the Heavenly Twins.

She looked at the clock: almost three. Somehow, she had made it through the remainder of the party with her smile fixed in place, polite laughter produced at the silliest of jokes, and with a succession of partners ready to whisk their hostess off to the dance floor. But at least six of them — seven, if you counted Harry — knew it wasn't just the decade that had come to an end.

At last the door clicked quietly open. Harry seemed surprised to see her still up, and when he came further into the light she could see a tightness to his form, and his smile was strained. Helen's heart shrank until it felt like a burning pebble in the centre of her chest. Not tonight, please not tonight ... She needed more time, just one more day of knowing him the way she always had. She wasn't ready to lose him yet. She wanted to blurt out that she would forgive him, no matter what he'd done, but her pride kept the words in check.

'How long?' she said instead, turning away from his outstretched hands.

'What?'

'How long has it been?' She made a supreme

13

effort to sound calm, but heard the rising hysteria in her own voice.

He played for time, crafting his excuses. 'How long has what been? I don't know what—'

'I know about it, Harry, so don't bother to lie.'

Silence, then a heavy sigh. He was right behind her now. 'Just about two months.' His hands rested on her waist, and she whipped her head back, so fast it sent her hair flying in their faces, and shoved him away.

'Don't!'

'I'm sorry.' He remained at a distance, but his face was wreathed in sorrow. 'Darling, we must talk about this, it affects us all. The children too.'

The children. Helen gave an agonised moan. Benjamin was old enough to understand, perhaps, but Roberta at eleven and Fiona at just five ... their lives would be destroyed, all because their father found a pretty face irresistible. 'Will you tell them the truth?'

'Of course. Hels, how did you know? Who told you?'

'I have eyes! I saw you and Jeanette talking out there. What was she doing, begging you to tell me?'

'I would have anyway, but she said it had to be now.'

'So you're just doing as you've been told. Well done, Harry Fox.' The sarcasm fell between them with all the unbearable weight of a broken heart. Helen's breath caught in a sob, and she tried to walk away but Harry took hold of her arm.

'I didn't want to keep it from you, but Adam said it would—'

14

'Adam?' Helen stared. 'He's known too?' Her children's godfather, her own childhood friend, and he'd said nothing. *Eight*.

'Of course he's known, he's . . .' Harry let go of her arm and sank down onto the bed. For a moment he sat in silence, just looking at her. 'You don't know what you think you do, do you?' he said at length. 'I wondered how you could possibly have found out.'

'Found out what?' Helen's dismay was turning to a colder feeling now, at the broken voice and the helpless expression as he raised his eyes to hers. 'Harry, what's happened?'

'It's all gone,' he said. As he spoke the words his eyes grew bright with unshed tears. 'Every last penny. I'm so sorry, Hels. We're ruined.'

2

Bristol Royal Infirmary
March 1920

'We're so sorry, Mrs Fox . . .'

Helen felt a hand on her arm and one at the small of her back, but didn't know who they belonged to. More mumbled words, explanations that meant nothing. She heard another voice from somewhere behind her, urging her to come away, to sit down, to drink tea. She had no idea who was speaking. Her legs moved, but only instinctively, to keep her balance as the hands pulled her towards a seat; if they hadn't, she would have stayed exactly where she was, where those calm, long-practised words had scratched deep, acidic wounds into her heart: *We're so sorry . . .*

Three words that brutally separated the Heavenly Twins forever, three words that they must say dozens of times a week. But this was *Harry* they were talking about. Harry with the wide smile, the glinting eyes, the quick wit . . . Harry whose breath she could still feel on her cheek, whose hands were as familiar to her as her own. This morning he'd eaten breakfast with her, laughing as his fork slipped and the piece of egg he'd saved for last had skidded off his plate. He'd forked it up again, and winked at her as their eldest daughter had rolled her eyes in the excruciating embarrassment only an eleven-year-old could express. They'd both sti-

16

fled their laughter, but she'd read in his eyes what she knew was in her own: the sweeping knowledge that they would forever be the best of friends as well as the closest of lovers.

Now he was gone. All that laughter, all that love. The world darkened, and Helen suddenly felt as if she were falling through ice-cold cloud. She fumbled beneath her for the solid safety of the seat edge, and closed her eyes as she dragged a deep breath in. *Help me, Harry, I can't —*

'It will have been quick, darling.'

Now Helen recognised the voice. Dazed, she looked up to see Adam Coleridge, still dressed in his racing clothes, his helmet strap twisted around his oily hands, his face smudged and blackened and a deep graze down one cheek. Behind him Jeanette stood, pale and shocked looking.

'Quick?' How could he know such a thing? Harry had lain on the track for several long, horror-filled minutes before anyone had managed to get close enough to roll him onto his back and smother the flames. He'd died at the scene, certainly, but how could anyone know what he had suffered?

'They said the fuel pipe leaked,' Adam went on, as if knowing the reason for it all would bring Harry back. 'It sprayed petrol back over the exhaust and caught—'

'Stop it.' Helen's voice was dull.

'He didn't check it, Helen.' Adam lowered his voice. 'The thing is he shouldn't even have been riding.'

'I said stop!' She stood, and pushed past him to leave, but he stopped her.

'I'm only telling you because . . . Look, you have the right to know.' Adam put his lips close to her ear under the guise of a comforting embrace. 'He had brandy in his jacket pocket, I found the bottle when I ditched my bike and went back to him.' He patted his own pocket. 'I took it. I've told no one, all right?'

Helen stared at him, numb. 'But he doesn't . . . He never ... How do you know he'd drunk any?'

Adam started to speak, but clamped his mouth shut and Helen followed his gaze to see Jeanette looking at them with narrowed eyes.

'Not here,' Adam said. 'I'll come to Burleigh tonight, we can talk then.'

'What about the children?' Helen muttered, anguish sweeping over her again. 'How do I tell them?'

'I'm their godfather,' Adam said quietly. 'Do you want me to be with you?'

Helen didn't reply, her mind was already filled with too many fresh realisations. 'Oh God, Fleur ...' Harry's mother would have to be told before word reached her, it was bound to be in the papers.

Adam looked helpless. 'Darling, I'm so sorry.' He bent to kiss her cheek, but she pulled back and her voice was cold.

'If it wasn't for you, he'd still be alive.'

Adam's eyes darkened. 'By the time I realised what had happened I was a long way ahead of him. I couldn't have saved him, Hels.'

'Don't call me that.'

'I couldn't get to him any — '

'I'm not talking about the fire!'

18

Adam stared at her, clearly uncomprehending, but she couldn't say any more. She shook her head, and Jeanette stepped forward and took Adam's hand.

'You know where we are if you need us, Helen. We're both utterly devastated for you all.'

'I'll come around later,' Adam repeated, as Jeanette pulled him away.

'Don't.'

Helen returned home and gathered the children to her, and, somehow, broke the news. She held the girls as they sobbed, keeping her own tears in check until, exhausted by bewildered grief, they fell asleep. Benjamin tried harder to be adult, to hide his tears, but they built in his eyes until the slightest movement sent them spilling down his newly shaven cheeks, and when Helen drew the boy to her, he wept as hard and as freely as his sisters had.

Much later that night Helen lay down on her bed, with her head on Harry's pillow, and fell into the abyss that had been waiting for her from the moment she had heard Jeanette's scream.

The funeral was predictably well attended. At Burleigh Mansions, after the service, the rooms that just three months ago had been festooned in fairy lights were now draped in black. The optimism and laughter that had greeted the new decade had turned to shock and grief, as Harry's friends and colleagues gathered to honour the memory of a sparkling, joy-filled, but far too short life. There was some speculation about why

Harry had refused his mother's pleas to be buried in the family crypt in Trethkellis, but Helen had firmly honoured his wishes – he'd fallen in love with Bristol, so why not be buried here?

Press interest had scarcely waned in the intervening days, and the death of Harry Fox was built up into a glamorous, though tragic affair; the *bon viveur* former playboy, and the woman who'd apparently tamed him, had drawn interest from the moment they'd moved into Burleigh Mansions as newlyweds in 1901; everyone had been looking for a flaw in their marriage, a sign that Harry had returned to his former ways. The fact that he'd remained friends with Adam Coleridge — who certainly *hadn't* been tamed, no matter how fondly Jeanette believed otherwise — only added to the certainty that Harry would fall by the wayside before too long.

But three children and a war had not dented the Heavenly Twins, and now Harry had been so cruelly wrenched from the world there was very public speculation as to what Helen would do next. Would she sell Burleigh and move away? Would she sell Harry's shares in the various companies he owned, and take her children on a cruise to give them a chance to heal? Would she invest it all in something new and exciting?

Invest it all? If only they knew. The three months since New Year's Eve had been a strange time. So great was her relief at discovering she'd been wrong about an affair, she had succeeded in convincing herself that, as long as she had Harry, everything would be all right. Money wasn't important, their lifestyle wasn't important. After all, before they'd

20

met she'd been a nobody, and she'd happily go back to that life . . . Provided she was a nobody who had Harry Fox at her side.

But if her own past had been ordinary, Harry's hadn't. His entire life had been spent in a comfort bordering on luxury, and it was a struggle for him to come to terms with losing it all, and with failing his family. So he'd fought. Hard. She'd watched, lost in admiration, as he pulled himself back up, exerting himself like never before, clawing back what he'd lost and never once, in those three months, showing the public any other face than the smiling, confident Harry Fox they all knew and admired.

It was only when, immediately before that fatal race she had mistakenly opened a letter addressed to H Fox, that she realised he'd lied to her as well.

Helen circulated after the service, pressed black-clad arms and thanked people for coming, and tried to avoid speaking to anyone for more than a few minutes. Harry's elegant mother had shunned everyone's attentions and taken her leave early, eyes bright with fresh tears, and begun her lonely return journey to Cornwall, to the hotel on the coast that Harry had loved so much, and that might have saved his life.

Helen looked around the crowded room, and her heart cracked a little to see her three children sitting statue-like on the couch, the two eldest clutching cups of tea, their set faces discouraging well-meaning advances from friends and relations. Sarah, the nanny, sat beside six-year-old Fiona, with a protective arm around the little

21

girl's shoulder.

All three children had done themselves proud today, even the still-shocked Roberta, who Helen had worried about the most. They'd all deeply loved their father, and been equally cherished in return. He was the stone pillar around which all his children grew like ivy, and now he was just a name, a memory, a wisp of remembered love.

But Roberta had found a particular place in his heart, strenuously as he would deny it. Benjamin, the first-born, had been greeted with indescribable joy by both of them, and as soon as he was old enough Harry had begun taking him to meetings and to his club, proudly showing off the heir to the Fox dynasty. The boy had lapped up the attention and rewarded it with complete obedience and with the best of his sparsely given affection.

Fiona, the youngest, had held him in a different way; he would laugh at her determination to crawl away from him, seeking the freedom of any open door they happened to be near, and would scoop her up again without once fearing it was him she wished to be free of. She only had to begin her baby-babble to him, leaning on his knee with her chubby little elbow and staring earnestly up at him, for him to start grinning.

But between the two, when Roberta had come along, Harry had taken one look at the angrily pinched face and jerking fists, and fallen under her spell. As a toddler she'd seemed to become aware of this, and would happily climb into his lap, safe in the knowledge that he would not immediately put her down again, or scold her for creasing his newspaper. But she had tested him, that was

22

for sure; she was the one who had the power to make him think the hardest, and to check his temper the most. They'd enjoyed a complicated, but devoted relationship, and now Roberta was adrift and seemingly alone. But today she had comported herself with a dignity beyond what might be expected of an elevenyear-old, and Helen made a silent promise that she would go to her later and tell her how proud she was.

When the last mourner had left, and the children had gone gratefully to their rooms, Helen closed the front door and leaned against it for a moment. She stared absently up at the coats on the pegs and wondered why her throat had thickened again, until she realised: the fine, black wool one was Harry's; his smell would still be on it, that curious mixture of oil and Pears shaving soap . . . She brushed her hand down the sleeve, clutching at the cuff for a moment, then went through into the sitting room, craving only peace, and time to think, before she went upstairs to find Roberta.

'Helen?' Adam Coleridge moved away from the window, glass in hand, his expression nervous.

Startled, Helen recovered quickly. 'What are you still doing here?'

'It was the only way I could think of to talk to you. You've been avoiding me all day.'

'Oh, do pardon me,' Helen said tightly. 'I've been a bit distracted burying my husband.'

Pain flashed across his face. 'I didn't mean to —'

'I meant what I said.' She moved past him to sit down, but did not invite him to do the same. 'If it

23

wasn't for you, he'd still be here.'

'I know.' His quiet voice made her look up. She had expected an argument, or puzzlement, at least.

'Do you?'

'The investment was my idea. I'll regret bringing him into it, until my …' He stopped, and took a deep breath. 'I didn't realise he'd ploughed everything into it though, Hels, I swear.'

'Really? Where do you suppose he got the money?'

'I didn't know he was down on funds. He told me it was a breeze, getting it together.'

Of course he did. He can make anyone believe anything. 'And you told him it was a sure money-maker.'

Adam nodded. He looked twice as old as he had on New Year's Eve, his blond hair, usually pomaded to within an inch of its life, messy now where he'd been dragging a hand through it. 'I thought it was.'

Helen gave a hollow laugh. 'Well I suppose you were right, in a way. It's made money for someone, and it's given Burleigh Mansions right back to the mortgage company.'

'What?' Adam put his glass down and sank into the armchair opposite. He rubbed his face with both hands. 'Are you certain?'

'I found the letter before the race.'

'God, what will you do?'

'Throw myself on Fleur's mercy I suppose. Harry inherited his father's share of the hotel, so he owns … *owned*, half of it. Now that half is mine.' The pain was sharp, and she caught her breath with it, but Adam hadn't noticed, he was still lost in dismay.

'Why didn't he go to her when he first knew he was in trouble?'

'That's what I wanted to know,' Helen said grimly. 'We had some terrible rows about it, but he refused, said it was her home and he couldn't ask her to sell, or re-mortgage, because of his foolishness.' The memory of those arguments, as heated as they'd been, seemed to belong to someone else now.

'But just selling his own half would have helped,' Adam persisted. 'Anyone would have been happy to buy into somewhere like that.'

'I suggested that, too. I mean, she hadn't yet signed his half over to him, but that wouldn't have taken much to remedy. So in the end he agreed to get that much done, just in case, but by the time it was signed over he said he didn't need it anymore, that everything was all right.'

'That's what he told me, too. Not that he'd have asked for my advice. But Fleur would have helped him, and gladly.'

Helen nodded. 'I forgot you knew her so well.'

'Since Harry and I were twelve.' Adam's mouth flickered in a little smile of memory, but it quickly faded. 'I spoke to her earlier, she's in pieces.'

'That's why I can't ask her yet.' Helen hesitated, not sure she really wanted to know, but she had to ask. 'About that brandy.'

He looked at her warily. His pleasant, open features were strained now, the blue eyes shadowed, the mouth tight. 'I told you, no one will ever know. Not from me.'

'How do *you* know though? That he'd actually drunk any, I mean.'

Adam was silent for a moment, and she let him gather his thoughts. He *couldn't* know, it was just speculation. Otherwise he'd have just come out and said he'd smelled it, and if that was the case he'd have stopped Harry from riding.

'How was he, on the day of the race?' he asked at last.

'Cheerful. Optimistic.' Helen's heart ached as she remembered. 'He spent some time with Benjamin teaching him to shave, then with Roberta, showing her his motorcycle pictures.'

'And Fiona?'

'She'd dragged the nanny outside to play the moment breakfast was over.' Helen frowned, growing suspicious at these questions. 'He just seemed content.'

'Doesn't even that seem strange, given your situation as you know it now?'

'Not at all. He was wonderful with the children, you know that. Look, Adam, I'd have known if he was drinking a lot. You know Harry, always in moderation.'

'Precisely. He wasn't a drinker, so it wouldn't have taken much. Not enough to make it obvious anyway. And it didn't impair his riding.' Adam paused. 'But he should have smelled a leaky fuel pipe, and have you ever known Harry not to go over his motorcycle with a fine-toothed comb before a race?'

'This was the first one I'd been to,' Helen reminded him, feeling a little tremor run through her.

'He came late to the trackside, and gave his motorbike the briefest looking over.' Adam shook his head. 'I assumed he'd already checked it beforehand.'

'And you didn't ask?'

'Why would I?' Adam was growing defensive now, she could read it in the way he sat up straight. 'I had my own machine to check, and he didn't come over to speak to me anyway.'

'But you were his friend,' Helen countered hotly. 'He'd have looked out for you, stopped *you* from riding if he'd had the slightest —'

'But I didn't!' Adam slammed his hand down on the arm of his chair and rose to his feet. 'I *didn't* have the slightest suspicion, and neither did you, did you?' He turned away, but not before she saw his jaw tense with anger. 'If you're saying he died because I didn't care enough to mother him, then you're as much to blame as me.'

He evidently mis-read her silent acceptance of that truth as shock, and turned back, his face reflecting his remorse. 'Helen, I'm . . . that was unforgiveable. I'm sorry.'

She waved it away. 'What did you mean when you said he wouldn't ask your advice? He always did. To his cost,' she added bitterly.

Adam sighed. 'Harry wasn't the only one to lose his shirt in that investment. Why would he trust me when he knew I'd lost everything too?'

'Everything? How?' She couldn't find a shred of sympathy for him, no matter how close they'd once been.

'The shipping company he told you about, Blue Ensign, was floated on the stock market just after the war. I could see it had the potential for a monopoly on freight, and freight was the future.' He shrugged. 'I still believe that now. Anyway, I put everything I had into it, and for a while everything was rosy, the risk paid off. Then other, better companies sprang up, the Union Castle Line got bigger and stronger—'

'Yet you persuaded Harry to invest in Blue Ensign too?' Helen's voice was tight.

'He's so well respected in investment circles, just his name on the board of directors should have helped, let alone the money he ploughed into the company. I honestly thought it would raise the value of shares.'

'And instead they fell.'

Adam nodded. 'Plummeted, it's fairer to say. The company was hit by one disaster after another, and finally the big one. An entire shipment lost at sea, thanks to an engineering fault. The line was sued by both buyer and seller, and after that we couldn't give the shares away.'

'Harry never told me why you weren't insured against that kind of loss or litigation.' In fact he'd snapped when she'd asked, which was so distressingly unlike him that she had never asked again. 'What kind of company doesn't set up insurance?'

'Blue Ensign was insured for that voyage. If the ship had sailed as planned, three days later, we'd have been fine. We'd have lost the cargo, yes, but we'd have been covered, and indemnified against lawsuits too.'

'But?'

He looked away. 'But there was an opportunity for return freight if we delivered early, and

28

we couldn't turn that down.' He shook his head. 'The dates on the policy document didn't cover us for those three days.'

Finally they were getting to it. Helen tensed as she asked, with deceptive calm, 'And whose decision was it to sail early, yours or his?'

'Neither.' He sounded momentarily defensive. 'We were on the board of directors, we didn't run the company.'

'But whose *idea* was it? Who told the board that the insurance was valid? It was you, wasn't it?'

Adam still couldn't look at her, and she leaned forward, her words a hiss in the otherwise silent room. 'Answer me!'

'Helen, I'm—'

'Get out.'

'Let me explain.'

'You've had your chance and you danced around it.' She rose, stiff and aching, and close to tears. 'Get out. I never want to see or hear from you again. I'm glad you've lost it all.'

He picked up his hat, and looked at her for a long moment. When she didn't apologise, he gave her a faint, sad smile. 'I don't blame you for that.'

'I don't care if you do.'

Helen followed his gaze as they reached the front door, and caught sight of a framed picture, one of Harry's favourites, hanging on the wall. The three of them together just after the war; Harry in his blue convalescent uniform, his good arm slung around Adam's shoulder, and Helen standing in front of them both, stiff and formal, terrified of ruining the photograph by smiling.

'I loved him too,' Adam said softly. For a second

Helen saw the pain in his eyes and in the stoop of his shoulders, and almost relented. But a glance at Harry's coat hanging on its peg, never again to be worn by the man she loved, killed that momentary weakness. She barely waited until Adam had stepped over the threshold, then slammed the door behind him.

3

November 1920

Eight months already. Eight months of looking up expectantly whenever the front door opened in the early evening, only to feel the knife of loss slicing through her each time she remembered: he wouldn't be returning from some meeting, or a day out at the races with Adam and his other associates. He wouldn't come sweeping into the sitting room on a wave of purpose and energy, to kiss her lightly and pour a glass of brandy, chattering nineteen to the dozen. Eight long, empty months that also seemed to have passed in a brief flicker of broken light – Pathé news: your life is shattered, but your children need you to be whole.

So she'd tried. Day after day she'd found a way to make it easier for herself to pretend, and the children had gradually come out of their own shadowed little worlds. The day she'd heard one of them laugh again, unguarded, natural, innocent, her pretence had shifted into a kind of weary reality. Harry was gone, but Benjamin, Roberta and Fiona were here, and she loved them with a new kind of desperation that frightened her sometimes. Thankfully they hadn't noticed the panicky way she would follow them with her eyes when they were doing something even mildly dangerous, particularly little Fiona, who knew no fear.

The most difficult summer of her life had

passed, somehow. On Harry's forty-second birth-day — she couldn't bring herself to think of it as, *what would have been* his birthday – she had taken herself upstairs and hoped that the nanny would realise she needed to be left alone. Walking along the landing to her room she had heard muffled sobs coming from Benjamin's room, and stood outside his door, her forehead resting against the wood, her fingers wrapped around the handle, but she hadn't gone in. Her eyes had prickled and swum with the tears she tried so hard to keep in check, and while part of her yearned to take her son to her breast and cradle him as she had when he was little, she knew her presence would stop him from giving vent to his grief.

If Roberta had been her daddy's favourite, Harry had been this boy's inspiration. The girls would, with luck, find such men later on in life, and they would no doubt cling to them just as fiercely, but Benjamin must now grow up with the expectation that someday he would have to be someone's Harry. How was he to do that, when his own father was no longer there to guide him?

'Oh, Ben,' Helen whispered against the door. 'I promise I'll try.'

And now November had come, with all its flimsy grey light threatening to disappear beneath lowering clouds and ever-imminent rain. Helen stood in the hallway of Burleigh Mansions for the last time. The house had been repossessed in March, though thanks to Harry's life insurance she had managed to pay rent to the mortgage company, but now it was sold, and she had been given notice to move out. All summer she'd put off talking to Fleur about Harry's inheritance; it had never felt like the right time, but now she was ready to claim what was hers. If Fleur herself couldn't buy out Harry's half, finding an outside buyer for fifty percent of such a prestigious property shouldn't pose any problem, Adam had said as much. Then Helen and the children could move back to a more modest home in Bristol and begin their lives again.

Reluctant to put such a delicate request into writing, or even speak it over the telephone, she'd written to ask Fleur if she could bring the children to stay for a little while. Let them get to know one another again, in their new roles without Harry, before she broke the news. Fleur had been touched and even eager, and now here they were, their furniture sold, their books and other smaller belongings stored in the attics and basements of some of Harry's friends, and their clothes in boxes and cartons ready for the trip to Cornwall.

Benjamin was upstairs somewhere, Helen could hear his feet thundering up and down the landing between bedrooms, and Roberta and Fiona stood by the collection of small suitcases by the front door, peering out and waiting for the car that was to take them all to the station.

'Has she got a big house?' Fiona wanted to know.

'Don't you remember *anything*?' Roberta said. 'We were only there last summer. It's the big hotel on the cliff.'

'It's not so big really,' Helen put in, 'it's just

33

quite grand-looking. It only has twenty-five guest rooms.'

Fiona frowned and pursed her lips, then she paled, and whispered, 'The place with the ghost?'

'There's no ghost,' Helen said quickly, and made a note to question Benjamin about that one later. 'There's lots of room to play, but you must remember people are paying to stay there. So if Fleur, I mean your grandmother, tells you not to run in the lobby, you're not to run.'

'Will there still be guests in the winter?' Roberta wanted to know. She sounded hopeful, and Helen realised she had been too preoccupied to spare a thought for what her children were leaving behind; this vibrant, growing city, their friends, their schools . . . It was a lot to demand of them, but they were all going to have to adjust. And they'd be back in a few months in any case, in the heart of everything once again.

'There's always someone staying there,' she said, 'even if it's not as many as during the summer. Fox Bay attracts a lot of arty people at this time of year, they like to paint seascapes, and harbour scenes, and it's better for them when there's hardly anyone else around except those who work there.'

'And because Fleur puts the prices down in winter,' Benjamin put in, jumping down the last few stairs. 'The car's here, I spotted it from the landing window.'

'You're not to call her Fleur,' Helen said absently, and looked around her at the empty house. It was unsettling what a stark difference the lack of furniture made to such a familiar place; voices echoed in the bare rooms, joining the wispy remnants of those who'd lived here before. For a moment she almost heard them: Victorian gentlemen bellowing at house boys; bells ringing as ladies called for maids; children shrieking as they illicitly ran up and down the wide staircase; housekeepers grumbling as they shuffled about with armloads of laundry; butlers greeting guests at the door.

And then the young newlywed Foxes had arrived, and their three children were born in this very house. The war had come and gone, blessedly leaving them unbroken, if not untouched, and the parties they gave had been the talk of Bristol. There must surely be imprints of all this in these old walls. Whispers of their past. Helen pulled the door shut behind them and turned the key in the lock. Even if there were no ghosts at Fox Bay Hotel, they were leaving plenty behind at Burleigh Mansions.

★ ★ ★

Fox Bay, Cornwall

The hotel was set high so it overlooked the sea, but with a generous stretch of immaculate grounds to separate it from the cliff path. Harry's father had bought the abandoned Trethkellis Abbey in the 1860s with the idea of creating a hotel that bore his family name, but had been determined not to alter the external appearance of the former monastery more than necessary. It still stood strong and square after centuries of being battered by the sea gales, but was saved from a forbidding appearance by the graceful arches of the cloisters that ran the length of the building.

Nowadays garden chairs lined up where once the Benedictine Order of monks had walked to prayer in the little chapel at the far end, but there was still a strangely peaceful air about the place; guests who found themselves there rarely chatted, but sat quietly reading, or just listening to the sea, lost in their own thoughts.

Helen stood on the cliff's edge and stared out over the choppy grey sea, with the bitter November wind tugging at her hair and her coat, and wondered why she was putting off the warmth and welcome she knew would be waiting for her indoors. The children had gone eagerly inside, out of the cold, but Helen had been unable to bring herself to do the same. Perhaps because she had never been here without Harry, and her mind kept showing her his laughing face when he'd told her about the private beach, and she'd sat there like a fool with her mouth hanging open. Private *beach*?

'Only a little one,' he'd said, still grinning. Then he'd drawn her close, to the disapproval of the others in the train carriage, and his voice dropped as he'd murmured against her ear, 'But still, very, very private ...'

The memories gave her such a swift, breath-stealing pain that she'd turned away from the hotel's front door, and let her feet carry her away across the wet grass. The cliff path beckoned, and she hoped the wind and the drizzle would blow some of the melancholy away and replace it with something fresher. She walked a little way, and felt the ache ease, to be replaced with a gratitude that she'd at least known such a love, even if it had been cut away from her so soon.

He'd stood behind her, that day, on an outcrop of the cliff a little farther along, and wrapped his arms around her. She'd felt safe, and blissfully happy, barely able to believe she deserved such joy. She'd shivered in the wind that gusted off the sea, and he'd held her tighter.

'The Cornish wind favours the fisherman.'

'What?' She twisted in his arms and looked up at him, but he was staring out over the water.

'It's a local saying. When there's a stiff wind it's harder to control the boat, and it's more dangerous to go out, but the fish bite better. There's a rhyme,' he went on, "Wind from the east, fish bite the least, wind from the west, the fish bite the best.' There's more, but I can never get that bit right. Something to do with bait. Anyway, when the wind comes off the sea in this part of Cornwall it's coming from the west.'

'So, when things get difficult, but you persevere, the rewards can be greater?' Helen felt pleased with her interpretation, and gratified when he gave a soft laugh.

'Exactly. It took a while for me to persuade you I was worth a chance, but here you are.'

'Here I am,' she repeated softly now, blinking back tears. The grief came in waves every bit as unpredictable as those that wore away imperceptibly at the rocks below, and Harry felt so close here . . .

'Mum!'

Helen turned to see Roberta, her arms wrapped

37

around herself to hold her coat closed, and she found a smile for her. 'I'm coming, love. Give me a minute.'

'Granny says it's time for tea.'

Granny? Since when had Fleur consented to such a title? She was head-to-toe pure style, looked half her age, and lived with all the glittering abandon for which the Fox family was famous. The groups Harry and Helen had brought down from Bristol had been composed entirely of the wealthy and the well-known, but, almost without exception, these hard-to-impress people went away talking in glowing terms of Harry's mother, and making plans to invite her to every event in the social calendar. *Granny* indeed.

'Is she that much changed since we last saw her then?' she asked.

'Not at all, which makes it even odder. But quite nice.'

Helen held out her hand. 'Come on then, take me to see … Granny.'

As they walked back towards the hotel Helen looked around at the vast open spaces on all three sides of Fox Bay. 'Daddy always wanted to build a golf course here,' she said, surprising herself by her readiness to talk about him.

'Did he?' Roberta sounded astonished. 'I didn't even know he played golf.'

'He didn't.' Helen smiled. 'He was just very keen to learn, and told me there was no better incentive than to have his own golf course, where he could teach himself without anyone ever seeing how bad he was.'

Roberta squinted through her blowing hair.

'That does sound like him. I don't know where he'd build it though, that's all farmland up there, isn't it?'

'I think so, yes. Higher Valley Farm starts up by the main road, from what I can remember, and comes all the way down to meet the hotel's land at the back.'

'He could probably persuade them to sell,' Roberta said, and Helen looked at her shrewdly.

'Do you think so?'

'Oh yes. Knowing Daddy he'd only have to chat with them for ten minutes, and they'd go away believing he was doing them a favour even making the offer.'

Helen couldn't help smiling at that. The girl knew her father well.

They stepped onto the deeply carpeted floor of the lobby, and Roberta went off, presumably to explore a little more, or perhaps to find Ben; they'd grown so much closer since the loss of their father, though it was only evident in the way they picked at one another.

Helen looked around her, remembering the last time she had been here, just last summer when the children had spent almost the entire week on the beach. She and Harry had entertained, of course, and life had been on an even keel, with tenderness in the bedroom and fun with their friends, and there had still been plenty of money then too. Dinner conversations had been the same as ever: would Harry think about getting a job? Laughter up and down the table, and Harry's shrug speaking volumes. Why should he? He was having too

39

much fun letting his investments do the work, and racing his beloved motorcycles. *Prize money's like a wage, isn't it? Well then, Mother, I do have a job! Besides, Adam has an incredible opportunity he's going to tell me all about, haven't you, Adam?*

The lobby looked the same as it had back then. Formerly the room where the monks had gathered to eat, it was bigger than many purpose-built hotel lobbies, with a much wider staircase that wound up through three floors from the wildly expensive, luxurious en suite rooms on the first, past the smaller rooms on the second, and up to the private, family and staff rooms on the third. A small mechanical lift had been installed in the space where a dumb waiter had once carried food to the upper rooms to where, according to the little brass plaque on the wall, the precentor had bent to his monastic writings over the centuries, rarely disturbed by such trivia as mealtimes.

The décor at Fox Bay had, for many years, favoured the influence of both Charles Rennie Mackintosh, and his wife Margaret; the stark edges and elongated shapes of the high-backed chairs were softened by sumptuous embroidered cushions, featuring the wildflowers to be found all along these Cornish cliffs. Polished walnut cabinets with glass fronts housed silver cocktail shakers, and stylish portraits of honoured guests, painted by acclaimed visiting artists, adorned the walls.

Through the double glass doors that led to the lounge, Helen could see the glossy white grand piano Harry and Adam had so often hammered into submission, in accompaniment to bawdy songs that had sent more than one guest from the room in appalled disgust while others roared with laughter. A long, walnut-topped reception desk with brass fittings saw the comings and goings of the guests, and behind that was the office door, which opened even as Helen watched.

'There you are, darling.'

Fleur Fox crossed the lobby, as elegantly presented as ever, but as she drew closer Helen saw Roberta had been wrong; Harry's mother had changed, but it was all in the eyes. The same green-flecked hazel as both Harry's and Ben's, they were glistening as she drew Helen into her rather angular embrace, and they were . . . softer, somehow. She still didn't look like a *granny* though.

'It's so good of you to have us,' Helen murmured.

Fleur held her at arm's length. 'You make it sound as though you're here on holiday. You're family, this is as much your home as mine.'

A spasm of guilt went through Helen at those words. 'Yes, I understand.'

'Then there's to be no thanking me. You and I are equal here.'

Not quite, Helen thought. I am a guest. For now. Aloud, she simply said, 'I'll be very happy to do anything to help out with the running of the hotel.'

Fleur looked a little shifty, and Helen suspected there might be a list of *little jobs that need doing, if you have a minute*, at some point, but thankfully it wouldn't be today.

'Where's Fiona?' she asked, looking around.

'Gone to bed. Poor mite was so tired from

travelling.'

'And Benjamin?'

'Probably still in the cellar with the bar manager.'

Helen grimaced. After the New Year's party she had forbidden Benjamin to go anywhere near alcohol, as if his appalling hangover hadn't done that job for her. Now here he was with an entire cellar at his fingertips, and he'd only been here for half an hour.

Fleur seemed to read her mind, and smiled. 'Don't worry, Guy will make sure he behaves responsibly.'

'Guy? Guy Bannacott?'

'You sound surprised.'

'I didn't realise he still worked here. After . . . you know.'

'That incident was a never-to-be-repeated piece of tomfoolery,' Fleur said archly. 'He knows he was walking on very shaky ground.'

'Although in some absolutely stunning shoes.' The words were out before Helen could stop them, and there was a long silence during which she could have bitten her tongue out.

'Not to mention my best gown,' Fleur said at length, and as they both relaxed into laughter, she gave Helen a sidelong look and her voice dropped. 'Whatever his proclivities, legal or otherwise, Guy is not only a first-rate bar and restaurant manager, he's my closest friend, I'd have been lost without him these past few months.'

Helen nodded, and squeezed Fleur's arm. 'I know, and I like him a great deal. I'm glad you've had him to lean on.' She almost apologised for not being there herself, but just stopped herself in time. She wouldn't have been expected to be there, after all, and she didn't want to start from a position of weakness, this was going to be hard enough.

'He'll look after Benjamin,' Fleur said, 'don't worry. Now, I sent Roberta to bring you in for tea, so shall we go in?'

'Are we eating in the main dining room?' Helen hung back, suddenly unsure.

'And why wouldn't we? We only have a certain number of serving staff, and to pull them off the dining room, to cater specifically to us, would be a little foolish don't you think?'

'I suppose. I hadn't thought.' Over the summer she'd become accustomed to simply serving herself and the children anyway, the last of her staff had long since departed, though Sarah had clung on, without wages, until the very last of her own money had run out.

Fleur pushed open the door. 'Oh, it looks as if Ben's come back up. And Roberta's in there now, too. I'll join you shortly, I just have one or two things to sort out.'

Helen was no stranger to hotel restaurants, and certainly not this one, but here it was different; she felt conspicuous, as if everyone knew who she was, and would start whispering behind their menus. But no one spared Helen a second glance, certainly not the group of eight guests seated at the big round table at the far side of the room. There were very few occupied tables this late in the season, but the group made enough comforting noise to allow a feeling of invisibility as Helen

43

wove her way through the room.

Despite the small number of off-season guests, each table was laid with a pristine, snow-white cloth, fresh flowers, gleaming silverware, and a crystal-clear water jug, as if every one of them would be occupied. Helen realised she was beginning to look at everything with the eyes of a proprietor, and to appreciate the work that must have gone into preparing this one room, for this one meal, on this one day. It made her head spin just to think about it, and her respect for Fleur grew.

She made her way to the table in the corner where her two oldest children sat waiting, and slid into a seat facing outward. 'I want to keep my eye on you,' she told Benjamin, who looked pained. 'And what's all this you've been telling Fiona about ghosts?'

'That was ages ago,' he protested. 'Last summer. And it was just a joke anyway.'

'Still, remember she's only six. If I hear you've been —'

'I won't! I've got more interesting things to do now.'

'Like what? We've only just got here.'

'Mr Bannacott is going to teach me all about wine.'

'He is not!' Helen saw the man in question approaching their table, and dropped her voice. 'Have you learned nothing after that party?'

'No, I mean he's going to teach me all about it properly,' Benjamin insisted. 'Did you know that Dom Pérignon, that champagne we had at the party, was really a monk? Just like the ones who lived here. He was …' He broke off, frowning, but by the time he'd recalled his earlier lesson Guy was beside their table.

'Mrs Fox,' he said quietly, and Helen smiled up at him and took his proffered hand.

'Helen,' she reminded him. 'We've known each other long enough.'

'I was so sorry to hear about Harry.' Guy's expression told her these weren't just the same polite words she'd become accustomed to hearing from near strangers since March. 'He was an example to us all.'

'Thank you,' Helen said, feeling her throat thicken. 'He often spoke well of you too.'

After a solemn silence Roberta spoke up, and it sounded rather as if she were forcing herself to sound excited. 'Can we really order anything we like, Mr Bannacott?'

'Anything.' He smiled, and his brown eyes crinkled as he cleared his throat and reverted to his usual formal tones. 'May I take your order, Miss Roberta?'

Roberta looked at Helen with a questioning little smile, and Helen nodded, appreciating the girl's efforts at normality. 'Go on.'

'And at breakfast tomorrow?'

'Of course.'

'Tomorrow I'm having three boiled eggs,' Roberta said, with satisfaction.

'Three?' Helen echoed, appalled, but the ever-professional Guy didn't blink.

'Very good, miss.'

'Pay no attention to her.' Helen shook her head. 'She'll have one, and make no fuss.'

Roberta pouted, and handed her menu back. 'Soup, please.'

While the children finished ordering their meal, Helen's attention was drawn to the two ladies who were just settling in at the next table, and whose voices were raised far more than was necessary for two people so close to one another.

'Of course, I told them I wouldn't stand for it,' the closest woman was saying. She picked up one of the thick white napkins, folded intricately into the shape of a boat, and shook it out. 'The noise coming up from the laundry in that place was *frightful*.'

'Really?'

The woman gave a little smile, and waited until Guy had taken Helen's order and left. 'No, not really. But the view wasn't all I'd hoped for, and this was the only thing I could think of, so I called the manager, and I said, 'I insist on being moved into a quieter room.' And they did, of course. The master suite in fact, and at no extra cost.'

Her companion nodded. 'These places expect to shoulder the added expense. I made sure all my dining room bills were waived the last time I stayed at Cliffside Fort, in Caernoweth. They dug their heels in, of course, saying they couldn't possibly do that on the basis of one cold soup, but I told them how fast word spreads, and how they'd lose business if people knew their chef wasn't up to the job.'

'It's only the truth.' The woman caught sight of Helen's wide eyes on them, then glanced at the children, and gave Helen a friendly, if somewhat pitying, smile. 'Hello, dear. Travelling with young-

46

sters can be tiresome, can't it? And expensive.'

'Well, we —'

'A word of advice.' The woman patted her mouth with her napkin. 'Don't pay full price for anything, you're out of season now so it should all be reduced by at least half. The hotel can afford it.'

'But surely some of it would be more expensive, not less,' Helen countered, 'if, say, the vegetables are out of season?'

'The cost of importing a few beans is more than compensated for by the prices they charge for some of these rooms.'

'And,' her friend put in, 'if you still think the food bill is too expensive, ask to see the manager, then tell her you're a good friend of the owner. You'll never have to pay for another meal.'

'Actually, the manager *is* the —'

'Take this place,' the first woman went on. 'Mrs Fox is nice enough, but she has no idea how to keep her customers happy.'

A timely burst of laughter from the large group belied that, and Helen smothered a smile, but before she could reply the door opened again. She looked over, expecting Fleur and already anticipating the discomfort on the ladies' faces, but it was a woman of roughly her own age, perhaps a few years younger. Blonde hair was piled high and secured with a huge feather, and she wore a tripled rope of pearls about her neck, and a lacy green gown that wouldn't have looked out of place on the stage. She glided across the room and stopped at the table next to them.

'Good evening, Misses Bentley,' she said, nodding at each of the women in turn. Her accent was American, which evidently caught Roberta's fascinated attention at once. 'It's so nice to see you again.' She drew out the word so in a long, low drawl. The blatant sarcasm was staggering, and Helen picked up her napkin to stifle a laugh.

The woman glanced at her briefly with cool grey eyes, then moved on to join the noisy table. Her distinctive voice could be heard raised in laughter, and prompting it in others, though they couldn't hear what she was saying – Helen found herself straining to do so, and she could see Roberta was doing the same. The woman was quite frightening in her glamour and borderline rudeness, but oddly fascinating for all that, and Helen realised, with a little jolt of surprise, and even guilt, that her own smile and laughter were real.

The Bentleys, presumably sisters, resumed their talk, but frequently broke off in order to express their dislike of 'those artistic buffoons', who were making their mealtime so unpleasant.

'If they keep this up, I shall go over there,' one of them warned, 'and then they won't know what's hit them.'

'I shall tell the manager.'

Helen felt some sympathy for them; they were entitled to peace and quiet, after all, and the blonde newcomer had certainly livened up an already boisterous party — perhaps if the Bentleys hadn't been so scathing about Fleur, Helen might even have taken up their cause and offered to carry their complaint across the dining room.

Fleur's arrival caused the expected agitation on the next table as the sisters realised their mistake.

When she then took a seat at Helen's table, they kept darting nervous glances at them, no doubt waiting for Helen to relay their penny-pinching schemes, and probably preparing their defences between mouthfuls. Helen said nothing to Fleur, but she did look up once to see the blonde's eyes on her mother-in-law, and a wicked little grin on her lips. The Bentleys had clearly made their opinions known before, and it seemed Fleur's cause was not going unchampioned.

'Who are they?' she asked, gesturing at the group.

'They're the Trethkellis version of the Newlyn School,' Fleur said.

'Ah,' Helen nodded to the children. 'Remember I told you how artists like to come off-season?'

'They're only here for a few weeks though,' Fleur added, 'and they don't have their own premises, luckily for Fox Bay. They'll be here until the middle of December, I think.'

Bubbling laughter erupted again from the group, in response to something the blonde had said. It was infectious, and Helen couldn't help smiling again herself. 'And she's their leader, I suppose.'

'Who is?' Fleur twisted in her seat. 'Oh, her. No, she's not an artist, nor even part of their group, she's just a guest here. Now, young Fox cubs, what are we eating tonight?'

The meal ended on a surprisingly cheerful note, made more so by the blonde American stopping at their table on her way out of the dining room.

'Mrs Fox, might I be permitted to tell you once

49

again just how much I appreciate everything you do for your guests?'

Fleur's lips twitched. 'That's very kind of you. This is my daughter-in-law, and my grandchildren.' She made the necessary introductions.

'Oh. You must be Harry's widow. I'm sorry for your sad loss.' The blonde held out her hand to Helen. 'Millicent Scripps, wife of Edward Scripps. You know, the US newspaper magnate?' She dropped her voice to a conspiratorial tone, that nevertheless carried across the nearest two tables. 'He's a personal friend of the president, you know.'

Helen confessed to not knowing who Edward was. 'But it's lovely to meet you, Mrs Scripps.'

'Oh, you'll meet him soon enough. He's planning on coming over here and writing a huge article about this gorgeous English hotel I've told him so much about, and all its fascinating guests.' Mrs Scripps beamed at them all, and then turned her attention to the Misses Bentley. 'I do hope we weren't too noisy for you, ladies.'

Helen tried not to laugh as the two women fell over themselves to deny everything they'd been complaining about. 'No, of course not!'

'Absolutely enchanting to listen to.'

'Don't give it another thought.'

'Good!' The woman gave an exaggerated sigh of relief. 'Creative people must have an outlet, right? I can see you understand that. I shall tell Edward as much, and I'm sure he'll want to interview you both for his newspaper, as ladies of such distinction. Friends of the arts, too, he's going to *adore* you!'

The Bentleys glanced at one another. 'And you

say he knows the president personally?'

'Oh, he and Woodrow are the best of friends!'
Millicent clapped her hands, and Helen had to
bite down on another grin; she didn't believe the
woman for one minute, but she was certainly
entertaining.

'I must leave you, ladies.' Mrs Scripps bestowed
a brilliant smile on Benjamin. 'And gentleman, of
course. I have *so* many letters to write, not least
to darling Edith. Wilson,' she added, and Helen
watched the Bentleys practically wilt with admiration.

'Well she's . . . interesting,' she said with a smile,
watching Millicent sway from the room, waving
at her artist friends as she vanished through the
door.

'Isn't she just.' Fleur turned to her granddaughter, who was starting to flag a little. 'You look done
in. Off to your room with you, and your mother
will see you settled into bed in a little while. You
too, Benjamin.'

She must be the only person who could still
treat Benjamin like a child and get away with it,
Helen reflected with an inward smile. As they left
the dining room, she could still hear the artists'
group from halfway across the lobby. 'Those ladies
might be awful snobs,' she mused, 'but they did
have a point about that party. They're very loud.'

'They're also paying twice as much as the Bentleys.'

'That shouldn't matter ...' Helen trailed off
as she saw Fleur's expression close down. If the
thought had been tapping at her mind to broach
the subject of the inheritance, and get it over with,

51

now was definitely not the time. In fact she had no idea how she was going to do it; Fleur was clearly more than just a live-in owner, she had a strong role to play in the day-to-day running of the place too. Helen selling her half would mean more to Fleur than losing half the bricks and mortar, just as Harry and Adam had known it would. But without the money from Harry's share she herself would have no home, and the children no future. She couldn't put it off forever.

Her jaw cracked in a yawn. It had been a long and emotional day and she abandoned her idea of relaxing in the lounge in favour of an early night. After she'd tucked Roberta into bed, and made sure Benjamin's late-night ambitions towards the wine cellar had been nipped in the bud, she retired to her own room on the third floor; one of those set aside for family and the few live-in staff. She sat for a while, looking at the photo of Harry that had lived on her dressing table at Burleigh, and that now graced her dressing table here, and then reached out and stroked the smiling face, captured forever behind glass. Although her heart contracted as fiercely as ever at the loss of him, she realised with a leap of relief that she was starting to feel less helpless now that she had a purpose. This drifting along through life, and longing for a return to the past, would soon be over.

The following morning Fiona came into Helen's room even before she'd risen. Helen pulled herself up against the pillow and blinked owlishly at her youngest daughter, who was already dressed.

'Can we go out?' the girl asked.

'Out where? Don't open that curtain!'

Fiona ignored her and pulled the heavy purple fabric back to let in the light. 'The beach?' she said hopefully, but without much expectation.

Helen hesitated; it was a grey and gusty day out there. Then she saw the disappointment begin to creep across Fiona's face, and relented with an inward shudder. 'Yes, all right. But you'll have to wrap up warm. Does Roberta want to come?'

'She went to the village with Guy and Benjamin.'

'Go on then. Go and find your big coat, and your scarf and gloves.'

The girl bounded off, and Helen hauled her aching body from the bed; she'd had no idea yesterday had taken such a toll on her, but there had been a great deal of lifting and carrying, once the train journey was over. She found herself grateful to Fiona after all; a good walk would loosen her up a bit, at least, and build an appetite for breakfast.

Soon the two of them were helping each other down the cliff path, and onto the narrow stretch of sandy beach that lay below the hotel. The tide was on its way out, and the rocks that separated Fox Bay from Trethkellis were covered with sharp mussels and pale brown and white limpets; the sand strewn with black and green bladder wrack seaweed, slimy and bulbous. In the distance Helen could see the Trethkellis lifeboat station with its huge granite pillars securing the slipway, and the slipway itself, extending out several hundred feet past treacherous-looking rocks. On a day like today it was all too easy to imagine small fishing boats getting into difficulties out there … Helen shivered and turned away.

She watched Fiona peering into rock pools and picking up pebbles, and let her mind wander. For once it did not immediately go to memories of Harry, instead she rehearsed her opening gambit to Fleur, thinking of all the different ways she could bring the subject up, and all the ways Fleur might respond to each one.

She brushed wet sand off a large, smooth rock and sat down. All this was made harder by knowing Fleur would do all she could to help, and to secure her grandchildren's future; if she'd been a cold woman, with her own interests closest to her heart, it would have been much easier. Back in Bristol it had made so much sense, all neatly laid out: Fleur would keep her own half of the hotel, which meant Benjamin would still inherit something of the family's Cornish legacy, at least, and on paper it was all perfect. But here, face to face with the reality of it all, everything seemed to tilt and slip, built on ifs and buts.

What if she couldn't sell only half of the interest in Fox Bay? It would probably be a lot more complicated than she'd thought, but if it was too complicated, what then? Would she have to persuade Fleur to sell her half too? That would put an end to Ben's inheritance and would put Fleur out of her own home. No, that wasn't something she could consider either.

Helen thought back to the reading of Harry's will, but it had sounded as if death was not something he'd truly believed could ever touch him. *To my children: this, this and that.* His motorcycle books to Roberta, his watch and chain to Benjamin, Fiona would have his favourite ship-in-a-bottle, the *Cutty Sark* ... small but precious gifts he knew his children would treasure. *All else, including any properties, to my wife.* Of course, she realised now, at that point he'd probably been in the process of trying to work out what he actually owned, and what he'd had to sell off. Let alone what was about to be repossessed.

The grey water swelled towards her and she watched it break on the shoreline, sending foam fizzing up the sand before chasing itself back out to sea. Again, and again. If only life were so simple. And death, too.

Helen frowned herself into concentration again. Maybe just selling the beach would be enough to afford a little townhouse? Then she'd still have the hotel to fall back on when the children were grown, if she wanted a change of lifestyle. She looked around at the small inlet and sighed. No, it would be worthless by itself, with its only access through the hotel grounds. Her brother David and his wife had always been keen on Fox Bay, but they hadn't the capital; David had always said as much whenever Harry had mentioned any of the investments with which he'd become involved.

What about Guy? Helen sat up straight as the thought came from nowhere. He lived at the hotel, so had no rent to pay out of his wages; he was sure to have something put away. If *he* bought Helen's inherited share there would be no question of him turning Fleur out; lifelong friends, they'd become partners in business too. She felt a tremor of excitement at the perfection of the idea, and as it grew, she stood up and waved.

'Fiona! Come on, that's enough now. You'll catch a chill out here!'

Fiona's mouth turned down, and normally Helen would have laughed, watching the girl drag her feet, pretend to lose her glove, and then spot an interesting stone that must be closely examined. But she wanted to be there when Guy returned, to explain her dilemma and talk to him about her ideas before she took them to Fleur; it would be so much better to go with a plan already in place.

'Come *on*,' she urged. 'When we get back you can have some breakfast and look at Roberta's fairy book, all right?'

That put a wind behind Fiona, and they returned for a late breakfast in the near-deserted dining room. Helen decided that, for the remainder of their stay, they would eat in the little suite of private rooms on the ground floor; it was ludicrous to be waited on like guests, no matter what Fleur said. Jeremy Bickle, the head barman who was standing in for Guy, was pressed into telling Helen that Roberta had, indeed, had three boiled eggs for her breakfast.

'She said you'd approve,' he told her, embarrassed. 'And since you weren't here, we — '

'One, tomorrow,' she said firmly, 'whatever she tells you.' But she couldn't help smiling behind her hand, nevertheless.

After breakfast, she and Fiona sat in the lobby and Helen turned the fragile pages of Roberta's favourite book, murmuring the required exclamations of delight at the sight of gossamer wings and delicate features, but all the while keeping an

56

ear open for the sound of Guy's car on the gravel outside. At last she heard it, and stood up to meet him, but her anticipation was short-lived.

'Where's Guy?'

'He sent us back in a taxi,' Benjamin said. 'He met someone he knows, and as it's his day off he decided to go off into Bude with him. He bought me some books about French and Italian wines to read, look!'

Helen swallowed her disappointment and admired the books he showed her. It seemed he was genuinely interested after all, and not using Guy's offer of tuition as an excuse to repeat his New Year's Eve shenanigans, which came as a huge relief.

Roberta glanced at her little sister. 'Why's Fiona got my book?'

'Never mind that, Miss three-boiled-eggs!'

Roberta flushed. 'I did eat them all,' she offered, by way of mitigation.

Helen shook her head in defeat. 'I don't know if that's worse or better! Go and get changed, both of you. And take Fiona upstairs too, she needs to change into dry clothes.'

It was silly to be impatient, she reminded herself as the children went up, the two older ones swinging Fiona between them on the stairs, it was only their first day, there was plenty of time to arrange things with Guy. But the thought of going up to her room to finish her unpacking didn't appeal at all, it just made her stay here feel more permanent.

She had also discovered that each room she went into, for the first time since they'd returned, held its own memory of Harry. The piano and the dining room had been one thing, and had even made her smile a little, but some of the other rooms had dealt her fragile healing a numbing blow. The cloisters had been the worst.

The chairs put away for the summer, she'd stood instead next to the pillar against which he'd been leaning on that bright autumn day in 1903, when she'd told him she was expecting their first child. He'd looked at her, uncomprehending for the space of a couple of heartbeats, and then gathered her to him with the deepest sigh. She'd heard that sigh again, echoing through the stone and feeling it against her hair, and had turned away from the cloisters, unable to bear the weight of fresh grief.

Other rooms held echoes of his voice, shadows of his presence; his lanky frame sprawled in various chairs, with casual elegance and the utter confidence he'd also inspired in others. This was his home, and Helen was certain the memories would become a comfort when they visited Fox Bay in the future, but for now, despite her earlier reluctance, she found herself eager to get back outside in the fresh air.

She checked to see Fiona was still happily annoying her siblings, then strolled outside into the grounds, following the path which led around the back to the tennis courts, little used at this time of year. The courts themselves were surrounded by a wide stretch of grass and a low stone wall, and on the other side of that wall lay the small church dedicated to St Adhwynn.

'Adh*wynn's*,' Harry had told her. 'Pronounced just like that. Most of the locals just call it St

58

'Dwinn's now. She was a fifth-century virgin, apparently.' He'd dropped a kiss on her forehead. 'Aptly enough, she's the patron saint of sweethearts.'

Helen's chest tightened now at the memory. On Saturday 17th August 1901, this tiny stone building, with room for possibly twenty in its knotted wooden pews, had been packed from altar to bell tower. The congregation had spilled over and out into the churchyard, despite hers and Harry's wish to keep the event small, and after the ceremony the two of them had emerged, so certain of their immortality, into the windblown churchyard with its leaning stones, a churchyard inhabited by the dust and bones of all those other immortals.

She stared at the sharply arched, carved wooden door, as if she expected it to open and the phantoms of her former life to come tumbling out, and part of her wished they would; if she could see her happy young self now she would beg herself to make the most of every precious moment. But would she have listened? She thought of all the fearful nights she'd spent when Harry had been overseas serving in the army, the days when she had dreaded the arrival of a telegram and had eyed every boy on a bicycle with throat-clenching dread. That Helen would have listened, and believed, but then the war had ended, and she'd been so sure she now had him forever ... How could he have survived all that horror, only to fall to a stupid, leaky fuel pipe? It was madness.

She crossed the overgrown grass, ignoring the cold wet streaks that brushed her stockings, and tried the door handle. The clunking echo of the latch bounced around the tiny porch on the other side of the door, and, as she stepped inside, the memories awoken by the musty smell took her breath away. She wasn't just remembering now, she was re-living. She could hear the muffled noise made by too many people in a confined space trying to remain quiet; shifting feet, suppressed coughing, rustling hymn books, the stern hushing of a parent to their bored child. She could even see Harry just ahead of her at the altar, Adam Coleridge at his side, could see the stiffness in his shoulders as he forced himself to remain facing the front, until, finally, he had twisted to look at her coming towards him down the short aisle.

His smile had seemed such a long time coming, and she'd stopped, suddenly certain he'd changed his mind. But then his lips curved upward and it seemed, for a second, as if all the meagre light in this place was concentrated on his face and everything else had disappeared. He'd ignored eti-quette and held out his hand to her, the organ had struck up the *Bridal Chorus*, and Helen's eager, satin-clad feet had moved her towards the altar, towards Harry, and towards her future.

Now those feet were anchored to the cold stone floor, and there was no one to smile on her, or to hold out their hand. Helen stifled a sob, and that too echoed through the tiny building, such a lonely sound it frightened her. She turned away from the altar again, not even sure how long she had been here, lost in the past, and suddenly hat-ing the church with all its empty promises. She left by the south door and passed through the kissing gate at the top of the churchyard, and the air, chilly though it was, tasted fresh and slightly salty blowing up from the sea.

As she followed the low stone wall around to the path that would take her back to the hotel she heard something. A voice. She stopped and turned her head to lessen the sound of the wind and the sea, and a light, almost ethereal voice drifted to her from the empty graveyard. For a moment her blood chilled to match the spots of rain that batted against her face; had she really been so keen to find ghosts? But she realised almost at once that the woman's voice was real, and although she couldn't make out the words Helen felt oddly comforted by it. She walked towards the wall and saw the top of a felt, cloche-style hat, but the head upon which it sat remained bowed.

'... always come back,' the woman was saying. Helen saw a pale hand reach out and brush dry leaves away from the top of the neat, upright stone, one of the few left like it. Not a grave, but a memorial. 'I don't want you to worry about me.' Now she could hear the voice properly, Helen realised it held a light Welsh accent. 'I still take you with me, wherever I go. I always will.' The voice broke on these last words, and Helen stepped back, reluctant to intrude on such a private moment, but the woman must have heard her feet in the grass, and looked up, sitting back on her heels.

Helen blinked in confusion; the owner of that gentle Welsh voice was the bold American woman from the dining room the night before. 'Mrs Scripps?'

The woman seemed disorientated for a moment, then came back to herself. 'Marshall, actually.'

61

She sat silent for a moment, then kissed her fingertips and pressed them to the memorial stone. She rose to her feet and held out her hand. 'Leah Marshall.'

'Then all that last night?' But it didn't seem to matter now. Helen shifted her gaze to the memorial and spoke softly. 'Your husband?'

Mrs Marshall opened her mouth to speak, but closed it again and turned to look out over the sea. Helen waited for a moment, then touched the woman gently on the arm. 'I'm sorry, I don't mean to intrude.'

'No, it's all right.' Mrs Marshall looked back at her, seeming to size her up, then she nodded. 'His name was Daniel.'

'Was it the war?'

'How did you know? Although, I suppose so many are.'

Helen hesitated. 'Well, it's only that I noticed it's a memorial stone and not a grave.'

Mrs Marshall's lips tightened, and once again Helen wished she'd not spoken.

'You're right, of course,' the woman said at last. 'He's still out there, somewhere.' She blew out a harsh breath and looked back at Helen. 'I lost him at Arras in '17. His tunnel collapsed.'

Helen winced. 'How awful. I'm so sorry.' There didn't seem anything more to say, so Helen waited while Mrs Marshall arranged her coat, knocked mud from her knees, and gathered herself.

'He was born here,' Mrs Marshall said, and it seemed to Helen that now she had begun, she wanted to talk. Perhaps, brassiness and laughter aside, she actually had no one else. After all, despite being such a lively part of the artists' group, she'd arrived and left alone last night.

'You're Welsh, aren't you? Was Daniel local? Where did you meet?' Helen held up a hand. 'Stop me if I'm being nosy, Mrs Marshall, you must tell me to mind my own business.'

Mrs Marshall offered her a brief smile. 'I don't mind. It's nice to talk about him actually. Yes, Daniel was from Trethkellis, but we met over there, in France. And since I suddenly seem to be telling you my life story, you should probably call me Leah.'

'I'm Helen. Were you a nurse during the war then?'

Leah nodded. 'Before it, too.'

'And now?'

'I can't. Not now.' Leah sat on the wall and swung her legs over to stand next to Helen. 'It's not that I don't want to help people, I just . . . I can't.' She threw a little smile back towards the lonely memorial beneath the wall, and dropped her voice to a conspiratorial murmur. 'Daniel would rise up, swim back, and haunt me if he knew I'd given up.'

Helen smiled. 'Do you come here a lot then?'

'Whenever I can, but it's a long trip from Mountain Ash, lots of changes on the train. I don't come in the summer though, it's too busy.'

'It must be difficult, having him so far away.' Helen thought of Harry, lying in a churchyard up in Bristol; agonising in itself, but how much worse it would be if he were in another country.

'It can get to me a bit,' Leah admitted. 'But even when I can't get here, he's always with me.'

63

She pulled a locket out from beneath her coat and opened it. 'See, I've got a lock of his hair. I cut it just before he joined up, while he was asleep. He went mad when he found out, but he forgave me. He always forgave me.' She stared for a moment at the fair curl, trapped behind a glass oval just as Harry's face was, then snapped the locket shut and turned to look out over the sea again. 'I've never truly felt at home here, but it's where I can feel him the closest. Do you know what I mean?' She looked back at Helen. 'Of course you do.'

'We married in that church,' Helen said, indicating St Adhwynn's. 'I'd forgotten it was so close to the hotel.'

'It's so pretty, I've always loved it.' Leah's face told a deeper story, but she smiled away the sudden shadow. 'Must be a very special memory.'

Helen looked again at the studded door, and nodded. 'I might be able to see it like that one day.' They began to walk, by unspoken agreement, back towards the hotel, and she searched for a way to banish the melancholy of those memories. 'Do you know Fleur well? Last night you seemed keen to stand up for her.'

'She's very kind, isn't she? She keeps Daniel's memorial tidy for me, when I can't come down.'

'And last night, when she went along with your Mrs Scripps act?'

Leah gave a little laugh, and the mood lightened further. 'She knows the little games I like to play, and why.'

Helen's curiosity was piqued again. 'And will you share that with me, too?'

'It's hard to explain.' Leah pondered a moment,

as if she'd never really thought about it before. 'Coming down here, to be with Daniel, it's something I need to do, and it brings me some kind of peace for a while.' She shrugged. 'But at the same time it turns me into something like a ghost, myself. You must understand that feeling.'

'I do.' Helen remembered the way the sounds had echoed at Burleigh. They seemed to reflect the hollow feeling Harry had left behind in her own soul.

'It's such an awful, empty feeling,' Leah went on, 'so I fill it with as much fun as I can. And even with mischief sometimes. It helps.' She smiled. 'And it amuses Fleur too, though she'd never admit it.'

Helen laughed outright, surprising herself. 'I imagine it does. Millicent Scripps, indeed!'

'Edward Scripps actually exists though,' Leah said. 'But I don't know if he's friends with President Wilson, and I'm pretty sure his real wife's called Nackie.'

'Well Millicent certainly did Fleur a favour last night. Those Bentley sisters might have a point about the noise, but they were being quite horrible.'

'I enjoyed seeing them squirm, Fleur doesn't deserve the way they treat her, but since she won't say a word, Millicent's doing the job instead.'

'Well,' Helen ventured, her hostess instincts rising to the fore again, 'they *are* paying guests.'

'So's everyone else.' Leah shrugged. 'You can't please everyone, so what's the point in trying?'

Helen blinked. 'Because it's what a decent person does, I suppose. Even if it doesn't work, one ought to try, don't you think?'

'Up to a point I suppose,' Leah conceded. 'But you'd be spreading yourself awfully thin, and you have to think of your own state of mind sometimes. Anyway,' she waved that off, 'speaking of Fleur, do you two get along all right?'

'Surprisingly well, actually. Why?'

'She talks about Harry a lot, of course, and the kids, and I feel I know them all. But ...' She trailed off, looking embarrassed for the first time.

'But not me?' They had reached the gravel drive now, and Helen stopped, reluctant to go back inside just yet, and face Harry's ghost around every corner.

Leah gave her a sidelong look. 'Truthfully I think she's a bit wary of you.'

'Wary?'

'I can see why, mind. You've got an air of . . . something about you. Not sure what.' Leah gave a little laugh. 'Don't look like that, I quite like it. In fact I've decided I quite like you.'

'That's comforting,' Helen said, a little dryly, and Leah laughed. They both looked up as a magpie landed, chattering, on the gate by the tennis courts, and Leah saluted it and muttered,

'Bore da, Mr Pioden, sut mae eich wraig?'

When Helen didn't do likewise Leah raised an eyebrow. 'Not warding off bad luck today, then?' Helen thought back to the magpie she'd saluted just before Harry died, but didn't want to break the breezy lightness of the moment; it was too new, and too precious. 'The day a magpie salutes me, I'll salute him back.'

'I see. You've clearly got the right idea of your

66

own worth.' Leah looked at Helen thoughtfully for a moment, then slipped her arm through hers. 'Magpies aside, I think we're going to be great friends, Mrs Fox.'

'Do you?' Helen returned the speculative look. 'We've only just met, and I won't be staying long.'

'Nor will I,' Leah pointed out. 'But I'm sure you know how a pen works, as do I. As for us only having met last night, all I can say is that … well.' Her brisk, almost brash manner fell away, and her voice softened. 'I don't share my confidences with just anyone. Do you?'

'No,' Helen admitted. 'Harry had *his* friends, and plenty of them, but he was all I ever needed.' She blinked away the sudden sting of tears, and Leah hugged her arm closer.

'Likewise with Daniel. But I found a way to fill the space he left, and you need to find a kindly soul to help ease yours. Us meeting like that,' Leah gestured behind them towards the church, 'I like to think that was fate's way of making sure you do. Or maybe even Harry's.'

Helen wasn't so sure; Harry still filled her heart and her mind, and what was left over belonged to Roberta, Benjamin and Fiona. But as they parted company in the lobby, and she watched Leah's steps drag a little on the stairs, she wondered if perhaps that didn't matter. Perhaps it was Leah who needed the help, after all this time of being alone, in which case Helen was more than equal to the task. Wasn't that what she did best? And if it helped her in the process then she wouldn't have spread herself too thin, as Leah had suggested, for nothing.

★ ★ ★

That evening Guy returned, and an impatient Helen reluctantly gave him a chance to settle in before seeking him out. She followed him into the lounge bar, and chatted with him briefly as he prepared her gin and orange juice, but then she took it away to an alcove so she could straighten everything in her head first. She'd ask him, subtly of course, if he had any plans for opening his own premises one day, and that would naturally lead to the subject of finances, so, depending on his response she'd be able to casually—

'Mrs Fox! So lovely to see you again!'

She looked up to see Millicent back, in all her considerable glory. 'Good evening, Mrs Scripps.' She hoped she didn't sound brusque, but the interruption wasn't at all welcome just now.

'Do you mind if I sit with you a while?'

Helen remembered her earlier determination to help, and gestured to the chair opposite. 'Do you do this every night?'

Leah shook her head and reverted to her own voice. 'Just when I need to pick myself up a bit. Although the visit to Daniel today ended better than usual, thanks to meeting you.' She looked away, ostensibly studying the bar, and Helen wondered if she felt she'd opened her heart too readily, but when she turned again the faintly wicked smile was back. 'I thought I might have a bit of fun with our favourite guests tonight.'

'You really shouldn't, you know,' Helen reproved.

'Oh, nothing too awful. Just a little diversion,

don't worry.'

But Helen had the sense that she might have made Leah think twice, and it was a good feeling. 'It does sound strange,' she said aloud, 'hearing your voice come out of that face.'

'This face?' Leah gave her an affronted look and adopted Mrs Scripps's accent once more. 'Darling, I'll have you know this is the finest face Max Factor can produce.'

'Stop it!' But Helen couldn't help but smile, and Leah grinned back and picked up Helen's drink.

'So, what brings you into this little den of iniquity tonight?'

'I … just wanted a chat with Guy.'

Leah's eyes narrowed. 'Why do I think there's something shifty going on?'

'I don't know.'

'Is there?'

The question was blunt, almost rude, given the newness of their acquaintance and Helen hesitated. It was as she'd told Leah earlier; over the course of her marriage she had never felt the need to grow friendships; leaving her childhood behind in Exeter had been the start of almost twenty years of needing no one but Harry. Perhaps it would all have been different if she'd cultivated her own trusted circle. All those people who'd known something at the party before she had, if they'd been closer, might they have told her? Adam hadn't, but then he'd had his own selfish reasons and she could no longer count him as trustworthy.

The closest she'd come to a girlfriend was Jeanette Duval, and that friendship had fallen far short of the kind of conversations she'd already had with

Leah. But could she really trust this woman she'd known for less than a day?

'Don't tell me if you don't want to,' Leah said, as the silence drew out. She looked embarrassed now, and as if she might leave at any moment. 'It's just that you looked a bit lost. I'm a good listener, but don't let me bully you.'

'I don't want to be rude, it's just —'

'You're not being rude. You're being sensible. I could be anyone.'

Helen raised an eyebrow. 'Like the wife of a celebrated newspaper magnate?'

'I could definitely be that,' Leah agreed. 'And that's the sort of person you certainly *don't* want to be telling secrets to.' The atmosphere relaxed a little, and Leah leaned forward to pat Helen's arm. 'I'll be here if you do decide you want to unburden yourself, but I don't want you to think I'm being pushy.'

'You've stolen my drink,' Helen pointed out with a little smile. 'That's quite pushy.'

'It just means I feel comfortable with you,' Leah assured her, and winked.

Helen gave a laugh. 'You did say you know Fleur quite well, would you steal *her* drinks?'

Leah's eyes shot wide. 'I said comfortable, not reckless!' She put down Helen's glass and adjusted the neckline of her dress, and just before the material fell back into place and covered it again, Helen saw the chain of the locket containing Daniel's hair. She recalled the frank honesty Leah had shown her in the churchyard, and made up her mind.

'I have to ask Fleur something delicate.'

70

Leah's face registered curiosity, but more so it showed a flicker of gladness that Helen was ready to confide in her. 'Go on,' she murmured.

Haltingly, Helen began to explain about Harry and his disastrous investments, and then, as if someone had opened the sluice gates of a dam, it all came pouring out. She couldn't stop it, even if she'd wanted to. She told Leah about Adam's role in it all, about Harry's pointless death, the loss of their home, and finally she laid out her hopes for the future. 'So you see, I need to release the money somehow, but I doubt Fleur could afford to buy me out, so I thought perhaps Guy —'

'Stop.' Leah leaned across and put her hand on Helen's. 'Stop, love.' She sat back, chewing at her thumbnail, and her eyes drifted closed as she let out a huge sigh. 'You can't do any of this.'

'Why?' Helen tightened up again. 'Because of Fleur? I told you, I don't intend to make her homeless, and I've lived on a pittance all summer waiting to ask, but it's my children's inheritance, and mine, and that's why I —'

'No, I mean you literally *can't* do it. Fleur can't sell the hotel, to Guy or to anyone else.'

'Why not?'

'Because it's not hers to sell.'

71

4

Leah watched Helen's expression freeze, but she couldn't take the words back now. She'd undone all the good she'd done so far in helping this outwardly calm, but desperately sad, woman to unburden herself, and it was a wretched feeling.

'I'm so sorry.' How thin that sounded.

'What do you mean, it's *not hers*?' Helen could barely get the words out.

'Just exactly that. It belongs to a man named Ronald Gardner. He owns hotels all over the place. London, Manchester, here in Cornwall too. He owns the Cliffside Fort Hotel down at Caernoweth actually, bought it from the Battens after the war.' Leah stopped, suddenly aware she was babbling. 'Anyway, Fox Bay is a Gardner hotel as of last year.'

'Last year?' Helen blinked slowly, as if trying to order her thoughts. 'I still don't understand, last year Harry was still … She must have gone behind his back.' Her eyes opened wide. 'No wonder he wouldn't, or couldn't write to ask her for help!' She stood up and started to walk away, then swung around and came back. 'How well do you know Fleur, really?'

'Reasonably well. Like I said, she tends Daniel's memorial, and I help out sometimes, when she's short-handed.'

She was about to go on, but Helen held up a hand, frowning. 'And that's another thing. Why is

72

she still here?'

'I don't know anything more really. Just that she manages this place, but she doesn't own it.'

'And the beach? Is that still in the family?'

Leah shrugged helplessly. 'You'd have to ask her. I'm sorry.'

'Not half as sorry as Fleur is going to be,' Helen said grimly. 'She knew I'd be asking for my share at some point. I mean, Harry was her son! He must have been devastated. She destroyed him!' Helen's face was pale, and Leah wished she hadn't donned her Mrs Scripps persona tonight, she felt quite ridiculous to be dressed in this way when Helen was so distraught. She compared the drawn, tight-lipped woman of today with the one she'd met just last night in the restaurant, her sherry-coloured eyes shining over the top of the napkin behind which she'd not quite hidden her laughter, and her heart contracted in sympathy.

'What will you do?' she ventured at length.

Helen took an age to come back from wherever her thoughts had taken her. 'Do?' She gave Leah a bright, empty smile. 'I'm going to talk to Fleur, of course. See how long it takes her to tell me the truth about what she did to Harry.'

'Perhaps it's better if you wait, at least for tonight.'

'Why?'

'There's a big dinner party, some local dignitary, or MP, or something. Fleur won't have time to turn around, let alone talk properly.'

'Then she won't have time to think up any lies either,' Helen pointed out grimly. 'No, tonight it is.'

There had turned out to be an unexpected iron core lurking inside Helen Fox's polite, faintly timid exterior, and Leah actually felt an unexpected flicker of sympathy for the formidable Fleur. She stood up and found her Millicent Scripps voice.

'Honey, it looks like you've been cheated, and I am behind you every step of the way.'

Helen gave her a wan smile. 'Probably safer there than anywhere else.'

She seemed to be struggling to maintain her composure as she left the lounge, and Leah reflected that it must take an awful lot of strength to appear so collected in public while inside she was clearly on the point of collapse. She found it oddly warming to realise that she was probably one of very few people to have glimpsed that side of the renowned Mrs Harry Fox, but at the same time it put her in a position of responsibility; out of a simple desire to help, she had drawn the truth of Harry's death out into the open where Helen would finally have to meet it head on. Now, whatever happened, Leah would have to ensure she was there to help steady her new friend, and in her own secret mind she knew she wasn't the steadiest of people herself. All she could do was hope she was up to the job.

She sipped at Helen's drink, and let her thoughts drift back to two years ago, to the first time she had seen the Bristol Foxes and their entourage. They usually came in the summer, and back then the hotel had still belonged to Fleur and her son; the elder Mrs Fox had been as much part of the noisy party as the hangers-on who had burst in, on a wave of excitement and laughter, just after

74

the end of the war. Ready to celebrate the first peacetime Christmas in four years.

Rationing hadn't stopped this crowd from having the time of their lives, and Leah, sitting alone just as she was now, had watched it all, invisible and wracked with envy. Harry Fox, the centre of it all, had struck her as the kind of man she wouldn't have trusted for one minute: never alone, always laughing, and with the kind of good looks that drew people to him just so they could find out if his company was as appealing as his appearance. Evidently it was.

His wife, pretty enough but lacking the glamour of most of their guests, had looked on with proud indulgence, and at first a cynical Leah had rolled her eyes. *Foolish woman if you think you can hold that one.* But before the first night was over, she'd realised Harry Fox was utterly devoted to his family, and that he wasn't hesitant about showing it. Leah had overheard him talking to his friend Adam, presumably the same Adam who'd persuaded him to invest in that doomed shipping company, and as the slightly sozzled but genuine love poured out of him it was as if she'd been listening to her own sweet Daniel. It was more than Leah could bear, and she'd checked out the following morning and returned to Wales, aching for what she'd lost.

Blinking back tears now, she looked up to see Helen's older daughter hovering on the other side of the glass doors. Eventually the girl came hesitantly in, and stood just inside, looking around.

Leah stood up. 'Roberta?'

Roberta turned in the direction of her voice

and Leah gestured her over. The poor girl looked as if she'd rather be anywhere than here, but she obediently crossed the floor.

'Hello, Mrs Scripps. Have you seen my mother?'

'She's gone to find your grandmother.' Leah noted the look of puzzlement on Roberta's face, and realised she had spoken in her own voice. 'Your mum knows my little secret,' she said, tapping the side of her nose. 'My name's Leah Marshall, I'm from Wales, I'm certainly not rich, and I've never been to America in my life.'

Roberta looked blankly at her for a moment, then giggled, and the shy colour faded from her cheeks. 'How did you learn to talk like that?'

'Mam and I had a doughboy staying with us, after he was invalided out of the war. Why don't you sit down, so we can get to know one another properly?'

'A doughboy?' Roberta took the seat recently vacated by her mother, and sat forward eagerly. 'Is that a soldier, then?'

Leah nodded. 'Our lads were Tommies, right? Well, Australians were diggers, and Americans were doughboys. A lot of us with spare rooms took in convalescent soldiers, and I'd been a nurse before, so it made sense. He was a nice enough boy.' She didn't want to confess how she'd hated him at first for not being Daniel, for only joining the war after Daniel had already been killed, and most of all for living through it. It was wrong to feel that way, she knew that, but it didn't make the feeling of injustice any easier to bear.

'Now, enough about that. Roberta's a fiddly name, so tell me, are you secretly a Bobby? Maybe even spelling it with an 'i'?'

'I'm just a Roberta. I was named for Dad's father, the one who built this hotel.' The girl's eyes darkened for a moment as she said, 'Daddy always said it sounded silly and should be shortened, but Mum says Bobbi Fox sounds like a music-hall girl.'

Leah grinned, wanting to banish that shadow. 'Nothing wrong with that if it did. Have you heard of Lucy Kempton? Lucy Batten that was?'

'No.'

'Well she's not music-hall, strictly speaking, but she's raised a few eyebrows on the stage, put it that way. Local girl, too. From Caernoweth. She and her husband sometimes stay here.' She looked the girl over with a critical eye. 'You'll find the right name when you're older, I'm sure.'

Roberta looked around. 'I thought Granny was working tonight. What did Mum want with her?'

'Oh, this and that.' Leah changed the subject quickly. 'You look famished. Would you like to go into dinner with me instead?'

'Oh, yes please! I'd love to.'

'Even though I'm not a glamorous American?'

Roberta smiled. 'You're still very glamorous.'

'That is absolutely the correct response, well done.'

On the way to the dining room Leah saw Fleur, looking harassed and moving urgently in the direction of the dining room, and before long it became obvious that it was the head chef who was in her firing line today. Raised voices from the kitchen had the few guests looking at one another in embarrassment, and Roberta's eyes were wide as she stared in the direction of the sound of her grandmother in full voice. Thank goodness the local dignitary hadn't yet arrived, and even more so that the Misses Bentley were elsewhere.

'That's not like your granny, is it?' Leah observed. 'She's normally very discreet when she has to berate someone.'

'And does she ... berate a lot?' Roberta sounded nervous now.

'Only those she pays to do a good job,' Leah soothed her. 'You're her granddaughter, she wouldn't raise her voice to you. But Mr Gough's reputation affects the hotel, and that's different.' She picked up her menu. 'Now, what will it be? Your grandmother tells me you have a liking for boiled eggs.'

Roberta's raised eyebrow made her look just like Fleur herself. 'Only for breakfast.'

'Of course.' Leah watched the girl consulting her menu, and admired her composure. She was very much like her mother in that regard, it seemed; the unguarded moments of sadness were quickly quashed, but not banished. Merely hidden.

'Where's your brother tonight? And little Fiona?'

'Ben's putting Fiona to bed, she had her supper ages ago.' Roberta lowered her menu. 'Ought we to wait for him?'

'It would be polite,' Leah agreed, and Roberta put her menu down with an exaggerated sigh.

'He'll be ages, he always reads too many stories to Fiona, she can twist him around her little finger.'

Leah smothered a smile, and looked up as Guy

78

Bannacott approached their table. 'We're waiting for young Mr Fox.'

'Very good.'

'I understand he's keen to learn the trade?'

'I believe he might have an aptitude,' Guy said. 'He's picked up quite a lot already. What about you, Miss Fox? Would you like to learn all about the wines of France and Italy?'

'No fear,' Roberta said, then flushed. 'I mean, no thank you, Mr Bannacott. I don't like wine.'

'Roberta's still a little bit young to go tasting that sort of thing. What does interest you?' she added, as Guy withdrew.

Roberta's face reflected one of those moments of shadow again, and her eyes, so like her mother's, darkened for a moment. 'I like looking at Daddy's motorcycle books,' she ventured quietly. 'He loved to ride. Perhaps I could learn too, someday.'

Leah didn't know what to say to that, but she had an idea Helen would be the first, and biggest, obstacle to that ambition. To her relief Benjamin chose that moment to saunter in. He caught sight of his sister and waved, but hesitated as he saw Leah sitting beside her. Leah waved him over.

'We're just choosing,' she said, gesturing for him to sit down. 'There's a menu there.'

'Where's Mum?'

'Talking to Granny,' Roberta put in. 'Come on, I'm starving.'

Once again, she had pushed sadness to the back of her mind, and Leah wondered if she ever let it out for longer than a moment. She studied Benjamin surreptitiously over the top of her menu; at seventeen he bore a striking resemblance to what

79

she remembered of his father; the same abundance of thick, dark hair, the same easy manner . . . he would probably have the same carefree, booming laugh, too, but at five years older than Roberta, and a full eleven over little Fiona, Leah suspected he felt the burden of surrogate fatherhood while still being regarded as a boy.

So over dinner she made a point of talking to him like an adult, drawing out a hitherto well-hidden wit, and before too long even Roberta was giggling. There was a closeness between these two, Leah realised, and she wondered if it had always been there, or if losing their father had strengthened their bond. As an only child herself, she couldn't imagine being so close to someone who wasn't your parent, who was an ally in times of despair, either real or imagined.

'What's Mum talking to Granny about?' Benjamin wanted to know.

Roberta shrugged. 'Maybe talking about how long we're staying here. Did she tell you?'

Her brother shook his head and forked up another mouthful of potato. 'She never does.'

'Well I hope it's not very long.'

'Why not? It's great here.'

'All right for you,' Roberta complained, 'you've got Mr Bannacott to teach you stuff. Fiona's got Mum and Granny fawning all over her, and who've I got?'

'You've got me,' Leah put in, without thinking.

'It's not the same,' Roberta said, and although Ben looked horrified at what he probably saw as rudeness, Leah suddenly understood the melancholy that had accompanied that mention of motorcycles . . . Roberta had been her daddy's girl. She took a gulp of water to help swallow a lump that rose in her throat.

'I'm sure your mum and Fiona would like to spend time with you too, while you're here,' she said. 'And you'll be home before you know it.' Even as she spoke, she realised, with a sinking feeling, that tomorrow was her own last day at Fox Bay. Possibly for a long time to come; her savings would not stretch much further, and her widow's pension was insultingly small. She had to get a job, whether she wanted to or not.

'Well when we go home, I'm going to sell all my dolls,' Roberta was saying, chasing a stray pea around her plate, 'and I'm going to buy a bicycle instead.'

'Mum will never let you,' Benjamin said mildly, but it had the sound of an old discussion. 'She wouldn't let me have one until I was fourteen, so you've got ages yet. Besides, bicycles cost a lot more than you'd get from selling your dolls.'

'Well Mum said we're going to have enough money to buy a whole new *house* when we go home.'

'So? That doesn't mean we'll have enough to buy you a bicycle.'

Sensing he was deliberately needling his sister, Leah changed the subject quickly; from what she gathered from Helen there would be no new home except perhaps another rental in time, and certainly no bicycle. But as dinner went on she had the suspicion that leaving tomorrow was going to be harder than usual; quite aside from her new friendship with Helen Fox, she felt a growing

81

warmth towards these children, whose loss had
been even greater than either of them yet realised.

★ ★ ★

Helen peered through the swinging dining room
door now and again, and she caught a glimpse of
Leah and Roberta studying their menus. It was
a relief to know the two of them were keeping
each other company, and she just hoped Benjamin would be able to settle Fiona all right, and
that the little girl wouldn't come downstairs looking for her instead; as tightly wound as she was,
Helen was just as likely to blow up at the wrong
person. But perhaps that feeling would prove useful, it might help her to say what must be said,
and more importantly, to find out why Fleur had
done it. How *could* she have?

Eventually Fleur reappeared, fussing with the
cuffs of her blouse as if she'd been waving her
arms around like a madwoman. It was entirely
possible she had been.

'I'm glad I've caught you.' Helen was able to
smile quite convincingly, but Fleur's expression
was wary, nevertheless.

'I've just had to have words with Mr Gough,' she
said. 'He's considered one of the best in Cornwall,
but my goodness he's stubborn. Artistic temper-
aments! You haven't met him yet, have you? You
should, I'll introduce you—'

'Fleur!' Helen was not to be deflected. 'Might I
have a word? Somewhere private.'

'Now? I'm quite busy with arrangements for an
important dinner.'

'This is important too. It won't take more than a few minutes.'

Fleur regarded her steadily for a moment, then gestured to the office. 'Come through.'

Helen followed, wondering what it would be like to be one of those people, like Adam Coleridge, who could come out with something cryptic and watch their victim squirm as they tried to wriggle free.

But she only just managed to wait until the office door had closed behind her before she blurted out, 'Why has the hotel been sold to that Gardner man?'

Fleur sat down heavily. 'I had the feeling you were going to ask me about your share,' she admitted, 'and I wasn't sure what I'd say. But how did you know about the hotel?'

'It doesn't matter.'

But Fleur had already guessed. 'Leah, I suppose. I thought she must have known. Helen, love, you have to admit you've kept your own cards close to your chest. You didn't just bring the children for a visit.'

'No, I didn't.' Helen felt a dull flush spread over her face. 'Why didn't you say anything, if you knew why I was here?'

'I was too glad to have you here. I didn't want to risk pushing you away again so soon.'

'How long would it have been before you told us?' Helen's voice had risen, and, aware of the receptionist just beyond the door, she lowered it again. 'This hotel was the only thing we had left! Harry could have been saved if you hadn't been so selfish —'

'What?' Fleur's eyebrows shot up.

'You knew about his debts.'

'Of course I did! That's — '

'And he said he'd never asked you for help, because he couldn't ask you to share your own home, and relinquish control of the business. But he *did* ask, didn't he? Only it was too late, you'd already sold it from under him!'

Helen couldn't look at Fleur anymore, and turned to stare out of the window instead, but the pathway stretched out towards St 'Dwinn's church, and she closed her eyes on that, too. 'He must have felt so ... so helpless, with nowhere to turn.'

'If you're suggesting he took his own life, you're wrong.' Fleur's words thickened with tears, and despite everything Helen had to steel herself not to offer her comfort. How could she have done this to Harry?

'No, I'm not suggesting that,' she said tightly. 'But he might not have felt the need to numb the fear with drink.'

'Drink? Harry didn't drink to excess, he never has.'

'That's why it affected his judgement so badly.'

'But he knew he was racing on that day, why would he do something so foolish?'

'He'd just had a letter to say the mortgage company was taking back Burleigh Mansions.' Helen looked Fleur full in the face now, her jaws aching with anger. 'We both know that if he'd had the security of the hotel to fall back on, they wouldn't have repossessed us. Your grandchildren are homeless now because of what you—'

84

'I didn't sell Fox Bay from under him, love,' Fleur said quietly. 'I gave it to him.'

Helen fell silent and simply stared at her. 'What?' she managed at last.

'Last summer, when you all came down together, I gave him my share of the hotel.' Fleur came closer and took her hand, and Helen was too stunned to pull away even if she'd wanted to. 'He didn't want to accept, but I told him he had a duty to you and to your children. He was supposed to do exactly as you suggested, use the asset to raise some capital and pay off his debts. Keep the bank at bay. But instead he sold it.'

'*That's* where he got the money for the Blue Ensign investment?'

Fleur shook her head. 'I don't know that part. Just that he contacted Ronald Gardner, and they struck a deal. Gardner got the hotel for far less than market value, on the understanding that no one knew about the sale, that the name wasn't changed, and that I have a home here for as long as Gardner owns it.' She squeezed Helen's hand. 'I think it was Harry's way of showing me his gratitude.'

'And what about his wife, his children? Didn't we deserve the same kind of assurance?'

'He was probably so certain of the success of his new venture, this Ensign thing you mentioned, he didn't think for one moment you'd need anything more.'

Helen withdrew her hand and fumbled her way to the chair. Whichever way you looked at it, she had no home, and now no hope of one either.

'What will I tell the children? How will we live?'

'You can all stay here.'

Helen looked up in disbelief. 'As *guests*?'

'There will be a roof over your heads for as long as you need one. And food. You won't have to pay a thing.'

'And your lovely Mr Gardner will accept that, will he?'

'He will if I offer you a job.'

Helen's mouth opened and closed while she struggled for words. The rug had been whipped out from under her feet so fast she felt she was still running on thin air. 'What job?'

Fleur thought for a moment. 'I don't have an assistant manager.'

'And can you make a case for one, with Mr Gardner?'

'I don't have to; I have full autonomy here — Mr Gardner never even visits. So, would you like that job? With a view to taking over as manager when I retire, of course. And,' she pushed on, finding her stride, 'perhaps Benjamin can be trained in Guy's role, for holiday cover and suchlike. We usually hire locally, but Ben has a good head on his shoulders. He'll do well.' She crouched by Helen's chair. 'Look, Helen, you and the children are all I have left,' she said in a choked voice. 'And I'm all you have. You came here to claim what was yours and, well, I'm it. Will you stay?'

'What choice do we have?' Helen knew she sounded bitter and ungrateful, but all her dreams of a compact little home in Bristol, where she knew people, and where her children had friends and schools, were crumbling into dust. Her gaze fell on the plaque on the wall: a simple, stylised fox's head carved in wood, with the ornate Latin engraving on a brass strip beneath it: *Vulpes latebram suam defendit.* The fox protects his lair.

Does he though? The voice in her head was light and mocking. *Or does he sell it, and leave his mate and cubs homeless?*

Helen straightened her shoulders. 'Maybe so,' she murmured aloud, 'but there's a new Fox in charge now.'

The following morning before breakfast, while she was preparing herself to break the news to the children, another disappointment waited in the lobby in the form of Leah, her two suitcases, and her regretful expression as Helen approached her.

'I'm sorry I didn't tell you, but I didn't see you after you went in with Fleur.'

Helen shook her head. 'No, I should have realised, but I was too preoccupied last night to ask how long you were staying.'

'I'd almost forgotten myself, what with everything,' Leah said sadly, 'but Mam's expecting me back.'

'I understand.'

Helen had gradually, through the dark hours of the night and into the drizzly grey morning, been coming to terms with the shattering of her plan and the new direction her life must now take, but in the back of her mind had been the comforting thought that at least she had an ally here. She'd begun to accept that Leah might even have been a friend, but now she was vanishing too. Helen felt herself retreating once more into her own mind, reliant on no one but herself after all.

87

'How did things go last night?' Leah asked, pulling on her gloves.

'Not well, but I won't trouble you with it. Suffice to say you were quite right, the hotel is owned by someone called Gardner now.' Something stopped her from blurting out that Harry's final betrayal had been so much worse than she'd thought; that was her own private sorrow. No one else needed to know, and even now Helen couldn't bear the thought of someone else judging him – betrayal it might have been, but it would have been out of desperation, not greed. Only herself and Fleur would understand that. And maybe the two older children, but she couldn't tell them either.

'I'll write,' Leah said. 'Every week if you like.' She took Helen's hands. 'I meant what I said about us being great friends. I'm certain we will.'

'Me too,' Helen said, knowing it was politeness and nothing more. But there was no point in parting on a sour note, so she squeezed Leah's fingers and smiled. Her party smile. Her hostess smile. *Do call again won't you, darling? It's been divine to see you ...*

'I'll look forward to your letters,' she said aloud, mechanically. 'And I'll write back and tell you how things are going.'

'You must be sure to give me your Bristol address when you move back.' Leah looked at her closely. 'We'll be much nearer to one another then, too, it's just a hop and a skip from Bristol to Mountain Ash.' She picked up her cases. 'Until then I'll write to you here, and Fleur can send anything on once you've left.'

Helen's practised smile slipped, and Leah put

her cases down again. 'I knew it! What else happened last night?'

'It's not your problem to worry over,' Helen said, stepping back as Leah tried to embrace her. 'You must go, the taxi is waiting.'

'Blow the taxi!' Leah turned away, and an openmouthed Helen saw shades of Millicent Scripps in the way she removed one glove and dinged the bell on the reception desk. 'I'd like to send a telegram, please.'

Ten minutes later they were sitting in the lounge bar, in the same alcove they had sat in last night, and Helen was telling her everything Fleur had said. Leah watched her, expressionless except for a flicker of anger when she learned that Harry had lied for so long. But she said nothing.

'So,' Helen finished, digging around for that bright smile again, 'it looks as if you'll be able to keep writing to me here after all.'

Leah nodded, not returning the smile. 'And how do you feel about that? Really?'

Helen blinked. Leah had immediately seen past the lightness, and she recalled her earlier dismissive thoughts about friendship with a pang of guilt.

'I don't know,' she said truthfully. 'One minute I'm optimistic, the next I'm so angry I forget to breathe. I'm grateful to have somewhere to live, of course, but—'

'But it's not the same as having a home of your own.'

'Burleigh Mansions wasn't mine either, at the end, but it was private, and I could do what I wished. It's different here.' She looked around her. Fox Bay was the last word in luxury, but she would be nothing more than a live-in employee here.

'Right,' Leah announced. 'I'm staying.'

Helen looked at her blankly. 'What?'

'I'm going to stay a while, and help you settle in.'

'But ... what about your mother?'

'The telegram I sent just said I'd missed the train, but I can send another to explain I'll be staying another week or so. Aunt Mary will understand, and there's nothing preventing her from staying with Mam. They'll have a great time telling each other what a let-down I am.' Leah sat forward and put a hand on Helen's arm. 'You're going to need help for a little while, and that's what friends are for.'

Helen couldn't stop the tears from spilling. Not since childhood had she felt the warm touch of genuine friendship from anyone except Harry and Adam, but even Adam's had been tainted by his betrayal. Leah Marshall had effortlessly settled into Helen's life in the space of a few hours, as if she had always belonged there, and Helen was unprepared for the conflict that brought; on one hand it was comforting, and a huge relief, but on the other there was the undeniable fear that she was putting herself entirely into the hands of a stranger, and risking that awful sense of loss all over again someday. Only time would tell.

Leah, with the kind of no-nonsense, no-fuss attitude Helen was already starting to recognise, handed over a cotton square. 'Blow your nose, Mrs Fox, this is no way for your guests to see you.' She called one of the bell boys over. 'Take my cases back up to room eight please. Don't worry,' she added to Helen, 'I can just about pay for another week, though I'll have to move to a smaller room after a day or two.'

'You won't!' Helen was so deeply moved she had trouble forming her words, and she took a moment to compose herself and finish wiping her eyes. 'I'm making my first decision as assistant manager of this hotel. Any bills incurred in the service of any member of the Fox family will be waived.'

'Then I'm moving in.' Leah laughed at the look on Helen's face. 'Not really, don't panic. But I can help you with the children while you're getting used to your job. I can introduce you around Trethkellis – they'll only know you as 'Harry Fox's widow', no doubt.'

'Mostly. We didn't go far from the hotel often when we stayed. They knew Harry though, since he grew up here.'

'Just the same as with Daniel and me. They knew him well, and me hardly at all, but I met a few people after he died, and they were very welcoming.' She gave Helen a sad little smile. 'There can only have been a few years between Harry and Daniel, it's odd to think they must have known one another.'

'I wonder what they'd have thought of us meeting like this.'

'They'd both have been delighted, I know it.' Leah pressed her arm. 'Right then, while Fleur is teaching you the ropes, I can act as a secretary and send letters out to anyone who needs to know your plans have changed. Will that do, to begin with?'

Helen nodded, smiling and wiping the last of her tears. 'That will certainly do.'

'Good. Now I'd better go up and unpack.' Leah took off her coat and draped it over her arm. 'Go and talk to the children, and I'll see you after breakfast. Bring your address book.'

5

Leah sent another telegram to Aunt Mary: *Friend in need. Staying to help. Call hotel if needed. Will write soon. L.* Then she settled down in the lobby, still dressed in her smartest travelling clothes, and idly flicked through a copy of *The West Briton and Cornwall Advertiser* while she waited for Helen to finish breakfast. But it wasn't holding her attention.

The momentary impulse to stay had surprised her as much as it had Helen, but there was something about her new friend that both impressed and touched her. The residual happiness of her former life seemed to hang about her like a protective cloak, and the ache of loss was gentled by it — the love of Harry, and for him, seemed to somehow help compensate for the loss of him. Leah ran her locket up and down its slender gold chain, and realised she could learn a great deal from Helen.

Her eyes were just glazing over when the revolving door moved, and the bell boy leapt forward to take the bag of a tall, well-dressed woman who looked around her, a little smile cracking rather too much make-up. Leah turned away again, and back to her thoughts, but when the woman spoke it was in a voice that carried right across the lobby. The voice of a woman used to being obeyed.

'I wish to take room eight.'

'It's taken, Madam,' the receptionist said.

'Room six is — '

'Nonsense, see here.' The newcomer pointed at the book. 'Someone checked out only this morning.'

'I'm so sorry. But we have plenty of rooms available at this time of year, and four more first floor *en suite* — '

'*Eight*,' the woman said, as if the poor man hadn't heard her. 'I insist. Or do I have to put in a complaint?'

Leah found herself on her feet and walking across to the reception desk. Without planning it, her voice came out in a passable English Home Counties accent. 'I'm sorry, Mrs . . . ?'

'Marlowe.'

'Mrs Marlowe. That room is taken. By me.'

'It's not reserved, and you haven't checked in.'

'But I do have the key, look. Martin just hasn't had the chance to update the book yet, it was a really last-minute decision.'

Mrs Marlowe eyed the numbered fob with exasperation. 'Room eight is closest to the lift.'

'Room six is closer to the stairs,' Leah said helpfully. 'And it's *en suite* too.'

'Then might I suggest *you* change rooms?'

'No. Might I suggest you call ahead and reserve it next time?'

A frosty silence descended between them, and then Mrs Marlowe turned to the receptionist. 'Martin, is it? You have been singularly unhelpful, not to mention inefficient. I'm putting in a complaint with Mrs Fox, and you'll more than likely be out of this establishment by teatime.'

It was the Bentleys all over again, and Leah lost

her temper. 'You can't threaten him!' The short outburst had disguised her own accent, so she slid smoothly back into English and added, 'My husband is a part owner of this hotel.'

She felt her own eyes widen with the unexpected audacity of this claim, and turned it into a belligerent glare. Mrs Marlowe froze, quite satisfactorily, and Leah fought not to laugh. That was twice in as many days she had stilled some acid tongue with the same ruse; oh, the power of having an influential husband! 'Now, are you going to apologise? Or are we going to have to refuse your stay, and . . . and ban you from staying here?' she added, in a further burst of recklessness. Might as well throw caution to the wind.

'*Your* husband? And you are . . . ?'

'Mrs Ronald Gardner. Grace.' She held out a hand, not the slightest bit surprised when it was ignored.

'Mrs Gardner,' Mrs Marlowe said stiffly, 'I don't know what your husband has told you, but this hotel is owned by the Fox family.'

'Ronald is a recent buyer.'

'I don't know the name.'

'Nor should you, yet, but if you wish to continue staying here, you'll soon learn it.' Had she pushed it too far? The woman clearly knew the hotel well, and it would be the work of a moment to uncover the lie. Which meant you could really only class it as a prank, nothing more serious, Leah consoled herself, and she felt sure Helen would appreciate the joke. Heaven only knew where Grace Gardner had come from, but Leah quite liked her.

Martin unhooked the key to room six and

passed it across the polished desktop. 'I'll have a boy bring your bag, Mrs Marlowe.'

'Oh, I can't be bothered to argue.' Mrs Marlowe snatched up the key. 'But I suggest you ask your husband some searching questions, Mrs Gardner, because he most certainly does not own any part of this hotel.' As the bell boy pulled the lift gate closed behind them Leah saw the woman's eyes on her, hard and appraising, and she gave her a little wave. Ah well, it had worked, even if the woman hadn't believed her, and it had passed an entertaining few minutes while she waited for Helen. She rather thought she might keep Grace Gardner for another day, when Millicent had grown boring.

After breakfast she and Helen sat together in the office, making a list of those people who Helen needed to inform of her new circumstances. 'I'll draft and type the letters,' she offered, 'and you can sign them. If there are a lot, I could take them in to Bude to be printed.'

'No, there aren't too many.' Helen looked a little crestfallen at the realisation. 'Are you sure you're happy to do it though?'

'Absolutely. It's time-consuming and you have better things to do. Besides,' she confided, 'the shop where I worked closed down a few months ago, so I plan to find work as a secretary when I go home. This will be good practice.' She hadn't mentioned it to her mother or her aunt yet, and had the feeling it wouldn't go down too well with either of them, since they had both been urging her to take up nursing again ever since the war.

'You can keep it short and simple,' Helen said, 'something suitable for the salutation, according to who they are, and then: *I am writing to inform you of my new permanent residence, to take effect immediately.* And then the address, and telephone number. I can write later to anyone who deserves a more thorough explanation. I'll have to write to Harry's friends who've been storing our belongings, and decide what to do with it all.'

Leah noted it all down, registering the reference to Harry's friends. Not *their* friends. She was starting to understand a little more about Helen every time they spoke. 'Did you manage to talk to the children at breakfast?'

'I did. It was hard, and I didn't go into details, so I'd appreciate it if you don't pass on anything I told you this morning.'

'Of course not. How did they take it? It's such a huge change for them all.'

Helen nodded. 'Fiona's thrilled — she'd live outdoors if she could, and in Bristol she could never even go into the garden alone. Roberta's in a bit of a funk, but I'm sure she'll come around, and Benjamin's still a bit withdrawn but he's got his father's, um ...' She blinked and cleared her throat, and Leah waited quietly. 'His father's pragmatism,' Helen finished, after a moment. 'He knows there's nothing to be done about it, and he's got this new interest in the hotel to focus on. I think he'll be fine, eventually.'

Leah nodded. 'He'll make an excellent trainee manager, I should think, even if he then goes off to work somewhere else.' Right away she could see this was the wrong thing to say, by the flash of

97

fresh pain on Helen's face, and she silently chided herself for it. 'I mean, a long way down the road, of course. Oh, I must tell you.' She smiled, hoping to banish Helen's sadness. 'I was a bit naughty myself this morning, so you might get one of your guests complaining about me. She'll be calling me Mrs Gardner.' She said the name in her new Home Counties accent, and was rewarded by the little smile that touched Helen's lips.

'Where did *that* come from?'

'I suppose it was just at the front of my mind, after what you told me,' Leah said. 'I just blurted it out in the heat of the moment.' She briefly outlined the new guest's bullying behaviour towards poor Martin. 'I had to do something to bring her back down, she was coming across as if she owned the place.'

'Well I don't suppose it matters, anyway,' Helen said, 'since I certainly don't own it.' She shook her head, her smile becoming more natural as she imagined the scene. 'That's cheered me up, actually. I think you staying here will be a tonic.'

'That's the intention,' Leah said. 'Now, let's finish this list, and then you can get on with learning the ropes.'

Her pen worked quickly, noting down the few names Helen gave her, and the addresses. Just one or two Bristol friends, insurance companies and bankers, and then family.

'My two uncles on my mother's side, Ernest and Clive Britton.' Helen tutted as she checked the book. 'I'll have to dig out the addresses though, I think they're in my old book. Oh, and my brother David, he lives in Exeter.'

98

'David … ?' Leah paused, waiting for the surname.

'Marlowe. And you'd better add his wife, Kay, in the salutation.'

Leah stopped writing, and swallowed a sudden sick feeling. 'Marlowe?'

'Yes.'

Leah wrote it slowly, almost afraid to ask, 'And what does Kay look like?'

'Tall, quite thin, wears silly hats and a lot of make-up, usually. Why?'

'And do you two get on?'

'Only for David's sake. She's a bit patronising for my taste.' Helen skimmed through her address book. 'Why are you so interested in my sister-in-law?'

'Because I think she checked into the hotel about an hour ago.'

Helen looked startled, and none too happy. 'Alone?'

'It looked like it.'

Helen sighed. 'That's all I need. I know exactly why she's —' She stopped, and raised an eyebrow.

Leah chewed at her lip and nodded. 'Sorry.'

'So now she knows the place has been sold on.'

'Is that so terrible?'

'To be honest I was hoping to avoid the embarrassment a little longer,' Helen said. 'I know it would come out eventually, but my pride has taken a bit of a battering lately, I would have preferred not to let anyone know we're penniless.'

Leah winced at the term. 'You're not penniless, you have a respectable job. And anyway,' she pointed out, 'she doesn't know she knows.

99

She thinks I was lying. Which I was,' she mused, distracted by the complication she had caused. Then she came back to the matter at hand. 'Are you going to keep her from finding out the whole story?'

'I'm going to try, for a while at least. But that's going to be hard, now she's bound to bring the subject up with … Hell!' She closed her address book and stood up. 'I'd better find Fleur before she does.'

* * *

Now that the weather had turned dull and grey, most of the guests tended to use the lounge bar and the lobby in the evenings, rather than the guest sitting room on the first floor, or the small open lounge on the second. The views from these rooms in the summer was spectacular, but at this time of year they afforded little in the way of sunlight sparkling on calm seas. Some guests however, particularly the artists, enjoyed watching the white-capped swell from the warmth and comfort of the hotel, so there was always a discarded cup or glass, and usually a crumpled newspaper, to dispose of. It was Fleur's habit to personally sweep these rooms after breakfast every day, and this morning Helen found her tutting over a spilled drink on one of the side tables.

'We have a visitor,' she said, going over to help clean up the mess. 'My brother's wife has checked in.'

'I didn't think you two got along particularly well,' Fleur said. 'Is David with her?'

100

'No, I'm assuming she's here because she still thinks I've inherited the place.'

'Ah, I see. And she wants to make sure she takes advantage of that?'

'Partly, perhaps. The thing is, I'd rather she didn't know about what Harry did. She won't be able to stop herself from telling everyone we've ever known, and gloating about it while she does.'

'Gloating?' Fleur dropped a cloth over the puddle of tea on the table and began patting it. 'Why on earth should she do that?'

'She's always disapproved of Harry, kept saying he was a playboy and I shouldn't trust him.'

Fleur's face tightened. 'Did she now?'

'But I think it was partly jealousy,' Helen hurried on. 'She knew him before I did, and I think she'd set her cap at him from the start.'

'I wouldn't have thought they moved in the same circles, I certainly don't remember her from before you and I met.'

'You know Harry, Adam and David were at boarding school together?'

'I knew that's how you met Harry, at David's wedding.'

'Well Kay had met him a few years before that, and evidently thought she'd struck it lucky. Not that there was ever an understanding between them, from what Harry said.' Helen pondered a moment. 'Having said that, I don't think she was jealous of Harry himself. Once she accepted that he wasn't going to give up his racy lifestyle for her, she'd have been perfectly happy with David.'

'*Would* have been?'

'Kay used to patronise me something awful

101

when I was just David's insignificant little sister. You've seen how much more glamorous she is than I ever was —' She held up a hand to forestall the polite protest she knew was coming. 'It's true, you know it is. Kay stopped short of patting me on the head, but there was always the sense that she only invited me to parties to show everyone how nice she was.' Helen shrugged, and passed a dry cloth to Fleur, taking the sodden one in return. 'I don't know, maybe I'm maligning her. She might not have been that cynical, just clumsy at being nice. But when I first met Harry he made such an obvious play for me, it must have rankled.'

'Well yes, probably, but it was her *wedding*! She'd already made her choice. And to rub salt into the wound, you succeeded where she hadn't.'

'I never set out to change him, you know that.'

'But he did change,' Fleur pointed out, 'and more importantly he didn't care who knew it.'

She gave the table a final wipe with the dry cloth and straightened the coasters. 'He had no regrets in giving up his wilder ways.'

'That didn't stop Kay from warning me every time we met. It reached the point where I started to think she was hoping rather than warning.'

'That's quite likely the case.' Fleur dropped the cloth back into her basket. 'Though not because she still wanted Harry, because it sounds very much like the dog in the manger to me. But from what you've said she'd be only too pleased to be able to take poor, broken little you back under her wing.'

'Which is the main reason she's here now, I'm sure of it.' Helen sighed. 'Besides, this place was the one thing Kay coveted above everything else. She used to tell us we were mad for living in Bristol, when Fox Bay was here waiting for us. That she'd never take it for granted like we did.'

'Do you think she's hoping to take some share of it? To ingratiate herself now she believes you're the owner? After all, to her mind you owe her so much.'

'It's possible.'

'Then surely it's better she realises you're not the owner.'

'Ordinarily it would be, yes. But she'd make such a song and dance over making sure everyone knows what a kind soul she is, taking care of me after my nasty husband showed his true colours after all and threw away everything we owned . . .' Helen turned pleading eyes on her mother-in-law. 'I can't do that to Harry, Fleur. He was duped by Adam, but he gave off such an air of being in control that no one would believe that for a minute. They'd think it was greed, and his memory deserves better, don't you think?'

'The truth will come out eventually,' Fleur said gently. 'This sort of thing won't stay hidden forever.'

'I know. But it's too fresh just now. Give me a little bit longer to get used to the knowledge myself. Please? I only found out yesterday, after all.'

Fleur nodded. 'Of course. She won't hear of it from me ... What's that look for?'

Helen told her about Leah, and Fleur rolled her eyes, but a smile creased her face. 'I'd have loved to have seen that,' she confessed. 'Leah can be the most convincing person in the world when she wants to be.'

'Which can be unfortunate at a time like this.'

'Well it sounds as if she knows Kay didn't believe her. But at least I'll be on my guard when the subject comes up.' Fleur picked up the basket of cleaning things. 'Come on, we have to get started on your education. With any luck we'll manage to stay in the office and avoid her altogether for a while.'

Luck was indeed on their side, but not for long. At dinner time, Helen met Kay in the lobby on her way to the dining room. Feigning surprise, rather well, she thought, Helen asked whether her brother was also visiting.

'He has work to attend to,' Kay said shortly.

'Oh, what a shame. Shall we eat together?' Helen saw Leah approaching down the staircase, and shot her a look and a minute shake of the head. *Not now ...*

'I do love it here,' Kay sighed, looking around the dining room as she picked up the menu. 'Especially at this time of the year, when there are so few people around. Will you open for Christmas?'

Helen's heart gave a jolt, and she swallowed hard. 'Fleur's arranged for us to have a quiet one this year,' she said. 'It's going to be a difficult time, particularly for the children.'

Kay looked mortified. 'Of course, I'm so sorry.'

For a while an awkward silence prevailed as they both studied their menus with more concentration than was necessary, then Helen cleared her throat. 'So yes, we're closed on Christmas Eve,

Christmas Day, and Boxing Day, and we re-open on Monday the twenty-seventh. We'll stay open for New Year, of course, if you and David would like to come and stay.' She crossed her fingers under the table, and thankfully Kay shook her head.

'We'd have loved to, but my cousin has invited us to the city for the week.'

'That's a shame.' Helen looked up and signalled to the loitering Guy, who'd just finished preparing the Bentleys' usual table. 'Have you chosen?'

'Yes, thank you.' Kay's face visibly tightened as Guy approached, and her smile was polite but chilly. 'Good evening, Mr Bannacott.'

'Good evening, ladies,' Guy said, as smooth as ever. Kay looked as if she were questioning her own recollection of the scandal for a moment, and Helen had some sympathy for that; it was hard to equate this suave professional with the man Kay had seen off-duty last summer, drunk as a lord but dressed very much like a lady, drifting down the upper corridor to his room and singing *My Old Man (Said Follow the Van)* in a strong cockney accent.

'Are you ready to order dinner?' he now asked politely, pouring iced water from the jug.

Kay made her choice, then handed him her menu. Helen did the same and picked up her glass to ease the sudden dryness in her mouth; it appeared from the look on Kay's face that the time for polite small talk was over.

Kay waited until Guy had walked away, then she faced Helen squarely. 'When were you going to tell me Harry had gambled away my nephew's inheritance?'

Helen's heart sank. It was worse than she'd expected. This much information hadn't come from Leah, and she was certain it wouldn't have come from Fleur. 'He didn't gamble,' she said quietly. 'He never would.'

'Investment is still gambling, only under a cloak of respectability.'

'Who told you about it?'

'I met Mrs Gardner this morning. Though I must admit I didn't believe her when she said her husband owned the hotel.'

'Well then —'

'So I called Adam.'

Helen put down her glass. This was something she hadn't even considered. 'Adam?'

'Coleridge, of course. He assumed I already knew, since I told him I'd met Mrs Gardner.'

'I didn't realise Adam even knew, himself,' Helen said. 'He seemed surprised enough when I told him about Burleigh Mansions being repossessed by the mortgage company, so how did he know about this?' *And if she hadn't kept him at arm's length, would he have told her anyway?*

'I think he only found out a few weeks ago,' Kay said. 'He hasn't shown any interest in anything much since Harry died, but you know how it is in the business world. He might be down, but he still has friends.' She sounded hesitant now. 'Helen, he loves those children, and they love him. Why would you cut him out of their lives?'

'That's my business.' Whatever Adam had told Kay, he was sure to have left out his own part in Harry's downfall, and Helen saw no reason to tell her either. It would make no difference any-

106

way; Kay's original opinion of Harry would not be shaken, especially now she'd been vindicated in that view.

'But he — '

'I don't want to talk about Adam bloody Coleridge!' Helen hissed, surprising herself as much as Kay. 'And I'd rather the rest of our friends didn't find out yet that I've been left in this ... *difficult* situation.'

'Difficult?' Kay flapped her napkin and spread it on her lap. 'Harry has done exactly what I always told you he would do! He wasn't satisfied with losing your lovely Bristol home, he reverted to type and left you homeless and penniless, and he robbed his own son of his inheritance!' She waved a hand to encompass the hotel.

'Why did you come here, Kay?' Helen asked tiredly. She was close to tears now, her own despair had been rising again steadily throughout the day, and it was a struggle to remain outwardly optimistic.

'To help you,' Kay said, calming somewhat. 'You're going to need someone while you settle in, and I'd done David's books and finances for years before he took up this job at the War Office. I know you've had no experience of working for a living.' *Too busy throwing parties and chatting up financiers*, was the unspoken end to that sentence.

'And now that you know the hotel isn't mine after all? Do you still want to ... *help*?'

Kay's eyes widened. 'That's actually quite insulting. Of course I'll still stay, and give you the benefit of my own experience.'

'That's very kind,' Helen said, making a supreme

effort not to apologise, 'but there's no need. Fleur is teaching me all I need to know.'

'Fleur's not as young as she likes to think she is,' Kay said. 'I'm sure she'd rather retire, now you're here to take the strain.' She pressed Helen's hand, and her voice softened. 'Let the poor woman have some time off, darling.'

Helen had to steel herself not to pull away; how dare Kay accuse her of exploiting her elderly mother-in-law? 'Fleur is absolutely fine,' she said, hiding her irritation. 'I'll learn best from someone who knows the hotel, after all. But you're welcome to stay as my guest,' she hurried on, seeing Kay's face shut down again. Kay was right, word passed quickly around the business world, especially if it was assisted by a disgruntled sister-in-law. 'Is David well?' she went on, hoping to change the subject.

'Perfectly,' Kay said, and Helen detected a sharp note in that single word.

'Are you two all right?' she pressed. 'It's unusual for him not to come down here if there's an opportunity.'

'I told you, he's busy. You know what these government departments are like.' Kay draped her napkin over her side-plate. 'Actually I don't think I can stay, after all. Please have my bill drawn up.'

Surprised but relieved, Helen didn't try to persuade her sister-in-law to change her mind. 'You won't have a bill, you haven't stayed the night.'

'I've taken up a room for the whole day,' Kay pointed out stiffly.

'We're not busy, I can't take payment for —'

'Don't you dare feel sorry for *me*!'

108

Helen blinked. 'What?'

'Oh, I know how you and that playboy laughed at us! You with your big house in Bristol, us with our little home in Exeter. Well we might not have had your advantages, but at least we still have that home, David has a very good job now, and I can still pay my way.'

'Kay, I didn't mean —'

'No.' Kay took a deep breath and stood up, ignoring the curious glances they were getting from the other diners. 'You never do, do you? But did you ever stop to think about how it felt for us? Being invited to your revolting, ostentatious parties, watching you swan around as if you were the one paying for it all.'

Helen could only stare at her, shocked at this sudden outburst.

'*David* was Adam's friend,' Kay went on, her voice low but tight, 'until that insufferable Harry Fox stepped in and took over. *He* might have been the one to benefit from Adam's connections—'

'Connections which were the ruin of everything we had!'

'Well you can be sure he wouldn't have thrown it all away like Harry did! He'd have invested intelligently.'

'Even though it's just gambling under a cloak of respectability?' Helen was grimly gratified to see the flush on Kay's face, but her sister-in-law was in full flow.

'Harry's sense of entitlement was his undoing, and you were too besotted to see it, no matter how many times I tried to warn you.' Kay pushed her chair back into the table, hard enough to send

109

the water jug shaking, and the cutlery crashing. People were starting to stare. 'Well you made your bed, Helen, but Harry sold the mattress from under you.'

Helen stood up too, realising she needed to backtrack if she were to salvage something from this. 'Kay, look, I know you're still in touch with Adam, so please … could you ask him not to tell anyone what's happened here? With the sale, I mean.'

'Why on earth would he?'

'You've said yourself; the business world is small. We were a prominent family, so there's sure to be —'

'Don't keep fooling yourself,' Kay said tiredly. 'David said it, and he was right: the great and magnificent Fox family is just the same as the rest of us now.' She sounded as if she truly pitied Helen, and not in the patronising way Helen was accustomed to.

'Does David really feel like this?' Helen asked, following her to the door. Her anger was on the rise again. 'Or are you simply putting words in his mouth, the way you always have done?'

Kay whirled, and Helen was taken aback by the tears that stood out in her eyes. 'I have supported David since the day we met. I could have gone off with Harry if I'd wanted to, but I chose a man with integrity over charm. And if Adam had just *once* thought to bring him into one of those investment opportunities —'

'You didn't have the capital,' Helen pointed out. 'You said so. No one kept any secrets from you, for goodness sake!'

'No one bothered to ask, either. Well I hope now that Harry's gone, you'll see what a fool you've been.'

Helen felt the words like a slap, and her first instinct was to lash out in return, but she struggled to suppress her temper; Kay might be insufferable at times, but she was still married to David, and deserved civility at the very least.

'You're set on leaving then?' she said tightly. 'The last train out of Trethkellis is long gone, where would you go?'

'There's a nice little guest house in the village, as I recall. Sandy Cove. I'll go there.'

'But it's late.' Reluctant to let Kay leave under such a cloud, certain it would only provoke the woman into gleefully spreading the tale of Harry's downfall, she found a conciliatory tone. 'Let's go into the sitting room and talk.'

Kay looked across the dining room, where the artists had fallen silent and were picking at their food, no longer staring but certainly straining to hear what the row was about. 'All right,' she said at length. 'Perhaps privacy is best. I'll stay awhile.'

'Go through, I'll join you in a minute. I'll just tell Mr Gough we don't want dinner after all.'

After a quick visit to the kitchen, Helen went into the office and telephoned the Marlowe house. 'David? It's Helen.'

'Ah.'

'Presumably you knew she was coming down then?'

'I guessed.'

'And you knew why?'

'I only realised after she'd gone.'

111

Helen frowned. 'What do you mean?'

'I didn't realise she'd found out; I'd have given anything to spare her that, but after she'd gone I discovered she'd found the letters. I don't know how long ago.'

'Letters?'

'Well, from Clare. Didn't she mention them? I thought that's why you were calling.'

Helen thought back to the way Kay had reacted when Helen had asked about David. She groaned. 'What have you done, you idiot?'

'Just look after her,' he pleaded. 'Make sure she stays a few days. A week, even. She just needs something to concentrate on. If staying there to help you will do it, there might be a chance we can salvage something from this almighty mess. Look, Hels, for what it's worth, it's not serious. With Clare, I mean.'

'Somehow I think that might be worse.' Helen sighed. 'All right, I'll try. But just remember she gave up a lot for you, David. More than you think.'

In the sitting room she pulled the curtains closed, shutting out the winter night that pressed against the window. 'I'm grateful to you for coming down to help me out,' she said, hoping she sounded sincere. 'How long will you be staying?'

'I'm not sure.' Kay seemed to have calmed down, thank goodness. 'I'd be happy to talk you through the books though, I meant that. I'd also like to go into Bude tomorrow.'

'Perhaps Guy could run you, in his motor.'

Kay shot her a cool look. 'I don't think so.'

'Guy is a perfectly nice man,' Helen said, trying not to sound impatient. 'He and Fleur are the best of friends.'

'It's his other *friends* I'm not sure about.'

'Oh, don't be so …' Helen took a deep breath. 'The train from Trethkellis leaves a little after ten o'clock, I believe.'

'Thank you.'

'About what you said,' Helen ventured after a short silence, 'you've clearly been holding on to that for some time. I just want you to know Harry and I have never thought ourselves superior to you and David, or to anyone else come to that. It's . . . it was, just Harry's way. He liked to enjoy what he'd earned, and to share it with friends and family.'

'He was a conceited playboy,' Kay snapped. 'I *warned* you —'

'At least he wasn't having an affair!'

A silence fell between them, and Helen wished she could take the words back, but they were out now.

Kay's face was pale. 'How did you know?' she asked at last, her voice barely above a whisper.

'David told me.'

'When?'

'I telephoned him just a few minutes ago.'

Kay subsided. 'I didn't realise he knew I'd found out.'

'He said something about someone called Clare.'

'She works in his London office. He probably spends all his time with her when he's there.'

'Presumably that's why you came down then, not to help me at all.'

Kay regained her composure, and tapped a cig-

113

arette out of a silver holder. 'Actually, no.' She flicked her lighter. 'I came to find out if Fleur would sell to David and me.'

Helen stared, sure she'd misheard. 'What?'

'When I found out about this Clare woman, I thought, what could I possibly do to get David away from London, and focus him back on our marriage? The answer was simple: buy Fleur's half of the hotel. Just think,' Kay gave a soft laugh, 'we might have been partners, you and I, if your reckless husband hadn't thrown it all away.'

Helen tightened up at that, but it was nothing new from Kay. 'You could have bought Fleur out?'

'There's no need to sound so sniffy about it! Despite what you said about us lacking capital, we're not destitute.' Kay dragged deeply on her cigarette. 'It would have taken everything we have, and a lot more besides, but it would have been worth it for this place. So you can imagine how cross I was when I met Mr Gardner's wife.'

'I know you've always loved it here, but—'

'I stayed here before you knew it even existed,' Kay told her, dismissing her with a wave. 'Harry invited David down, with Adam, in the summer of '98. It's where I met them. David and I had been courting for a few months at that time so naturally I was invited too.'

'Partners,' Helen mused, distracted from the much colder reality by curiosity of what might have been.

Kay regarded her quizzically. 'Do you suppose we'd have worked well together?'

'We might have surprised one another.'

'Now we'll never know,' Kay said, and it sounded as if she oddly regretted that.

114

'More importantly, do you think it would have saved yours and David's marriage?'

'Undoubtedly. But we'll survive anyway.' Kay sighed. 'We've survived it before.'

'You mean David's had other affairs?'

Kay drew on her cigarette again and gave Helen an amused look. 'No, darling. I mean *I* have.'

'With whom?' Helen couldn't believe what she was hearing.

Kay had gone from snarling assassin to self-satisfied cat. 'There have been a couple,' she admitted. 'But David knows, so don't go thinking you can run to him with all the gossip.'

'I wouldn't,' Helen protested. 'Were you … in love?'

Kay's smile faded. 'No,' she said shortly, stubbing out her half-smoked cigarette with unnecessary vigour. 'That's not what it was about. It was during the war, anyway. Things were different then.'

'So your lovers were, what? Conchies? Or in reserved occupations?'

'One was a pacifist. The other was back on a Blighty, we met when I was a hospital visitor.'

'Did he return to the Front?'

'Yes.' Kay picked up her bag. 'It doesn't matter. Anyway, David's decided to show his teeth and do the same, and I've decided I don't like it. Which makes me a hypocrite of course.'

Helen shrugged in agreement. She was so astonished at the thought of Kay's other life, she found it hard to remember how the conversation had taken this turn. 'So, now you've found out about the hotel what will you do?'

'Go home. Tell him he's being an idiot, that he hadn't half the excuses I did, and that Clare probably has dozens of admirers and he hasn't a hope in hell of keeping her. I expect he called her down the minute I left, and told her he had the run of the house.'

Helen's eyes narrowed as she remembered her brother pleading with her to keep his wife out of the way for a while, and wondered how she could have been so gullible. 'Then you should go back tomorrow, and catch them at it,' she suggested.

'That's a novel way of getting rid of your guests,' Kay said with a tight smile, 'sending them home after one night.'

'I mean it. He asked me to keep you here, and said it would help you both to give you something to focus on.'

'Wily old goat,' Kay said, but now her smile had a hint of admiration about it. 'I'll leave first thing. Don't worry, I won't breathe a word about the hotel. I can't say the same for Adam, of course, but I'll ask him.'

She leaned in to kiss Helen's cheek, and after she'd left Helen sat in bemused silence, pondering how little she really knew her brother and sister-in-law. Kay had always struck her as distant, a little snobbish, sour-tempered but predictable. Her brother, the same. But it seemed they were made for one another in more ways than that after all.

The following evening, she was sitting with Leah in the lounge bar when she was called to the telephone. When she came back, she was smiling.

'My brother David,' she explained. 'Apparently his devoted wife returned to his side this evening, all ready to forgive and forget, and walked into quite the scene.'

'What did she do?'

'She picked up Clare's clothes and threw them out of the bedroom window, apparently. Then she told David she never wanted to discuss it again, and that they were going out to dinner and he was to be ready in ten minutes. David is now terrified.'

Leah's eyes shot wide. 'This is the same woman I met yesterday morning?'

'The one Grace Gardner met,' Helen corrected. 'It makes you wonder if *anyone* is actually who they seem, doesn't it?'

A week later Leah broke the news that she finally had to return home. 'Mother and Aunt Mary are getting on each other's nerves,' she explained. 'They're far too alike to get along for extended periods of time, I'm afraid. I'll have to go first thing on Wednesday morning, to meet the train from Temple Meads back to Wales.'

Helen's heart sank. 'I understand, but I shall certainly miss you.'

She tried not to sound like a dismayed child, learning her mother was leaving her at boarding school, but that was how she felt. Several long evenings by the fire, sharing stories of Daniel and Harry, had lifted each of them out of their own little worlds, and as grief and tears had turned to affectionate smiles for the memories of their lost loves, Helen had felt some of the weight lifting from her heart, and a flicker of purpose creeping in. She felt the comforting tendrils of true friendship uncurling, and knew Leah was experiencing the same. She could only hope it would survive being separated by Leah's return to Wales.

Of her children, only Roberta was still showing any sign of rebellion at being wrenched from her former life. Benjamin had fallen silent, characteristically distancing himself from the family while he thought about things for a day or two, and then reappeared with a determined set to his features and thrown himself fully into learning whatever Guy Bannacott was prepared to teach him.

Fiona hadn't yet had the chance to build a group of friends in Bristol, so when she'd learned she would be attending a school with a playground that looked down on Trethkellis Beach, she had even given a whoop of delight. Roberta, by contrast, was quiet and withdrawn, spending long hours in her room writing to friends, few of whom had so far written back. But it was early days yet, and they had busy lives – which was part of the problem, no doubt. The other part, and less easy to put aside, was that Helen was painfully and helplessly aware that Bristol was where Harry was.

If only she could persuade the girl that what lay in the churchyard near Burleigh Mansions was not her father, that his spirit remained in this place he'd loved, but Roberta was just twelve, and such a concept might not be the comfort it would be to someone older. She remembered Benjamin's teasing comment to Fiona that the hotel was haunted ... Perhaps he was closer to the truth than he'd realised; the impending departure of her new friend made Helen wonder if she'd soon begin talking to the walls instead, imagining Harry to be listening, and waiting for him to give advice. It was a disturbing thought.

'I know you have to go, but I don't think I'm quite ready,' she confessed to Leah now. 'We must make the most of the next few days. You haven't even shown me around Trethkellis yet, remember?'

Leah smiled. 'Well, since I've already fallen down on that promise, let's go for a walk today. I'll let Fleur know I'm stealing you for the morning. And fetch the middle cub, it's a waste of the last of the dry weather to lock herself away like this, and it'll do her good.'

Helen went to find Roberta who, predictably enough, put up a protest. 'It's cold out. Besides, I'm tired. I don't want to go for a walk.'

'Not even with Leah? She has to leave the day after tomorrow, so this will be your last chance.'

That did the trick. Leah exerted an effortless fascination over Helen's eldest daughter, even though Millicent Scripps had not reappeared since that second night. Still mumbling, but now under her breath, Roberta unhooked her coat from the back of her bedroom door, and trailed Helen downstairs.

Fiona was already bouncing up and down with impatience, eager to be outside despite the heavy, overcast sky. 'Is Benjamin coming too?'

'No, because he's a *boy* and he doesn't *have* to,' Roberta pointed out. 'Come on then, let's get it over and done with.'

Fiona looked shocked, but Helen and Leah

119

exchanged a glance, and Helen read her own thoughts in her friend's expression: *she's grieving, let it pass.*

'Right,' she said, slipping her own coat over her shoulders. 'Where are you taking us?'

'We'll go by St 'Dwinn's first, then follow the road around by Trethkellis Farm and into the village that way.'

'That's miles!' Roberta stared at them, horrified.

'You've got decent shoes on your feet,' Leah said airily. 'It'll be good for you to get to know the roads around here. Especially for when you learn to drive a motor car.'

'Leah!' Helen shot a look at her daughter, cringing at the thought. 'She's only twelve!'

But Roberta had perked up. 'Can I, Mum? When I'm older, I mean.'

'You'll need to,' Leah pointed out. 'This isn't like Bristol, where you have everything on your doorstep. I wish I'd learned, but I can't afford a motor car anyway.'

They set off across the hotel grounds towards the church. Fiona skipped ahead past the tennis courts, while Roberta walked more sedately with the older women, reminding Helen with a little jolt that, while she might be 'only twelve', she was fast leaving her childhood behind. Not so long ago she would have taken Fiona's hand and skipped with her.

They reached the church, and Leah went to say her goodbyes to Daniel while Helen took the girls to find the Fox family crypt. In the back of her mind was the hope that something so solid, in memory of their family, might give them a focus when they couldn't visit their own father's grave whenever they wished. That they could come here whenever they wanted to be close to him, instead.

'All of Daddy's family have been buried here, since before the monastery was turned into an hotel,' she told them. 'They've lived around Treth-kellis for centuries.'

'And they made the monks leave?' Fiona was clearly perturbed at the thought. 'Did our family just . . . send them away, to find somewhere else to live?'

'Not at all,' Helen soothed. 'Your grandfather didn't buy the abbey until 1864. Henry the Eighth had already sold it in the mid-sixteenth century, to raise money for his military campaigns. Roberta, have you learned yet about the dissolution of the monasteries?' But any hopes she had of involving Roberta in the conversation, or raising any interest at all in the hotel, were short-lived; her daughter was steadfastly staring into the distance, over the top of the leaning headstones, and her face was blank though her eyes shone. Helen went to her and put an arm around her shoulder. It had been foolish to bring her this way, after all, but there was nothing to be done for that now.

She looked at the names engraved in Cornish granite, and felt another pang of regret that Harry's name had been carved into smooth marble, and so many miles away. Of course, now she knew why, but what had he hoped to achieve by keeping it all such a secret anyway? Did he think he might buy the hotel back someday? Or had he just accepted that once his mother was gone all ties

121

with Cornwall would be cut forever? She would never know now.

Leah was getting up from her knees and brushing at her skirt, and Helen called the girls over. 'Come on, we'll take the exit by the north gate.'

Leah had already begun walking in that direction, and Fiona scampered after her. Helen glanced down at Daniel's memorial stone as she passed it. Daniel Marshall, beloved son of William and Jane. 1883–1917. So many young men with the same sad stories on their memorials, or, if their families were a little luckier, on their headstones ... Her ruminations were cut short as a shout went up over by the gate.

'Help!'

Fiona had tried to climb the dry-stone wall instead of following Leah through the kissing gate, and her coat was caught on a jutting stone. She clung on to the wall, buffeted by the strong westerly wind in the exposed churchyard, and her feet were in danger of slipping off the wet stone. 'I'm stuck!'

Roberta ran to help, and Helen joined them, not sure whether to scold the little girl or hug her, as her sister lifted her down to safety. She settled for brushing Fiona's coat down, a little more roughly than was warranted, and sighing heavily to make her point. Secretly she admired the child for her adventurous spirit — something she herself had never possessed and could not take credit for passing to her children. That trait was all Harry's.

'That boundary marks the edge of Higher Valley Farm,' Leah said, pointing as they joined her.

122

'We'll follow it around, and it'll lead us to the road into the village. We could perhaps visit the tea shop, girls, if your mother has no objection?' She directed this at Helen, who nodded.

'No objection at all.' In fact the wind was starting to bite through Helen's coat, and she almost relented and allowed Roberta to go back to the hotel, as she saw the girl turn up her coat collar. But Leah was striding away, holding on to Fiona's hand, so Helen ignored Roberta's faintly mutinous look, and followed.

The track led them the long way around two fields, and as they turned eastwards the wind at their backs seemed to fall off, and helped them along their way instead of battering them sideways. After a while, moving farther inland, they began to notice more outbuildings, and the odd barn.

'Look, Mummy!' Fiona pointed. 'Skinny sheep!'

'They're goats,' Leah said, drawing her over to the wall so she could lift her for a closer look. 'There are no sheep on this farm anymore, nor cows, except for a few milkers. Since the start of the war it's mostly been crops, and some smaller livestock.'

'You know the farm?' Helen asked, coming alongside.

'Beth, the farmer's wife, was quite friendly with Daniel's mother and we met her at the memorial service. She was very kind, I remember that.'

'I'd like to meet her,' Helen said. 'It'd be good to get to know someone living so close.' The germ of an idea planted itself.

'Perhaps, if I discuss it with Fleur, we can even

123

talk about the farm supplying Fox Bay's kitchens.'

'You can certainly meet her husband,' Leah said, squinting into the distance. 'It looks as if he's doing something in that barn. The door's open, anyway.'

Roberta sighed. 'Do we have to? Can't we just go to the village now and have tea and cakes?'

'We're going to introduce ourselves to our neighbour,' Helen said firmly, 'and you're going to be polite and friendly.'

Roberta cast a quick, embarrassed glance at Leah, and followed without further demur.

The farmer came out of the barn as they approached, and stopped in his tracks, no doubt astonished by the sudden arrival of four strange females on his land. He was tall and well-built, with a shock of dark hair sticking up all over his head, and dark, bushy eyebrows. His face was pock-marked and weathered-looking, and when he smiled his welcome Helen saw he had several missing teeth, but it was a wide, unselfconscious smile.

'Mornin' to you,' he called. 'Are you lost?'

'Good morning, Mr Nancarrow.' Leah held out her hand. 'Leah Marshall. We met once before, briefly. I'm acquainted with your wife.'

Nancarrow shook her hand, and then Helen's. He bobbed his head at Roberta, and winked at Fiona. 'Don't normally see such pretty visitors at the back end of nowhere,' he observed.

'Mrs Fox has moved into the hotel,' Leah went on. 'She's Harry's widow.'

Immediately Nancarrow's face sobered. 'I was proper sorry to hear about Harry.'

'You knew him?' Helen asked.

'I did. 'Twas his fault my boys got interested in motorcycles. Not that I ever 'eld it against him, mind,' he hurried on, perhaps remembering the cause of Harry's death.

Helen made herself smile past the sudden, sharp pain. 'Well it's good to meet you, Mr Nancarrow.'

'Call me Toby, since we're neighbours.'

'Toby then. You have sons?'

'Twins. Just like me and their Uncle Alfie. He lives in Porthstennack, down the coast.'

The conversation was interrupted by a spluttering roar that burst through the open barn door. Helen's heart slithered against her ribs at the sound, and for a moment she thought she might black out. The last time she had heard that ...

'Quiet that thing down!' Toby bellowed. 'S'cuse me, ladies.' He vanished into the barn.

'Helen?' Leah's voice cut through the sound, and Helen felt a hand on her arm. 'Are you all right?'

The engine-sound faded to a rattle, and then died altogether. All Helen could hear now was the rustle of wind in the trees, the distant bleating of Nancarrow's goats, and the murmur of voices from inside the barn. She blinked and looked around at Leah.

'Sorry. It's just that sound. It took me back to the racetrack for a minute. I'm fine, honestly.'

'Can I go in?' Roberta sounded animated for the first time in days, and Helen looked at her, surprised to see a light in her eyes she hadn't seen in a while, but she wasn't sure it was a good thing; close proximity to the one thing Harry had loved above all else might not be the best way to help her cope with her grief.

'Perhaps another day,' she said. 'Mr Nancarrow has his work to do.'

Toby came out of the barn, followed by two young men of around eighteen. Identical, down to the oil that covered their fingers and streaked their shirts, they grinned around at the newcomers.

'Glad to meet you. I'm Jory,' offered one.

'Jowan,' the other said. 'We'd offer to shake hands, but … ' He waggled his blackened fingers at Fiona, and laughed as she shrank back. 'Just teasin', miss!'

'Didn't you want to discuss something?' Leah reminded Helen. 'Something about the farm and the hotel working together?'

'Oh?' Toby looked interested. 'What's that, then?'

'It's something I have to think about first, and talk over with the … with my mother-in-law, before I put it to you. Perhaps I might call tomorrow morning, and speak to you and your wife together?'

'Can't pretend I'm not intrigued,' Toby mused, squinting at her. 'Me and the boys've got ploughing to do early, so after breakfast do you?'

'I'll see you around nine o'clock then,' Helen said, shaking his hand again. 'I hope we can do each other some good.'

Leah held out her own hand. 'Please give Beth my kindest regards and tell her I'm sorry I haven't had a chance to catch up with her this visit. I have to return to Wales tomorrow.'

They took their leave, treading gingerly through the long grass back towards the road. Roberta was hanging back and twisting to look over her shoulder, but Helen couldn't see the Nancarrows anywhere. Then she realised they'd gone back inside the barn, and the motorcycle's engine started up again. After a moment the machine itself emerged; a skinny, black contraption with a sidecar attached. The twin in the sidecar gave a whoop, and the one riding it rose on the foot pegs, and the motorcycle roared off across the grass, belching thick black smoke and coughing its way to the end of the field. Toby Nancarrow came out of the barn, and stood watching and shaking his head, but Helen knew there would be a look of indulgent pride on that weathered face.

She looked at Roberta, whose wide eyes were following the motorbike's progress, and whose skin was flushing with excitement, and there was no mistaking the look on the girl's face as she turned back to her mother.

'I think I might quite like living here after all.'

6

Higher Valley Farm, Trethkellis

The following morning, standing at the farmhouse door, Leah glanced at Helen and for the first time she saw nervous anticipation on her friend's face. 'Are you quite sure you're ready for this?'

'Not in the least,' Helen said, then gave her a rueful smile. 'But you mustn't ever tell Fleur that. She's always assumed I was nice but hopeless, so she thinks this was a wonderful idea.'

'Then she might have come along,' Leah said reproachfully. 'It's not fair to put it all onto you.'

'Us,' Helen corrected her. 'I think she sees you as part of the Fox family already. Whether you like it or not,' she added with a little grin.

Leah felt an unexpected warmth at this; it wasn't as if she didn't have her own family, but she'd never met one like this before. Grieving or not, they were open and friendly, chaotic in their way, with three children who were at one another's throats one minute, defending each other to the death the next. She thrived on the energy that had suddenly arrived in Fox Bay, the way she'd soaked up that of the groups of artists, and once more she wished she could stay longer.

'Don't look so worried,' she said now, 'I know Beth a little, which should help.'

The door was opened by a pleasant-looking woman, with the wind-reddened, slightly rough-ened skin of one who spends a great deal of time out of doors. She stood looking at them blankly, then recognised Leah.

'Oh, it's you, Mrs Marshall! Not seen you for a good while. Come in.'

'This is Helen Fox, who's moved into the hotel,' Leah said, following her into the stone-floored hallway.

'Glad to meet you properly, Mrs Fox. I've seen you round and about here before.' Beth's bright blue eyes, and the friendly smile that lit them, made her appear younger than she must be to have two grown sons. 'Toby said you'd be along. Didn't expect it so soon, mind.'

'Is this a difficult time? I don't want to intrude.'

'But you do have business to discuss,' Leah said firmly.

'Yes, I do.' Helen shot her a look, part embarrassed and part grateful, and visibly squared her shoulders. 'I hope to do us both some good, Mrs Nancarrow.'

'Come through.' Beth led them into the large, warm kitchen. The smell of carbolic soap clashed with that of boiling lamb bones, but the effect was surprisingly comforting, and Leah could almost believe she was at home, listening to her mother and her aunt bickering over the best way to make a good stock.

'Toby's been kept out for the time being.' Beth busied herself with cracking eggs into an ancient-looking pan. 'But you can talk to me. How can you party do us any good, then?'

Helen opened her bag and took out the notes Guy had prepared for her. She shuffled them for a moment, and Leah saw her hands shaking. She wordlessly placed one of her own over them. *It's all right*, she mouthed. *Take a deep breath.*

Helen cleared her throat. 'I have some figures here, which my restaurant manager has provided.'

Beth's eyes narrowed. 'Figures for what?'

'I thought perhaps we might be able to come to some arrangement, whereby you would supply a certain amount of your produce to our kitchens.'

'We already have customers for our produce,' Beth told her. 'We send it up to Plymouth on the train, and then some of it goes even further than that.' But Leah had noted a sudden interest, and she gave Helen an encouraging nod.

'Naturally,' Helen said smoothly. 'And we wouldn't be taking a great deal in any case, but the thing is, our guests mostly come from those cities you're sending your produce to, so for them to be given an egg for breakfast that was laid *that very morning* … well, they'd gladly pay extra. Not to mention vegetables they can see in the field one day, and on their plate the next. We'd be able to put a percentage of that profit back into the price we pay you.'

Helen had hit her stride now, and Leah relaxed as she saw Beth's attention turn briefly inward, working out how this would benefit the Nancarrows and their livelihood. She knew how difficult it was for farms right across the country; several near her home in Mountain Ash had been sold off since the war, and Cornwall was a county so rich in agricultural heritage it must be suffering greatly. The Corn Production Act had passed just three years ago, but farms were still crying out for

130

help just to survive.

Helen was winding up her spiel now. 'If you and Toby agree, Higher Valley would sign a contract with Fox Bay to supply eggs, milk and vegetables to begin with. If, at some point in the future you find yourselves in a position to buy more live-stock, we could consider adding beef, mutton and bacon to that list.'

Before Beth could respond, a cry came from outside. A bloodcurdling sound that made all three of them jump and stare at one another in shock. Then Beth dropped the knife she was holding and moved towards the kitchen door, stumbling in her haste. The grunting and sobbing grew louder as the front door crashed open, and another hoarse scream echoed down the hallway. Instinct drove Leah out into the hall where Toby, supported by his two sons, was cradling his left arm to his chest, drenched in blood from neck to waist.

'Hot water!' Leah shouted back to Helen. She ran to where Beth was trying to usher one of her boys away so she could take the burden of her husband, but the white-faced twins refused to yield him.

'Bring him into the kitchen,' Leah told them grimly. 'Fetch some scissors. And one of you boys go for the doctor.' The entire family was in shock it seemed; they would need careful handling. Helen could do that, while Leah did what she knew best, but first she had to get Toby somewhere where she could see how bad his injury was.

Jowan and Jory helped their father into a chair by the window, and Beth handed Leah a huge pair of scissors. 'Fetch the little green table for Mrs

Marshall,' she said, in a shaky voice. 'Hurry! And go for the doctor, like she said!'

One of the twins vanished, and the other went into the next room and returned with a small square table, which Leah positioned beside the chair before gently drawing Toby's arm away from his chest. Trying to ignore his groans of pain she laid his arm on the table and began to cut away the shredded shirt. His head nodded onto his chest and Leah saw sweat dripping off his brow and mingling with the rich crimson of his blood. He mumbled something incoherent.

'How's that water coming?' Leah asked Helen, keeping her voice calm.

'Heating,' Helen said, 'but slowly.'

Leah nodded. 'Can't be helped, we'll just have to take it as it comes. Be ready to bring it over as soon as I say.' She finished cutting the blood-soaked sleeve, and carefully peeled the material away to reveal a deep gash that began just above Toby's wrist, and crossed his forearm, ending inside his elbow.

Toby swore and cried out, and his head fell back against the head rest of his chair. Leah lifted his arm to tuck the ragged sleeve out of the way, and he howled again as his right hand doubled into a fist and slammed down onto the arm rest.

Leah turned to Helen. 'Now!'

Helen appeared at her side with a pan of water. Leah dipped her finger into it; it wasn't anywhere near hot enough, but it would have to do. Beth gave her another clean cloth from the washing basket, and Leah knelt on the floor and began to clean Toby's arm. Toby hissed, but this time he kept still, and she knew his eyes were on his wife rather than what she was doing. Beth was kneeling at his right side now, her hands clasping that tight fist, and her face pale.

'What happened, Toby?' Leah asked in that steady, calm voice she'd forgotten she possessed.

'Something ... stuck ... land wheel,' he said through gritted teeth.

'What wheel?'

'Plough,' he managed, and let out a sharp cry as Leah tried to grip and pull out some of the grass that was deeply ingrained in the wound. 'Old cloth. In the land wheel. I was trying to free it.'

The wound had clean edges, but there was a great deal more earth and grass driven into it than Leah was happy with. 'Get him a drink,' she told the hovering twin. 'It doesn't matter what. Beth, I need something to bandage this with. Then what happened?' she prompted Toby as she resumed cleaning. She wanted to keep him talking so she would hear if he was about to pass out.

'The horse was . . .' He stopped, and Leah looked up sharply to make sure he was still conscious. He was, but his eyes had slid from his wife to his son, who'd poured ale from the jug on the sideboard. 'She was startled.'

'Oh God, Dad,' the boy said in a broken voice. 'We're so sorry.'

'What?' Beth looked at him, her face twisted in confusion. 'Sorry for what?'

Tears poured unchecked down her son's muddy cheeks. 'We were in the next field, fixing the bike, and when we finally got the engine to start, we revved it. Just to make sure. We didn't know Dad was still … The horse shied and took off.'

'Oh, Jowan, you — '

'We heard Dad screaming. The horse had stopped a little way away, but the share caught Dad's arm.'

Beth rounded on him, her face dark with fury and fear. 'You shouldn't even have been doing that! You should have been *with* him!'

'T'ain't their fault,' Toby murmured. 'Told them they could break until breakfast.'

'Helen, take Mrs Nancarrow and Jowan into the sitting room,' Leah said. 'Toby, are you ready?'

He nodded, and then looked at Beth who had not moved. 'Go on, love,' he said gently. He didn't look at Jowan as the boy stumbled from the room, still sobbing. Leah remembered the young men's carefree laughter and their good-natured teasing just yesterday, and wondered how everything could change so quickly. She had seen wounds like this all too often, and although Toby's arm wasn't broken, she knew he would be lucky to keep it.

'What'll Beth and the boys do?' Toby muttered. His chin was beginning to droop onto his chest again, and Leah tapped his face gently.

'Stay with us. I need you to be alert just now.' She shifted, and pain shot through her knees where they pressed against the cold stone floor. 'Are you ready?' she asked again.

'Yes.'

Leah tipped the water from the bowl over Toby's arm, and felt his entire body tense as he fought not to cry out. She wrapped the arm as tightly as she could in the bandage Beth had laid on the table. It had old, amber-coloured stains on it, though it had clearly been washed and put away against the day it might be called into use again.

Toby was watching her as she pulled the bandage tight. 'From before,' he told her. His voice was faint and slow. 'When I came back from France. Beth was all for throwing it away.' He gave a strange little laugh. 'But I'm superstitious, see. I thought if we kept it, we'd never need it.'

Leah tied off the end. 'I'll bet you're glad your boys were too young to join up.'

Toby ran a hand over the thick bandage, and swallowed what was probably a surge of nausea. 'At first, when we went out there, I was wishing they could come with me. For the glory, you know how it was.'

Leah nodded. 'I remember. But by the time any of you reached my clearing station you'd already discovered the truth.' How well she recalled the dead-eyed and weeping men who'd passed through her hands in those days. Just as Daniel would have passed through some unknown nurse's in his own little patch of hell — if the tunnel's collapse hadn't been so catastrophic.

'They must have only missed by a matter of months, in the end,' she said. 'Beth must have been beside herself, to have you home wounded, but alive, and then to face losing Jory and Jowan.'

'When the War Office extended it, that spring, to include seventeen-year-olds, we didn't know what to do.' Toby was lost in the past for a moment. 'They were sixteen at that time, but they turned seventeen in the October. We even thought about hiding them. Lying. Anything.' He raised his eyes to hers, and they were swimming with tears of remembered terror. 'Then it was all over. Just like that.' He sighed, and lifted his torn arm to cradle it once more against his bloodstained shirt. 'I thank you for what you've done here today. You've likely saved my arm, so you've saved the farm too.'

Leah shook her head and rose stiffly from her kneeling position. 'I'm just glad to have been of help.'

Beth appeared in the doorway. 'Jory's back. Doctor Rowe'll be here d'rectly.'

'What did Mrs Fox want to talk about?' Toby asked her, eyeing the water that pooled around the legs of his chair.

'Oh, that'll keep for later, for crying out loud!' But when she turned away to fetch a mop Leah could see the relief on her face that he was ready to talk about other things.

'He'll be all right, Beth,' she said. 'The doctor will be able to stitch him up.'

'You should never have stopped being a nurse,' Beth told her, and Helen, coming into the room with Jowan, nodded in agreement.

'Promise me you'll look into going back to it.'

'I don't know —'

'You must! Look at the way you stepped right back into the role today.' Helen crouched to look at Toby's neatly bandaged arm. 'No hesitation. Think how many people you could help.'

Leah's heartbeat quickened as she considered Helen's words. It was true she'd not thought twice today, and the memories of the clearing stations had been there but hadn't rendered her helpless, as she'd always expected they would. Could she? She looked at Toby, whose face was white and lined with pain, but who sat upright in his chair, and then at Beth's relieved smile. Perhaps she could do it, after all.

The doctor arrived ten minutes later, and Leah and Helen left, assuring Beth that Helen would return when Toby was well enough to discuss the business proposal.

'Doctor Rowe seemed to approve of what you've done,' Helen said, as they walked back across the yard towards the road. 'He looked quite impressed, actually.'

'It was as if no time had passed since the last time I was in that position,' Leah admitted. 'I didn't have the chance to wonder what I should do, although all I could do was to clean it and close the wound. Poor Toby, he's in for a rough morning while the doctor stitches that up.'

Helen shuddered. 'And the boys are in for a rough time from their mother too, I should think.'

'Quite likely. They've already been punished quite enough though. They're in pieces.'

They walked in silence for a while, but as they reached the hotel, Leah stopped Helen with a hand on her arm. 'I'm going to do it,' she said. 'I'm going to go back into nursing.'

'Good!' Helen smiled. 'I'm so glad. I can't think of a better outcome for this awful thing that's happened, you'll do so much good.' She slipped her arm through Leah's. 'Now we both have a whole new life to look forward to.' There was a faintly melancholy tone in her voice, and Leah hugged her close.

'You'll be all right. Those children of yours are absolute darlings. Your . . .' She trailed away,

137

uncertain, then went on, 'I never met Harry, but he would be so proud of you, I'm sure.'

Helen nodded. 'I hope so. You'll still come back, won't you? To visit, I mean.'

'Any time you'll have me.'

'And you can have room eight whenever it's free.'

'I don't want to turn into your sister-in-law,' Leah laughed. 'But it is a special room.'

'And you're a special person. I think you were right when you said you thought we'd be great friends.'

Right up until the letter dropped onto her door mat three days later, Leah had meant what she'd said about a return to nursing. She'd planned to visit the local hospital that very day, in fact, and stopped on her way out of the house to pick up the post, recognising Helen's clear, neat handwriting on the envelope tucked in among the two or three others. With a smile she pulled the paper out and read it, her smile fading as the words washed over her. Then she tucked it back into its envelope, removed her hat and coat, and went to make her mother a cup of tea.

Dearest Leah

It hurts my heart so badly to write to you with such sad news. Toby Nancarrow died this morning, of an infection that had reached his heart before anyone knew of it. You mustn't for one moment blame yourself, the doctor said you did everything perfectly ...

PART TWO

PART TWO

1

Fox Bay Hotel 26th July 1929

'Twenty-one today!
Twenty-one today!
She's got the key of the door,
Never been twenty-one before —'

'Hush!' Helen chastised Guy, but couldn't help smiling at the look on Roberta's face as the other guests in the dining room began a faintly bemused, but good-natured, clapping. 'Happy birthday, darling.'

'Thank you.' Roberta blushed furiously, her habitual hauteur failing her under the nods and smiles of total strangers.

Guy threw his snow-white cloth theatrically over his arm. 'Your choice off the menu today, Miss Fox. What will you have?'

'She gets to choose every day,' Fiona pointed out. 'We all do.'

'Ah, but Mama has always had the power of veto,' Guy said in a mock undertone. 'Until now, that is.'

Helen threw him a look, and inclined her head towards her daughter. 'You are an adult,' she conceded, 'so if you insist on having three boiled eggs there's nothing I can do to stop you.'

Roberta handed her menu back to Guy. 'Three boiled eggs, please, with plenty of toast and butter.'

'Ugh.' Fiona pulled a face. 'Just toast and marmalade for me.'

'Boiled egg for me too,' Fleur said, 'but just the one.' She sounded subdued today, not like her usual self at all.

'And I'll have the same as Fiona,' Helen said.

Guy took the rest of the menus and, watching him move off towards the kitchen to place their order, Helen remembered their first night here and had one of those occasional, tingling moments of acknowledgement. After all she and her broken little family had overcome, all they'd lost and struggled to recapture, here they were, all breakfasting together on the day of her daughter's twenty-first birthday. Almost all of them, anyway.

'Has anyone seen Ben this morning?' she asked.

'Sleeping?' Fleur suggested. 'He's on duty tonight, after all.'

Fiona shook her head. 'He doesn't go to bed until after lunch this time of year. Does he know we're eating in the dining room today? He might have forgotten it's Roberta's birthday.'

'I don't see how.' Helen opened her napkin and spread it on her lap. 'The party preparations have been going on for weeks.'

'Exactly! He's so used to it, he might just be sitting in the breakfast room wondering where we all are.'

Guy returned to pour the tea. 'Are you talking about Ben? I've sent him into Bude with Jeremy Bickle and a list.'

'Heaven help Bude then,' Roberta said with a grin. 'I should have gone with them, it would have been a lark.'

'You have guests arriving before lunch,' Helen reminded her. 'You can't just go gallivanting off to town, even on your birthday.'

'She's got the key of the door,' Guy sang again, then glided away to take another breakfast order before Helen could say anything. He was especially chirpy lately, Helen noted, but today there seemed to be a brittle edge to it that made it seem forced. Perhaps he was having trouble with his new particular friend? Fleur would know, if anyone did.

But breakfast with at least two of her children was such a treat for Helen these days that she put such conjecture out of her mind, determined to make the most of it. Fiona, now fifteen, was watching her older sister with a fascination that seemed to grow by the day, and Helen noted how she'd tried to emulate Roberta's fashionable spit curl. But Roberta's hair was sleeker, shinier, and Fiona's bouncy curls, just like Helen's, wouldn't obey. Perhaps one of the younger chambermaids might be persuaded to help her with it before the party.

Helen gave a little sigh of contentment as she looked around the crowded dining room. Fleur had stepped back from her role around a year after they'd arrived, and in the time since she had taken over as full-time manager Helen realised the hotel had begun to feel like her own. It still held all the old memories, but now they were gentle and comforting, rather than aching reminders of happier times, and in her turn she had lavished all her attention on perfecting the details, and was rewarded for her efforts as the reputation of Fox

Bay began to permeate the wider world.

Guests now came from Europe, America, even New Zealand, and two years ago they'd had their first visit from a Hollywood movie star. The staff had almost erupted in feverish excitement, but Helen's insistence on giving him the peace he so desperately sought meant that he took word home with him: here was a hotel where a guest, no matter how famous, truly would be left alone, where they could take in all the beauty of moorland and coast, yet still enjoy the crispest, whitest sheets, the freshest food, and the best champagne.

Tonight's party would be a private affair, but Helen knew it would be covered in the local press nevertheless, and possibly even in some of the smaller nationals, so she crossed her fingers beneath the breakfast table that nothing would go wrong. Then, with a smile she uncrossed them again; luck would have nothing to do with the success of this party, or its failure; that would all be down to her. At least now she could admit to herself that she was more than capable of doing it well.

Roberta began talking about the friends she had invited; mostly girls from the telephone exchange in the village, where she worked, and Helen listened at first but gradually became aware of a conversation happening at the table behind her.

'You know the one,' the gentleman was saying. 'Just across the way. Higher Valley.'

'What about it?'

'Well half of it's been sold, apparently. See here?' There was a rustle as he passed a newspaper across the table to his wife. 'A developer, no less. I tell you, the countryside is going to rack and ruin. There'll soon be nothing left at this rate.'

'We don't know they're going to build houses,' the woman said reasonably. 'It might stay as it is.'

'Don't be dense, Alice! A *developer* doesn't buy half a farm just for the pleasure of muddy walks and renting out a field or two. No, mark my words, that open farmland will be a village, or even a town, before we come down next summer. That's if we do come again; I mean, if we want to look at houses we might as well stay in the city.'

Shaken, Helen returned her attention to the conversation at her own table. The Nancarrows had struggled even more since Toby's death nearly ten years ago, and they'd sold part of their woodland off already, but she'd hoped the arrival of Toby's brother was a sign that things were improving. She'd certainly never considered their financial straits might lead to something like this, and if more people thought like – she sneaked a glance over her shoulder and stifled a groan – Mr and Mrs Walker, two of her wealthiest regulars, then Fox Bay's profits would soon start to fall as well.

'Mum!'

'Sorry,' Helen said, and smiled at Roberta. 'Miles away. What was that?'

'I was just asking what time the first car is due to arrive?'

'Around eleven, I think.'

'Good, I have time to take a quick ride out before I have to get changed.'

For most young ladies that would herald a morning's gentle hacking along the lanes and across fields, on the back of a gentle-natured horse

145

or pony, but for Roberta Fox it meant something very different.

'Must you? Today of all days?' Helen tried to keep her tone light, but it was difficult. 'You'll get so dirty. And what if you fall off?'

'I never have yet,' Roberta pointed out.

Your father never had, either. But Helen didn't voice the thought.

Instead she simply nodded and concentrated on spreading marmalade on her toast. 'Will you be able to help with the last-minute arrangements, Fleur?'

'I would, darling, you know that, but it's my meeting day. Did I tell you we've got the funding for the war memorial at last?'

'You did, yes.' With fast-dwindling hope, Helen turned to her youngest child. 'Fiona, what will you be doing?'

'Going to Trethkellis,' Fiona said, as if it were obvious, and Helen supposed it should have been. So, while Roberta was riding that rattling old machine around the lanes, frightening the seagulls, Fiona would be hanging around the lifeboat station and getting under people's feet there. It would be a miracle if she even arrived home in time for the party.

Thank goodness for Benjamin, now twenty-six, already an experienced night manager and formally training as a sommelier. Helen sometimes worried that he might be poached by some other hotel, such was his growing reputation, but tonight he would be on hand here, to advise, pour, and discuss. The perfect gentleman, just like his father.

Helen smiled to herself; Harry would have been

146

immeasurably proud of all three of his children, and for the very reasons that gave Helen the shudders. In the years since his death she had learned to hide it better, and she had the strength of his memory to thank for that; she could picture him raising an eyebrow at her whenever he sensed she was about to curb an activity, then disappearing behind his paper again without saying a word. So now she merely nodded and hoped for the best.

As the leisurely meal progressed, her mind kept playing with that snippet of overheard conversation behind her, and the moment breakfast was finished, she went out to the lobby and took a copy of the local newspaper from the pile on the reception desk. In the office she spread it out and began turning pages with growing relief; if anything big was happening to Higher Valley Farm, it would almost certainly have been closer to the front.

But she'd almost reached the last page, and was starting to convince herself Mr Walker had been mistaken, when she saw it. A small, boxed-off article announcing the sale of one hundred acres of land from Higher Valley Farm, Trethkellis, to a company called Hartcliffe Developments . . . The company clearly had no interest in advertising their purchase, to have instructed for it to be buried so far inside the paper like this, and it was likely they had only done so at all out of some legal obligation.

Helen remembered how Harry had dreamed of building his own golf course; firstly to learn on, and then to open to the hotel guests . . . It looked as though he wouldn't have had to rely on his legendary charm after all, just on the collapse of the Nancarrows' livelihood.

Her first impulse was to telephone Leah, but she quickly dismissed that idea; Leah had her job, and her aunt, and even if she could drop everything and come to hold Helen's hand, what could she do that was of practical help?

The door clicked quietly open and Fleur came in, and when her gaze fell on the crumpled newspaper she showed no surprise. 'Awful, isn't it? Just devastating.'

'You've read it then?'

'No, but Guy told me. I'm sick over it, Helen. What are we going to do? It's bound to have an impact on us, our guests come here for the wide-open spaces and the fresh air.'

Somehow hearing it from the usually optimistic and unflappable Fleur made it seem even more starkly real than reading about it.

'Mr and Mrs Walker won't be back, for a start,' Helen told her grimly. 'And they're only the first that we know of. Once word gets out that'll be it.'

'Does it say who's bought it?'

'It just says the company name, presumably from up the line somewhere. Cliff-something.' Helen looked again, and frowned. 'No, Hartcliffe. Actually, that sounds familiar, I wonder if I've seen their signs up somewhere else? It might be worth finding out, so we can see what kind of buildings they favour.'

'It doesn't make a difference really, does it?' Fleur said, and sighed. 'Whoever it is will soon be digging up the land, and planting bricks instead of barley. We're ruined.'

'We'll find a way to fight it,' Helen said, summoning a briskness she certainly wasn't feeling, 'and in the meantime we will not let it spoil Roberta's twenty-first.'

Fleur seemed ready to give up, but Helen would not; she had worked too hard in the intervening years since her timid and hopeful arrival, and she knew she had become someone of whom Harry would have been fiercely proud, because she felt that pride in herself.

She stood up and brushed down her dress. 'We'll worry about this later, but just now we need to put on the greatest acting performance we can manage.' She even managed a tight smile. 'It's at times like this we could do with Leah being around.'

The party was a runaway success. Helen had stood in her bedroom earlier, looking out of the window and watching the marquee go up against a balmy, late July sky, and her thoughts had naturally turned to what Harry would think of it all. Pride in his daughter for all she had become would have been at the forefront of his mind. Her adoption of that silly shortened name she'd chosen, and which Helen refused to use, would have made him roar with laughter. Helen could hear it now, that way his voice had of becoming high and squeaky when he tried to speak mid-guffaw, and the echo brought a faint smile to her face. He would have loved watching his eldest daughter moving among her friends and invited guests from the village; popular, and at ease in a way she rarely was around her own family – except her brother.

Music from a local seven-piece band, Billy Lang and the Pure Blues, blared well into the night. Some of the hotel guests wandered out to see what was going on and ended up joining the celebrations themselves. Helen encouraged it, in the hope that being welcomed to a family function would cement relationships so that, even if the landscape around them changed, they would remember that personal connection to Fox Bay, and keep coming back.

She ventured into the marquee in search of Roberta, blinking in the blue haze of swirling smoke. The crowd was still dense, despite the lateness of the hour, and Fiona was staring in awe at the fringed and sparkling dresses of the women, and at the astonishing and exuberant dancing on the hardwood floor. Lindy Hop, Charleston, Jumping Jive … Helen found it exhausting just to watch, though Leah would have loved it if she hadn't been stuck at home in Wales.

It was still a deep source of disappointment that she had retreated once again from her natural nursing vocation, but nothing Helen had said had made a difference; not even caring for her mother until her death three years ago had driven her to reconsider. To offset her frustration with her office job she'd have thrown herself right into a party like this, and been cutting a rug with the best of them. Even the vicar of St 'Dwinn's was joining in, out of breath but laughing, as one of Roberta's telephone exchange friends flung him around the floor.

The guest of honour was nowhere to be seen so Helen went back outside. Benjamin, on duty tonight but taking a well-earned break, was in conversation with some of his friends, by the gate that led to the tennis courts.

'Ben?' Helen crossed the yard. 'Have you seen the birthday girl? The Houghtons want to say goodbye to her before they leave.'

'She went that way,' Ben said, gesturing towards the courts with his wine glass. 'She was holding a note.' He grinned and dropped a sly wink. 'Going to meet a secret admirer, perhaps? I can't see Jowan Nancarrow, come to think of it.'

Helen followed the path to the tennis courts, where she'd had a wooden gazebo built a few years ago. Players would usually gather there while awaiting their turn on one of the full-sized courts, and Helen could see two figures in it now, thrown into relief by the lights strung around its edge.

One of them was Roberta, and the other ... She stopped dead and drew a breath sharp enough to hurt. The figures were a respectable distance apart, and low voices carried across the summer night air though the words were indistinct; there was no sign of any impropriety whatsoever, but that didn't stop the anger from boiling the blood in Helen's veins.

'Roberta!' she called, her voice tight. Her daughter turned towards her, and Helen saw a pale, slim hand rise to her mouth. The girl knew, then. She knew how this would make Helen feel. 'Your guests are leaving.' Unable to speak further, Helen turned away and hurried back down the path. She didn't much care now if Roberta said goodbye to the Houghtons or not, but the thought of her there, in the half-dark with that —

151

'Mum?' Ben had clearly noted her agitation as she drew level, and levered himself off the gate post. 'What's wrong?'

'Did you know he was here?' Helen demanded. 'Did you know he'd sneaked in here, and, and—'

'Wait!' He came closer. 'Who are you talking about?'

'Adam Coleridge!' Helen spat the name out as if it were poisoning her. 'Out there in the gazebo with *your sister*!'

He threw a shocked look towards the tennis courts. 'No! Has he been in touch with her?'

'I haven't a clue,' Helen said coldly. 'I take it he hasn't approached you, then?'

'The last time I saw him was at Dad's funeral.'

'Likewise. He's not called or written.' Though even if he had sent a letter she'd have sent it right back. 'So why is he here now?'

'Mrs Fox?' A voice crept out of the semi-darkness. 'Please do tell Roberta we've had a lovely time, but we must get back for the nanny.'

'I will, Mrs Houghton,' Helen promised. 'Thank you for coming. You too, Father Trevelyan,' she added, seeing the pink-faced vicar hovering nearby.

More guests drifted away, and when Helen looked over at the gazebo it was empty. Adam had sensibly slipped off, presumably the same way he'd slithered in, the snake. Helen was trembling with a mixture of rage and dismay; not satisfied with causing the death of Roberta's father, now he was skulking around in the dark with her. And worst of all, *what if Roberta liked it?* Adam had snared many a dizzy girl the same way, Helen had seen it so often since they'd become adults; a lazy, indulgent appreciation; a certain way of skimming from crown to shoes, returning to the face at leisure; a tiny half-smile that lurked at the corners of his mouth. Calculated, confident, infuriatingly compelling —

'I'm sorry.' Roberta appeared at her shoulder. 'I didn't know he was coming.'

Helen had to fight not to break down in tears. The emotions of the day were piling up, and she was perilously close to the edge. 'Has he gone?'

'Yes.'

'What did he want? Please tell me he wasn't —'

'Honestly, Mum!' Roberta's voice lost its conciliatory tone. 'He's our godfather! He didn't do anything improper, or even suggest it. He was like ... like he used to be, when we thought of him as our uncle. Nothing else.'

Helen wanted desperately to believe her. 'Do you swear on your father's memory?' she asked, in little more than a whisper.

'Why do you hate him so much?' Roberta sounded exasperated, though genuinely interested, but Helen couldn't bring herself to explain, even now, what only a handful of people had known all this time.

'It doesn't matter. We've not thought of him for years, and now he's gone again.'

'But he —'

'You have guests waiting,' Helen reminded her again. She cleared her throat and looked away, searching for an escape. 'I have to speak to Mr Skinner; he was late on reception duty tonight.'

'All right. But you're wrong about what Uncle

Adam wanted.' Roberta went back to the party, and Helen watched her go, almost forgetting Ben was still there until he moved to stand in Roberta's place.

'Makes you wonder why he was really here then, doesn't it?'

2

The following morning Helen set off across the field to Higher Valley Farm. Sometime in the early hours, after falling into bed exhausted from the party, she had awoken remembering where she had heard the name of the development company before: Hartcliffe was one of the more ancient areas of Bristol. Adam turning up at the party was probably a coincidence, but darkness always magnifies unsettling thoughts, and Helen lay awake wondering if it were possible that he had somehow rebuilt his fortune, and was now trying to do to her what he had done to Harry. But why? Anger? Peevishness? Revenge for the way she'd cut him out of the children's lives? All of those?

She'd flung herself over in bed, from one side to the other, trying desperately to shake off the thought, but in the end she'd just lain staring upward with burning eyes, tracing the faint cracks in the plaster as the sun began its slow climb. Eventually she abandoned all thoughts of sleep, and bathed and dressed, leaving a message explaining that she would not be at the family breakfast table, and asking Fleur to cover her early duties.

Now, with Higher Valley Farm coming into view, she slowed her steps. What was she going to ask, exactly? Who's bought your land? Why did you let them plan a development on it? Do you realise you're putting us out of business? Of course, they would apologise over a nice cup of tea and some fruit cake, then they'd contact the estate agents, explain they'd made a mistake, and it would all go back to the way it was. Helen allowed herself a bitter little laugh, but the fact remained: she had to know if Adam was involved.

Beth Nancarrow was hanging washing along the line at the top of the sloping garden. With three working men in the house this must be a mammoth daily task, and Helen hurried across the grass to help. Beth looked around as she approached and nodded her welcome. The bright smile Helen remembered from her first visit, so long ago, had been absent for some time after the accident that had taken Toby's life, but in the past year or so it had returned.

Helen suspected that was largely due to the arrival of Toby's brother Alfie, whose position on Priddy Farm in Porthstennack had become redundant just over a year ago. The boys and Beth had tried their hardest at Higher Valley, but had been glad to surrender the running of it to Alfie, who'd sadly fared no better.

Helen had only met him a couple of times since his arrival last spring; the boys still did all the deliveries and Beth still took care of the money. Alfie generally preferred to keep himself to himself. He was as like Toby as his nephews were alike, with Toby's height and mass of dark hair but without the pocked skin and missing teeth, and Beth was as naturally drawn to him as she had been to his brother when they'd all been young together. As far as Helen knew nothing had yet come of this attraction, but perhaps now that the pressure of trying to save a failing farm had been eased, they

156

might find time for one another. Dark clouds for Fox Bay, silver linings for Higher Valley.

'Let me take this end,' Helen said, helping lift a heavy sheet from the huge basket at Beth's feet.

'Have you come to talk about our arrangement?' Beth asked with her customary bluntness. She stuck two dolly pegs into her mouth and hefted her end of the sheet over the line.

'Not quite, although . . .' Helen hadn't considered that far, but the sale would doubtless have an effect on how the farm supplied Fox Bay. 'No,' she said at length. 'Not yet. It's about the sale of your farm.'

Beth took the pegs from her mouth and pushed them over the sheet, her manner noticeably cooler. 'You'd best talk to Alfie about that.'

'Do you know anything about it? Like who it is who's bought it?'

'It says in the paper, doesn't it? Hartcliffe Developments.'

'From Bristol.'

'I reckon. Pass me that shirt?'

Helen did so. 'Do you know who runs the company?'

'No. Like I said, you'd best talk to Alfie.'

'Did Mr Nancarrow know they were going to develop the land?' The question was out, and Helen wished she'd not uttered it after all; Beth's face lost its last trace of friendliness.

'You don't know what it's been like.'

'I know how it is to lose a husband, and to be left without money or a home.'

'Things were bad long before Toby died, you know that.' Beth took the last pair of corduroy

157

trousers and flapped them straight.

'Alfie's done his best, but he took on a dying duck.' She pegged the trousers so hard that Helen heard wood split, as the peg gave way beneath Beth's fingers. 'We had to take what we could, and I know folks around here think we've sold to the devil, but you can't lay the blame at Alfie's feet.'

'I wasn't going —'

'It's still my farm. Alfie's just doing what I asked him.'

'But he's the one who negotiated the deal?' Helen persisted. 'The one who met with the Hartcliffe people?'

Beth pursed her lips. 'If it makes a difference, yes. You'll find him down the river, fixing the fence by the weir.'

It was clearly a dismissal, and Helen looked down at her shoes; the soggy path by the river would make a mess of them, but she wasn't going to put it off until she had suitable footwear. She *had* to know, or drive herself mad.

'Beth,' she began, but stopped when Beth turned betrayed eyes on her. They'd never been proper friends, even after that awful time that had brought them together just after she'd moved here, but there had at least been a mutual respect between them. Now it was fractured on both sides. She turned away with a sigh of regret, and made her way down across the steep garden, sensing Beth Nancarrow's eyes burning into her back. Hopefully the woman would realise the question had come from a place of desperation and not judgement, but there was no time to try and convince her now.

Helen heard him before she saw him. The sound of hammer against nail, and, occasionally, wood, drifted up from the river, cutting through the gurgling of the weir and accompanied by some decidedly colourful language. She emerged from the meadow onto the path, where the farmer was ensuring the livestock would be able to drink without slipping into the fast-running water. A lively-looking collie nosed among the scrubby little bushes, no doubt hoping to flush some entertainment out of them.

'Mr Nancarrow!' Helen called, during a pause in the hammering.

He looked up, squinting against the early morning sun, then tested the piece of wire fence he'd been securing and came up to join her. 'Mrs Fox. What can I do for you?' From the wary look on his face, he'd already guessed but was hoping he was wrong.

'I understand why you've sold your land,' Helen said quickly, anxious to avoid more pointless conflict, 'but I just have some questions about who's bought it. Do you have a moment?'

He shrugged. 'Not much I can tell you, but all right. Reynard! Come!' The dog bounded up the slope, and Helen looked at it, amused despite everything.

'Reynard?'

'What of it?'

'Well, that's a fox, isn't it?'

'Is it?' Nancarrow looked down at the dog. 'Jowan named him that. It'll be on account of his pointed little face though,' he added, 'not because of your hotel.'

159

Helen felt foolish, and changed the subject back to the one at hand. 'I just want to know a little bit about the people behind Hartcliffe Developments.'

Nancarrow tucked his hammer into the canvas bag hanging off a fence post. 'All I know is it's based in Bristol and run by someone called Simon Hill.'

Helen felt her chest loosen in relief. She'd been jumping at shadows after all. 'Simon Hill,' she repeated. Did that name ring a bell somewhere in the back of her mind? Maybe, but the chances were she'd just have heard it bandied about during the days when Harry moved in those kinds of circles. 'That's the name on the transfer deed?'

'That's the one.'

'No other? I thought it would have needed two signatures at least.'

Nancarrow sighed. He sounded impatient now. 'Yes, there was one other. A co-director by the name of Jean Hill. His sister, I believe. And it was witnessed by some solicitor or other. Anything else you'd like to know?'

'No, and thank you.' Helen let the relief out in a smile. 'I'm sorry to have troubled you. Perhaps we can talk sometime about the arrangement between Higher Valley and Fox Bay?'

He looked startled. 'What about it? Are you cutting it off?'

'Not yet. Although that will happen if we close, anyway —'

'Close?'

'Obviously, once the area is developed.' But it seemed it hadn't been obvious to him at all, the way it had been to Beth; he hadn't been acting callously, just thoughtlessly. Not that it made a difference to the outcome. 'Anyway,' she went on, 'about the contract. Since you're selling part of your concern I wonder if you'll still be able to fulfil it for as long as we're open? Or whether you'd like to re-negotiate.'

He still looked nonplussed, so she shook her head and turned to leave. 'Just come to the hotel when you're not so busy, and we'll discuss it then.'

'I'm always busy,' he pointed out, gathering his thoughts at last, 'but yes, we can still fulfil it.' As she turned back, he went on, 'The farm was nearly sixty hectares, and all we've lost is the flat land up by the main road. Hundred acres or so. Our eggs and milk output won't change, and we'll still have plenty of room for growing potatoes and runner beans. Beth might even start planting out strawberries.' He gave her a taut smile, that made him look suddenly hard in the newly glinting sun. 'I suppose you'd have to call us more of a market garden now, than a farm, but what's in a name, eh?'

Helen didn't know how to respond to that, everything that crossed her mind sounded selfish, so she just nodded. 'Thank you, Mr Nancarrow.'

'You used to call my brother Toby, didn't you?'

'I did, for the short time I knew him.'

'Then I suppose you should call me Alfie.'

'Alfie, then. Thank you again.'

She started back up the slope, and heard him clearing his throat in a marked manner, so she turned back to see him looking at her with his heavy eyebrows raised. 'Yes?'

'I've invited you to call me Alfie,' he said patiently.

'Yes, I did — Oh.' She smiled. 'Please, do call me Helen.'

'Oh, I couldn't possibly, Mrs Fox.' His face was expressionless, but for an amused tilt to his mouth.

'Well,' she countered, 'as a wise man once said, what's in a name, eh?'

He grinned, then bent and scratched Reynard's ears, and as he walked back down to the river, Helen heard him whistling. It seemed she'd been right; the easing of the financial pressure had given him a lighter heart, and Beth's patience in waiting for him might very well be rewarded at last.

★   ★   ★

Mountain Ash, South Wales
10th August

Leah shoved the letter back into its envelope and then into her coat pocket. Aunt Mary, who'd moved in after Mam died, was moving about upstairs in what was now her own room, and it sounded as if she was once again dragging furniture across the uncarpeted section of the floor. She was never happy unless she was changing something. Leah looked up at the ceiling as if she could see through it and silence the racket with a glare, but the bumps and slides continued. At least it meant her aunt was feeling strong and healthy, which lessened Leah's guilt about leaving her at a moment's notice.

'I'm off then, Aunt Mary,' she called. 'I'll be back Wednesday.'

'Right you are,' her aunt shouted back. 'Don't you worry about me, mind. I've got the number for the hotel.'

'And you'll use Mrs Carter's phone?'

'Yes! Go on with you or you'll miss your train.'

Leah pulled the front door closed and ran lightly down the steps, giving a deliberately cheery wave over her shoulder to where Aunt Mary would be watching from the window. She didn't want her aunt to see how the letter was weighing her down, like a brick in her pocket, and even the prospect of three days added to her usual Saturday and Sunday break didn't stop the sick churning she felt in the pit of her stomach. But at least those days would be spent far away from here. The farther the better.

Travelling to Fox Bay these days was more like coming home than returning to Mountain Ash ever was. Over the past nine years the friendship she'd found with the family had drawn her back without fail at the tail end of each year, and in between those times they were such regular correspondents that she felt part of all their lives, not just Helen's. Missing Roberta's special birthday had disappointed them both, but now, two weeks later, she was determined to make the most of the days ahead, and knowing it would be a surprise for Helen and the children made the anticipation all the sweeter ... She shook her head; Roberta had just turned twenty-one, she must stop referring to them as *the children*.

The journey down wasn't too awful either. Not too hot, considering it was summer, and the time passed pleasantly enough, especially after the change at Plymouth, in the company of two younger women who were on their way to Bude to join the cast of a play.

'It's Mae West's *Diamond Lil*,' they told her proudly. 'Will you come and see it?'

It sounded just the thing Leah needed to take her mind off things, and as she rose and lifted down her bag, she promised to discuss it with Helen. 'She's so busy, I'm sure she'd appreciate a night out. Her daughters, too.'

'Tell the man on the door you're our friend!'

'See you soon, Leah. Come backstage!'

The young women waved madly after her as she alighted at Trethkellis, and she waved back, grinning at their infectious excitement and looking forward to seeing them on the stage. She watched the train chuffing off into the distance and felt the tension lifting from her shoulders, until she hefted her bag and started up the platform towards the gate. She was used to being here in November and December, but at the height of the summer season there were no empty taxis to be seen, and it would be a long wait in this heat, even in the little station café.

'Mrs Marshall?'

She turned around and for a split second she was back in the Nancarrows' kitchen nine years ago, with the hot, coppery smell of blood in her nostrils and the greasy feel of it under her fingers. Then she blinked and reality reasserted itself: it wasn't Toby Nancarrow who'd hailed her, but his

164

brother from Porthstennack. They'd met the last time she was here, the only time he'd ever brought his farm's produce to the hotel, and they'd got along quite well while she'd helped him unpack the boxes in the kitchen.

He was a friendly sort, intelligent, and even quite nice-looking in a smiley, shaggy-dog sort of a way. He'd told her stories about doing a similar thing further down the coast, where the farm on which he'd worked had supplied the big house at the top of town, the one that had caught fire before the war. 'Of course, it was horse-drawn cart back then,' he'd said, and she'd detected a hint of nostalgia as he'd looked at his van.

'Can I drop you at the hotel?' he asked now, and she wilted with relief.

'Oh, yes please! You've saved my feet, thank you.'

'Righto. I'm just here to pick up a package, give me a minute.' He disappeared into the office and emerged a few minutes later with his parcel. 'You've picked good weather for it, this time,' he observed. 'I thought you said you don't like to come down during the summer months.'

'Not usually, no. I prefer it much quieter. But this time it's a surprise, since I missed a birthday party.'

'Ah, young Miss Fox's twenty-first. Yes, that was quite something, so I heard. The boys talked about it for days. Music and dancing like it was — '

'Don't rub it in!' Leah settled into the passenger seat. 'Helen doesn't know I'm coming. Although I realise now that might be a mistake,' she added. 'I should have realised it's peak sea-

165

son and she'll be busy.'

'She'll probably welcome the distraction,' Alfie said. He drove slowly through the crowd towards the main road. 'She's told you about the development, I take it?'

'Development?' Leah looked at him, startled. 'No, she hasn't. What development?'

'Beth's told me to sell off another part of the farm. This time it's a sizeable bit of the top fields, and it turns out the company that bought it plans to build houses on it.'

'What?' Leah's heart sank. 'Oh no, poor Helen.'

'People need houses,' Alfie pointed out, a little sharply. 'Not everyone's lucky enough to have a great big posh hotel to live in.'

'I appreciate that,' Leah said, matching his tone. 'But a housing development right there will take away the hotel's biggest benefits. Clear, open countryside for miles. Not to mention all the noise and disruption when the building starts.'

He didn't reply, but he pulled his cap further down over his nose, and his gaze was as stony as the road to which it was fixed.

'And what about your contract with the hotel?' Leah persisted. 'What'll happen then?'

'We'll have to cross that bridge when we come to it,' Alfie said, and added defensively, 'The bloke I dealt with never said he was going to build on it.'

'Did you ask?'

'No.' He sighed. 'But, in all fairness I suppose the company name should have told me.'

'And that's ... ?'

'Hartcliffe Developments,' he muttered, flushing slightly. 'But it could have meant anything.

166

Could have meant a ... nature reserve, or a zoo, or something.'

Leah ignored that. 'Hartcliffe. Are they from Bristol then?'

He nodded. 'Bloke named Hill, and his sister.'

'What's he like, is he married?'

'What difference does that make?' Alfie gave her a curious glance, then shrugged. 'Never met him, anyway. The sale was all done through solicitors.'

'He's not even been down here to see what he's bought?'

Alfie turned into the driveway of Fox Bay Hotel. 'If he has, I haven't met him.' As he pulled up to the front door, he looked across at Leah. 'It's like I told Helen, we didn't have a choice.'

'I just can't believe he hasn't even come down here to see what he's going to destroy.' Leah climbed out, and Alfie fetched her bag from the back.

'Not in person, he hasn't, but one of his directors knows the land well enough. Told him about it to start with, apparently, and persuaded him to put the offer in. He's the one who brought the deeds down for signing. Seemed nice enough.'

'*Seemed* sounds about right.'

'Look, I'm sure Mr Coleridge never intended to put anyone out of — '

'Wait.' Leah frowned. 'Coleridge?'

'It's not on the transfer deed so I might be mis-remembering. Give Helen my best,' he added, and climbed back into the driving seat. 'Tell Mr Bannacott there'll be extra eggs if he wants to order any before the next delivery.'

Leah couldn't answer, her mind was too full of

167

everything she'd learned in that five-minute trip from the station. She barely remembered to lift a hand in thanks and farewell as Alfie drove away. Adam Coleridge ... Helen must be distraught.

3

'So, what do you think?'

Bertie leaned on the motorcycle's handlebars to test the front suspension. 'It's not a bad price, for what it is. But still a lot more expensive than the four-stroke.'

'Not too many miles on it,' the mechanic pointed out. 'Considering it's three years old.'

'But those miles will have taken their toll more on a racer, than the same number would on a road bike.' Bertie walked to the back of the Flying Squirrel and crouched down, squinting down the length of the bike. 'What's the top speed?'

'We've had it pushing seventy, and that's in the last couple of months.' The mechanic wiped his hands on his trousers and thrust one of them out, inviting the deal. 'Come on, Bertie. You've ridden it, you know it's a good machine.'

'I've ridden it around *here*, Stan. No way of knowing what it can really do.'

'Get it on the track, you'll see then.'

'Are you saying you'll let me have a trial ride?' Stan looked trapped, and his hand fell back to his side. 'Well — ' 'If I like it, I'll pay the asking price.' 'And if you drop it?' 'The price, or the bike?' Bertie grinned at the look on Stan's face. 'Don't worry, I won't do either. You've known me long enough to trust me.'

Stan didn't smile back. 'It don't matter how long we've known each other, if you drop the bike, you'll either pay full price, or full cost of repairs.'

'Do you make this kind of deal with everyone?' Bertie asked. An innocent enough question, but Stan would know exactly what it meant.

'Not everyone's got the gall to ask for a test race,' he said, his expression giving nothing away.

He and Bertie looked at one another, and then Bertie looked down at the hand Stan had proffered earlier. 'Shake on that, then?'

There was a long pause, then the hand came up and grasped Bertie's. 'You'll sign something,' he warned.

'I'll sign whatever you like.'

Stan led the way into his office and dug around until he found some scrap paper. On it, he wrote:

1926 Scott Flying Squirrel. Loaned from Houghton Sales and Repairs for the duration of 1 week.

'Don't forget the race,' Bertie said, peering over Stan's shoulder. Stan sighed.

To include 1 (one) 500cc class race at Bude Racetrack.

He added the dates, Bertie's name, and the proviso that all repairs would be paid for if the loan did not result in a sale. He signed it,

Stanley Arthur Houghton.

Then he handed the pen to Bertie, who scrawled

170

across the page with careless elegance:

Roberta Fox.

Arriving home a little later, Bertie was surprised and delighted to find Leah in the family kitchen, talking to Ben, who'd come down early to help Guy with an inventory of the wine cellar. Bertie's friends, embarrassingly enough, couldn't stop talking about Ben. He wasn't unattractive, she supposed. They talked about him in the village, and in the telephone exchange in particular, and a couple of her friends spent far too much time asking questions about him. *Is he courting anyone special? He's so charismatic, and charming!* Bertie couldn't see it. He might hold a position of responsibility now, and know an awful lot about wine and fine dining, but he was still the same old Ben, still just as annoying as he'd been at fifteen, only taller. And she still adored him, though it would never do to show it.

Leah turned as Bertie came into the room, and a smile brightened her unusually solemn face. 'There you are!' She moved in for a hug, but Bertie stepped back, her hands raised.

'I wouldn't, I've been down at Stan's.'

Leah laughed. 'So I see. He's let you loose on his bikes again?'

'Better than that.' Bertie grinned. 'I've almost bought one.'

'Almost?' Ben raised an eyebrow. 'How can you have almost bought something?'

'I'm picking it up tomorrow for a trial and racing it at Bude next Saturday. If I like it, I'm buying it.'

171

'With your birthday money, I take it?' Ben whistled. 'Mum's not going to like that.'

'Oh, she doesn't like anything.' Bertie dismissed that with a wave and turned back to Leah. 'What brings you down here during the summer? We weren't expecting you, were we?'

'I had an unexpected extra few days, so I thought I'd come down and see how you all are.'

She sobered. 'I gather you've had some horrible news.'

'The hotel you mean?' Bertie nodded. 'It's awful. Mum's in a real state over it, and Gran's worse.'

'Where are they?'

'Gran's at a WI meeting, Mum's in the office.' Ben started towards the door. 'I'll tell her you're here.'

'Wait a moment. Does she know who's bought the farmland?'

'Someone named Hill. From Bristol.' Bertie went to the sink and rummaged beneath it for the soap. 'Why?'

'And it's absolutely certain he's going to build on it?'

'Mum seems sure. To be honest she doesn't talk to me about it much. She talks to the Almighty Benjamin though, because he's a man and therefore more important than me.'

'Or because I'm the night manager,' Ben put in mildly. He was used to her little digs, but it was still fun trying to rattle him. 'She knows you're going to run off and make a home somewhere else,' he went on, 'and so's Fiona.'

'And what if I don't want to get married and move away?'

172

'Who said anything about getting married? Who'd have you anyway?'

Bertie pulled a face and flicked soapy water at him.

'Touché, Ben,' Leah said, with a grin. She still looked tense though, and Bertie began to wonder if she'd underestimated the impact the land sale would have on them.

'Is it really serious?' she asked, drying her hands. She looked at the towel, then hurriedly tucked it back onto the rail, adjusting it so the oil smudge wasn't visible. 'I mean, we'll lose some guests, but we still have the beach, and the cliffs. And the hotel itself is beautiful.'

'But there are plenty of other beautiful beach-side hotels not being crowded out by houses, and where would you rather go, if you're looking for a quiet coastal retreat?'

Bertie felt the first stirrings of real disquiet. 'I hadn't really thought it would make that much difference. Bugger Alfie Nancarrow! Why on earth did —'

'Bertie! Language!' Leah looked around as if she expected Fleur to have returned from her meeting early, but the door was still firmly shut, and she relaxed a little. 'It's not Alfie's fault, he didn't know Mr Coleridge was planning to build.'

Bertie and Ben exchanged wide-eyed looks. 'Mr Coleridge?' Ben repeated.

'There are lots of Coleridges,' Bertie ventured, but her heart sank.

'Too much of a coincidence, surely,' Ben muttered. 'Bertie, did he say anything to you at the party?'

'You've seen him?' It was Leah's turn to look at them both in surprise. 'Is he still here?'

'He was the one who'll have paid for Bertie's new bike,' Ben said, and Bertie glared at him.

'Shut up! She'll only tell Mum.'

Leah frowned. 'Who's she, the cat's mother?'

'Don't tell her, please!' Bertie turned pleading eyes on her. 'Uncle Adam gave me some birthday money, but if Mum finds out she'll make me give it back.'

Leah didn't look at all surprised, considering this must have sounded like an odd assertion. 'She can't really,' she pointed out. 'It's your money, and you're an adult.'

'Well even if she lets me keep it, she'll make sure Stan doesn't sell me that bike.'

'Do you know why Uncle Adam and Mum don't speak anymore?' Ben asked, his train of thought clearly following Bertie's. Leah shook her head, but Bertie wasn't sure she believed her.

'Is Mr Coleridge still here?' Leah persisted.

'He's staying in the village,' Bertie said. 'Why?'

'Perhaps you could arrange to see him. Persuade him to leave Trethkellis and go back to Bristol, for your mother's sake.'

'How did you find out so much about the sale?' Bertie asked. 'You must have only been here for ten minutes!'

'Alfie gave me a lift from the station. Will you do it?'

'I'll try,' Bertie said doubtfully, 'but it's not very fair. He'll be really upset. When he came to the party he kept asking if Mum ever mentioned him, or if I thought she might be glad to see him after

174

all this time.'

'She wouldn't be, we all know that.'

'Then since you know so much, I think you ought to tell us why.' Ben leaned against the closed door and folded his arms. 'Come on, Leah. Mum's never going to, and we're all adults here.'

Leah blew a heavy blonde curl away from her face, and looked at him, exasperated. 'It's not my place.'

'If you want me to persuade him to leave,' Bertie put in, 'you're going to have to give me a good reason, other than his buying up some local land. He was incredibly generous, and he was our father's best friend. I've never understood why she pushed him away after Dad died.'

She and Ben waited, and Leah sighed and sat down, patting the table for them to join her. 'All right. But not a word to your mother, and I want that man gone from the area before she realises what he's done now.'

Bertie listened, with growing dismay, as Leah told them what Helen had confided to her almost ten years ago. It was hard to believe; Uncle Adam had always been so much fun, always dropping in to Burleigh Mansions with trinkets and books for the three Fox children – he was the one who'd given her *Arthur Rackham's Book of Pictures* which she'd always loved so much, and which Fiona had devoured after her. Mum must have forgotten that part, because every other sign of him had been removed from their lives, like a face cut from a photograph.

'So *he* was the one who took all our money,' Ben said slowly.

Leah shrugged. 'Well, he convinced your father it was safe to invest, anyway.'

'No wonder Mum blames him for Dad's death, then.'

'Wait,' Leah said quickly, 'I didn't say that.'

'You didn't need to, it's obvious.' Ben stood up, his face grim. 'She could never hate anyone for this long unless it went as deep as that. Do as Leah says, Bertie, the sooner we get him out of Trethkellis the better. At least now I know why Mum was so upset when she saw him at your party. I never want to see her like that again.'

'Then let's make sure she doesn't find out. Tell me when you've arranged to meet him,' Leah said to Bertie, also rising. 'I need to know when he'll be gone, so I can keep Helen out of the village until then.'

'She'll find out in the end anyway, and she's stronger than you think,' Bertie pointed out.

'I know how strong she is, but you heard what your brother said. Why put her through it when she's already got enough to worry about?'

'He left me the telephone number of the guest house where he's staying.' Bertie patted her trouser pockets. 'No, it's in my coat. I'll call him now.'

'And I'll go and see Helen.' Leah disappeared with her bag, leaving Ben and Bertie alone in the kitchen.

'Do you think I should give the money back?' Bertie asked.

Ben shook his head. 'Not in a million years. He owes us.'

The door opened again, and Leah popped her head around. 'Ben, darling, how long have you

176

got before you start your shift?'

He checked the watch on his waistcoat. Their father's watch, and as usual Bertie's heart shrank a little to remember him wearing it. 'A couple of hours yet, it's only just four. But I'm supposed to be helping Guy.'

'Would you be a sweetheart and drive me into Bude, before I see your mother? I'll have a word with Guy and explain.'

'Can I come?' Bertie asked, perking up again. 'I need some new gloves from the leather shop.'

'Certainly not! You'll spoil the surprise.'

'What surprise?'

'Honestly.' Leah looked at Ben and rolled her eyes. 'Who's recently had a special birthday, can you think of anyone?'

Bertie grinned. 'Ah.'

'Ah, indeed. Right then, young man.' Leah smiled at Ben. 'Let's go, and when we get back Helen and I can have a nice chat.'

By the time Leah and Ben returned, with a glorious-looking strawberry sponge, Mum had learned her friend was visiting and the heavy air of approaching disaster had lifted.

'There's a little bakery just near the theatre,' Leah said, slicing into the sponge. 'I didn't expect them to have something so wonderful left at this time of day, but someone had ordered this and not picked it up.'

'Lucky us.' Mum grinned. She toasted Bertie with her forkful of cake. 'To the birthday girl, all over again!'

The arrival of Fiona, home from Trethkellis lifeboat station, made it easier for them all to put the darker news of the day to one side, and they sat around the kitchen table, chattering about boats, while they made inroads into the strawberry sponge.

Bertie waited until Mum and Leah had vanished into the private sitting room, and Ben had gone off to begin his shift, before hurrying upstairs to the quiet study on the first floor. She placed the call to Sandy Cove, and hung up feeling an odd kind of guilt at the pleasure she'd heard in Uncle Adam's voice. Would she be able to tell him, face-to-face, what she thought of him?

Before that there was the motorbike to pick up. It was a very different machine from the AJS she'd bought off the Nancarrows a few years ago and she'd need this week to get used to it, not to mention fiddle with the tuning to get it just right for her own riding style. A low buzz of excitement ran through her at the thought of the mid-August meet next week; she'd devoured the reports of this year's Isle of Man TT races, where the Squirrel had done so well, and now she was just hours away from bringing one home herself. It was scarcely believable! She was leaning on the reception desk, daydreaming about lifting the trophy, when Leah emerged from the sitting room and threw her a wordless, questioning glance.

Bertie nodded, and sobered, remembering where the money for her dream had come from. Damn the man. 'Ten o'clock tomorrow morning, by the well in the village.'

'Good girl.' Leah looked back at the closed sitting room door and lowered her voice. 'Your mother still doesn't know, and I think it's best we

178

keep it like that if we don't want to add to her troubles.'

'Mrs Marshall? the receptionist called. 'There's a telegram for you.'

Leah grimaced and went over. A moment later Bertie's mother came out of the sitting room, and a miserable-looking Leah indicated the telegram. 'Helen, I'm so sorry, but I have to go again.'

'Already?' Mum's face fell. 'You've only just arrived.'

'This is from my neighbour. Aunt Mary's got this thing about not asking for help when she wants to move something, and she's been rearranging the furniture in her room again.'

'Oh my goodness! What happened?'

Leah handed her the flimsy piece of paper. 'They think she's dislocated her shoulder. Honestly, I've told her time and time again to just ask!'

'But you won't be in time for the last train out, now,' Mum said worriedly.

'It's all right, I'll go first thing in the morning. She's being looked after by our neighbour tonight. I just feel bad for being so far away, and she'll need my help when Mrs Carter has to leave.'

'And you might be able to help, with your training and all,' Mum pointed out, ever hopeful of Leah's return to her vocation.

'Perhaps. I'm sure the doctor has done everything that can be done, though'

'I'll ask Guy to drop you into the station early, you'll be able to catch the ten past eight.'

Bertie turned away, as disappointed as her mother; Leah was the brightest, liveliest thing about Fox Bay at the moment, and whenever she

179

turned up things just seemed . . . better. More exciting. Now she was about to disappear again already, and the gloom would descend once more with no distractions to counter it.

She'd miss Bertie's race, too, and besides that, Bertie had hoped to persuade her to come with her tomorrow to confront Uncle Adam, but if she was catching the early train she would be long gone by then, and Bertie would have to do it alone after all. Despondent, she went back upstairs, leaving Mum and Leah to talk, and flopped across her bed. How long did she have left, to be staring at this ceiling? How long before the hotel was nothing more than a vague memory, the same as Burleigh Mansions?

She closed her eyes and tried to remember her old home in Bristol, but it kept merging into this one; the staircase would lead clearly enough from her old bedroom, but by the time she reached the ground floor the big hall had turned into the lobby here. It seemed that despite years of denial, Fox Bay had come to mean more to her than she'd ever wanted it to. Uncle Adam had ruined them twice over.

4

Sandy Cove Guest House, Trethkellis

Adam looked around the small, slope-ceilinged bedroom, and wondered how much he would miss it when he went home. Not much actually, he decided; he would miss being at Trethkellis, certainly, the sea air seemed to be good for his chest, but Sandy Cove had been built for much smaller people, and when he'd first booked in he'd given his head an eye-watering bash, just trying to look out of the window. The egg was still there, and he rubbed at it now; perhaps it was fate, delivering a well-deserved punishment for telling Simon Hill about the Nancarrows' farm. It would be worth it in the end, though, it had to be. Bumped head notwithstanding.

The phone call from Bertie had come as a surprise, and sparked a hope that she wanted to thank him properly for the birthday money; Helen spotting him at the party had meant Bertie had had to go before she'd seen what the envelope had contained. Fifteen pounds was a substantial sum, particularly as he wasn't nearly as flush as he pretended. But it was her twenty-first, and whether or not her mother regretted it, he was still her godfather ... he could have done nothing less. For a moment he wondered what she'd spend it on, then he grinned. No, he didn't wonder at all; after the brief chat they'd managed on the night of her birthday he knew damned well that money would soon find its way into the greasy hand of Stan Houghton. This particular apple had not fallen far from the tree.

'Mr Coleridge!' Mrs Finch's voice had drifted up the narrow staircase, as Adam was opening his suitcase to begin packing. 'Telephone!'

The guest house still favoured the old-style candlestick telephone, and he'd picked up the mouthpiece, hoping it wasn't Jeanette on the other end of the line. Not today, please . . . 'Adam Coleridge speaking.'

'Uncle Adam? It's Bertie.'

'Bertie! What can I do for you? Have you spent that money yet?'

'I wondered if we might meet again before you leave.'

Did he imagine the emphasis on that last word? 'How did you know I'd still be here, after two weeks?'

There was a pause, then she said quietly, 'Because I think I know why you came.'

Adam stilled. 'Do you?'

'*Can* we meet?'

'Your mother would prefer not.'

'She needn't know.'

Adam frowned. Going against Helen's wishes was the last thing he wanted, especially now she must hate him all the more, and with good reason. But Bertie was a grown woman who could make up her own mind, and he missed all the Fox children painfully. He would just have to try and emphasise that Simon Hill was in charge of Hartcliffe, and all decisions came from him. No matter

182

who pushed him towards them.

'I'd love to meet,' he said. 'How about tomorrow morning? Can you get into the village? We could meet on the seat by the old well, if the weather holds.'

'All right. I have to go to Stan's, but I should have finished there by ten.'

So, he was right about the money then. He smiled. 'I look forward to it.'

He had replaced the receiver and gone back upstairs to finish packing. Tomorrow he'd say his goodbyes to Bertie, and then drive back to Bristol and hand over Simon's copy of the signed transfer deed: one hundred acres of ground at Higher Valley Farm. After that ...Well, after that anything could happen.

He checked his watch now and crossed the village square towards the well that stood at its centre. The weather was still warm, and he was comfortable in shirt sleeves and a waistcoat, so it was no hardship to sit on the carved wooden bench in front of the well and watch the comings and goings of the holidaying visitors and the locals while he waited for Bertie.

The thought of saying goodbye gave him a surprising pang. He'd missed being part of this family, and his brief contact on Bertie's twenty-first had re-awoken the wish that he'd persisted with Helen when, in the depth of her grief, she had pushed him away. Since starting boarding school, he had come to look on the Foxes as his surrogate family, welcomed without question at their home at holidays and Christmas, when his own parents had found children a social impediment. The sense of belonging had only intensified when Harry had married one of Adam's own dearest childhood friends, and moved to Adam's home city, and he had spent almost as much time at Burleigh Mansions as the family themselves.

Until now he'd successfully fooled himself into believing he'd moved, without regret, into his new life; albeit a life that was little more than a slowly recovering professional one, and even that much he owed entirely to the brother of his erstwhile fiancée Jeanette Duval. Or Jean Hill, as she was more properly called. It occasionally made him smile that she'd long ago decided 'Hill' was too too common and had adopted a French name that was at least close to it in meaning. Especially now that 'Hill' had become a name to be reckoned with in Bristol, and she'd gradually reverted to it as if no one would notice.

Smiling again now, he twisted his head as he became aware of an engine rattle that lifted above the few motors that pottered about the village on this Sunday morning. It was coming from a lane that led out towards the moors, and after a moment the motorcycle came into view over the rise, and despite the goggles that obscured the rider's features he immediately knew who it was. He recognised the bike as a Flying Squirrel, and nodded in approval, looking forward to discussing it with her.

Bertie was oil-streaked and dressed in plus fours, with her short coat open and snapping in the wind. She pulled up outside the post office across the square and killed the engine, and before Adam could go over to offer help, she had pulled the motorcycle back onto its rear-wheel kickstand. Looking at the ease with which she did it, he reflected that it was just as well he hadn't offered — she'd have given him short shrift, no doubt.

She pushed the goggles up over the front of her leather helmet, and he rose to greet her as she came over, complimentary words about her choice of motorbike on his lips. But she ignored his outstretched hands, and her face was expressionless as she sat down and pulled off her helmet. She stared up at the sky for a moment, then closed her eyes against the bright sunlight.

He cleared his throat, sensing trouble on the horizon. 'Thank you for coming to — '

'Why did you do it? Why buy that land?'

He looked away, stung by her abrupt manner and her refusal to look at him. 'Look, I don't know how much you've heard, but Simon Hill is head of Hartcliffe, not me.'

'But you work for him.'

'Not on everything.' Better not to mention his seat on the board of directors. 'I just offered to tie up some loose ends as I was coming down anyway, for your birthday. To which,' he added pointedly, 'I was not invited.'

'Are you surprised, after what you did?'

'Bertie, that farm was in trouble. They've welcomed a chance to pay off their debts, and they can still function as a working concern.'

'So you did it all for them.' Bertie gave a short, scornful laugh. 'How kind.'

'Simon was looking for land. I know the area

185

and knew that the Nancarrows have been struggling for years. It made logical business sense, so I just suggested Simon get in touch with them to find out if they were open to a deal.'

'Utter tosh! And besides,' her voice faltered, 'I'm not just talking about the farmland.'

'What then?'

She finally turned to face him, and to his dismay he saw her eyes were brimming with tears. 'It's taken almost ten years, but Ben and I know now why Mum hates you so much. It's because of what you did to Dad. The investment that ruined him.'

Adam's heart turned over. 'I never meant to push him to the point he'd lose everything,' he managed. 'He told me he had the money to invest.'

'He did have it! Because he sold the hotel!'

'But I never knew that!' Adam stood up and shoved his hands into his pockets. He kicked at the stones around the well, searching for the words he needed. It was like trying to explain to Helen all over again, only now it was harder. Because over the past ten years he'd done nothing but agonise over it, looking for a way to excuse himself, but Helen had been right. He should have asked, he should have sat Harry down and really talked it through with him, but he'd been too eager to take the money and throw it at Blue Ensign. And then the decision to risk the insurance …

'I just came here to make sure you're leaving.'

He nodded, swallowing past a tightness in his throat. 'I'm going later today, don't worry.'

'Good. And I'm going to repay every penny of that birthday money.'

186

'Don't — '

'I don't want your guilt money.'

'Guilt money? Roberta, you're my *goddaughter*!'

'It's Bertie,' she reminded him. 'I've already paid Stan the deposit on that bike, or I'd give it back to you right now.'

'I don't want it.'

'Then give it to someone stupid enough to fall for your lies.' Bertie stood up. 'I'm going home, while I still have one. I just wanted to tell you that no one wants you around here, so, if you've signed your filthy documents, you can stop hanging around now.'

Watching her stride away, Adam knew he should call out, say something to make her stop and listen, but he couldn't find anything to say except that tired old, *but I didn't mean to*. Like a schoolboy who has hurt a classmate and lost the friendship of everyone in the playground as a result.

Bertie didn't look back as she rode away and he could have kicked himself for being too wrapped up in searching for excuses to reach out to her and just say sorry instead. Maybe if he'd done that it would have stopped her in her tracks, at least long enough for him to think of something to say that would show her how he regretted everything. It wouldn't bring her father back, but it might take some of the poison from her veins. And Helen's. That hurt more than anything; he'd always claimed she irritated him as a child, but he'd secretly enjoyed it when she tagged along during the holidays, even when she'd pushed him out of a tree for saying her hair was too curly.

He sat a while longer, lost in the past, then made

his way reluctantly back to Sandy Cove to finish packing. As he walked, he found he was smiling a little at that childhood memory, even though he'd been furious at the time, at being bested by a girl ... Not to mention the sprained wrist, and the torn coat he would have to explain. It had taken all David Marlowe's nine-year-old diplomacy to quell the row: *If you tell Mother on Helen, I'm telling your mother on you!* Good old David, it was a shame their friendship hadn't survived the three-way pull that boarding school, and meeting the charismatic Harry Fox, had created.

He reached the guest house, still deep in memories, and was brought up short by the sight of a slender woman dressed in a simple but elegant summer dress and wearing a neat little flower-garlanded summer hat. A bag, with an unusually pretty handle bedecked in butterflies, sat at her feet, and she was peering closely at a piece of paper in her hand, and then up at the front door.

'Can I help you, miss?'

The woman turned, and Adam was disturbed to see her eyes were red and swollen. Her nose was pink, too, and he found it oddly touching that she gave him a bright smile, as if it could possibly disguise the fact that she'd been crying.

'Oh, I was just wondering if this is Sandy Cove Guest House,' she said, in a pleasantly low voice with a faint Scottish accent. 'I can't see a sign.'

'It is.' He held out a hand. 'Adam Coleridge. I'm staying here. Well,' he amended, 'I've *been* staying here. I leave today.'

She shook his hand. 'Susannah Paterson. It's nice to meet you.'

188

'You're from Edinburgh?'

'Morningside. You have a good ear for Scots.'

'I have family in Leith.'

She blinked in surprise. 'Well, that's a coincidence.'

'What brings you to Cornwall?'

She looked away quickly. 'Just a holiday.'

His glance dropped automatically, and he saw a slim gold band on her wedding finger. He looked around. 'Is your husband with you?'

She withdrew her hand gently. 'I'm widowed.'

'I'm sorry to hear that. Was it recent?' That would explain the tears.

'No, the war. A gas attack.'

Adam's skin tightened in cold, sickening memory of his own experience of poison gas, and hoped it didn't show on his face; it was likely she'd been told her husband's death had been quick and relatively pain-free — he'd had to write letters to that effect himself, to those his men had left behind. He didn't want her to ask questions, or to have to disabuse her of that notion . . . He still felt the effects of it after nearly thirteen years.

'Allow me to escort you inside.' He pushed open the door and gestured for Susannah to go first. 'There are some lovely rooms, but I would make sure you pick one at the front of the house, if there are any left.'

'Oh?' She turned to him. 'Is that because of the noise, or the view perhaps?'

'No.' He pointed to the raised bump on his forehead. 'The roof.'

For a moment the smile that touched her eyes was more natural, but it soon faded, and she consulted the paper again. 'It says here that the landlady is a Mrs Finch.'

'I'll introduce you. She's very sweet.'

'And you're very kind,' Susannah said, and her voice shook a little bit. 'Thank you.'

'Not at all.' He hesitated, unsure whether to address the tear that was trembling on her lower lashes. But it spilled before he could say anything, and she wiped it away hurriedly.

'Please, don't mind me. I'm just tired.'

'This is more than tiredness,' he said gently, surprising himself. 'Mrs Paterson, I believe you need to talk to someone. Will I do?'

'Hello there!' They both turned as Gladys Finch came out of the dining room, a stack of napkins in her hands. 'Just let me put these in the laundry and I'll be right with you.'

'Mrs Finch, this is Mrs Paterson. I believe she has a reservation.'

'No, forgive me if I gave the wrong impression, but I don't have one,' Susannah said. 'I was just given the name of this guest house by a friend. I know it's the height of the season, but I'm hoping you'll have a room.'

'You're in luck, this gentleman is leaving today, if a room at the back will suit you.'

Susannah looked at Adam, and he saw her suppress a smile as she removed her hat. Beneath it was a cap of sleek dark hair, shaped into a neat bob and cut very short, and she passed her hand over it to subdue any flyaway strands. 'That will suit very well, thank you.'

'I'll leave you to book in,' Adam said. 'I must finish packing so I can vacate the room.'

'Thank you ever so much for your kindness, Mr Coleridge.'

'Not at all,' he said again, mentally rearranging his timetable to allow for a leisurely afternoon; he was in no real rush to return to Bristol, after all, tonight would be just as good ... It wasn't long before he idly began to wonder if anyone else was leaving Sandy Cove Guest House with a spare room tonight.

★ ★ ★

Fox Bay Hotel

'... And so Mr Glasson says he can use me as part of the launching crew when I'm a bit older.'

Helen looked at her youngest daughter doubtfully. The girl was as slender as a twig, largely due to her constant climbing of the cliff path from the hotel down to the beach and back, and her arms didn't look strong enough to so much as lift one of those ropes, let alone haul on it with any effect. Particularly when it was heavy with sea water.

'And this is the captain who said this?'

'The coxswain,' Fiona corrected. 'Yes.'

'How much older is 'a bit'?'

'He said another two years.'

'And in the meantime?'

Fiona shrugged. 'I'm still allowed to go down there and watch, and sometimes help with fetching and carrying. And cleaning, too.'

'And you're happy to do this?'

'Yes!'

Helen needn't have asked, really; since she'd left

191

school last year, Fiona came home from Trethkellis every day positively glowing.

'You let that girl run wild,' Fleur had said then, with a rare show of disapproval. 'She needs to be working. Miss Tremar said we could make use of another pair of hands.'

The cleaning supervisor never stopped saying that, no matter how well staffed they were, but Helen had been reluctant to clip Fiona's wings when she was so happy, healthy and determined to help others. Before she'd lost Harry, she'd have bowed instantly to Fleur's disapproval and her indifference to it now was another of the ways in which she'd grown.

'She is working,' she'd replied airily. 'She's doing a good job for them and learning a lot.'

'Learning isn't earning.'

'She doesn't need to. Not yet, anyway. She's fourteen, Fleur! There's plenty of time to put her to work. I'm sure the enthusiasm will burn itself out eventually.'

Fleur had looked unconvinced. 'Do you really think so? She loves it there.'

'I know. The RNLI's exciting, and it's heroic, but it's a charity, staffed by volunteers. Fiona's going to want an independent income one day, and she'll look to the hotel for it.'

But the girl's enthusiasm hadn't waned, if anything it had grown, and now that their future at both hotel and seaside were uncertain, she needed to add some strings to her bow.

Fiona persisted with her pleas to be allowed to spend more time at the lifeboat station. 'They all say I'm really useful down there —'

'We'll discuss it later.' Helen peered out of the sitting room window, which looked out onto the tennis courts. She'd always assumed all motorcycles sounded the same, but the sound distracting her now was steadier, and even a little quieter, though still a blatting racket. Sure enough, the bike that rounded the corner of the hotel and made for the tool shed was a different machine from the one Roberta had bought off the Nancarrow boys; instead of peeled black paint, a long, narrow tank, and handlebars that came back towards the rider, this machine's tank was painted red, and seemed to sit right atop the engine, and Roberta was leaning forward across it in order to grasp the handlebars.

Helen frowned. Where had the money come from for a new motorcycle? Roberta had been complaining just last month that she hadn't enough for a summer hat, but yesterday she'd been talking about some new leather gloves, and now this.

Fiona usually hurried off the moment any discussion like this was over, but Helen suspected she was more interested in seeing her sister come under scrutiny than in making her own escape.

'I'll see you before dinner,' she said firmly. 'In the meantime, go and find Miss Tremar and tell her you're available to help in the rooms until we take on another chambermaid.'

Fiona's face turned mutinous, but she knew better than to argue with her mother and as soon as she'd gone, Helen hurried out to the shed.

'That's new,' she observed, pushing the door a little wider.

Roberta was crouching by the front wheel and turned as Helen came in, but did not rise. 'It's not mine yet.'

Helen relaxed a little. 'Yet?'

'I've paid a deposit, and Stan's letting me race it next week. If it works out, I'll buy it.'

Race? 'With what?' She hadn't meant to sound so abrupt, and saw the effect it had had by the way her daughter's hand stilled as it was running over the tyre. 'I just meant I hadn't realised you'd been saving up for a new bike. It's very nice.' It sounded falsely jolly to her own ears, and Helen wished she wasn't constantly trying to smooth things over. Roberta wasn't a difficult young woman by any means; she was no longer argumentative, or unreasonable, or sulky or rude. She was just . . . unknowable. Enigmatic, often stubborn, but with flashes of sweetness that reminded Helen of the child she'd been, and sometimes surprisingly thoughtful. But on her own terms, and rarely when it was expected. She was something of a stranger, living under Helen's roof but poised for flight at the first opportunity. No wonder it didn't seem to worry her too much that the hotel would soon be out of business.

'When's the race?' she went on, ignoring the little voice inside her head that told her to just be quiet and leave Roberta to it.

'Next Sunday. The eighteenth.'

'Oh.' A faintly awkward silence fell between them, which Roberta filled with additional checks to her machine. Helen braced herself, but had to ask. 'Where *did* you get the money from?'

'Does it matter?'

'Your job at the exchange doesn't pay a great deal, so I'm just curious.'

'I didn't steal it, so it doesn't matter.' Roberta stood up at last, and her expression was mild enough, but Helen knew her well and could see a tension in her jaw. Her own irritation prickled as she followed her daughter out of the shed.

'If you weren't so secretive about it, I wouldn't even be asking.'

Roberta sighed. 'It was a birthday gift, all right? Someone gave me birthday money.'

'Who, though? Roberta, what are you hiding?'

'Nothing!' But she glanced over at the gazebo by the tennis courts, and it was like an electric light going off in Helen's head.

'It was Adam, wasn't it?' she breathed. 'That's what he was doing here.' She struggled, for a moment, to find the words. 'How could you take money from a man like that?'

Roberta swung around, her expression suddenly furious. 'If it wasn't for Leah I wouldn't have a clue what kind of a man he was!'

Helen stared. 'What's Leah told you?'

'Everything.' Roberta looked as if she couldn't decide between blame and sympathy. 'That he caused our ruin, that you blame him for us having to leave Bristol — '

'She had no right!'

'And what about us? All we knew was that you and he had had a falling out, and that you only tolerated him at the funeral because of what people would say if he wasn't there.' Roberta was breathing hard now, and tears were standing in her eyes. 'If I'd have known the full story, I would never have accepted the money.'

'Well now you do, are you going to give it back?'

'I told you, I've used it as a deposit for that!' Roberta jerked her thumb over her shoulder towards the shed. 'And I'd say he owes us, anyway, wouldn't you?'

'I don't want a damned thing from him,' Helen said, her voice low and hard.

'Well it's a good thing he gave it to me then, not you.'

Before Helen could respond, Roberta strode across the yard to the back door and vanished from sight. She followed, slowly, trying to fight the rising sense that she was losing control of her carefully re-constructed life once again. They'd had nearly ten years of peace, quiet prosperity, and expectations that every day would bring more of the same; was that all she was allowed now? Should she accept that everything must be turned on its head, or was there something to be done about it?

Two weeks ago, she had told Fleur she wasn't going to sit by and watch her world collapse, and now here it was, crumbling at the edges and tilting beneath her feet. Well, clearly it was too late to do anything about Adam and his guilty birthday gift, but what about the rest of it? An objection against the development, perhaps?

It was disappointing and frustrating that Leah had had to return home, Helen would have welcomed her friend's support, but Leah wasn't the only one who could cause a stir. If it didn't work at least Helen would have tried something, rather than rolling over the way she did with Roberta.

What was it Harry had said, years ago, when he'd first brought her here? The Cornish wind favours the fisherman. Well, things were certainly getting choppy at Fox Bay.

'What's bitten Bertie?' Ben asked, stifling a yawn as he came into the office later. 'She's been throwing things around in her room most of the afternoon, slamming doors, growling at anyone who comes near her.'

'Did she keep you awake?'

'A bit.'

'I'll tell her to keep the noise down,' Helen promised. 'She's not a child, she should know better.'

'So what caused it? Did you two have another squabble? I gather she's thinking of buying a new bike.'

'She's moved past the thinking stage. Did you know where she got the money from?'

He nodded. 'Sorry.'

'She told me what Leah told you. About Adam.'

Ben seemed to relax a little at that. 'Thank goodness. I've been worried about how to keep it under my hat. It's awful, but it's better now that you know.'

'Of course I know,' Helen pointed out, and turned the page of her ledger to begin a new week. 'I'd have sooner kept it from you though.'

'It was so sneaky and underhand,' Ben went on, sliding into the chair opposite. 'I can't believe he had the brass neck, not to mention the lack of conscience.'

Helen looked up from the page, frowning. 'Well,

lack of conscience, yes. But I don't know about brass neck.'

'Really?' Ben shrugged. 'What would you call it? The slimy bastard —'

'Ben!'

'Come on, Mum! As if he hasn't cost this family enough. He knows *exactly* what building on that land will do to this place.'

Helen froze. 'What?'

Ben had a trapped look about him now. 'What?'

'Adam Coleridge is part of Hartcliffe, is that what you're telling me?'

'I thought you said Bertie had told you,' he muttered.

'She told me Leah had explained why the mistrust exists between us, nothing more.'

Ben rubbed his tired face with both hands. 'Damn. Bertie always said I had a big mouth.'

'Well put it to good use now,' Helen said grimly.

Ben sighed. 'All right. Alfie Nancarrow gave Leah a lift from the station. Toby would have recognised Adam of course, from when they were all kids here, but Alfie doesn't know him from … um, Adam.' He gave a nervous half-smile, but Helen did not return it, and he went on. 'He told Leah that Adam had brought the transfer document down for him to sign.'

'So he is part of Hartcliffe.'

'Must be. You'll have to ask him how involved he is. Except you're probably too late; as far as I know he's leaving Trethkellis.'

'He's been *staying* here?' Helen snapped the ledger shut, and Ben groaned.

'I've done it again, haven't I? Look, he's been

198

here negotiating things, as far as I can make out. Leah told Bertie to make sure he leaves today, and Bertie was meeting him this morning to do just that. I assumed she was successful, although listening to that racket she was making, perhaps not.'

Helen couldn't believe what she was hearing; the entire family, and her best friend, had been scurrying around behind her back as if she were too fragile to cope. And for two whole weeks Adam Coleridge had been living right under her nose while he plotted the Foxes' downfall – he must have been laughing up his sleeve at them the entire time.

'Is there anything else you haven't told me?'

He shook his head. 'What do you want us to do?'

'All I can think of is raising a petition in the village, to put a stop to the development.'

'Then let's do that.' Ben stood up. 'We have a voice around here, let's ...' he paused a moment, then smiled, 'put my big mouth to good use.'

5

Trethkellis Beach

'I'm sorry to hear about your car,' Susannah said, shifting her parasol to her other hand so she could slip her arm through Adam's. He looked down at it, resting on the striped material of his shirt, and dismissed a little pang of guilt at the lie.

'I'm sure it'll be easily fixed; Stan Houghton has an excellent reputation as a mechanic. In the meantime, I'm just relieved to have got a room, since *someone* moved into mine.' He grinned at her look of remorse. 'I'm joking. And my forehead is spared any further bumps, thanks to Mr and Mrs Cotton's nice big, front-facing room.'

'How lucky they'd decided to move on early.'

He nodded, looking away to disguise the little smile that wanted to break across his face. He'd been doing the Foxes a favour too, really, slipping Mr Cotton an ill-afforded few pounds, and urging them to try Fox Bay for the last few days of their holiday. Mrs Cotton was thrilled when her husband had suggested it; Adam was able to secure their room until Wednesday at least; Stan Houghton would be paid for doing next to nothing with Adam's Austin Twelve, and Fox Bay would have two extra paying guests. Everyone came out smiling. With the exception, perhaps, of Adam's own bank manager, but some things made it worth putting oneself under financial strain, and one of them had just wrapped her hand around his arm.

As for Susannah herself, she had been flatteringly pleased when he'd told her, over lunch in the dining room, that he'd had to extend his stay after all. Even her little show of regret just now was belied by the way she'd moved closer as they walked along the sand.

'You're looking brighter this afternoon,' he said. 'I expect it's the sea air, but dare I hope that a little companionship has helped?'

'Oh, it has,' she said. 'I'm so sorry for appearing such a weepy fool before.'

Adam was about to dismiss her description, but at the last moment he realised it would sound exactly that: dismissive. Instead he covered her hand with his own and said quietly, 'I wish I knew what it was that had upset you so much.'

'No, you don't.' Susannah gave a shaky little laugh. 'It's nothing you could help with, and it's nothing romantic or even something you could sympathise over.'

'How do you mean?'

'I mean it's not that I've ... I don't know, lost all my life's savings to some charming rogue, or the love of my life to a storm at sea.'

'An interesting insight into an interesting mind,' Adam observed, but he felt that little twist of guilt again at the mention of life's savings. 'All right, I understand. But if you do want to tell me I promise I'm a very good listener.'

'You are, aren't you?' She looked up at him quizzically, scrutinising him as if she wasn't quite sure of him yet. That was understandable; they'd shared lunch, and a little walk, and that was all.

But something about her sadness was pulling on a wire deep inside him that he'd never known was there. He wanted to banish the shadows from those solemn eyes, and to free her thoughts from whatever was holding them prisoner.

'So, you've not told me what you're doing here, either,' she said now. She bent and picked up a shell, and in doing so her hand slid away from Adam's arm. He missed the warmth of it and wondered if she'd put it back again.

'I'm just here on business,' he said. 'Very boring. You're the most interesting thing that's happened in two weeks. Except for my goddaughter buying herself a new motorcycle,' he added, unable to help talking about Bertie even now. Susannah was a pleasant distraction, but always in the back of his mind lurked the memories of those contented and happy years in Bristol.

'A *motorcycle*, gosh.' In her gentle, refined Scots accent the word took on an almost exotic sound. He wanted to tease her into saying it again, but when he smiled down at her she was staring away over the water, and he realised she was clutching the shell tightly and in danger of cutting herself. Her interest was delightful, polite, and utterly feigned.

'Susannah.' He loosened her fingers and removed the shell, seeing the dents in her skin where it had all but cut through. 'Please. Talk to me.'

She shook her head, still facing the rolling seas, but appearing oblivious to the laughing children who frolicked in the shallows, chaperoned by mothers in wide-legged beach pyjamas and sun

hats. 'You'll hate me, and I've enjoyed this afternoon so much, I couldn't bear that. You'll go back
home in a day or so, let's just enjoy a little ... what
did you call it? Companionship?' She nodded, as
if he'd answered. 'Yes, let's just enjoy that. I hav-
en't had any in such a long time.'

She moved off along the beach and he followed,
trying to think of something amusing to say,
something to bring back that smile he had had
such a tantalising glimpse of just once or twice.
He couldn't, and all too soon it was time to turn
back. The sun was slipping into the sea and the air
was turning cooler, and although there were still a
lot of people milling around the beach, most had
begun packing up their hampers and knocking
sand off shoes, ready to slip them back on for the
long trek back up the cliff path.

Despite the melancholy veil over their walk, it
had been companionable. Susannah had asked
him about his business, and then his goddaughter,
and why he wasn't staying with her and her family.
That had taken him unawares, and he mumbled
something about them having no room. He told
her about the land at Higher Valley Farm he'd
brought to his business partner's attention, and
how he'd combined a visit to Bertie with obtain-
ing the signature on the land transfer document;
she'd been interested, and asked questions, but as
before he had the sense that she was merely talking to stop herself thinking. Or to stop him asking.

They crossed the square and were almost at the
guest house when Susannah stopped to peer at a
sheet of paper tacked to the post box in the wall.
'Is this the land you were telling me about?'

'Where?'

She pointed, and read aloud, 'Sign the petition in the shop, to stop the development of Higher Valley Farm by Hartcliffe Developments. Is that you?'

'My partner,' he said, reading the sheet. Now he could see there were others too, dotted around the village; in the post office window, on the side of the well, and even pinned to the wooden rail that ran along a row of cottages, all directing people to the village shop to sign the petition. Since the shop was now closed it was impossible to tell how many had signed it, not that it would make the slightest difference. Still, he couldn't help but admire Helen's spirit, the spirit of the curly-haired girl in the tree. She was going to put up a fight, that was obvious.

They arrived back at the guest house, and Adam asked Susannah if she would join him for dinner, confident of acceptance since she'd seemed so pleased to learn he was staying. But she shook her head.

'I don't want to eat anything, it keeps me awake. I need to sleep tonight, I have a lot of thinking to do. Perhaps we'll bump into one another in the morning?'

Adam gave her what he hoped was a convincing smile. 'Of course. Pleasant dreams.'

Back in his own room, after a dinner that was no lonelier than any he'd had in the past ten years, but had felt weighed down with solitude, Adam tried to read his book. But it was a dull and dry book on business strategies, and his mind kept straying to what could possibly be distressing

Susannah Paterson to the extent she could neither eat nor sleep. Was she running away from a violent situation at home? Or searching for a lost loved one? No, she'd have taken any help she could find, were that the case. She'd said it would make him hate her ... surely that was impossible. Unless she'd done something so utterly evil that her life depended on remaining hidden.

Eventually he gave up on his book and tossed it aside with a little grunt of frustration. The window was open, and it let in a cool breeze that carried the distant crashing of the sea and the screams of the gulls searching for their supper. He could hear the chattering of a magpie too, and, remembering Helen Fox's lifelong habit, he was about to salute it to ward off bad luck, when he heard its mate's response, and relaxed. *Two for joy*. About time.

The sun had all but disappeared now, and the light that spilled across his bed was golden orange — he wished once again that he'd had a front-facing room from the start, and he hoped Mr and Mrs Cotton had a nice room at Fox Bay; they were even closer to the sea there, and the sunset would be rich and beautiful, spilling across the grounds.

He lay back on his bed, fully dressed, picturing it and listening to the birds, and was just falling into a light doze when another sound drifted up through the window. Startled, he swung his legs off the bed, propelling himself to the window where he leaned out to stare downwards. Sure enough there was the bowed head of a weeping woman, hatless, her dark hair catching the last of the sun's rays and absorbing it, so it looked like glowing coal in the half-dark.

'Susannah!' he called in a low voice.

She looked up, her face pale and her mouth open in dismay. 'Oh!' She wiped at her eyes and tried on a smile. 'I'm all right. Go to sleep.'

'Wait there, I'm coming down.'

'No, there's no need, really.'

'Don't go anywhere.' He padded downstairs in his stockinged feet and slipped out through the front door. Susannah was where he'd seen her, huddled against the wall, and when he reached her he saw her eyes were as red as they'd been this morning, and still streaming.

'My dear girl,' he said gently, 'why won't you —'

'I'm so sorry!' She dissolved into tears again, and this time put up no protest as he drew her into his arms. 'You shouldn't get mixed up with all this, it's not fair.'

'I'll be the one to decide that,' he said, with a firmness he didn't really feel. *Mixed up with what? What was she hiding?* 'Will you at least tell me, now you've kept me awake?'

'I just don't know what to do.' She shook her head against his chest, and he smoothed her hair. It was thick and soft beneath his fingers, and he wanted to keep doing it, but she pulled away and ran her own hands over it instead. The habit seemed to calm her, and she looked up at him steadily. 'If I tell you everything, you must promise me you won't breathe a word to anyone. Or tell anyone I'm here, if they come looking.'

Growing alarmed now, he could only nod. She looked around, then took his hand and drew him around the corner of the building, to where a

206

lean-to shelter protected piles of cut wood beneath tarpaulins.

'I told you about my husband,' she said, fixing her gaze on the lumps and bumps shrouded in canvas. 'He came from a wealthy family.' She gave a short, humourless laugh. 'A ridiculously wealthy family, in fact. They own an enormous estate near Inverness, which ... Anyway, I have a son, who's about to turn twenty-one and come into his inheritance.'

Susannah wiped at her eyes and took a short sharp breath that shook on the way out; she was clearly struggling to control her voice as she spoke. 'I don't know that I should be telling you this —'

'You should,' he urged her. 'Please, you'll feel better.'

'The thing is, I don't have any family of my own, and my husband's family wants nothing to do with me. They blame me for Timothy going to war.'

'That's madness! How could they blame you?'

'He joined up before conscription came in, and told them it was because he was embarrassed about his wealth. He said he could never be sure I loved him for who he was, and he just wanted to make me proud of him as a man. Oh, and I was proud! I watched him going off in his officer's uniform, and I told everyone he was my husband, and that he was going to sort out the Germans ... And then when he died, his family cut me off. They've not spoken more than a dozen words to me since it happened.'

'Oh, Susannah.' Adam reached for her, but she

moved away.

'No, I have to tell you it all now.'

'All right.' He waited a moment, then prompted gently, 'You and your husband have a son?'

'I said I have a son,' she said quietly. 'I didn't say we did.'

'Ah.' Adam watched her carefully, she was twisting her wedding band around her finger, lost in the past again now.

'They don't acknowledge me, but Gregory's the apple of their eye. Their only grandson. He's been living with them since he was sixteen, and they spoil him rotten.' She gave another short laugh and wiped her eyes on her sleeve.

He handed her a clean handkerchief from his pocket. 'Well, that's something. Are you able to keep in touch with him?'

'Aye.' She dabbed more delicately at her eyes. 'We write letters, and sometimes I'm able to get him away from his grandfather, and he'll get the train down alone to meet me in Edinburgh. Once or twice, savings permitting, I've travelled up there. The thing is ...' She hesitated, then spilled it all out in a rush. 'Someone is threatening to tell Timothy's family everything unless I pay him, and that will mean Gregory won't inherit a penny. Worse, he'll be cut out of the family, just as I am. I know he'd manage without the money, but he shouldn't have to. And he'd be devastated to lose his only family.'

Adam stared, eyes wide. 'You're being *blackmailed*?'

'This man doesn't believe I have very little money. He saw Gregory saying goodbye to me at the station and recognised him as the Patersons' heir. He's demanding I pay him five hundred pounds, or he'll go to the Patersons and tell them the truth.'

'How does he know the truth?'

Susannah turned away. 'Glynn, that's Gregory's father, was ... not a nice man. I thought he was exciting, and a wee bit dangerous, and I couldn't resist that, after the life I'd had, but he was more dangerous than I thought. This man was one of his accomplices. I think he might have been planning to do something to Gregory. A kidnap for ransom, maybe. But he recognised me, too, and put two and two together. This way probably seemed easier and less of a risk.'

'But what are you doing down here alone?' Adam was stunned by this revelation, but he couldn't understand what running away, without her son, would achieve.

'Gregory's quite safe for the moment, my deadline isn't up yet. I came to find Timothy's Aunt Gloria. She's the black sheep of the Paterson family, she despises the way they treat outsiders, so we always got along. I knew she'd lend me enough money to pay off this man, and then I'd repay her from Gregory's inheritance next month. In fact, I'd be able to pay her back twice what I'd borrowed. Probably a great deal more.'

'And, assuming Gregory knows nothing about this blackmail, wouldn't he mind you taking such a big slice of what's his?'

It was Susannah's turn to stare. 'I don't think you understand. Gregory's the Patersons' only grandchild. His father was their only son. He will inherit everything that was Timothy's. Adam, he'll be one of the richest men in the country!'

'*He* will be, yes.'

Her voice sharpened. 'And you suppose he'll leave me destitute, do you?'

'Of course not, but — '

She sighed. 'I'm sorry. It's just that it's hard to explain how it is with us. He lives with his grand-parents now, but until he was sixteen he was mine. It was just the two of us, ever since Timothy joined the army, and after Timothy died, he watched me sacrifice everything to make sure he didn't go without. He knows how it was, and we're still very, very close.' Her voice broke as emotion got the better of her. 'As soon as he learned about his legacy he promised me a very generous income indeed. At least two thousand pounds every year. More than I could ever need, and he wouldn't even miss it. No,' she finished more calmly, as if realising how intense she sounded, 'there would have been no risk whatsoever to Aunt Gloria. Not that she'd have hesitated even if there was. But it doesn't matter now.'

There was a sudden sadness in her voice, and she reached into her purse and withdrew an enve-lope which she handed to him silently. 'I found a small pile of unposted mail at her home, and this one was addressed to me.'

Adam took the letter out and handed the enve-lope back, noting how Susannah ran her fingertips briefly over the Morningside address before she put it back into her purse. She must be missing her home greatly, not to mention her son. He pressed her hand and read the letter.

210

Dear Mrs Paterson,

Forgive a stranger for writing to you with sad news, but Mrs Gloria Paterson has been recently taken into the hospital and is not expected to return. She has asked me to inform her family, and to say that, should anyone enquire, her will states that all her monies are to be donated to the hospital to further their good works. I am sorry for your loss.

Alice Mitchell, neighbour.

'I visited the hospital, just in case,' Susannah said. 'Some silly part of me thought it must be fate that I had arrived before the letter was posted, and that I might have the chance to see her one last time, even if the question of borrowing money never came up. But I was too late.'

Adam handed the note back. No wonder she had been distraught; to lose her only close family member, as well as all hope of securing her son's inheritance. It was a cruel blow. He wanted to offer comfort, but there was nothing he could think of to say; it was pointless telling her everything would be all right. If he'd had the money to lend her himself, he would offer it, but in the face of her predicament he felt helpless, and that was something he'd never been able to accept.

Susannah was speaking again now, and he turned his attention back to her.

'Aunt Gloria had the name of this guest house in her address book,' she said. 'She must have stayed here at one time. Adam, I don't know how I'm going to break it to Gregory! I'm sorry, I

211

shouldn't have burdened you with this. I told you you'd hate me, didn't I?'

'Hate you? Why in the world would I do that?'

'I had an *affair*! With a villain.' She looked around quickly, but they were still alone.

'And where is he now, this villain?'

'In prison.'

'And you're not. So presumably you never shared his criminal tendencies.'

'No. Just his bed.' Susannah looked embarrassed. 'I'm sorry,' she said again. 'That was crude and unnecessary. I'm just . . . at a loss.'

'What's this man's name? The blackmailer, I mean.'

'He just calls himself Tommy. But I don't even know if that's his real name.'

'And he's from Inverness?'

'What makes you say that?'

'Well, I've never heard of the Patersons, but he has, and I imagine if I lived in the same area I would have too.'

She nodded. 'Yes, I hadn't thought. I suppose so.'

'Well you have a great deal troubling your mind,' he said, 'it's hardly surprising. But how are you supposed to let him know you have the money, if you don't know where he lives?'

Susannah fumbled for the handkerchief he'd given her and pressed the cotton square to her nose. Her eyes were too bright again, and he remained silent while she brought herself under control.

'He's coming down to Edinburgh next Monday,' she said. 'We're to meet by the Ross Fountain in Princes Street Gardens.'

'Surely you won't go, not if you don't have the money?'

'No!' She looked horrified at the thought. 'I'll just stay down here and hope he doesn't discover where I've gone. But I'll have to contact Gregory and warn him to leave, to go overseas or something. In case this Tommy decides to try his original kidnap plan after all. I'll send a telegram first thing.'

'And what if the Patersons start asking him questions about why he's leaving so suddenly?' Adam's voice rose, and when she looked around in panic, he lowered it again, and took her hands. 'Susannah, this is lunacy. The only way you can safeguard Gregory, not to mention his inheritance, is to pay the man off.'

'But I don't have the money! And now I have no hope of getting it either. It'll be too late next month.'

'He won't wait?'

She shook her head. 'He has people after him. He's as scared as I am, to be truthful, but that doesn't help me. It just makes him more dangerous.'

They stood in silence for a while, listening to the sea pounding against the cliffs below the village. The gulls still swooped and shrieked, but night was almost fully on them now, and the sounds were fainter.

'I should go to bed,' Susannah said at length. 'Thank you for listening.'

'What will you do?'

'I'll have to send Gregory a telegram, as I said,

213

and hope that he's able to leave the country without alerting his grandparents.'

'But you might never see him again!'

'At least he'll be safe.'

There was no answer to that, and a silence
descended for a moment. 'Will you sleep?' he
asked at length.

She gave him a strained little smile. 'Probably
not a great deal, but talking has helped. So thank
you.'

He nodded and stepped back so she could
move past him out into the yard. 'Mind your head
on the ceiling,' he reminded her as she went in
through the front door, and the smile relaxed a
little.

'Aren't you coming in?'

'Not just yet.' He turned to look out towards
the sea. 'I have some thinking to do. Perhaps I'll
see you at breakfast, if you feel you can eat something then?'

'I'm sure I'll be hungry enough by then. Goodnight, and thank you again.'

He put his hands in his pockets and waited until
the door had closed behind her, then turned to
walk down the road towards the beach. His mind
was taking all manner of twists and turns, and he
wished this had happened ten years ago, when he'd
had the money to give her. Before Blue Ensign. As
the thought crossed his mind, his vision darkened
slightly. No, he didn't have the money to help her,
but Simon Hill, or, more particularly, Hartcliffe
Developments, did.

Could he? He could have it back into the
firm's accounts before Simon ever missed it.

He would have to disguise it somehow, but Jean might even help with that, maybe even add it on to the documented cost of Higher Valley. But no, the price paid to the Nancarrows was noted on the transfer ... He sighed. It was hopeless, after all.

He stopped walking. A glance down the coast showed him Fox Bay Hotel, standing high and bright on the cliff, like a lighthouse; its warm light would be bathing the summer evening, and extending the playtime of the guests as they sat outside under parasols, and played tennis by the light of lanterns strung along the fences and around the gazebo. He couldn't see any of these details tonight, but he'd spent enough time there to know, and the thought brought him back to Harry, and of course, Blue Ensign.

He kicked at a stone in sudden anger. Damn that company! If it wasn't for them, he'd have been able to play the knight in shining armour for Susannah Paterson, and reap the more tangible rewards too. But then, if Harry hadn't lost everything Adam wouldn't have ended up working for Simon, or convinced him to buy the farmland, or been here at all. Fate was complicated and confusing, and he was tired of trying to unravel it.

He trudged back to the guest house and let himself in quietly, then looked at the book he'd been reading earlier. He picked it up again; perhaps it would put him to sleep this time, and help quash the niggling feeling that, if he could only lay his hands on that money, everything would change for the better. He began to read.

Higher Valley Farm

'I thought you'd never finish.' Bertie swung down from the gate and followed Jowan into the barn. It was almost pitch dark now, and work in the fields had only just finished, the workers dispersing into the night towards their homes, to snatch a scant few hours of sleep before it all began again.

'You've heard the phrase, make hay while the sun shines,' Jowan said, grinning at her in the light of his lantern. He stretched up to hang it on the nail above his head, and Bertie took the opportunity to move closer and slide her arms around his waist.

'I'd rather be making something else,' she murmured against his neck.

'Well now, Miss Fox.' He draped his wrists over her shoulders and bent to place a soft kiss on her lips. 'You'll have the village in uproar.'

'Let them roar.'

Jowan Nancarrow had pursued her for the past three years, since she'd turned eighteen, but until last autumn, despite being increasingly attracted to him, she had been reluctant to spoil the friendship that had grown between them. Then one day Granny had seen them in the lane, just chatting, and later that afternoon she had taken Bertie to one side.

'That's a fine young man, Roberta. You could do worse, you know.'

'Jo's just a friend, Gran. And he's six years older than me!'

216

'Six years is nothing! Besides, friends don't look at one another the way you two were doing this morning. I might as well have been Scotch mist for all the notice you took of me!' She'd patted Bertie's arm. 'Don't waste your best years ignoring what's under your nose, my girl.'

So she hadn't, and she had never once had cause to regret the moment she had climbed off the borrowed bike, walked over to where he stood watching, and kissed him full on the mouth, to the amusement of his brother who had just joined them. For one heart-stopping moment she had panicked, wondering if she had kissed the right twin, but as she drew back and looked up into his face, she relaxed. Identical as their features might be, Jowan's blue eyes were as familiar to her as her own, and they'd looked down at her with stunned delight before he'd dragged her back to him and returned the gesture. He'd never told her he loved her; his voice seemed to stick on the words, but it was in every look and touch, and, when she had boldly led him into the barn last Christmas night, it was in the fierce heartbeat she had felt against hers, and in the way he had twined his fingers into hers as he had taken her, body and soul, in the chilly night air.

Now she reached up and plucked at the bits of hay stuck in his hair, with the easy familiarity of the lover she had become that night. 'Are you going to ask me if I've picked it up, then?'

'Oh, I know you have.'

'How?'

'I haven't been skulking indoors all day, you know.' He grinned. 'We all heard you, roaring

217

back down the lanes from Stan's. Anyone would think you had hellhounds on your back wheel!'

Bertie laughed, but the memory of what had made her ride so ferociously gave the laugh a melancholy edge, and Jowan, as always, heard it.

'What's wrong? I hope you weren't riding angry, you know what I've always said about that.'

Bertie considered for a moment, then decided he had the right to know what kind of man his uncle had just done business with. 'I told you I'd been given some birthday money, and that's how I could afford the hefty deposit Stan wanted.'

'Yes, and that you're paying the rest in instalments if you decide to buy.'

'But I didn't tell you who gave me that gift, and I only found out yesterday why I should never have accepted it.' She told him everything, moving out of the comforting circle of his arms, and peeling long splinters of wood out of the rail that ran the length of the barn, as she spoke.

'So he's the one Uncle Alfie was showing over the land,' Jowan said when she'd finished. 'Your mother must hate the sight of him.'

'Before he sent me that note to meet him, at my party, we hadn't heard anything from him since Dad's funeral. She wouldn't have him anywhere near us.'

'And he's the one who suggested Hartcliffe buy up a section of this place?'

She nodded. 'I'm sorry. I don't know why he's intent on destroying the hotel, but he should never have made your farm part of his plan.'

'But he's saved us,' Jowan said quietly. 'I know it's at your expense, which is unforgivable and I'd like to pound his head through a wall for doing it, but you can forget any idea that we've been dragged into ruin through this. We still have a home, we still have a lot of land, live-stock, a living —'

'Lucky you,' Bertie cut in, her voice sharper than she'd intended.

'Didn't you listen to the pounding-his-head-through-a-wall bit?'

She turned to him, and saw that despite his exasperated words, his eyes were soft on her. He came over to where she stood and touched her face. 'I just meant that you don't need to add guilt to your burden, because Higher Valley will be all right.' He smoothed the back of her head, press-ing her to him, and she sighed heavily against his shirt. He was right, it wasn't bad news for every-one, just her family.

'I hate him,' she muttered. 'For what he's done to Mum as well as what he did to Dad.'

'Speaking of your mum, what does she think about the Flying Squirrel?'

Bertie drew back and gave a little laugh. 'She's trying desperately hard not to show how much she hates it. But I know she does.'

'You're a bit hard on her sometimes,' Jowan reproached. 'She's scared. And understandably so.'

'She needn't be. If anyone is scared it should be me! I'm the one riding, after all.'

'But she's the one who saw your father ...' He trailed off, and Bertie felt a lance of pain and regret.

'I know,' she said softly. 'She saw him crash,

right in front of her.'

'And no matter how well you think you can imagine what that looked like, and felt like for her, you'll never really know.'

Bertie heard the catch in his voice; he and Jory had never been able to put aside the guilt they'd felt at causing their father's accident, no matter how much their mother and their uncle tried to reassure them.

She took his hand and brought it to her lips. 'I'm sorry,' she whispered.

'Don't be. But will you perhaps go a bit easier on her?'

'I will,' she promised.

'When can I come and look at the Squirrel?'

'Anytime you're free. I'll leave the key for you if I'm not there. But I'm racing at Bude on Sunday, so when I'm not at work I'll be tuning and testing. Want to take her out for a run?'

'If you trust me.'

'Well Stan's trusting me,' she said, 'so I suppose I ought to be at least as gracious.'

'You? Gracious?' Jowan gave a snort that earned him a sharp finger in the ribs. 'Ow! Okay, I take it back. You're the very queen, you are.'

'And don't you forget it.'

Bertie had been feeling the pleasurable, deep pull of his physical presence, until the subject of her father's death had come up. She had been aware of her breath becoming shallower and lighter, and her fingers had wanted to trace the line of his jaw and to feel the beat of his heart, but now she just felt small again. And sad. All she wanted was to hold him, and be held by him, and as she looked up she could see he understood, and that very nearly brought her to tears too. He drew her to him again and gently pressed her head to his shoulder, resting his cheek on her hair.

'I love you, Jowan Nancarrow,' she murmured, and when he merely tightened his grip, she knew his heart was saying what his lips could not.

6

Trethkellis
14th August

'I'll lend you the money.'

'What?'

It was Wednesday afternoon. Adam had extended his booking again until Sunday, and he and Susannah were standing on the small, hump-backed bridge at the bottom of the village, overlooking the river that led down to the sea. Groups of summer visitors ebbed and swelled around them, like the tide that foamed white against the rocks on the headland, and Adam's skin was tingling; things were coming together at a speed he hadn't previously dared to hope for.

'I can get it together in a day or two. I want to help, Susannah. Please, let me.'

'Are you sure?' Susannah's face was incredulous and filled with hope, making him feel ten feet tall. 'It's five hundred *pounds*!'

He took her by the shoulders. 'Look, if this is going to buy some peace for you and Gregory, it's a small price.' Then, just to be sure he hadn't misunderstood, he went on, 'Besides, it's only a loan, isn't it? You'll be able to repay it as soon as Gregory's inheritance comes through.'

'Of course,' she stammered. 'Twice over. More!' She bowed her head, overcome with it all. 'Oh, Adam, I can't thank you enough.'

She had a way of making him feel he was doing a grand thing, and it didn't even seem to matter, at that moment, that he had as much to gain from it as she. He held her awhile, wondering whether to explain what he was going to do, or to just do it anyway. 'You do trust me, don't you?' he said at length.

'Trust you? It's you who should be trusting me.' Her words were muffled against his chest. 'To lend me so much money without knowing a thing about me.'

'I do know you,' he said gently. 'Be patient while I get the money together. It'll take all I have, but it'll be worth it.'

'It will, I promise.' She looked up at him, her eyes streaming. 'Gregory will be so grateful, he'll give you anything you ask for.'

'As long as you're both safe, and happy.' Moved by impulse, Adam dropped a gentle kiss on her brow. 'I have to make a telephone call, but I'll meet you back at Sandy Cove later, and we'll talk more. You can tell me about this Tommy, and the place where you're going to meet him. I hope there'll be a lot of people there. Maybe I could come too?'

Susannah was staring at him, her fingertips hovering near the place where his lips had briefly rested, then she visibly pulled herself together. 'No, it's better if you don't. He'll probably be watching me for a while, to make sure I'm alone. I don't want him to be suspicious of anything at all.'

He nodded. 'All right. If you're sure.'

'I am. I'll see you later, I'd like to take a little walk, anyway.'

223

She reached up to touch his face. 'Thank you, you might think you know what this means to me, but it's so much more than you could imagine.'

He watched her as she crossed the bridge and disappeared into the crowd, her parasol bobbing gently before it became swallowed up in the dozens of others, then he hurried back to the guest house and placed two telephone calls in quick succession.

★ ★ ★

Fox Bay Hotel

Helen had taken refuge in the first-floor laundry store, and to help Miss Tremar she was checking off the linens against a list, when Guy found her. He looked unusually grim, and Fleur was with him, looking much the same.

'Can I have a word?' Guy said quietly.

'Of course.' Helen frowned. 'Is it more bad news?'

He fidgeted, and didn't speak for a moment, which was also unlike him. Then he gently took the clipboard out of Helen's hands. 'I have to tell you something, but you must promise to keep it between us, at least for now.'

Helen didn't like the look on his face any more than she liked his words. 'What is it?'

'It's the hotel,' Fleur blurted out. 'Mr Gardner is selling.'

'Already?' Helen's heart sank. She tried to keep her voice steady. 'This is directly due to what's happening at Higher Valley Farm, I take it?'

Guy nodded. 'He hasn't officially listed it yet, but he has a buyer lined up.'

'I see.' She cleared her throat. 'Do you think he'll want to move his own staff in, this new owner? Or might we be able to stay on?'

Guy looked downright miserable now, and exchanged a glance with Fleur, who shrugged and gestured for him to go on. 'I'm sorry, Helen. He's planning to convert it into seaside flats.'

'Flats? Who … Well that's …' She couldn't complete the sentence, and settled for just staring at him, silently demanding answers.

'He's called Norman Pagett. From London originally, but now lives in Cornwall. He spent the pre-war years converting old buildings into hotels, like the one down at the old Caernoweth fort. That's how Gardner knows him, he owns that hotel now. But evidently Pagett's realised that holiday homes are quite the coming thing.'

Helen's eyes narrowed. 'You know quite a lot about this.' Then she realised. 'This source of yours, is it Pagett himself? Are you *courting* him?'

'No! I mean, it's not Mr Pagett.'

'Then he works for him.'

His flush told her she had guessed correctly, but he shook his head. 'Please, you can't tell anyone.'

'Is he trustworthy?'

'Of course he is! I would never — '

'I mean, can you trust his *knowledge*, I'm not bothered one way or the other about his integrity, that's your concern.' Helen was aware her words were harsh, but dismay and anger had pushed aside her usual attention to the feelings of others.

'His name's Philip Rose,' Guy said. 'He's Mr

225

Pagett's architect, and he'll be sacked on the spot if Mr Pagett finds out he's told anyone.'

'How brave of him to tell you then,' Helen said acidly.

'I suppose if anyone is party to the man's building plans it'll be his architect,' Fleur put in, perhaps to smooth the tension, though she sounded hollow. 'What are we going to do? Will Mr Gardner tell us officially, or do we wait until it's all gone through, and we're thrown out?'

'I don't know.' Guy looked at them both helplessly. 'I'm as cut up about this as you are, I just wanted to give you —'

'I'm sure you'll find yourself with a job and a nice little flat to live in,' Helen said. 'Your lover isn't going to leave you homeless, is he?'

'Helen!' Fleur turned to her, shocked. 'It's not Guy's fault!'

'Maybe not, but he won't have to worry about having his home torn out from under him *again*, will he? And it's not his son who's going to lose what's rightfully his.'

'Harry was the one who gave that away,' Fleur reminded her. She put a hand on Guy's arm. 'Don't worry. Mr Gardner won't know you've told us, at least he won't hear it from me.'

'Thank you.' He looked at Helen, who battled with a complicated mixture of anger and hopelessness for a moment, before she subsided, and nodded.

'Nor me. And I'm sorry.'

Guy left them, still looking uncertain, and Helen pursed her lips. 'I think I'll telephone David and ask for any advice he might have. He'll be in the

226

city today, but Kay can pass the message on.'

She chose not to give Kay any details when her sister-in-law answered. 'Could you ask him to telephone me when he has a minute?' she said, hoping she sounded as if it didn't matter too much one way or the other.

'Of course, dear. Can I tell him what it's about?'

'Nothing important. Just a little brotherly advice.'

A pause. Helen could almost see the eyes rolling heavenward, but the voice was bland enough when Kay replied. 'Of course. I do hope everything's all right. I'll tell him to call you as soon as he can.'

'Thank you.'

But when David telephoned her back, he could provide little advice other than to 'Sit tight, sis, it might not go through. You never know.'

'There's nothing at all I can do?'

'Can you afford to put an offer in yourself? Push this Pagett cove out of the running?'

'Don't be ridiculous!' A thought flashed through her mind. 'What about you and Kay? She mentioned once before that it was something you'd considered.'

'Out of the question, I'm afraid, all our money's tied up in the house. Besides, back then the hotel was a thriving business.'

'But you've always loved Fox Bay.' She could hear the pleading in her own voice now, and tried to quash it. 'That's what you've said, anyway.'

'We've loved the *hotel*, darling girl, it's far too big and expensive to be a private residence.'

Helen hung up, deflated and adrift. The petition against the development had come too late;

it wouldn't make a jot of difference to Pagett whether it went ahead or not, since a development wouldn't scare off someone looking to build holiday flats.

Added to her worries about Roberta racing that motorcycle on Sunday, this latest news was enough to make her want to crawl into a dark hole and just stay there until everything went away. But she had a hotel to run ... For now, at least.

★ ★ ★

On Friday the news became official. Ben and Helen were just in the process of handing over from day shift to night, when Martin Berry knocked at the office door.

'Mr Gardner to see you,' he said, in tones of such reverence he might as well have been introducing Ramsay MacDonald.

'Thank you, Martin. Do show him in.'

Ronald Gardner had made an appearance at Fox Bay perhaps four times since Helen had moved in. A nondescript man of medium height, he favoured subdued clothes in neutral colours and Helen couldn't help reflecting how that suited his presence. Despite owning so many successful businesses he was like an ineffectual little ghost, who lived in the attic and only came out now and again to rattle his chains. He came into the office now, and looked relieved to see both his managers there.

'Good, good,' he muttered, shaking their hands. He sat down opposite them, his manner typical of one who is about to impart bad news; he fidgeted, played with his cufflinks, mumbled about the weather, and darted frequent glances back at the door, as if he wished he were already retreating through it. It took all Helen's self-control not to snap that she already knew what he was going to such lengths to avoid saying.

Eventually he found the words. 'I'm afraid I've decided to sell the hotel.'

In an effort to protect Guy's Mr Rose, Helen adopted what she hoped was a suitable look of shock, and Ben did the same — his response two days ago, when Helen had told him the news, had been far less restrained. She'd never heard such language but had, unusually, withheld any remonstrations.

'When is it going to be advertised?' she asked Gardner now.

'I don't know that it will be. I've received an extremely generous offer already, and I'd be a fool not to seriously consider it.'

'So you haven't absolutely decided to accept?'

'Whether or not I accept this particular offer is immaterial. If I do turn it down, I will still advertise the hotel and invite further offers.' He sounded so clinical that Helen wanted to shake some feeling into him, to make him understand what he was doing to her family, but it would do no good to antagonise him.

'As you'll know,' Gardner went on, 'the clause under which I purchased the business from your husband stated that his mother was to have accommodation and employment here for the duration of my ownership. That was as far as he could legally help her, and you. But this means that it's

229

entirely down to the new owner as to whether or not he keeps you on.'

Helen almost blurted that they all knew damned well there would be no jobs for them in Pagett's vision for the hotel, but just bit it back in time. Now that the news had come from the horse's mouth, the faint hope she'd been entertaining over the past two days died. She could think of nothing to say, and did not trust herself to speak in any case; the slightest slip would only cause trouble for Guy and his architect friend.

'Who is it that's interested in buying the hotel?' Ben asked. Thank goodness, he was keeping a clear head, even if she wasn't. It was a perfectly natural question to ask, after all, though the answer wasn't what she'd expected.

'A company called CP Holdings.' Gardner stood up and tweaked his waistcoat straight. 'I'm sorry, Mrs Fox, Mr Fox, but I can't stay any longer. I shall be in London from tomorrow until Monday, but I'll be making my decision over the next two days, and I'll bring it to you before the end of the day on Monday. I just thought it only fair you should be told.'

Helen wasn't sure whether she ought to be thanking him; after all he'd just calmly informed them they'd be losing their home and their livelihoods, yet he thought it a favour that he was telling them three days in advance. She settled for rising and nodding, and asking Ben to show him out.

'Well,' Ben said, coming back in, his face sombre. 'That's that, then.'

'I thought it was Pagetts who were buying?'

'He said CP Holdings, so it'll be a subsidiary.

230

Pagetts will be the controlling firm.'

'Oh, I see. So the P would stand for Pagett, but what about the C? I thought Guy said his name was Norman.'

'Probably be a partner, or maybe a spouse. It'll all be to do with tax, I expect, you know what these big firms are like.' Ben looked tired, and beaten, and for that alone Helen wanted to drag Gardner back in and chain him to a chair until he changed his mind. She sighed and shook her head. He was the owner, it was his prerogative to sell when, and to whom, he wished. And, being honest, she didn't blame him; whatever Pagett was offering now was likely to be a lot more than Gardner would get if he waited six months, when Hartcliffe had done their damage.

'What do we do now, Mum?' It was the first time Ben had asked for help or advice in years, and Helen's heart twisted to hear the helplessness in his voice; she was supposed to be someone he could turn to, no matter how old he was. She should know exactly what to say to make him feel better, it was still her job as his mother. But she had absolutely no idea.

7

Bude Racetrack
Sunday lunchtime

The field set aside for car parking was already almost full, and the first race wasn't due to start for another hour. Bertie puttered into the enormous yard, where countless motorcycles were being checked, revved, and sat on by people clearly not about to ride; women in ankle-length dresses, and children with shining eyes. There was an air of tension and excitement, and Bertie felt a rush of pleasure to be part of it. The press was also out in force; men with box cameras exhorting the prettiest and best dressed of the women to pose on various bikes, and several more moving among the riders themselves, taking candid photographs for magazines and newspapers.

Stan Houghton had clearly been watching for her arrival, and detached himself from the group of mechanics by the open doors of the huge shed. 'What have you done to her then?' He nodded at the Squirrel.

'Nothing! Just this.' She ran her hand over the hand-painted emblem of a fox's head on the tank.

'Very nice.' Stan nodded in approval. 'Did you do it?'

'Yes, I copied it from the photographs of Dad's bike.'

'And what if you decide you don't want to keep her after all?'

'I can always paint it out.' Then Bertie grinned. 'I've been riding her for a week, Stan, we both know I'll be keeping her.'

'Quite right, too.' They shook hands. 'Your first payment will come due first Monday in September. Done anything else to her?' He tried to sound casual, as he cast what Bertie knew would be a deceptively discerning eye over the machine.

'Well, I just cleaned the plugs and points, eased off the pistons, you know.'

'Why? They weren't seized, were they?' Stan crouched beside the bike and began tinkering, and Bertie shook her head and smiled, looking around to see who else she recognised.

There were a few other female riders, for the different classes, and most of these eyed her openly; they were likely seasoned racers, and curious about the new woman who'd arrived among them in this male-dominated world, but Bertie couldn't approach any of them. She felt tongue-tied and shy, and they soon turned away to talk to the reporters and spectators who flocked around them.

Bertie left Stan clucking over his motorcycle and went in search of Jowan, who'd promised to try and get away from the farm today. There was no sign of the farm's van, and she looked up at the sky. Apart from a few warm and sunny days August had been quite cool and mostly dry, but today the clouds were gathering out over the sea, and with the hay harvest in jeopardy Bertie knew Alfie Nancarrow would be expecting all hands to play their part. It looked as though Jowan would miss her race after all.

'Why so glum, chum?'

Bertie jumped; the voice had spoken almost directly into her ear. She turned to see a blond young man in racing clothes, swinging his goggles from one hand. Nice-looking and very confident, he was smiling at her, so certain of a smile in return that she couldn't help giving it.

'I'm waiting for a friend,' she said, 'but I don't think he'll be able to come after all.'

'Damned shame.' He didn't sound as if he meant it, and the way his unsettlingly direct blue eyes swept over her seemed to confirm it. 'What time are you on?'

'I'm down for the last race of the meeting. The 500cc.'

'Not the women's?'

'I didn't know there was one,' she confessed. 'It's my first time racing. Officially.'

'What are you riding? Sorry.' He held out his hand. 'Should have introduced myself. Xander Nicholls.'

Bertie shook the hand, suddenly even shyer than ever. 'Bertie Fox.'

'Ah, Stan's little protégée.'

'No.' Bertie's nerves dissolved immediately in her indignation. 'Stan's customer, thank you very much! What's he been telling you?' She quite forgot, in that moment, that she was talking to someone she'd previously only read about in the newspapers. Xander Nicholls was widely discussed, and much admired, and to have him racing at Bude no doubt explained the press

234

presence and the number of spectators already assembling.

'Simmer down, darling!' Xander laughed. 'I misunderstood, that's all. I gather you're racing his Scott Squirrel?'

'I'm testing it, and if I like it it'll be *my* Scott Squirrel.'

He raised a hand to his mouth, not quite hiding his grin, and looking rather like a chuckling schoolboy at the attempt.

Bertie bristled. 'What is it?'

'Nothing.'

'Something's clearly amused you,' Bertie pointed out, somewhat archly.

'It's just … I was just … No, it's too crude.'

Bertie felt the flush creeping up her neck even though he hadn't elaborated. 'Well now you're going to have to tell me.'

He lowered his hand, and the smile was still there. Bertie tried not to notice how appealing it was. 'All right. I was just contemplating the physical difficulties involved when a fox tries to ride a squirrel.'

Bertie started to frown, then her eyes widened. 'Oh!'

'I'm sorry,' he pleaded, 'you must forgive me.' But he was still laughing, and she couldn't stop herself from joining in. It occurred to her that Jowan would appreciate the joke, but not that it came from this flashy film star of a man.

'Xander!'

Xander turned towards the voice, and Bertie saw a glamorous woman with a stunning confection of feathers and beads in her hair. The woman

235

waved him over, and Xander waved back. 'My sister Lynette,' he said to Bertie. 'Insists on following me all over the country, convinced some handsome racer chap is going to whisk her off to Milan, or even the Isle of Man.'

'She's very beautiful.'

'She's an absolute horror,' Xander confided. 'Which is why she's still hoping.'

'I'm sure she's not,' Bertie said, smiling at the description.

'You haven't met her. Well, I've been summoned, so I'd better go. Apparently there are fifty million influential and fascinating people waiting to speak to me.' He rolled his eyes. 'I'd much rather be talking to you.'

'Because I'm neither influential nor fascinating, of course.'

Xander's bright blue eyes focused on hers for a moment longer than was comfortable. 'I have no idea if you are, or will become, influential,' he said, in a lower, more thoughtful voice, 'but you are certainly fascinating.' Before Bertie could respond he walked away. 'Good luck in your race,' he called back over his shoulder.

Fiona appeared at her side, and she stared after the departing Xander. 'Who was that?'

'Xander Nicholls. Current South East champion in about four different classes. I've told you about him.'

'You never told me he was quite so handsome,' Fiona murmured, and Bertie looked at her in surprise; it was the first time her little sister had expressed any awareness of male beauty, and it was quite disconcerting.

'I'd never seen him up close before,' she said. 'The newspaper pictures are terribly grainy, and this is only the second time he's raced this far west. Have you seen Jowan?'

Fiona shook her head. 'I think they're hurrying to get the harvest in before it rains. Guy's going to pick me up again at six, so if you haven't raced by then I'll miss it too.'

'I'm sure I will have.' Bertie squinted at the sky again. 'That's if it's not rained off. The track will be too dangerous if that lot falls.'

'Do you mean I might have wasted an entire Sunday?'

Bertie didn't have to ask what she'd have been doing otherwise. 'The lifeboat isn't going anywhere,' she pointed out. 'She'll still be there tomorrow, and the next day.'

'But I won't be,' Fiona said despondently. 'Mum has insisted I start work as a chambermaid from next week.'

'Well you're not at school any longer. And besides, cleaning up at the lifeboat house can't be that much different to cleaning up someone's bedroom.'

'*You* don't have to do it!'

'I have a job,' Bertie reminded her. 'You could apply at the exchange too, if you like. You might have to work on toning down that accent though, you sound quite the little Cornishwoman.'

'Well I grew up here, which is more than you did,' Fiona retorted. 'And I'd rather work at the hotel than some poky little room listening to people squawking at one another all day.'

237

'Don't take your temper out on me,' Bertie said mildly, 'I have enough worries today, thank you.'

'It's so very exciting though, isn't it?' Fiona stared around her in awe. 'Almost as exciting as watching the *Lady Dafna* launch.'

'You and that boat!' Bertie couldn't help smiling. 'Look, I have to go and talk to Stan, are you sure you'll be all right?'

'Perfectly.' Fiona had caught sight of some friends she'd been at school with, and was off before Bertie could suggest a cup of tea in the refreshment tent. Bertie watched her go, touched that her sister had given up a day at the RNLI station to watch her in her first ever race. She knew Ben would have come too, if he hadn't needed the sleep ahead of tonight's shift. Mum, though ... even if she had been able to come, she wouldn't have.

The news about the hotel sale had rippled through the family, and, not surprisingly, cast a deepening shadow over them all. It was hard to remain enthusiastic at seeing the spill of new guests, and the departure of happy ones, when they all knew this was likely to be their last season at Fox Bay. Bertie tried to see things from her mother's point of view, and, contrary to what most of the others thought, she did feel the imminent loss keenly herself, it was simply that she didn't find it easy to show her feelings quite so readily. She remembered the promise she'd made to Jowan, to go a little easier on her mother, but it was proving hard to keep; surely it wouldn't have been so difficult for her to come and say goodbye and good luck?

* * *

Sandy Cove Guest House

Adam had joined Susannah for breakfast, but been disturbed by the way she kept checking the clock, and wiping her hands nervously on her napkin.

'Try not to worry,' he said. 'It will all be all right.'

'I have to meet Tommy tomorrow,' she reminded him. 'If I don't leave by the five o'clock train this afternoon, I won't meet up with the sleeper in Plymouth. And it's too late to warn Gregory to leave now.'

'I understand.' He took the teapot out of her shaking hand before she burned herself. 'Why not come with me to the race meet in Bude? You can get the train direct from there.'

'The race meet?'

'My goddaughter is racing her new motorcycle.'

'I can't bear motorcycles,' Susannah said, frowning at the clock again.

'But you sounded so interested when I told you Bertie had bought one.'

'I was, but that doesn't mean I want to go somewhere so noisy and dangerous to watch her race it, especially when I need to be away.'

Adam understood that, and why she was sounding so snappish, but he was absolutely not going to miss Bertie's race. 'The thing is, I'm collecting the money from a friend of mine who lives near there, so I can give it straight to you.' He sensed her decision faltering. 'Then I'll run you to the station and see you onto the train myself. How

239

does that sound?'

She considered his words for a minute. 'I just don't want to give Tommy any excuse to carry out his threat.'

'You won't, don't worry.'

Susannah relaxed, and even managed a smile. 'In that case I accept. Thank you.'

'Good! Then that's settled. Fetch your coat after breakfast, it looks like rain.'

He stood in the hallway twenty minutes later, with his own coat over his arm and his hat in his hands, and watched her run lightly up the stairs. He was faintly amused to realise he was already recognising certain of her characteristics; the way her slender hand trailed behind her slightly, hovering over the rail but not touching it, and the way she flicked her glossy hair back from her face to ascend the second short flight. She was an intriguing woman, and he looked forward, with increasing impatience, to getting to know her better once all this was over.

* * *

The sudden clamour of bells signalled that the riders were preparing for the first race of the day, and Bertie went down to the start and finish line to watch them line up. She had raced in small, friendly meetings over the past year or so, but this was something quite different and she was entranced by the sight of a row of bikes, like chained guard dogs, held in check by their riders. The air was blue with exhaust smoke, two of the riders had stuffed toys strapped to the backs of

240

their bikes, and at least four were talking to one another around cigarettes still plugged into their mouths. They squinted past the smoke at the official, who raised his flag, held it for what seemed like a painful amount of time, then finally dropped it.

The bikes leapt forward, and while most of them roared away, one or two coughed into silence and their riders sat in disgust until everyone else had roared off, before dejectedly scooting them to the side of the track. Bertie flinched; she couldn't bear it if she were the one to be doing that, in a couple of hours' time.

She hurried around to the first bend in time for the second lap, watching to see how the riders approached it, then cut across the ground and was in place at the third bend, for the next lap. She was so intent on studying the lines the more successful riders took, and trying to remember at which point they'd opened the throttle again, that she hadn't realised Xander Nicholls was beside her until he spoke.

'The Squirrel is lighter than most of these, you'll be able to take a wider line here and still get past the front runners.'

'I don't intend for there to be any,' Bertie said, surprising herself with her somewhat cocky response.

'That's the spirit,' he laughed. He offered her a cigarette and she shook her head. He shrugged and lit his own. 'Has your ... *friend* turned up yet?'

'Not that I've seen.'

Xander exhaled smoke slowly, his eyes burning through the air between them. 'Then he's an idiot,' he said softly.

'He lives on a farm. They have to get the hay in before the rain starts.'

'Then he's a loyal, dedicated, hard-working idiot.'

'Stop calling him that,' she said crossly.

'He's not here with you, in my book that makes him an —'

'Well he's not.'

Xander moved to stand closer to her. He leaned in very close, and murmured, 'I'll show you mine, if you'll show me yours.'

She stared at him, feeling the flaming in her cheeks. 'Wh … what?' She looked around to see if anyone had heard, and when she turned back to him, he was grinning. Again.

'Motorbikes,' he said. 'What else would I have meant?'

Damn the man! Bertie was starting to feel like a silly girl Fiona's age, instead of a grown woman. 'After this race,' she said, suddenly not wanting to be on intimate terms with him, even if it were just crouching beside him poking at suspension and gearshifts.

'Alas, I'm riding in the next one, and in two more after that. And then it'll be your turn. Perhaps next time.' Xander began drifting away again, his grin seeming to hang, Cheshire Cat-like, in the air between them.

Bertie wanted very much to have the chance to look over Xander's AJS; Stan had said it was the brand-new racing model, just out in April of this year, and the chance of seeing one before they became just another old bike was fairly remote.

'All right!' she called after him. 'I suppose I can come back down to the track later.'

'I would hope you'll be here anyway, to watch me beat the field,' he said, feigning affront.

Bertie was starting to read him more easily now, and arched an eyebrow. 'Some of these riders might surprise you.'

'We'll see.' He held out a hand, and Bertie unthinkingly took it.

It wasn't until they arrived at the shed where last-minute mechanical checks were taking place, that she realised some of the other women were looking at her with mistrust and envy. She sighed and released her hand from Xander's grip. The last thing she wanted was to alienate the very people with whom she'd hoped to forge a friendship, and in any case she was devoted to Jowan; Xander was just being friendly, if a little forward. But as she turned reluctantly away she felt a smaller, feminine hand slip into hers instead.

'Don't pay them any mind,' a low, London-accented voice said, and Bertie turned to see Lynette. Up close she was even more beautiful; the Nicholls clan were clearly a good-looking family. 'I'm in love with someone else,' Bertie said, 'I don't want word getting back to him that Xander and I are ... anything at all,' she finished.

'Then don't behave as if you are.' Lynette gave her a smile and her eyes, just like her brother's, crinkled at the edges and made her look much more friendly. 'Xander is a fiend for wrapping pretty girls like you around his bony little finger.'

Embarrassed, Bertie tried to dismiss the compliment by twisting to look at Xander's fingers, which were resting on the saddle of his bike while he crouched on the other side of it, and was amused to see Lynette was quite right.

'They really are bony!'

'And you should see his feet,' Lynette confided with a little giggle. Against all expectation, Bertie decided she quite liked her.

'What are you two sniggering at?' Xander demanded, bobbing back up.

'Nothing,' Bertie began.

'Your feet,' Lynette said. 'The ones you use to walk all over people when you're bored with them. Well you're not doing that to Beautiful Bertie.'

'Honestly, he's not —'

'Hush, Bertie. I'll take care of you. Now, let Xander show you his machine, so you can dribble over it and try to estimate how much it costs him to run, and later we can watch him crash it, together.'

Bertie's smile faded. Crashing was always in the back of her mind, but it had never become the subject of something as casual as a joke. Now the thought sent a lance of pain through her. The Nicholls siblings glanced at one another, and then Lynette squeezed Bertie's hand.

'Don't worry, sweetie. You'll be fine, and so will he.'

'It's not that,' Bertie muttered, and she told them what had happened to her father. They listened in horror and sympathy, and then in astonishment that she had taken up the sport he had loved and died for.

'I feel a bit as if I'm honouring him to be honest,' she said, only now realising the truth of it herself.

'I've always loved motorbikes, and wanted to ride them, but racing wasn't something I thought of doing until recently. It makes me feel … closer to him, I suppose.'

'I can understand that,' Xander said, and for the first time Bertie saw the man behind the flirtatious joker. 'I'd like to talk to you for a few minutes. Alone,' he added, looking at Lynette.

'I'll come and find you in a minute,' Lynette said. She gave her brother a warning look. 'Don't make any promises you can't keep.'

'What did she mean by that?' Bertie asked, when Lynette had gone.

'She means, don't offer her a place on the team if you think she's going to lose.'

'What team?'

'Look, Cornwall is a long way to come just for a day's sport,' Xander said, 'but it's worth it, because a little backwater like this is the place where I'm most likely to find what I'm looking for.'

'And that is?' Bertie was too interested to take offence at the 'little backwater' comment.

'Unknown but promising riders, to form a team that we can take around the country, and maybe into Europe.' Xander sighed. 'Lynette knows that sponsors like a pretty face they can put on their posters, and she thinks, for that reason, I'm going to ask you. I just want to reassure you she's wrong.'

'You're not going to ask me.' Bertie tried not to let the sudden deflation show; for a second her heart had started to beat fast.

'No, I *am* going to ask you. Just not for that reason. Only if you're placed top three in your race,' he went on quickly. 'I can't afford to take some-

245

one just because they have a novelty value.' He pulled on his gloves. 'Besides, the sponsors have already got a pretty face for their posters. Me.' He grinned at the way she rolled her eyes. 'But if you're placed in the top three, we'll talk afterwards. All right?'

Stunned, Bertie nodded. Top three . . . in a field of professional racers.

Her nerves intensified the more she listened to the people around her, they were so knowledgeable, had such impressive wins under their belts already. Before long Xander was donning his helmet, and giving her a last wink as he coasted side-saddle down to the start line, a cigarette wedged in the corner of his mouth. He acknowledged the cheers with a grin, nod, or wave, and blew kisses at some of the ladies, but Bertie was already learning that this was a blasé act, masking Xander's absolute determination to be the best. There was nothing frivolous about this rider, and his reputation proved it.

Bertie and Lynette watched every race together after that, Bertie squinting with even more concentration at the way the experienced riders took the curves and picked their moment to slide past rivals. The sky threw a few spots of rain down now and again, and she wasn't sure whether she was praying it would hold off, or that it would empty down in bucketloads and force the officials to cancel her race. But the clouds held on to their burdens, and soon she heard the race being called over the loudspeaker. She felt sick, and excited, and her hands shook as she pulled her new leather gloves over them, but Lynette had seen this all before.

'Just relax,' she urged. 'Honestly, darling, you're the only girl in this race, and you're new to the circuit, so most of the others will have written you off before you start. Harsh truths are still truths,' she added, as Bertie turned to glare at her. 'What I mean is, no one in that field will be watching you, you'll have the advantage of all those years riding around bumpy fields with your farmer friends, and when it matters, you'll be able to cut through the pack and surprise everyone.'

'You seem to have a lot of faith in me, for someone who's never even seen me ride.'

'Listen, I was there when Xander was learning all the tricks. I can recognise grit when I see it.'

Bertie tightened the strap on her glove. 'Let's hope grit is enough. I've forgotten how to change gear, let alone slip the clutch.'

Lynette laughed. 'I'll be cheering you on. Off you go. And remember what could happen if you do well.'

Bertie had thought of little else since Xander had mentioned it, but she had to put it from her mind now. She freewheeled down to the start, and through the coughing and spluttering of the bikes coming to life around her she heard someone bellowing her name.

She turned to see Jowan, pushing through the crowd towards her, and her heart lifted. 'I didn't think you'd be able to come!'

'Me neither,' he admitted. 'Uncle Alfie took pity though, and sent me off.'

Bertie grinned. 'Did he really take pity, or did he accept that you were neither use nor ornament?'

'A bit of both.' He pushed her helmet back so he could kiss her, and as she felt the warmth of his lips on hers, and the curve of his proud smile, her nerves eased a little. A few minutes of fierce concentration, and then it would be over, come what may, and even if she didn't place in this race, she would do it in another. Now that her interest and her ambition had been piqued, she could look ahead to joining some team even if it wasn't Xander's. She tied her scarf around her face and dropped Jowan a wink, smiling behind the cloth as he blew her a kiss. There was no going back now.

8

Lining up, blipping the throttle and holding the clutch in, Bertie realised Lynette's prediction was correct: the other racers' eyes slid off her immediately but held far longer on others, sizing them up. They were dismissing her! The arrogant —

The flag dropped. Bertie twisted the throttle and let the clutch out, feeling the front wheel lift for a heart-stopping moment, before crashing down and finding traction again. Too fast; she'd almost performed a wheel stand without trying, and, crucially, without being ready for it. But as unsettling as that had been, it had taken her well into the front runners of the pack, and as she leaned into the first curve she relaxed again. The only thing different about this, compared to thundering around the fields and yards at Higher Valley, was the closeness of other bikes.

Exhaust fumes blew across her face, but her goggles and scarf kept her vision and her breathing clear. Bits of dirt spewed up from the back tyres of the bikes that had pulled ahead, and more than once there was a sharp crack against the glass of her goggles as a small stone bounced off. She hardly dared think about what would have happened if she'd forgotten to protect her eyes. Earlier she had seen one rider take off with his goggles still pushed up over his helmet, and he had almost tipped off fumbling them down one-handed. The race was lost for him before he'd taken the first bend, but at least he still had both his eyes.

A rider drifted too close coming out of a snaking section. On the outside, Bertie had to pull sharply away to avoid a collision, and she felt her back wheel slide, just for a split second. Her heart in her mouth, she eased off the throttle until the track straightened out again, and the other rider had pulled to a safe distance, but she had lost valuable ground.

Only if you're placed top three ... She pictured Jowan's face, how proud he would be if she could tell him she was going to become a motorbike racer, and as she approached the next bend she recalled Xander's other words: *The Squirrel is lighter than most of these, you'll be able to take a wider line here* ... She gritted her teeth, took the wider line, and kept up her speed.

Gradually the field fell back, now there were only four bikes ahead of her, and one on either side. There was one more lap to go; one more chance to take her courage in both hands, and remind herself that this machine was built to race. It wanted to lean hard, it needed someone to push its engine to the limit of its capabilities. It was made for this, just as she was.

The sun had disappeared behind lowering cloud, and with the glare on her goggles eased Bertie risked a glance behind; no one was close, she was at the back of the lead group. She just had to find a way to break through the seemingly impregnable wall of tyres and exhausts that formed the tight front row. Beside her, to her left, the rider who'd almost collided with her earlier was throwing quick glances her way. She wondered for a single paranoid moment if he'd intentionally come too close, hoping to frighten her off, though that was unlikely. But just to prove how useless it would have been, she nosed across the track until she was knee-to-knee with him, and kept hard on the throttle until she had pulled just ahead. *No fear, see?*

In clear fourth position now, she shot beneath the banner on the final lap. The line of bikes ahead began to break up just a little, as one of them inched ahead of the group and the others battled to regain the lead. Bertie's eyes were fixed firmly on them, searching for a way through. She could feel that the Squirrel still had something in reserve, knew that if she could only find a gap to squeeze through, the power would be there when she needed it. She couldn't risk looking, but she knew Jowan would be standing at the start–finish line, and Fiona, Lynette and Stan too, and that they would all be cheering her on. Would Xander be there? And would he already be regretting his promise?

A roar went up, as one of the three bikes directly ahead took the bend too sharply and went into the snake section at the wrong angle. The rider brought his machine back under control, but had already paid the price, and Bertie guided the Squirrel into the gap he'd left. Her breath was hot and damp through the scarf, and she could taste dust now, but her heart was racing as steadily as the machine beneath her. Third place . . . if she could hold this position her life would change forever. Abruptly an image of a burning bike flashed into her mind. Harry Fox, the same emblem on his tank as she had on hers, paint bubbling, metal melting and twisting … his life had not only changed, it had ended.

But hers would not. She glanced back over her shoulder and, realising she had eased off the throttle in her momentary panic, and that her nemesis had crept closer again, she hunched further over the flattened tank, cutting down every bit of wind resistance she possibly could. The final bend, and then the very last straight, lay just ahead. Whatever happened now she had done it. She had taken to the track for the very first time and she had not frozen, nor had she disgraced herself. And Jowan was here watching her.

The bend was a long, smooth curve to the left, and Bertie took it on the inside, where the angle was tightest. She leaned in still more, until she could swear she felt the whisper of the ground beneath her knee, and there was tension in every part of her as she prayed she hadn't taken it over too far. Still she kept hard on the throttle and the curve faded into the glorious sight of the long straight stretch to the finish line. To her right two riders were battling for first and second, she was content to take third. All she had to do was keep upright and not lose her nerve.

'Come on, you little beauty,' she breathed, her words damp on her lips against the scarf. The throttle was wide open, the finish line was there … She leaned forward still further, and it seemed that force of will alone carried her across it. She was aware of nothing now but the scream of the Squirrel's engine and the vibrations that ran through her entire body, and as the roar went up from the crowd she realised it was over. She had finished in — she looked around in amazement as she sat up and coasted to a stop — second position.

Hands pulled her from her saddle and tore off her scarf, and all around her people were yelling her name. Still dazed, her legs shaking, she felt herself pulled into an embrace, then someone lifted her steamed-up goggles, and a pair of cool, firm lips pressed briefly against hers. She removed her helmet as people slapped at her back and shoulders, and Lynette seized her hand and shook it madly. 'Well *done*, Bertie!'

'You did it! You little rocket!' It was Xander, and Bertie belatedly realised it was he who had kissed her. Frantic, she looked around for Jowan, but when she saw him being restrained at the barrier by officials, along with dozens of others, she wished she hadn't. His face was a mixture of pride and dismay; he looked as if he wanted to smile for her, but there was pain there too, and that was all because of Xander Nicholls.

'So, you'll buy her then?' Stan's grin was wide and happy. 'I'm proper proud of you, maid!'

She managed to smile back. 'I think it's worth the extortionate price,' she conceded, and he batted her affectionately on the shoulder.

'Will you be joining young Xander on his team then?'

'That depends if he was serious, or whether he thought there was no chance of me winning, so placed a safe bet.' Bertie looked at Xander, raising an eyebrow in challenge.

'Oh, I was serious all right,' he said, and his

253

voice was quieter now. So quiet that Bertie had to move closer again to hear him properly. 'Find me in half an hour, and we'll talk. You have friends and family to be with now.'

He and Lynette left her with Stan, who walked with her over to the barrier where Fiona and Jowan waited. Fiona looked at her in awe for a moment, then flung herself into her arms. Surprised and touched, Bertie hugged her back, then her gaze lifted to Jowan, who was glaring up towards the huge shed at the top of the slope where Xander was holding court.

'He's that flashy racer you keep talking about, isn't he?'

'Thank you, yes I'm pleased with how the race went,' Bertie said pointedly.

Jowan blinked and looked down at her, then his expression cleared, and he seized her and drew her close. 'I'm so proud of you,' he muttered into her hair. She knew it would smell quite awful, with sweat and the inside of the leather helmet, but it didn't faze him, and she loved him for that. 'You were fearless out there. Just as you are in the fields.'

'I wasn't,' she said, laughing a little now the tension was eased. 'I was terrified.'

'Then all the braver for pushing through.'

'And you're right, that is the flashy racer. But I need to tell you what he —'

'You don't need to tell me anything,' he assured her. 'Who's the pretty woman he's with?'

Bertie's mouth fell open, but no words came out, and then Fiona tapped her on the arm.

'Guy's here with the motor. Are you leaving

254

now too?'

'No,' Bertie said, still staring at Jowan, unsure whether he'd been teasing, or just seeking some kind of revenge. 'There's the presentation yet. I have business to talk about with Stan, too, and then ... something maybe quite exciting with Xander Nicholls.'

Fiona's eyes widened. 'Are you friends now?'

'Not at all. But I'm becoming friends with his sister,' Bertie said, stressing the last word and aiming it at Jowan. The grin on his face told her he'd been teasing after all. 'And there might be a future for me with Xander's race team.'

Jowan's smile vanished. 'What?'

'I'll see you at home,' Bertie told Fiona. 'I might be quite late, so tell Mum not to worry.'

Fiona left, and Bertie turned to Jowan. 'What's that look for? Aren't you pleased for me?'

'Racing for a living? With Xander Nicholls?'

'Does it matter who with?'

Jowan's face was tight. 'You always said he was an arrogant spoilt little boy.'

'Well I'd never met him,' she said reasonably. 'I could only go by what the papers say.'

'And now?'

'He seems all right.' She shrugged. 'But the point is, he's offered me a place on a team he's putting together, provided I was placed top three in my class.'

'Does this mean you'll leave Fox Bay?'

'Tell me what there is to stay for,' Bertie said, before realising how that sounded. 'I just meant ... with the hotel going under, and all.'

'I know what you mean,' Jowan said flatly.

'Miss Fox!' Bertie looked up in relief to see an official approaching. 'Mr Nicholls says he'll be free in ten minutes, if you'd like to wait in the refreshment tent. Then it'll be the presentation.'

'Thank you,' she called back. 'Jo, I didn't mean —'

'It's all right. It's been an exciting day. We'll talk later, after you've discussed ... *things* with Nicholls.'

Without waiting for her agreement, he walked away to talk to someone he knew. Bertie watched him go, then sighed and wheeled her bike back up to the shed, leaving it for Stan to check over while she went out to look for Lynette. Xander was deep in discussion with two men in smart suits, who looked completely out of place here, and he kept shooting amused, and undeniably provocative glances over at Jowan, who returned them with mistrustful ones of his own.

Bertie shook her head and turned away; contrary to what she'd always believed, it wasn't the least bit flattering to have two men behaving like children squabbling over the last sweet in the bag, not even if she were the sweet. But the thrill of coming second in her first major race still thrummed in her blood, and as her gaze swept the dwindling crowds her heart gave a little skip of added pleasure. Leah was here! She had returned to Cornwall just in time to witness Bertie's moment of triumph.

Bertie was about to go over to her when a gust of wind lifted the brim of Leah's hat, and instead of a riot of blonde curls she caught a glimpse of dark hair, and grinned; what was Leah up to now?

256

Her games had been few and far between lately, so this was a welcome return to form. She watched with interest, as Leah straightened her hat and then turned and smiled at the man behind her, but as Bertie followed her gaze her insides did a slow roll ... Adam Coleridge.

Adam pulled Leah to him, and lowered his lips to hers, and their embrace seemed to go on forever. When they broke apart Leah looked up at him with an expression of deep longing on her face that made Bertie feel like a voyeur. Whatever was behind Leah's adoption of the dark wig, her feelings for Adam Coleridge were as real as Bertie's were for Jowan. Adam took Leah's hand, and the two of them walked away, towards the field of parked cars. She probably wouldn't be coming to Fox Bay tonight then, after all.

Bertie backed away, unable to tear her eyes off Leah, until she stumbled over her own feet and had to turn and walk forwards, her heart hammering. In a moment she was back in the shed and unhooking her leather helmet from the Squirrel's handlebar. Somewhere in the distance she heard people speaking to her, offering congratulations and asking questions ... Heaven only knew what about. She dragged on her gloves and pulled the bike off its kickstand, and the crowd fell back as they realised what she was doing. She heard someone ask where Jowan was, and a laughing reply that he'd got himself into a scrap with the Nicholls lad, but it was all just noise now. She added to it, driving down the kick-starter, twisting the throttle and letting the engine voice what she was feeling. People were shouting now, telling her to pack it in, but she shifted the bike into gear and, sliding on the grass and barely keeping upright, she left them all behind.

* * *

Intriguing or not, Susannah had clearly not been exaggerating when she'd said she hated motor-bikes. She spent no time at all down by the track, despite Adam's urging, and remained a long way back until after the last race had finished, and the riders had taken their bikes back to the pit to be checked over. Only then did she venture down to the start and finish line, and that was apparently to escape some of the crowds who'd surged back hoping to get a close-up look at some of the machines that had been racing today.

Frustrated to have been forced by chivalry to stay by her side during the racing, instead of at the track, Adam stayed near the sheds, hoping to catch Bertie, but she was nowhere to be seen. The newest star of the show, she must have already vanished inside along with her fellow racers. He couldn't see Ben or Fiona anywhere either, so he checked his watch, waited another few minutes, and then returned to Susannah's side. He'd have to forego the presentation; it was time. He was starting to feel tense now, second thoughts creeping in, wondering if he'd be able to carry out his plan when it came right down to it.

'Are you ready?'

She turned and smiled, and moved unexpectedly, but easily, into his arms for a kiss. He was startled, but not too startled to make the most of it; it was largely relief and gratitude, but something in the way she leaned into him gave him the hope that it would develop into a more lasting feeling.

'Come on,' he said, taking her by the hand. 'It's time to go now. Are you all right?'

'I'm quite scared,' she confessed. 'Have you got the money?'

'Sorry, no. That's why we have to leave now, it's apparently back at the guest house. There was a change of plan and it was delivered there instead.' He could sense her frowning up at him, and kept his gaze forward, seeking his car among the dozens parked in the field. 'I'm sorry,' he said again. 'But if we leave now there's still time to catch up with the sleeper in Plymouth. If we miss it, I'll drive you to Edinburgh myself.'

'Why didn't you tell me it was back there?' Now she sounded agitated, and he realised this was going to be harder than he'd thought.

'I didn't know Bertie's race would be the last one,' he explained patiently, trying not to sound defensive. 'I didn't want to miss it, but if I'd known the money would be left at Trethkellis of course we'd have left right away.'

'We'd better hurry then,' Susannah said, and she barely waited for him to open her door fully before she slid into the passenger seat. He crossed around the front of the car, aware of her stony gaze on him through the windscreen though hardly daring to look at her, but he was doing the right thing. He knew it.

The drive back to Trethkellis was tense. Susannah was still clearly worried they'd miss the connecting train despite his assurances, and he tried to ease her fear by getting her to talk about

Gregory, and then, more importantly, Tommy.

'What does he look like?'

'He has a thick moustache,' she said, 'and he's tall, and very strong-looking.'

Adam didn't like the sound of that. 'Where did you say you were meeting?'

'West Princes Street Gardens. By the Ross Fountain.'

'Ah, yes. I know it. Just below the Castle. It was originally in Leith, you know.'

'No, I didn't.' But she was distracted and showed no further interest, staring out of the window at the passing hedgerows instead.

'What time are you meeting him?' Adam asked.

'Two o'clock. But I want to be there much earlier.'

'What time does the sleeper get in to Waverley?'

She twisted to look at him. 'Why are you asking all this?'

'Maybe if I can picture it all happening, it'll stop me imagining the worst.' He put a hand over hers. 'Are you sure you don't want me to come?'

She nodded. 'Please, Adam, can we go any faster?'

'It's starting to rain,' he pointed out. 'The roads have been dry for so long, and any wetting will turn them greasy in no time. Don't worry, we'll make it.'

She subsided and gave him a trembling smile. 'You're right. I won't be helping Gregory by ending up in hospital, will I?'

'Exactly.'

They arrived at Sandy Cove as the spots began to turn into real rain, and Susannah looked at him expectantly. 'Hurry,' she urged. 'I'll wait here. I have all I need.' She indicated her overnight bag.

Adam took a deep breath and fished in his pocket for his room key. 'I don't like this rain,' he said, handing it to her. 'Or rather, the car doesn't. I'll keep the engine running while you fetch the money. It's in an envelope in the top right-hand drawer of my dresser.'

For a moment she stared at him, exasperated, then she took the key. 'How did your friend manage to get the envelope into your dresser?'

'He told me he'd specifically asked Mrs Finch to put it there. Go!' He waved her away. 'You'll catch your death standing there!'

Susannah blinked raindrops off her eyelashes, and nodded. She hurried up the path, and as soon as she had pushed the front door open Adam shifted into gear and pulled away. He risked a glance into the rear-view mirror and saw Susannah standing in the rain, her eyes wide and betrayed. He saw her mouth his name — although it was probably a shout – and then his attention was back on the road, and on calming his pounding heart.

It was a beastly thing to have done, but he couldn't have let her go all that way, and face that awful danger; she would see the sense of it when he came back and told her Gregory and his inheritance were safe. Tonight Susannah hated him, but by tomorrow, when she heard what he'd done, she would be happy and grateful, and most importantly she would repay him. Hopefully before all his plans collapsed.

Riding the coast road towards home, with the long-awaited rain finally starting to spit from the sky, Bertie turned what she'd seen over and over, her anger growing with each twist and turn in the road. Leah was Mum's best friend! But she'd always treated Fox Bay like her home, so maybe she was secretly jealous of what Mum had? Not that she'd have it for much longer . . . And that too was down to Uncle Adam and his ferocious, insatiable greed.

The rain was coming down harder now, proper drops rather than the odd stray spit blowing in the wind. That damp, earthy smell of new rain filled the air, the smell Bertie usually loved and would go out walking in for hours, but now she hardly noticed it. It wasn't yet dark, but the sea was disappearing in a haze of grey, and the heavy, rain-filled clouds were lowering. The wind picked up, and Bertie pushed on. She adjusted her goggles in preparation for the even harder rainfall that was evidently to come, and some small, but sensible voice in the back of her head made her ease off the throttle.

She slowed down to pass through Crackington Haven, around a third of the way home, but emerging onto deserted roads she again pictured the treacherous Leah in the arms of Adam Coleridge, and her anger bubbled back. Leah's story about her Aunt Mary's injury was clearly a lie and Leah hadn't been called back to Wales at all. What was all that nonsense then, about sending Bertie to tell him to leave? Was it Leah's way of sending a warning to Adam that Helen knew he was behind the ruin of Fox Bay? If she found out that she was being used as some rotten little go-between ...

And what would she say to her mother? Should she keep it a secret? Tell Granny? How horribly ironic it was, that the one person she could normally have relied upon to give her good advice was the woman who had caused the dilemma in the first place. She tried to think more rationally, past the anger; it wasn't absolutely the end of the world. True it was a betrayal of sorts, but it wasn't as if Leah was *helping* Adam to ruin the hotel ...

The shock of that thought made her tighten her grip on the handlebars, and the bike leapt forward. Bertie's heart skipped as she applied the brake too hard, and the back wheel skidded on the greasy road. She throttled off again, breathing hard as the bike righted itself. If she didn't concentrate, she wouldn't have to worry about what she'd tell her mother when she got home. What did Jo keep telling her? *Don't ride drunk, and don't ride angry.* The thought of Jowan made her cross all over again; what was he thinking, getting into a spat with Xander? If he ruined her chance to join his racing team, he'd regret going to the race today. *I'll give you don't ride angry, Jowan Nancarrow ...*

Bertie took the turning that led to Trethkellis, still thinking hard. Ben might be able to think of some way of finding out what was going on, but she'd have to be quicker getting home if she wanted to catch him before the start of his night shift. Up ahead was a shortcut that would take her around the back of Higher Valley Farm, and bring her in to the hotel from the south. It would cut out the need to wind around to the front lane and creep slowly up the drive, as Mum always insisted, and she would be able to go straight to the shed and put the bike away.

The decision made, Bertie veered off the main road and followed the narrow, winding track down to where it crossed the river by the weir. The trees were dripping here, where the rain had evidently been heavier, and there were wide puddles that crept out from the verges on either side. Bertie winced as the water splashed up over her boots and wet her socks where the stitching was weak. Large drops of water ran off the leaves and down the back of her coat, and she glanced up in irritation and was rewarded with a splash right in the middle of her goggles. A grunt, a flick of her head, and then her heart leapt in shock, as a shape landed in the road directly in front of her.

She gave a breathless little scream. Her fingers once more tightened reflexively on the throttle, and then the road tilted up and slammed into her shoulder, and she was sliding along the road. The Flying Squirrel was living up to its name, spinning away from her to crash into the wall on the other side of the bridge, but Bertie did not stop. There was a sickening crunching sensation in her head as her helmet struck the ground and bounced, and then there was nothing beneath her legs at all, and she was falling ... A heartbeat later her right foot, leg outstretched, struck solid ground with all her weight behind it.

The crack seemed to fill the whole world, and pain blasted a line of fire up through her leg and into her hip. Bertie somehow dug the heel of her left boot into the ground, but all that did was spin her around until her back smashed into the trunk of a tree, winding her. All movement stopped, Bertie heard her own breath coming in short, terrified gasps, and somewhere below that, the gurgling of the river. Her leg blazed and burned, but a chill was racing through her, spiralling into her head and making her feel sick and dizzy. With an effort she lifted her head; facing up the slope now, instead of down, it was all too easy to see her right leg. Broken, of course. Her trousers were soaked in blood, had she speared her lower leg on a piece of sharp branch? It looked like it —

A whining yelp from the road brought her blurry eyes around, and she saw what had caused her to lose control of the bike. A dog. The Nancarrows' dog, it had to be, peering down at her, head on one side, panting.

'Reynard,' she whispered, and tried to summon the strength to shout; if Reynard was there, Alfie wouldn't be far away. But the movement, as she drew her head back to bellow for help, sent a shocking wave of pain through her, and her mouth flooded. She managed to twist onto her side so the vomit that rushed up her throat splattered onto the wet ground beside her, but before she could draw a good breath again, more came up. Hot, stinking, acidic. She gasped as she fell back, hoping it was over now, and pressed the heels of her hands to her eyes, wiping the tears. Now she could see properly, and what she saw made her moan in dismay and fear. That was no branch piercing her boot and her leg, it was her own shattered bone.

From somewhere in the distance she heard a

shout: 'Reynard! Come!' She looked up at the dog, who cocked his head to listen to his master, and prayed he would remain where he was until Alfie came to find him. But after a moment, when Bertie didn't do anything interesting apart from emit a feeble, useless cry for help, Reynard closed his panting mouth and turned away, loping off up the hill towards home.

Bertie stared at the place where he'd been, and then back at her torn and broken leg, and as the world faded around her and the rain fell faster, she closed her eyes and let fate have its way.

9

Fox Bay Hotel

Helen was passing through the lobby when Fiona arrived home. Her mind was, as usual now, on the CP Holdings company and when Mr Pagett was likely to contact her about the sale, but the sound of Fiona's excited chatter banished the thoughts for once.

'Well?' she asked. 'How did she do?'

'She came second! She had to stay behind and talk to Stan, so she said not to worry if she's late. *Second!* Can you imagine? Our Bertie!'

Helen felt she wasn't entitled to the rush of pride, but that didn't stop the smile from spreading across her face as she imagined Roberta's joy. 'That's wonderful.' She meant it, and she could feel the wideness of the smile, but her voice still sounded wooden and her words false. She wished there was something she could do about it, but her conscience was working against her.

Thankfully Fiona didn't appear to notice. 'Jowan was there too.

And Xander Nicholls! Do you know who he is? Oh, and the most exciting news of all —'

'That's Bertie's news to tell,' Guy broke in quickly, and Fiona subsided. The look on her face suggested that the news was something Helen might not be happy about after all, and indeed Guy's face reflected the same, but when Fleur

267

came out of the dining room the good news broke all over again, and the moment was gone.

Later Fleur found her in their private sitting room on the ground

floor. 'Bertie still not home yet?'

'Fiona said she had to stay and talk to Stan.'

'Yes, but it's getting dark.'

'It's only because of the rain.' Helen looked at the clock and frowned. 'Although it's almost nine. She should be back by now, I'd have thought.'

'She might have come back already, and gone straight upstairs.'

'We'd have heard that motorcycle in the yard. She's probably arranging to buy it, and if I know Roberta she'll be haggling over the price until sunrise.' But despite the light words Helen felt an uneasiness growing in the back of her mind. She tried to concentrate on the magazine she'd been reading, but found her gaze sliding off the page increasingly often, and towards the darkening window.

'I'm going to walk over to the farm and see if Jowan's back yet.'

'Good idea,' Fleur said. She too was peering at the premature darkness of the wet summer night. 'They're likely to have followed each other back. Maybe they're both at the farm enjoying a celebratory snifter.'

Helen hoped Fleur was right, although she didn't like the thought that Roberta felt more at home at Higher Valley than Fox Bay. She also wished Alfie Nancarrow had installed a telephone.

'I'll go and see.' She pulled on her raincoat

and rubber boots, and found a torch in the back kitchen, and soon she was trudging through puddles, and trying to bury that uneasy feeling under annoyance that Roberta hadn't thought to send a message. But it was hard to do; something deep inside her was pulling at her nerves and she couldn't shake the memory of Harry lying so horribly still, in the middle of the racetrack. But Roberta was only racing once, and had come through it not only unscathed, but triumphant.

Helen stepped around a large puddle that looked as if it might be deeper than her boots. Her torch swept the rough track ahead, and water dripped steadily off the brim of her hat; the rain was coming down straight and almost silent. Just a steady hiss, and now and again a louder splashing as it formed wide puddles in the path. The farmhouse was a glowing picture of welcome in the distance, and Helen hurried towards it, wishing she hadn't left Beth on such awkward terms the last time they'd met.

She knocked at the door and after a minute or two it was jerked open and one of the twins blinked out at her.

'Jowan?' she ventured.

He shook his head. 'He's out helping Uncle Alfie in the barn.'

'Oh. Is Roberta with them?'

Jory looked at her as if she were addle-headed. 'No, why would she be?'

'It's only that she's not come home. From the race, that is.'

Jory shrugged. 'Sorry, Mrs Fox. Can't help you. She did well though, so Jo tells me?'

'She did. Thank you.' Helen turned away from the warm light spilling from the farmhouse, and picked her way across the yard to the gate. She heard the door shut behind Jory as he went back indoors, and felt a moment's envy for the warmth and comfort he was returning to.

The barn door stood open and she could hear the two men shouting to one another inside. She poked her head around the corner to see Alfie up in the hay loft, and Jowan standing beneath, working his way through an enormous pile of hay, forking it up to Alfie who was spreading it to dry. They were working by the light of two lanterns, which gave the barn an eerie feeling, each lantern spilling just enough light in a patch for each of them.

'Excuse me?' she called. Jowan stopped with his pitchfork halfway, and turned. Seeing Helen, he frowned and lowered it.

'What's wrong? Has Bertie told you I behaved badly? Because I'm the first to admit —'

'No. She's not come home.'

'Helen?' Alfie appeared at the edge of the loft, and quickly swung onto the ladder and slid down. 'What's to do?'

'It's Bertie,' Jowan said, and he sounded worried now, which didn't help Helen's queasy stomach. 'She's not home from Bude.'

'Fiona did say she'd be late,' Helen said. 'I'm probably being silly.'

Alfie looked at his nephew. 'I thought you said she left a long while before you. Drove off in a temper.'

Helen's vision darkened. 'What?'

Alfie looked uncomfortable. 'Look, I probably got that wrong. Jo can tell you what really happened.'

Jowan came closer, and Helen saw he had a reddened mark on one cheekbone, and a cut on his chin. 'I got into a fight with Xander Nicholls,' he said. 'Otherwise I'd have stopped her.'

'So she *did* ride off in a bad mood?'

He nodded. 'She could see Nicholls and I were spoiling for a scrap, so she ignored us both. Then we got stuck in, and the next thing I heard she'd gone. Not that I blame her. She even missed the presentation — Stan's got her medal when she wants it.'

'Didn't you follow her?'

'Of course I did! She had a good ten minutes head start though, and I don't know whether she took the coast road or not. I assumed she'd come and see me here when she'd cooled down.'

'And no one's seen her since then.' Helen's voice was thin and shaky now. 'I think I ought to go home and call the police. Could you drive me back, Alfie?' She stood up, ready.

'I can do better than that,' Alfie said. 'I'll take you to see them myself, it'll be quicker.'

Feeling numb, Helen followed Alfie out to the van, and he settled her in the passenger seat before splashing around to climb in beside her. The van's lights cut a swathe through the darkness, but the rain made it impossible to see farther than a few feet off to either side. Helen didn't know why she was straining anyway; if Roberta were, by some miracle, coming the other way they'd see her motorcycle lights and probably hear the engine, even over the loud rumble of the van.

The police house sat at the bottom of the village, on the edge of the square. The rain was still falling steadily as Helen hurried up the path, but she barely felt it anymore though it was seeping through the stitches in her coat. Alfie stood beside her, in the same shirt sleeves and thin summer working trousers he'd been wearing in the barn; he hadn't even stopped to pick up a coat. The constable pulled open the door, took one look at the dripping pair, and gestured them inside.

★ ★ ★

From across the square Leah stood beneath the covered yard at the guest house, watching in surprise and growing concern. She'd only just lit her cigarette, cursing her stupidity at letting Adam go off to Scotland instead of giving her the money, when she'd seen the van on the lane opposite and recognised Alfie Nancarrow's farm vehicle. It was drawing up to the police house, which was worrying enough, but she was even more alarmed to see Helen jumping out and running up the path.

What had happened? Something at the hotel? But then Guy or Ben would have driven her, or she'd have telephoned. Leah had been planning to return to Fox Bay tomorrow, but now she was too worried to wait. She hurried into the guest house and up to her room, where she pulled her bag out and threw a few essentials into it. She would return for the rest, and to settle her bill, tomorrow. Hoping she wouldn't run into Mrs Finch and have to waste time explaining herself, she locked up her room and left, ducking her head against the rain as she ran across to Alfie's van. She slid into the passenger seat and waited, her heart beating fast, and only just remembered to pull off her short dark wig and shove it into her pocket as the police house door opened again.

Helen and Alfie stared, with identical expressions of surprise to see her sitting in the van, and then Helen gave a sob of relief and pulled open the door to put her arms around her. 'I'm so glad to see you!'

'What's happened?' Leah returned the hug.

'It's Roberta. She was riding back home from a race in Bude today, but she never arrived.'

'Oh, my God! What did the constable say?'

Helen climbed in beside her, squashing her in the middle of the three of them, and Alfie started up the engine. 'He didn't seem unduly worried. Said to wait until tomorrow morning, and if she's still not home we're to call him.'

'And will you? Wait, I mean?'

'No,' Helen said.

'Yes,' Alfie said, at the same time. 'Look, Helen, I think you should be at home with Fiona. I'll take Jowan and we'll drive to Bude, out one way and back the other.'

'But I can't just stay at home while —'

'Alfie's right,' Leah said gently. 'Fiona will be worried, and so will Fleur. I'll take care of her,' she added to Alfie. 'Just drop us at the bottom of the drive, and go and fetch Jowan.'

He did so, and when he'd driven off again Leah put her arm around Helen's shoulders, appalled at the way her friend was shaking. 'You're like an

273

ice block,' she said. 'Come in, have a hot cocoa and we'll tell the others what's going on.'

In the sitting room Leah helped Helen peel off her sodden coat. 'Go and have a bath before you catch a chill. I'll warm some milk.'

Helen shook her head. 'I want to be down here in case she comes back.'

'If she does, I'll come and find you. You'll be no good to her sick and feverish, will you?'

Helen didn't seem to have the energy to protest, and she went off to the bathroom. Leah sat down and ran shaking fingers through her flattened hair, trying to suppress her own fears; Helen would need someone calm and level-headed, at least on the outside.

'Aunt Leah?'

She looked up to see Fiona, who was staring curiously at Leah's coat pocket. 'Hello, darling.' She stuffed the dark wig down a little farther. 'Are you all right?'

'Granny says Bertie hasn't come back yet. Where's Mum?'

'She got drenched in the rain, she's having a bath to warm up. Would you like some cocoa?'

'Yes please.' Fiona followed her into the kitchen. 'Do you think Bertie went off with Xander Nicholls?'

'What?' That was something that had not occurred to Leah, and it gave her a flicker of hope. 'Is that likely? Who's he, anyway?' she added, remembering she was not supposed to know.

Fiona gave her an odd look. 'He's that racer. The last time I saw her she was about to meet him, to talk about joining his team. Maybe the

274

talk went on longer than she expected, and now she's waiting for the rain to stop before she rides home?'

Leah poured milk into the pan, trying to make sense of what Fiona was saying. 'His team?'

Fiona told her, and Leah relaxed. Of course, that's what must have happened. Bertie was too sensible to risk riding home in this downpour, and there would have been plenty to talk about, provided this racing team hadn't just been a ploy to get her attention.

'Is this Nicholls lad really going to offer her a place? He wasn't just teasing?'

'I'd say so. His sister seems lovely, I'm sure she wouldn't let him play a joke on Bertie.'

Leah spooned cocoa powder into a jug. 'Your mum will be relieved,' she said, 'and so will your granny. Where is she, by the way?'

'Here,' Fleur said from the doorway. She looked tense. 'Fiona, would you go and find Ben for me?'

When Fiona had left, Fleur sat down at the table and fixed Leah with a steady look. 'What were you doing in Trethkellis Square?'

Leah stirred the heating milk slowly, forming her reply. Helen had been too distraught to ask, but there was something about Fleur's direct gaze that she found unsettling. 'I'd just got in on the train, and was sheltering before I called the hotel to ask Guy to fetch me.'

'That's not Guy's job.'

'No, but he usually —'

'Your train must have been very much delayed. What time did you leave Plymouth?'

'Why are you asking me these questions? Isn't

it more important that we find Bertie?'

'If talking to you was stopping us from looking then of course I would agree.' Fleur got up to rummage in the larder for the biscuit tin. 'As it is, we're just doing what we can to care for Helen while we wait. How's your Aunt Mary?'

The abrupt change in direction was a relief, and Leah smiled. 'She's quite well, thank you. Back to normal, moving around without help.'

'Good.' Fleur opened the tin and pulled a face as she squinted into it. 'No custard creams. Shame.'

Leah watched her, suddenly uncertain again; there was something fragile about the light tone Fleur was using. Something brittle. 'Fleur? Are you —'

'How long have you been lying to us, Leah? Or perhaps I should call you Mrs Paterson.'

Leah's heart sank. 'I see.'

'I wish I did.' Fleur looked old, suddenly, as she never had before. 'Bertie is missing, and I'm worried half out of my mind about her, otherwise I'd send you away from this place and beg you never to return.'

'Come on, Fleur,' Leah said with a strained smile. 'You know me, and the way I like to play act sometimes. Why is this so different?'

'It wouldn't have been, if you hadn't gone through all that charade about pretending your aunt was hurt. We'd have understood if you just said you wanted to go off on a jaunt. But you lied to us all about Adam, and I can't forgive that.'

'Believe me, I'm sorrier than you'll ever know. You won't send me packing, will you?'

'Helen needs you. More fool her.'

'Fiona seems to think Bertie's stayed in Bude with this racer chap,' Leah ventured, and Fleur's eyes closed briefly.

'Let's hope Fiona's right.'

There was a long pause, then Leah spoke in a low voice. 'I want to explain, if you'll let me.'

'Good. Let's talk about the Mrs Paterson business first then.'

'First?'

'There's something else that's been preying on my mind, but for which I've supposed there would be a sensible answer. Now I'm not so sure, so we'll come to that later.'

Leah racked her brain for anything that might have prompted this outburst, but could think of nothing she'd done lately to give rise to any suspicions. Time would tell though, Fleur's face made that quite clear.

She nodded. 'Very well. Mrs Paterson was an invention of mine —'

'Obviously.'

'Are you going to let me tell you, or not?' Leah's voice was sharp now, and Fleur gestured wordlessly for her to continue.

'Thank you. Mrs Paterson came along with the sole purpose of delaying the building on that farmland. I'll tell you the details later, they're not important, but my ... an old acquaintance of mine has done this before. A confidence trick, they call it.'

'I know what it is,' Fleur snapped. 'I didn't just float down the Tamar on a log.'

'I'm sorry.' Leah took a deep breath, trying to sort the important parts from the incidental. 'I appealed to his sense of chivalry, then dangled a colourful piece of bait, in the form of a huge reward. I couldn't rely entirely on his altruism, after all. And I knew from things Helen had said that he's always looking for ways to make a profit.'

'Who isn't? And he believed this tale of yours?'

'He had no reason not to. I didn't approach him, he found me. I made sure of that. And I never asked him for any money. He offered.'

'It seems you have hidden talents.' Fleur spoke flatly and without admiration, and Leah flushed.

'I'm not proud of that side of me. But it was the only thing I could think of that would at least hamstring Adam and Hartcliffe so they couldn't build until we'd thought of something. If he was what Helen had said he was, the promise of a greater sum coming to him would have been enough to persuade him to . . . invest, if you like.'

'Like he did to Harry. But using lies instead of business.'

'I suppose.'

'And what went wrong?'

'How do you know anything went wrong?'

'Because you're here, and not in Gladys Finch's guest house pretending to be Scottish.'

'Ah. How did she know?'

'She didn't. Still doesn't. She belongs to the same Women's Institute as I do, and she mentioned you.' Fleur shook her head. 'Your trouble, Leah, is that, blonde or brunette, you're not easily dismissed from the mind. And Gladys is quite observant, you know, she particularly liked your travel bag. The one with the butterflies along the handle. All the same I wasn't sure it was you, until

278

you arrived here tonight.' Fleur took the mug of cocoa Leah handed her. 'You didn't say what went wrong.'

Leah sat opposite and stirred her drink. 'It turns out that Adam isn't just what Helen said he was, after all.'

'I might have told you that. He's as sharp as a tack. Saw through your scheme then, did he? Changed his mind about giving you the money?'

'No. Quite the opposite. I told him I needed it to pay a blackmailer up in Edinburgh, so he tricked me into staying in Trethkellis, and went up to pay the man himself.'

'Putting himself in danger, to spare you.'

'There is no danger! There's no blackmailer!'

'But he doesn't know that,' Fleur said grimly. 'The point is he genuinely wanted to help you, and not just for the profit.'

'You sound as if you're defending him!'

'No matter what he's done in the past, he was trying to help you.'

Leah sighed. 'Yes, he was.'

'And what would you have done with his, or rather Hartcliffe's, money?'

'Given it to Helen. It wouldn't have been enough to buy this place, but she could have bought a house for herself. Or,' she added, 'she could even have investigated the possibility of buying into the hotel as a partner, and then she'd at least have a say as to what happens to it.'

'It's too late for that,' Fleur said. 'It's already being sold, and the buyer's turning it into holiday flats.'

Leah groaned. 'Anyway, now there's nothing to

279

stop Adam developing that land the way he said he would. He'll be able to put the money straight back where he got it from, and they can move ahead with the build. What a waste of time.'

Fleur pushed her cup away. 'I don't know whether to thank you, for at least trying, or tell you to leave after all. You went behind Helen's back, with a man who's brought this family to ruin.'

'Don't make me leave,' Leah begged. 'I'll stay and help. I can think of another way, I'm sure of it.'

'We're beyond all that now. Mr Gardner's going to tell us tomorrow whether or not he's accepting Mr Pagett's offer, and he'd be a fool not to, what with the Higher Valley shadow still hanging over us.'

Before Leah could reply, the kitchen door opened and Fiona came in, white-faced. 'Mum's gone.'

'What?' Leah and Fleur both looked at the window, against which the rain was still beating.

'She's not in her room, and her bath is dry.' Fiona twisted her fingers into the front of her blouse. 'She must have gone straight out to look for Bertie.'

10

It's New Year's Eve, the night of the big party. The house is lit from top to bottom with fairy lights. So pretty. Roberta is eleven now, and still not allowed to stay up for the party; she'll be sent to bed soon. Benjamin can stay, but he's sixteen and almost a man. Why is it raining in the house? And why does her leg hurt all the way from her toes up to her hip?

Mummy looks beautiful tonight. She's not as pretty as Uncle Adam's girlfriend, people say so all the time when they think she's not listening ... But she's always listening. That's how she knows how to give them what they want at parties like this. She doesn't mind what they say though, because she's happy and she has Daddy. Daddy tells her she's beautiful and she believes him, but she won't believe anyone else who lies to her. Tonight though, Mum is lovely. She has a yellow ribbon in her hair.

The rain coming through the roof is cold.

Roberta sits at the head of the top staircase watching guests arrive. Fiona is running up and down the hallway behind her.

Singing. Annoying. Loud. She tells Fiona to stop it. Why is she shivering, in this warm house filled with light and laughter?

Oh, Mummy ... please, my leg ...

She should be happy. She won ... something. What?

There's Uncle Adam, with his lady friend Jeanette. Except everyone knows that's not her real name. She's what Mum calls a 'social climber'. But she loves Uncle Adam, who is laughing with Daddy. Daddy looks . . . frightened, behind the smile. But he's so handsome, and everyone wants to be his friend. The roof is leaking badly. Rain is coming in, but no one downstairs feels it. They laugh, they drink, they dance. Fiona is borne off, protesting, to bed. Mum tells Roberta she can stay for another half an hour.

Help me, Mum ... I can't stop shivering ...

Music plays in all the rooms. People are already dancing. The clock is ticking away the last hours of the year. A new decade. What will happen in 1920?

Daddy will die. Soon. He's down there talking, laughing still, but he's a dead man wearing a whole-body mask. The mask of a happy man. A loving man. One morning he will have his breakfast with Mummy and Fiona, and look at his books with Roberta. He will teach Benjamin how to shave, and then he will go off to ride his motorbike in a race, just like he's done a hundred times before. Only this time he will not come home. Not ever again.

I hurt, Mummy. I think I'm dying ...

The thought brought Bertie back to terrifying reality. She blinked up at the thin canopy of trees that lined the river and covered half the bridge. The disjointed memories retreated a little but did not fade, and the shivers that wracked her body brought waves of nauseating agony, sweeping through her and making her retch helplessly once again. Every heartbeat was magnified until it felt like hammer blows driving into her leg. She couldn't tell whether the water that dripped into her eyes was rain or sweat, but the sick heat that drenched her told her she was feverish and in grave danger.

She couldn't see the road; there were still two days to go until the full moon, but there was none visible to throw down any light tonight, not even faint silvery light that tricked the eye and made shadows and shapes in the trees. If only she could get as far as the road, she might stand a chance of being discovered. She tried to move, but the shriek that burst from her lips sounded like the loneliest noise in the world, and it was terrifying.

She lay very still for a moment, listening to the drips through the trees, and to the rushing water below, from the now rain-swelled river. She thought she heard something else, in the distance. She held her breath, straining through the night. A car? Was it someone passing this way, or was the night bending and twisting faraway sounds until they sounded closer than they were? No, it was definitely coming closer. Bertie managed to raise herself onto her elbows, her heart slipping and skipping as she readied herself to give the biggest shout she could manage.

The car chuntered slowly down the hill and onto the bridge, and Bertie took a deep breath. This was her one chance ... But the scream was choked off the instant she tried to utter it. No more than a faint, whistling hiss came from her dry, strained throat, and then the car was gone.

Bertie's tears fell, silent and despairing. She lowered herself once more to the drenched ground, and her mind began to close down against the terror that was crawling through her. As the rain fell on her upturned face Bertie squinted through it, and saw her father standing by the bridge, with his hand held out, beckoning. He smiled. He'd come back to them after all ...

She closed her eyes and went to him.

★ ★ ★

The coast road from Trethkellis to Bude was long and winding, and what if Roberta hadn't even come home that way? Or changed her route halfway so it took her through Crackington Haven and Boscastle? Helen had gone to find Guy, hoping he could drive her, but Ian Skinner, the night-shift reception manager, had told her Guy had gone out for the night after dropping Fiona home from the race.

'Do you know when he'll be back?'

'No, Mrs Fox. Sorry.' He had eyed her wet clothes with a hundred questions on his face, but none spoken. Faultlessly polite, as ever.

'If he comes back send him straight to Mrs Fox,' Helen said, and she'd walked out into the night once more.

It didn't matter that Alfie and Jowan were out looking, she would go mad if she simply sat at home waiting for news. Hearing that Roberta had driven off in a temper ... Harry hadn't been in his right mind either, that dreadful black day at the Bristol racetrack. The memory swept over her, and weakened her knees so she had to stop and lean on the wet wall at her side. How suddenly everything can change. A distraction, an oversight, a whole life lost and a family forever changed. *Please, God, if you're there … not again …*

She started walking again, and her boots rubbed the backs of her ankles until she felt certain she could feel blisters forming, then breaking. It seemed she'd been out for hours. The rain eased off after an unknowable time, and the clouds broke a little to reveal a faint glow of moonlight. Helen felt more hopeful of seeing something in the gateways along the road; perhaps Roberta had broken down, and had been waiting out the rain under the shelter of a hedge? But the reprieve did not last long; soon it was raining again. Great, heavy drops adding to the puddles that lay across the road, and full darkness descended once more.

She barely noticed the van until it was almost upon her. It pulled up just ahead and Alfie jumped out. 'Helen! For crying out loud, what are you doing? Get in!'

Helen did so, but reluctantly. 'I couldn't just stay at home,' she mumbled. 'You've found nothing?'

'No. I'm sorry.'

Jowan was staring out of the window, and Helen could feel the tension in his frame as she was squashed up against him. She put her hand on his arm. 'Thank you both for looking.'

'Well, like you, we couldn't just wait for the police to take action,' Alfie said. He looked at the clothes that stuck to her, and at the hair matted to her head. 'You didn't even change, did you?'

She shook her head. Rainwater dripped off her fringe and onto her nose, and she wiped it away with a wet sleeve. 'Nor did you. Where do you suppose she is?'

'We drove really slowly,' Alfie assured her, 'so you could take it as a good sign that we found nothing.'

'We ought to telephone the hospital.'

Alfie nodded. 'If I take you back home will you promise to stay there until morning?'

'It's almost morning now.' Helen squinted at the sky and the faint lightening along the horizon.

'You need to sleep. For a few hours, at least. Will you do that?'

'After I've called the hospital,' she promised. She could barely keep her eyes open, but that only made her feel guilty. How could she think of sleeping when Roberta was missing?

They arrived back at Fox Bay, and the familiar normality of the ground floor lights, always burning, seemed to make a mockery of Helen's fears.

'You might find she's telephoned, or even come home, while we've been out,' Jowan said, but he didn't sound hopeful.

'Wait then, while I ask,' Helen said. She hurried indoors, and found Fiona, Ben and Fleur all waiting in the private sitting room. They greeted her with relief, but she held off from embracing them, and when Fiona put forward her theory about Roberta having stayed with that racer boy she just nodded, and went back out to pass the idea on to the Nancarrows.

Jowan's face hardened when he heard Xander Nicholls's name. 'That superficial little —'

'Do you think it likely?' Helen insisted.

'She rode off in a bad mood, I told you. Everyone said so.'

'But might she have gone back? Fiona says she had some business to discuss with him, and it was something she felt deeply about.'

He looked away, but she saw his fist clench on his knee. 'Then for her sake I hope so, yes.'

'Where are they staying? The racers?'

'I have no idea. Presumably some hotel near the track.'

'We'll find out tomorrow,' Alfie said, then, more gently, 'Get some rest, Helen. You're all in.'

He squeezed her hands before getting back behind the wheel, and as they drove off Helen began to feel the weight lifting from her heart. The girl might be thoughtless and selfish, but Helen would rather imagine her staying in some hotel with a stranger than lying in a hospital bed alone. She called the hospital, nevertheless.

'She hasn't been taken in,' she told the others, returning to the sitting room. There was an odd kind of tension between Fleur and Leah, she noted with tired curiosity, but neither of them gave anything away, and they all soon dispersed to their respective beds. Helen peeled off her wet clothes with a little shudder, and wrapped herself in a large towel, then lay down. Just for a few minutes, to give her tired limbs a chance to recover before she put them to work again.

When she awoke, still wrapped in the towel, the sun was streaming through the window. Helen blinked at the clock, and sat upright with a little gasp; it was past ten o'clock. How had she slept so long? Why had no one woken her? She dressed quickly and with a fast-beating heart she hurried along the corridor to Roberta's bedroom, but her hopes were soon dashed; the bed was still made, and yesterday's clothes thrown across it from when Roberta had changed for the race. There was no sign that she'd been home since. She cleared her throat to rid herself of the sudden tightness there, and went downstairs in search of her family.

Breakfast was long since over, but she found Ben and Fiona in the sitting room, Fiona on the sofa, red-eyed and chewing at her knuckle, and Ben on the telephone. He looked even worse than his sister, his face pale and tight as he looked up and mouthed, *racers' hotel*, in answer to her enquiring look.

'He's found out where most of them are staying,' Fiona said. 'He called the newspaper offices.'

'Clever,' Helen said, hope rising again. She sat next to Fiona and took her hand. 'We'll find her,' she said gently. 'Maybe we'll find she stayed with this Xander fellow after all.'

Ben replaced the phone slowly. 'Xander didn't see her after she left.'

Fiona snatched her hand back and covered her face, and Helen drew her close, fighting back her own tears. 'Look after her, Ben.'

'Where are you going?'

'Back to the police house in the village. Do you know where Guy is?'

'He's out. I can call Constable Quick though.' Ben picked up the receiver again, but Helen shook her head.

'There's no point, he already knows as much as we can tell him, but he told me to come and see him today if Roberta wasn't home yet.' She eased herself away from her sobbing younger daughter, and dropped a kiss on the curly head that remained bowed. 'I'll be back as soon as I know anything.'

She was startled by the number of people in the lobby, until she remembered it was Monday, and she pushed her way through the milling, newly arrived guests with an urgency verging on rudeness, only to see the last of the taxis vanishing down the drive. Alfie had promised to take her back to the police house, though she hadn't wanted to trouble him again after all he and Jowan had done last night, but with Guy and his car also missing she had no choice. She scribbled a note to say she'd gone to Higher Valley Farm, then pulled on her boots, still wet from the night before. Each footstep made her wince as the blisters on her heels broke open again, and the edges of her toes flared and burned — she tried not to picture what was happening to them as she half-walked, half-ran to the farm.

Beth had thawed considerably, in the light of the news. 'I'm that sorry to hear about Bertie, Mrs Fox.'

'Thank you. I was wondering if I could trouble Alfie, or Jowan perhaps, for a ride in to Trethkellis, and then on to Bude?'

'I'm sure he'd be happy to, only they're all down at the weir again; the rains've brought down part of the bank, and Alfie needs to reinforce the fencing again before the goats get out.'

'Thank you.' Helen hurried down the field, slipping in the wet grass in her haste, but managing to keep her balance. Alfie was up to his knees in running water, and both his nephews were helping him to clear the debris and allow fresh fence posts to be driven into the soft ground. They all looked up as she approached, and Jowan's face was open and hopeful as Alfie called out, 'Any news?'

Two simple words, but so difficult to answer without giving in to fresh tears. 'Nothing,' Helen managed. 'She wasn't with the racers last night. I'm sorry, I won't take you from your work.' She turned to walk away.

'Wait!' Alfie shouted. 'I'll be a few minutes, then I can take you to the village.'

'I can walk,' she called back.

'To Trethkellis, yes. But if you have to wait for a train to take you on to Bude you'll be waiting for hours.'

'If you're sure?'

'I'll come too,' Jowan said immediately.

'You won't,' Alfie said. 'I know you're worried, but I need you and Jory here, and you won't be able to tell them anything Mrs Fox can't, anyway. Where's Reynard?'

Jory looked around. 'Dunno. He took off about ten minutes since.'

'I'll find him while I'm waiting,' Helen offered. It was better than standing around, driving herself to distraction with impatience. 'Which way did he go?'

Jory pointed towards the bridge. 'There's squirrels down there, mind, so he might not want to come away.'

Helen followed the direction he'd indicated, along a winding path that led alongside the river. She whistled now and again, and called out to the dog, and stopped to listen out for any sounds that might tell her where he was. Presently, she heard barking and quickened her steps. The path brought her out just shy of the bridge, and she saw Reynard standing at the side of the road. She peered more closely, but rather than squirrels she saw the flash of black and white that had once made her automatically look for another the same. The magpie stood alone on the stone wall of the bridge, pecking at some morsel it had found, and as it raised its head and looked directly at Helen with those beady black eyes her blood cooled. It was as if it were challenging her. Very deliberately she made her old salute. 'Good morning, Mr Magpie, hope your wife is doing well. Now where's my daughter?'

The bird ruffled its wings and hopped a few paces, then in answer to a chattering sound from across the road it flew off. Helen turned back to the dog, who was still staring into the darkness of the trees, not interested in the magpie after all.

'Reynard! Come!' She adopted what she hoped was a persuasive tone, patting her thighs and giving a little whistle. 'Come!'

Reynard looked at her, panting. Then he faced the river again and resumed his barking. Helen sighed and called again, but he would not budge. She saw a trailing bit of rope attached to his collar, and wished the Nancarrows had used it to secure the dog while they worked; this was wasting time now. Still, if she could grab hold of it, she could lead him away from those —

Something glinted in the early morning light, and as Helen peered at it her heart turned over and her knees almost gave way. Over against the shrub-covered wall, lying almost hidden at the bend of the road, was a motorcycle with a stubby red tank. A moan trembled on her lips, and she turned once more to where Reynard stood, and despite the way her feet had turned to lead she managed to cross the road. The dog's barking turned to hopeful little yelps, and he looked up at her, then down across the leaf-strewn slope. Helen grasped the stone wall of the bridge, and drew deep breaths, trying to banish the dark spots that bloomed behind her eyes.

Her daughter lay on her back, her face to the sky, eyes closed, still wearing her helmet. Her head was angled down towards the river, and her right leg was a mass of blood and splintered bone. Her hands lay limp, still gloved, the fingers open. Helen managed a shout, but she had no idea if it had been loud enough to reach the Nancarrows, and then she sank to her heels and slid down the slope towards the unmoving girl.

'Bertie,' she breathed. 'Please, darling ... please!' Her eyes burned, and a sense of unreality dropped over her as she knelt in the mud and the rain-stripped leaves and felt frantically for a pulse, or any sign of life.

'Help!' she screamed out, and Reynard gave a frightened little whine. He barked again. 'Go and find Alfie,' she begged, knowing it was useless; Reynard didn't move away from his spot by the side of the bridge.

292

Helen's trembling fingers pressed beneath the angle of Bertie's jaw, and her heart leapt as she felt a flutter there. She screamed again, more frantic than ever now, and leaned over to put her cheek to Bertie's lips. A faint gust of breath brushed her skin, and Helen burst into tears. 'Bertie, it's Mum. We've got you now. You're going to be all right, I promise.'

Bertie's skin was clammy to the touch, and Helen tore off the glove of the hand closest to her; the hand looked tiny and white, like that of a child, and Helen pressed it between her own, trying to warm it. Somewhere behind her she heard a cry of alarm, and then sliding boots, and then Alfie was beside her. A second later he was shoved to one side and Jowan took his place.

'Bertie!' He slipped a hand beneath her head and lifted it, pressing his lips to her forehead.

Alfie turned to Jory. 'Fetch the van down here. Now! Run for Christ's sake!'

Jowan was openly sobbing as he cradled Bertie to him. Alfie turned his attention to Bertie's shattered leg, and he winced and swallowed hard. 'We just have to pray she doesn't wake up until we've got her up the slope.'

He began to hunt around, and found two small, reasonably straight branches of about a foot long, which he twisted off their trees. 'Reynard! Come!'

Reynard yelped and began to slide down the slope towards them, and Alfie caught at the trailing rope attached to the dog's collar and began untying it. Helen, dazed and in shock, finally realised what he was doing, and laid the sticks either side of Bertie's right leg.

'That's the way,' Alfie said softly. 'She'll be all right, Helen.'

Helen tried to reply but could only snatch a hitching breath. She nodded though, and he spoke just as gently to his nephew. 'Lay her down, Jo.'

Helen held the sticks in place while Alfie wrapped the short rope around them as many times as it would allow, before tying it off. Thankfully Bertie did not move, although Helen found that just as worrying.

'Is she sick as well as injured? She feels feverish.'

'She's been lying out all night,' Alfie said, 'her clothes are drenched. Those trees overhead won't have protected her much even though it's summer.'

The sound of the approaching van brought a wave of relief, and Helen pressed a kiss to her daughter's temple. 'Hold on, love,' she whispered. 'We're going to get you out.'

Lifting Bertie up the slope to the waiting farm vehicle was the most horrific and terrifying thing Helen had ever tried to do. Jory supported Bertie's back, Helen was at her head, and Alfie and Jowan took the hardest part, doing all they could to stop her legs from dangling, but when they were halfway to the van Bertie woke with a harsh, breathless scream and her limbs jerked violently. Jowan took a glancing blow to his eye, and almost dropped her. He cried out and fell aside, and Helen slipped in the wet leaves and only kept hold of her daughter's upper body by her desperate and probably excruciating grip.

'Keep hold!' Alfie yelled, wrapping both arms around Bertie's knees. Bertie, lost in her own delirium, struggled harder, and no matter how they pleaded she did not stop fighting until she passed out again as they reached the road. By then Helen was sobbing, Jowan was red-eyed and silent, and even Alfie, who'd been the most solid of them all, looked shaken as they laid Bertie gently in the back of the van. He helped Helen to climb in, and she crouched at Bertie's side, taking her daughter's unresponsive hand once again. Jowan slammed the door and ran around to the front, and Alfie started after him.

'Hie, boy! Where are you going? I need you back here!'

'You stay, then.' Jowan started the van and, before anyone could move to stop him, he had pulled away, leaving his brother and his uncle in the road, staring after them in disbelief.

Bertie remained unconscious until they arrived at the hospital in Bude. Helen watched, helpless, as the doctors and nurses lifted her daughter carefully onto a wheeled stretcher and whisked her away, and as they disappeared down the corridor, she heard the heart-breaking sound of Bertie's voice raised in fear and confusion.

'Daddy?'

Tears once again flooded her eyes. She felt a strong arm go around her and for a moment thought it was Alfie, but of course he'd been left behind. She looked up at Jowan with overwhelming gratitude.

'I can't thank you enough,' she managed.

'Thank Reynard,' Jowan said with a little smile. He looked a great deal like his uncle in that moment. 'Did you know I named him after Bertie? He's just as stubborn and annoying as she is.'

Helen was surprised into a tearful laugh. 'Your Uncle Alfie said it was because of his funny pointed little foxy face.'

'That too,' he said solemnly. 'Bertie's face is funny and pointy. And beautiful,' he added, and his voice broke on the word. Helen held him until he gradually brought himself under control again. 'It's my fault. If I hadn't got into that stupid fight ...' He couldn't finish.

'Bertie is a headstrong young woman,' Helen reminded him, feeling a flash of fierce pride as she said it. 'You can't possibly blame yourself.'

'I don't know what I'd have done if the worst had happened to her.' He wiped his eyes on the sleeve of his shirt.

'Well she's in good hands now,' Helen said. 'Where can we wait, do you suppose? Or do you want to get back?'

'I'm going nowhere, I don't care what Uncle Alfie says.'

'Then it's a good thing Uncle Alfie isn't asking you to.'

They both turned to see Alfie by the door, his shirt as blood-soaked as Helen's coat, his hair sticking up as if he'd scrambled through a hedge. He came over to them, and first clasped his nephew's hand in thanks, then turned to Helen. 'Jory picked the bike up, and when we realised it was fit to drive, I brought it over. I'll put it back in the shed for her.'

A nurse showed them to a waiting room, where they could sit quietly until they were allowed to see Bertie, but Helen first went in search of a telephone to call Fleur. Passing through the corridor she felt a ghastly flash of powerful memory that took her back to that day nine years ago, when the doctor had told her Harry was gone. She swayed a little and stopped walking, letting the familiar smells and sounds wash over her while she told herself calmly and firmly that this was not the same. Bertie was going to be all right. She had to be.

When she returned to the waiting room Alfie and Jowan were sitting, tense and silent, in identical poses of waiting; bowed heads in their hands. They looked up sharply as she entered, then Jowan slumped again. *Oh, it's only you* ... But Alfie seemed to notice something was different about her, perhaps she was even paler than before, or perhaps something of those painful memories still showed on her face. He rose and came over to her, and took her hands in his, and when she looked up, she saw kindness had softened his hard features.

'She's a tough one, your racer girl,' he said in a quiet, but determined voice. 'She'll fight this out.'

'She was calling for her father,' Helen said, trying not to break down again.

'She's probably got a fever.' Alfie's fingers tightened on hers. 'Come and sit down. There's nothing you can do yet, but tough or not, she's going to need you to be her strength for a while.'

11

Bertie lay very still. There was white light above her, around her, pressing in on her. She could feel nothing below her neck, and above there was only pain and confusion. Her skin felt as if it were on fire, her head pounded and ached, and her throat was raw and inflamed. She tried to move. Couldn't. Tried to speak, but couldn't even part her lips, so she listened instead.

The voices that rose and fell around her were muffled, as if she were listening through thick pads of cotton that were clamped to her skull. The light pushed at her eyelids, trying to penetrate them. She wanted to open her eyes, to lessen the pain of that pressure, to let the light in to do its worst, but they remained obstinately shut.

Bertie drifted. The images that danced across her mind were ones of peace, and even happiness, but she couldn't focus on any of them, they slipped away too quickly. Faces came and went, and she tried to match them to the voices around her. Once she thought she heard laughter, but then she wasn't sure; it might have been a kind of wordless wail. Grief? Had someone nearby died?

She frowned. The noises were a little clearer now, there were doors opening and closing, stern voices, the faintly recognisable clatter of metal on china. And the bitter smell of disinfectant. She was in hospital.

All at once the memory of the crash swept

down, sending all other thoughts flying away. She recalled her mother's voice, calling her Bertie. She'd never done that before. Another vague memory of moving at speed, an engine rumbling beneath her, around her, through her. Mum's voice raised, telling someone to hurry, but also to take care. Another voice, unrecognisable, shouting something back. Pain, burning. Nausea and sweat. Her leg on fire ...

Her leg! She tried to move it, but was held firm by a numbing weight that covered her entire body. At least it no longer hurt. Was it daytime yet? How long had she been here? Voices again, raised now, protesting. But protesting what? Was she the only patient here, or was she in a full ward, and eavesdropping on the desperation of families she'd never met before? That laugh-sob again. It was so hard to tell which it was, and it suddenly seemed to matter more than anything; to connect to the living and to feel empathy, whether it was in joy or despair.

The swish of a door, opening or closing, and the sharp rat-tat of a man's shoes. The light momentarily brightened, and Bertie was sure she'd flinched, but she clearly heard the man say, 'No change.'

Frightened now, Bertie redoubled her efforts to open her eyes, to move her fingers, anything. What if they were going to straighten her leg and she regained all the feeling in it just at the crucial moment? But the voices faded again, and she felt a relieved tear trickle from the corner of her eye.

'Doctor!' It was a man's voice. *Jowan*? Bertie's eyes flew open at last, and although they shut again at once, against the harshness of the overhead light, she could still see the outline of Jowan Nancarrow's features on the inside of her eyelids. More tears spilled, soaking into her hair. She thought her heart would crack apart with the need to see him properly, and to touch him.

'Bertie?' He leaned in close and she could feel his breath on her cheek, but nothing else. Was he holding her hand? She would even welcome back the pain of her broken leg, if it meant she could feel his fingers tight around her own.

She tried once more to speak, but was unable.

'Don't move,' he ordered, and then his lips pressed to her temple and she could feel them trembling as he whispered against her skin, 'I love you, Bertie.'

Then his voice rose to a shout. 'Doctor! Nurse? She's awake!'

★ ★ ★

Fox Bay Hotel

Leah took the telephone call at the front desk. Helen sounded dreadful; hoarse, exhausted, and now frightened as well.

'They're worried about her,' she said. 'I can't stay on the line long, I must get back to the ward. Jowan's been with her since she woke up the first time, but she's running a high fever, and she keeps slipping in and out.'

'And they're worried because of this fever?'

'Yes, but more so that her leg's infected.'

Leah blenched, and once again she was back

300

in the Nancarrows' kitchen, pulling long blades of grass from Toby's dreadful wound. For all the good that had done ... She beat that memory away; it would do no good to dwell on it now.

'They're treating it as best they can,' Helen went on, and from the fear in her voice Leah guessed her thoughts had taken the same frightening turn, 'but she's very low, and they can't talk to her to ask her anything.' She sounded desperate. 'I know I should come back, but —'

'You'll do no such thing. Bertie needs you. We can manage.'

'But today we'll find out about ... oh. Did you know about Mr Pagett's offer for the hotel?' It sounded almost like an afterthought, like something that didn't matter, but Leah knew different.

'Fleur told me,' she said. 'I'm so sorry, Hels. Look, don't worry about things this end. Fleur's here, and you need to be with Bertie now.'

'How are Ben and Fiona?'

'Worried of course, but relieved she's all right. Fiona's the tough little thing she always has been, but Ben's refused to get any sleep, he's swaying on his feet.'

'Poor lad. Look, tell Ian Skinner he'll have to take on Ben's duties for now. He's more than up to the job.'

'I will. Give Bertie my love.'

'Of course. I'll call again if I have any news.'

Leah hung up and went to find Fleur, but as she crossed the lobby towards the reception desk, she abruptly remembered Fleur's intention to question her about something else that had been bothering her. She stopped in her tracks. Had

301

Fleur somehow found out? Had those little spies at the WI, whoever they were, been telling tales about something other than Susannah Paterson?

Leah turned away from the office and wrote a short note for Fleur, explaining what Helen had told her, and that she herself had urgent business to attend to in the village. That much was true, and as she walked towards the revolving door, she heard Fiona calling to her.

'Have you heard any news?'

Leah told her what Helen had said. 'I've left a note for your granny. I've just got to go into Treth-kellis for a little while.'

'I'll walk with you. I'm just on my way to the station.'

'Are you off to the hospital? Because I'm sure there's no need to take the train. Guy would be —'

'No. Mum says I can't visit Bertie yet.' Fiona's face fell.

Leah sighed and pushed a curl back behind Fiona's ear. 'I know it's hard, but I suppose that's for the best, for now at least. Especially with Bertie running a fever and not up to visitors. It won't be long though, and Bertie will be so pleased to see you when she's feeling a bit better. So, where are you off to?'

'The lifeboat station.'

'Ah, of course.' Leah felt a little surge of pride and love for the girl, whose fear for her sister was palpable, but who was determined to appear normal and not worry others in turn. 'A good distraction for you, helping others while the doctors take care of Bertie.'

She realised this would be a good time to put another of her questions to rest. It was one thing mingling with the crowds at the races, and risking the chance that someone might think she looked vaguely familiar, but quite another to be seen by someone who knew her as well as Fiona did, and who would see through any disguise in a moment. 'I'd love to walk with you. I'd enjoy the company, it's a while since we've had the chance to talk.'

'Better fetch your coat,' Fiona said, 'it's looking horrid out there.'

Leah looked out at the sky. It was clearing after the recent rains and she was tempted to risk it, but Fiona shook her head.

'I've got very good at reading the weather. You'll need your coat.'

Leah sighed and went to fetch it, feeling the girl's eyes on her as she climbed the stairs. She had the feeling Fiona had been rather left to her own devices, with everyone's attention taken up first with the sale, and then with Bertie. It was no wonder she had seized the chance to spend some time with Leah.

'Your mum tells me you were at the race when Bertie did so well,' Leah said, as they turned on to the Trethkellis road. 'Did you have a nice time?'

'Yes, I did,' Fiona said. 'Did you?'

Leah stopped. So much for bringing the subject up subtly. 'How did you know I was there? I didn't see you.'

'I don't think you were really looking though, were you?' Fiona dipped her hand into Leah's pocket and pulled out the wig. 'What were you up to?'

Leah's heart began to beat uncomfortably fast. Her usually nimble brain couldn't come up with anything, and just as she was about to unburden herself of everything, she realised Fiona was smiling. 'What's that look for?'

'You're a sly one,' Fiona said. 'Who was he?'

'Who was who?'

'Aunt Leah!' Fiona handed her the wig. 'I did see you with him, you know! He looked a bit familiar, is he local?'

'No, he's not.' Leah realised with relief that this girl had been little more than an infant the last time she had seen Adam Coleridge. Five or six years old at the most. 'What did you see?'

'I saw you both wandering around up by the big sheds, and then later I saw you on your own. I thought it best not to come over, because you were wearing that,' she nodded at the wig, 'and I guessed you were pretending to be someone else again. So, who was he?'

'Just someone who once played a trick on a good friend,' Leah said, giving Fiona a secretive little smile. 'I thought he deserved the same treatment.'

'You're so wicked! What's his name?'

'That doesn't matter, and it's no business of yours.' Leah tucked the wig away once more. 'Did you mention it to anyone else?'

'Only Guy, since he was driving me home.'

Leah tensed again. 'And did you describe him to Guy?' Fiona looked at her with a little frown, and Leah wished she hadn't pushed her luck. 'Not that it matters,' she added.

'Nothing to describe,' Fiona said at length, after

304

another curious pause. 'Just a man with blond hair and a smart taste in clothes.'

'You're right. I doubt Guy would know him anyway. As I said, he's not local. Now, tell me all about the lifeboat. What's she called?'

'The *Lady Dafna*.'

'That's an unusual name.'

'It's quite a sweet story actually,' Fiona said, thankfully dropping the subject and asking no more about Leah's mysterious victim. 'She was named by a little boy whose father was a helms-man on the old boat. When they got the new one, they let the boy choose the name, and he said he'd met a beautiful but mischievous fairy on the cliffs, and she'd told him she was called Dafna.'

'You're right.' Leah smiled. 'It's a lovely story.'

'I used to spend a lot of time looking at a book of fairy paintings,' Fiona said. 'Uncle Adam, he's not really our uncle, he was Daddy's best friend, anyway he gave Bertie this beautiful book —'

'It sounds the perfect name for something that's going to be dancing over the waves to help people,' Leah said quickly, a little light-headed with the way everything kept coming back to her deceit. It was as if the Fates were determinedly gathering up loose threads and following them back to their source, in order to tie them all together . . . or cut them.

She kept the subject firmly on the lifeboats for the rest of the walk, and they parted company at the outskirts of the village as Fiona took the road that led to the RNLI station on the sea front. Leah went on to Sandy Cove, and couldn't help feeling a little queasy as she looked around carefully for

305

Adam's car. By now he would have realised no one called Tommy was going to turn up, at the Ross Fountain or anywhere else, but there was no way of knowing whether he'd have come straight back, or waited another day in case he'd got it wrong. Another of those threads blowing in the wind, waiting for inquisitive fingers to find it.

She would get her things and hurry back to Fox Bay; there was nothing here to connect her to the family, and no reason for Adam to go to the hotel himself, so she'd never have to see him again. The thought gave Leah an unwelcome twist of regret, and she let out an irritated hiss. He was nice-looking, and he had taken it upon himself to be charming, even chivalrous; she was undoubtedly attracted to the man, and had responded to his kiss in a moment of unguarded desire, but she couldn't possibly like him, could she? Knowing everything he'd done to her best friend's family? No. He was a louse. A snake. And she'd had enough of those to last several lifetimes.

Just before she pushed open the door, she remembered her wig, and sent silent thanks to Fiona for making her go back for her coat after all. Perhaps not all the Fates were against her, at that. She hurried around to the log store and took off her hat, fitting the wig as best she could and hoping she'd pushed all her blonde curls up inside it. But with no mirror, hope was the best she could do.

'Mrs Paterson!' Gladys Finch was polishing the telephone table in the hall. 'I missed you at breakfast. You're up early.' The look on her face said, louder than words, *and I don't think you came back*

306

last night either, did you? But of course, she had been a landlady long enough to keep those kinds of thoughts to herself.

'I enjoy taking the air in the cooler weather,' Leah said glibly. 'It reminds me of Scotland. Mrs Finch,' she went on, adopting a regretful tone, 'while I was out walking I made a decision, and I'm sorry to tell you I shan't be staying the week after all. I'll just pack my things, and then I'll come and find you to settle my bill.'

Mrs Finch nodded. 'That's a shame. We don't often get glamour of your sort staying in the village.'

Guilt made it hard to respond appropriately to the compliment. 'I'm sorry,' Leah repeated, and hurried up the stairs to begin packing. But she realised almost at once that, as lucky as she'd been to have brought her wig, her travelling bag was still back at Fox Bay, sitting uselessly on top of the wardrobe in room eight. A knock at the door froze her as she took down her one good dress from its hanger, and she stood still, with her heart beating uncomfortably fast. What if it was Adam? What would she say?

But it was Mrs Finch, who looked at the small pile of clothes on Leah's bed with a little frown, but there was sympathy in her voice. 'I know the truth, my dear. *You* needn't feel you must run off.'

'The truth?' Leah wanted desperately to check her wig in the mirror, but she didn't dare move. 'What truth?'

'Your young man. That nice Mr Coleridge. At least, I thought he was nice.'

'And now you don't?' Mrs Finch had probably

seen him driving off, leaving her standing in the rain yesterday evening. 'Well, you're right, I suppose.'

'And he's not *your* young man, is he?'

'He's neither mine, nor young,' Leah said, with an edge to her voice.

Mrs Finch smiled a little at that. 'When you get to my age, dear, everyone under sixty is practically a child.' Her smile faded. 'No, I overheard him on the telephone.'

'Saying what? To whom?'

'You mustn't think I'm an interfering old woman, but ... Well, you're not the only one, I'm afraid.'

It was taking the last shred of Leah's patience not to snap at poor Mrs Finch to get on with it. 'Only one?' she prompted instead, folding the dress as neatly as she could manage.

'He was making an ... assignation, I suppose you'd call it, with a married lady.'

That caught Leah's attention, and she stopped again. She raised a questioning eyebrow, and Mrs Finch sat down at the dressing table and began playing absently with Leah's hairbrush. Leah's eyes widened as she saw how much blonde hair was woven through the bristles, and she gently took the brush out of Mrs Finch's hand and added it to the pile on the bed.

'Do go on,' she said. 'Please.'

'Well, I've seen how friendly the two of you are, going in to breakfast together, and then him taking you off for the day yesterday. I did have hopes, I'll not deny it. You seem so well suited. But last week he made a telephone call. To a lady.'

308

'When last week? What did he say?'

Gladys's brow wrinkled as she thought for a minute, then her expression cleared. 'It must have been Thursday, because that's the day I do the downstairs woodwork, and I was behind the sitting room door with the polish when he placed the call. To a number in Bristol, he told the operator.'

'And he said what?' Leah was aware she was sounding more and more snappish, but Mrs Finch didn't seem concerned.

'I can't recall his exact words, but they were something like, 'Make sure he's gone before I turn up.' And then he said, 'The longer he's away, the more time we'll have.' Oh, and then something about America, but that wasn't clear.'

'And how do you know it was a lady on the other end?' Leah's voice was steady, though she was feeling anything but.

Mrs Finch shrugged. 'Voices carry. Some are louder than others, and this one was quite … shrill, I suppose you'd say.'

'And could you hear what she said?'

'No. But she sounded quite agitated. Then Mr Coleridge just said she'd think of something.'

'You must have been listening very closely.' Leah adopted a tone of mild disapproval, but Mrs Finch shrugged again.

'At first I wasn't listening at all, but when I heard him say about visiting the lady, I did. And that's only because I like you, my dear. I didn't like to think of any man doing the dirty on such a nice, kind girl. And especially one so upset as you were when you came here.'

Guilt flickered again, and Leah sighed. 'Thank you for telling me all this. I did suspect, of course, which is why I was leaving. You understand why I must.'

'Where will you go?'

Leah was about to tell her, then stopped herself. Adam would charm the answer out of Mrs Finch in two seconds, no matter what she said she thought of him. 'I think I'll return home to Edinburgh.'

Mrs Finch looked around. 'Where's that lovely bag? I do like the butterflies on the handle.'

'I took a small picnic yesterday, and left it in Mr Coleridge's car.' She smiled and touched Mrs Finch's arm. 'When he brings it back, I'd like you to have it.'

The delight on her landlady's face made her feel even more wretched, but she couldn't have the worried woman trying to contact her to tell her he'd not brought it back with him.

Leah paid her bill, and accepted the gift of a small, plain bag to carry her things. As she walked back towards Fox Bay, she thought over what Mrs Finch had told her; she hadn't expected this lance of jealous pain at the thought of Adam with someone else. Had he even gone to Scotland at all, then? Perhaps he'd planned to share his windfall with this other woman? Well, they were in for a big disappointment. But who was this person, that Adam was prepared to steal for her, to risk his job, prison, and maybe even his life?

Leah's relief at being back at Fox Bay faded as she cheerfully greeted familiar staff on her way to her room but was met with one glum face after another in response. Her first thought was of Bertie, and she didn't bother unpacking, but left her bag on the bed and hurried back downstairs. Putting her fear of confrontation aside she knocked gently at the office door.

'Fleur? It's Leah. Can I come in?' When there was no reply, she opened the door anyway. Fleur was sitting at the desk, her head in her hands, and she looked up as Leah entered. Her eyes were red-rimmed and bright, and Leah's heart shrank.

'Is it Bertie?'

Fleur shook her head. 'No, thank goodness, but it's the next worst thing. It's all final. We've lost Fox Bay.'

'Oh, God.' Despite the relief it still came as a blow.

'CP Holdings put the offer in, Gardner couldn't refuse it, in the light of what's happened at the farm, and so that's it.' Fleur sighed. 'I've just had to hold a staff briefing before gossip gets out about it.'

'And CP are definitely planning to convert it into holiday flats?'

'So Mr Rose says, and he'd know, since he's Mr Pagett's architect. We're finished, Leah. If that's your real name.'

Leah stiffened. 'What do you mean? Of course it is.'

Fleur wiped her eyes again. She looked regretful but determined. 'It is time we talked about this, and now's as good a time as any.'

Leah thought it was anything but, and she held her silence as Fleur went on, 'I think I told you

311

about how my WI group has been trying to raise
the funds locally, for a war memorial in Trethkellis Square?'

Leah swallowed hard. 'Yes, you mentioned it.'

'Well, we've succeeded. A month or so ago, in
fact.'

'But that's wonderful! Isn't it?'

'Is it?'

'Of course.'

'Well perhaps you'll change your mind when I
tell you that we've spent the past months collecting the names and next-of-kin details of all the
Trethkellis servicemen we lost. It's proved sticky
in places, but that's where it helps that Helen's
brother works for the War Office. David has been
very helpful.'

Leah turned away, not because she didn't want
Fleur to see the flush that she could feel spreading
up her neck, because that didn't matter. What she
didn't want was to see that look on Fleur's face;
reproach, sadness, wanting to disbelieve what she
herself was saying while knowing it to be true. The
threads were still being gathered up, and Fleur's
next words proved it.

'Daniel Marshall was never married, Leah, was
he? Not to you or anyone else.'

Although it signalled the end of everything, it
left Leah feeling curiously light after carrying the
burden all these years. 'Not as far as I know,' she
said calmly.

'You're claiming a war widow's pension fraudu-
lently, aren't you?'

'No!' At least that much was true. 'Daniel
named me on the form.'

'He *named* you? Is that allowed?'

'You know the regulations, Fleur, you'll have done it yourself. The forms must be countersigned by a JP, and a police officer, it's not possible for me to have taken what Daniel didn't want me to have. Check *that* with David's office.'

'I will.'

'Daniel and I were . . . we loved one another. We were married in all but name.' That was true too, though it sounded weak. 'We would have married, if he'd lived,' she added, which wasn't.

'And what of Daniel's parents?'

'Both long dead now, you must know that.'

'Of course I do. I meant, did they know of your deceit?'

Leah shook her head. 'We told them we'd married in France. It seemed kinder.'

'His next of kin is his brother,' Fleur said, looking down at a piece of paper in front of her, 'and he moved away from the village when he was just fourteen. We haven't found him. Yet.'

Despite Fleur's deliberate emphasis on that word, that came as a relief for now. Leah's hand went to the locket she still wore, containing the lock of Daniel's hair. 'Please, Fleur, believe me when I say I truly, truly loved him. And he loved me.'

Fleur waved that away, as if it didn't matter, and it was all Leah could do not to snap at her for that, because it was all she had. Her entire life had been built on that love.

'And what about his memorial, here at St 'Dwinn's church?' Fleur went on.

'What about it?'

313

'Who paid for it?'

'Why does that matter?'

'Because *I've* been tending it, in the belief that you two were married in the eyes of the church in which you're commemorating him. I want to know how much of it is a lie.'

Leah nodded tiredly. 'All right. I paid for it, mostly.'

'What about his parents? They were still alive when he died.'

'They contributed what little they could, and I put forward the rest. It took everything I had. All my savings, and everything I inherited from my own father. He didn't leave us at all well off, and my job at the corner shop didn't pay much.' Leah looked at Fleur with a suddenly desperate need to make her understand. '*That's* the only reason I began claiming the pension. It was the only way I could afford to live.'

'Why did you lie to Helen all these years? To me? To all of us?'

Leah sat down, suddenly drained. 'It just came out, that first day you asked me where I went each day. You were so . . . respectable, I was a bit frightened of you.'

'Frightened?'

'Intimidated then.' It sounded so foolish now she knew the woman, but it was the truth. Part of it, anyway. Not just because Fleur had been the owner of Fox Bay, but because of the way she had drifted about with her glamorous family and guests, the wealthiest, the most discerning, the most confident. The ones who stayed in the big rooms on the first floor . . .

314

Abruptly Leah rose again, and had her hand on the door handle before Fleur called out to her. 'Leah, come back! We haven't finished this yet!'

But Leah ran across the lobby and was out through the revolving door in moments, all but oblivious to the spitting rain, her thoughts twisting away from the present and back to another time, and another world.

* * *

Fox Bay
March 1917

'Will they turn this place into a convalescent home, do you suppose?'

Daniel looked down at her in surprise. 'What's brought that question on?'

'I've heard that lots of places are giving themselves over to it,' Leah said. 'It's a good thing to do, isn't it?'

'I suppose. Maybe they will.' He tucked her hand more firmly around his arm as they walked towards the sea. 'Do you regret spending so much of our savings on this room, just for one night?'

'Not at all!' Leah laughed. 'To take a room on the *first* floor of Fox Bay ... we ought to come back here every year.'

'We could only afford it at this time of year,' he pointed out. 'Any time after April would be impossible. But I prefer it quiet anyway, so maybe we should.'

Leah tried to ignore the insistent little voice in her head, reminding her that this time tomorrow

315

they would be on their way to meet the boat that would take them back over to France. And that making plans for a future together was not only pointless, it was foolish. Instead she breathed deeply of the salt air, and enjoyed the rare closeness as she and Daniel walked through the kissing gate at the top of the St Adhwynn's churchyard.

'Did you know the hotel used to be a monastery?' he said suddenly.

'No.' She looked back at the building in the distance. 'But I can imagine it.'

'That pathway with the arches was the cloisters. I think, apart from having met you, I might have made quite a good monk.'

Leah couldn't help but laugh at that. 'Go on with you! A monk?'

'I think the peace and the tranquillity would have suited me.' Knowing how starkly such peace would contrast to what they were both returning to, Leah understood now why he'd brought the subject up. They reached the low wall that ran around the churchyard, and sat down, and Daniel bumped her shoulder gently with his.

'I'd like to marry you here, in this church.'

'Don't.' Leah turned away, but he caught her hand and pulled her back.

'I love you, Leah. I want to marry you at St 'Dwinn's, have our wedding party at Fox Bay, bring our children up by the beach, and then, when I'm a hundred and twelve, be laid to rest right here.' He kicked at the stone wall with his heel. 'So see to it.'

Leah gave a little laugh at his determined tone. 'I will. What will our children be called?'

'Our son will be . . . Oh, I think Gregory. Our daughter —'

'Susannah?'

'That's pretty. Susannah.' He stood up and tugged at her hand again. 'Come on, let's make the most of that room.'

Their lovemaking that night was tinged with real melancholy for the first time. Not even on the night before he'd joined up, the night she'd slipped from their bed and found her nail scissors to cut a lock of his hair, had they clung to one another with such sorrow.

That first night they had still been confident of a swift end to the war, and certain that Daniel had been going to some glorious battle where they would defeat the enemy and return victorious. Like the battles of old. Tonight, they knew the truth; that there would be mud, and blood, gas and flying debris, and screams that pierced the soul and left it darker and emptier than before. Leah's own work in the hospitals and clearing stations would bring her the remnants of men just like Daniel, young but turned old overnight. And so many of them would die beneath her blood-stained and helpless hands.

The next day Leah had returned to Reims, Daniel to Arras. Two weeks later the Americans declared war on Germany, and three days after that Daniel was dead.

12

Bude Royal Infirmary
1929

She'd drifted off again, but for how long there was no way of telling. There was silence all around her now, and the lights were dimmer. Bertie opened her eyes to stare at a clean white ceiling, and breathed slowly as she carefully turned her head on the pillow. She was in a room with several others, all sleeping except for a low murmuring at the far end by the window. There was someone in a chair by her head, but she couldn't see who it was without twisting further, and she was scared to do that just yet. It must be Jowan, and he hadn't noticed her movement so perhaps he too was sleeping.

Gradually she became aware of a wetness at her thighs, and in acute embarrassment she guessed she had soiled herself — but the humiliation vanished almost immediately, as she realised that meant she could feel her lower body again. Only now did she acknowledge the deep terror she'd had that she'd been paralysed, and now she knew she was not, she felt something building in her throat that was somewhere between a laugh and a sob. She swallowed it, not wanting to wake Jowan; he must be exhausted if he'd been with her all through the day and into the night.

As an experiment she tried to curl the toes on

her left foot. She wasn't ready to try the right yet, but if it was already set and encased in plaster of Paris she needn't worry too much; the worst was over. Her toes obeyed, and she shifted her left leg slightly, peering down the blankets in order to see the movement for herself and feed that heady sense of relief. There was a huge bump obstructing her view, and she guessed it was to keep the weight of the bedding off her broken leg, so she stopped moving in case she dislodged something.

'Bertie?' The voice wasn't Jowan's at all, it was her mother's. A hand gripped hers and Bertie turned to see her mother's face, tired and pale, the familiar dark curls now flat, making her tear-filled eyes look huge. 'You're awake ...'

'Mummy,' Bertie managed. She hadn't called her mother that in years.

'Don't move, darling,' Mum said unnecessarily. 'I'll fetch the doctor.'

Bertie looked blearily after her as she hurried away. Why bother the doctor? The nurse would be able to make sure she was all right, and perhaps give her something for the pain because there was an ominous burning sensation in her lower right leg now. She recalled the sight of the bone sticking out through shredded flesh, and fought down a surge of nausea. The burn began to intensify the more she thought about it, and became a twisting, cramping pain. Bertie bit back a little moan and reminded herself how lucky she was, but she hoped someone would come soon with something to help her sleep, or at least ease her a little.

At last Mum returned, and with her came a tall, narrow-faced man with a solemn, sympathetic expression on his face. He didn't appear to be carrying anything that might help dispel the pain, only a notebook and pen.

Mum moved the chair so she could look at Bertie properly, and sat down. She took Bertie's hand in her own chilled ones. 'Now you have to be brave, sweetheart.'

Bertie looked from her to the doctor, puzzled. She was being brave; if they knew how badly she wanted to cry —

'There was no choice,' the doctor said. His voice was quiet, to avoid waking anyone else, but his manner was more sombre than comforting. Bertie felt a twist of fear, making her heart race.

'What is it?'

'The infection was severe, and travelling rapidly towards your heart. I'm afraid we had to remove your leg, from just below your knee.'

Something tightened around Bertie's forehead. She couldn't think for a moment. The words meant nothing. Or maybe they were for someone else? Incredibly, her mouth wanted to smile, while her brain just screamed and screamed, drowning out everything else.

'No,' she said at last, very patiently, 'I can *feel* it. My leg is hurting, and it's getting worse. Can you give me something for it?'

'Roberta, listen.' Her mother's voice was high and shaky. 'You would have died, just like Toby Nancarrow, if they hadn't … hadn't taken it.'

Taken it where? The question seemed absurd, yet it brought a cold, sick feeling sweeping over her. Her leg wasn't part of her anymore, so it could be anywhere. It didn't need her. She heard a sudden

320

bark of laughter and realised it had come from her. *Where are you, naughty leg of mine?* Then, hard on the heels of that hysterical thought, another. Cold, dead, final: *I will never ride again.*

★ ★ ★

Helen watched Bertie's face go a pasty white. She threw a desperate look at the surgeon, who moved in to take Bertie's pulse just as the girl slipped into a faint. He nodded at Helen. 'She'll be all right,' he said. 'I'll tell the nurse to bring some morphine.' He walked away, leaving Helen and Bertie alone again in this room of sleeping patients.

After a minute or two Bertie stirred. 'I'm wet,' she mumbled, as though stirring from some deep sleep rather than a shock-induced faint. 'I'm sorry. I couldn't —'

'Hush, darling. I'll fetch someone.' Helen smoothed her daughter's hair, trying not to cry in front of her. She knew she should be relieved that Bertie was alive at all, especially after the fever had taken her so close to death, but the anguish she had seen on Bertie's face as the truth sank home had been like a fist, crushing her heart.

She turned to signal one of the nurses at the station at the end of the ward, and one of them hurried over. 'My daughter has ... She needs ...' She gestured at the bed, unable to find the right words without causing Bertie any further distress. 'Can you help her?'

The nurse realised immediately, and smiled at Bertie. 'Of course.'

Helen moved away, but couldn't block out the sounds of Bertie's anguish as the nurse cleaned her, and her own tears spilled over. Jowan had returned home after Bertie had been taken into surgery yesterday, and she knew he'd be wide awake and waiting for news, so she went out to call the hotel and ask them to send word to the farm.

By the time she returned to the ward, the surgeon himself had come back with a prepared syringe, and had just administered the morphine. Then, instead of hurrying away again he had taken Helen's chair, and was calmly explaining to Bertie how bad the infection had been, and why they hadn't been able to wait for her permission to perform the life-saving surgery.

'Then how long was I unconscious?' Bertie asked in a small voice. 'I thought I came in yesterday.'

'It's Thursday, you've been here for three days,' the surgeon said. 'During that time the infection spread, you were feverish and not able to give your consent, so we had to ask your mother to make the decision for you.'

Bertie turned to look at Helen, and there was suddenly something dark in that look. Something mistrustful. 'I'm sure she was happy to make it.'

That gave Helen a nasty twist, and even the surgeon looked taken aback by the flat tone and the cold words, and he must have faced this situation countless times. 'I don't think you understand quite how dangerous —'

'She's got her wish; I won't be able to ride my bike anymore.'

322

Helen's eyes stung. 'Roberta —'

'I was gon't be a racer, did you know that?' Bertie was slurring her words now, and Helen realised she was going under again, but she had to make her understand.

'I held off as long as I could, but the doctors said you might *die*!'

'Should've let me,' Bertie muttered. 'Don't worry. Now I can push mysh ... myself around on four wheels instead of two, and work at the exch ... change, and be a good daughter.' Her eyes slipped closed again.

'Don't worry,' the doctor said gently, seeing Helen's face. 'It's quite normal for a patient in these circumstances to look for someone to blame. I've given her something to help her sleep. She should be out until morning now, so you can go home and get some rest yourself.'

Helen shook her head. 'I'm not going anywhere. I couldn't sleep anyway.'

The surgeon gave her a long look, then nodded and left. Helen sat down heavily in the seat he'd vacated, and took Bertie's hand in hers. And she waited.

★ ★ ★

Leah put the telephone receiver back down with the utmost care, as if to jar it would bring Helen's broken voice back into the room. Bertie's leg; not just broken, however badly. Not knitting itself back together beneath a plaster of Paris cast, but gone. She stood up and left the office, her chest tight with apprehension, her mind scrabbling for the words she'd need when she found Ben and Fiona.

She'd broken all kinds of news in her time as a nurse. The worst possible. But this was even harder, because it was Bertie. Her mind took her back to that first night they'd dined together, while Helen confronted Fleur about the sale of the hotel. Bertie had been just twelve years old, terrified of the woman she'd met as Millicent Scripps, the confident American, but instantly at home with Leah Marshall from Wales. Since that night Leah had been, not like a second mother, but certainly a favourite aunt, to all three Fox cubs, as Fleur still called them. Now, having successfully avoided Fleur since the confrontation on Tuesday, it fell to Leah to gather the family together and give them the news Helen had struggled to tell her.

Guy Bannacott joined them in the sitting room, with Ben and Fiona, and Leah herself brought Fleur; the older woman had fear in her eyes as her gaze travelled from Leah to the others.

'What is it?' Ben asked. He stood by the window, suddenly appearing much younger than his twenty-six years, his hair unbrushed, and his shirt open at the collar, obviously pulled on in a hurry after being woken by Guy. 'Is it Bertie?'

Leah nodded. 'It is —'

'Mum said she was fine,' Fiona put in, her eyes wide and worried. 'Isn't she?'

'Please,' Leah began, still struggling to find the words. She took a deep breath, trying to ignore the four sets of eyes that bored into her. 'She's *going* to be fine, your mother seems sure of that.'

'Going to be?' It was Fleur's turn.

'She was very ill, with a fever,' Leah said. 'You all knew that much.' She didn't wait for acknowledgement, but plunged on. 'The infection was spreading fast, and sepsis had set in, and the only way they could save her life was to amputate her leg. The lower part. She still has the knee joint, so they'll be able to —'

'Stop it!' Ben stepped away from the window, white-faced and shocked. 'Stop talking like a nurse!'

'This is *Bertie*!' Fiona cried. Her grandmother pulled her close, and Leah swallowed the words she had been going to say, and nodded.

'I know,' she whispered. 'I'm so sorry. She really will be all right now.'

'How can she be?' Ben shoved his hands deep into his pockets. 'She's alive, yes, but her whole life is ruined. She lives to ride those motorcycles, just like Dad —' His voice choked off, and Leah's eyes prickled with tears as he twisted away to stare out over the tennis courts again. She saw his shoulders, rigid beneath the crisp white shirt, and heard the ragged catch of his breath as he fought to control himself for Fiona's sake.

She looked over at Fiona, who was wrapped in her grandmother's arms, her face buried against Fleur's shoulder. Fleur shook her head, perhaps thinking Leah was going to say more, but there wasn't anything she could say. She sat down in the nearest chair and laced her shaking fingers together, and the room was silent but for Fiona's shocked weeping, and the determinedly steady breathing of her brother. Guy had remained silent throughout, but the new shadows and lines on his face told of his dismay at the news. He had such a soft spot for the elder Fox girl, as much as for Ben, to whom he'd taught his trade with such fatherly care.

'I'll go and see her today,' Fleur said at length.

'I'll drive you,' Guy offered, and Fleur nodded her thanks.

'I'll go after the lunchtime shift. You and Ben can go later, Leah, after Guy drops us back.'

'What about me?' Fiona drew back and looked up.

'You can come with me,' Fleur said, after a moment's hesitation.

'I don't know if that's a good idea, Fi,' Leah said, 'I don't want you to be upset —'

'Bertie will be upset if she doesn't,' Ben said, his voice calmer now. 'Of course she must go.'

'Very well.' Fleur brushed Fiona's hair back from her forehead absent-mindedly, her face taut. 'Go and get ready so we can leave right away after lunch.'

'Someone ought to tell Jowan,' Ben said.

Leah stood up. 'He knew before Bertie did, he was there yesterday when they took her into surgery. But I'll send word to the farm that she's awake.'

'Poor Bertie.' Ben's voice was low, and still a little bit puzzled, as if he couldn't quite accept the news. 'How must she be feeling?'

'Glad to be alive,' Leah ventured, but immediately realised it was the wrong thing to say.

Ben blinked slowly at her. 'Eventually, perhaps. But you know her almost as well as any of us, do you truly believe that's how she feels now?'

326

Leah held his steady gaze for a moment, then turned away, shaking her head. 'Come and find me when you're back, Fleur.'

* * *

Helen greeted Fleur and Fiona with relief, but noted the paleness of her younger daughter's face with concern. She was about to ask if perhaps Fiona ought not to be here, but bit back the words as Fiona kissed her sleeping sister's cheek before kneeling down, holding Bertie's hand.

'Guy sends his love,' Fleur said, 'but says he'll wait outside. He doesn't want to crowd her. He'll visit later when she's had more time to recover. How is the poor lamb now?'

'She can't seem to stay awake for more than a few minutes.'

'Hardly surprising. Is the fever actually gone?' Fleur gently laid the back of her hand on Bertie's forehead. 'She feels much cooler now.'

'She's improving physically, but she still won't talk about her leg, and what they can do to help her once the … once it's healed.'

'Well she's only had a short time to adjust, you've had a couple of days.'

'When did you know?' Fiona asked, frowning.

'By Tuesday afternoon we knew the infection was spreading,' Helen said, remembering the awful scenes. 'We waited as long as we could, but she wasn't making any sense when she was awake. Jowan was here, he saw what she was like. So in the end I had to make the decision, and they operated first thing on Wednesday morning.'

327

Fiona bit her lip. 'Why did you wait a whole day to tell us?'

'I didn't want to say anything until it was all over and we knew the infection had been stopped.'

Fiona's attention returned to her sister, and Helen looked at Fleur. 'How's Ben taking it?'

'Badly,' Fleur said bluntly. 'He'll be along this afternoon.' She seemed on edge, even more so than expected. 'I can't stay long, but he's bringing Leah with him.'

'Good. She'll be just the tonic Bertie needs. She adores her, always has.'

'Everyone does,' Fleur said, in an oddly flat voice, 'no matter who she's pretending to be.'

They sat in silence for a while, watching Bertie while trying not to look at the ugly lump in the bed where her leg should have been. Her hair lay tangled and sweaty on the pillow, and her delicately flushed face made her seem like a child again, worn out with energetic play. Helen remembered those years, and how cross she had been with all three children at times, with their muddy clothes and torn coats, and she wished she could swallow a magic potion that would take her back. She wouldn't waste a moment being cross this time.

An hour passed, in a haze of half-started and half-hearted conversation. Around them the nurses and patients talked in quiet voices, now and again someone would cry out and be soothed, and occasionally a sudden loud noise would make Bertie flinch and mutter, but she always subsided again. Fiona said her knees ached, and she got up from her position on the floor and went to find a chair she could drag over to sit at her sister's side.

'I haven't heard anything yet from Mr Pagett,' Fleur said, 'about how long we have. He hasn't even written, let alone visited and officially told us we're going to have to leave.'

'He might assume Mr Gardner's done that.'

'And Mr Gardner will naturally leave it to Mr Pagett.' Fleur sighed. 'I think you'll have to call Mr Pagett yourself, to make sure of things.'

'I can't think about that now.' Helen turned back to Bertie. 'It will have to wait.'

'Of course. Unless you want me to do it?'

'He might not tell you anything, since you're no longer the manager, but it couldn't hurt to try. Do you know what time Ben will bring Leah?'

'As soon as I get back I'll take over from him, and he'll bring Guy's car.' Fleur sounded tense again. 'Speaking of which, we ought to go, Guy has been waiting long enough. Come along, Fiona.'

She leaned over and kissed Bertie's forehead, then pressed Helen's arm as she passed her. 'I'll come again tomorrow,' she promised.

Fiona looked back over her shoulder at her sister as she went.

Helen gave her a little wave, and Fiona waved back, and then she was gone, leaving Helen feeling strangely empty without her.

Bertie began to stir a few minutes later.

'You've just missed Granny,' Helen told her as she opened her eyes. 'But don't worry, she'll be back again tomorrow.' Bertie nodded, and Helen went on, 'I have good news —'

'Has my leg grown back?'

Helen winced. 'Darling, don't.'

'Then what's the good news?' Bertie looked

329

sorry for once, and Helen relaxed.

'Leah's back from Wales. Ben's bringing her to see you in a little while.'

Helen didn't expect cheers, and maybe it was too soon to hope for even a little smile, but the scowl that darkened her daughter's face came as a shock. 'What is it? You and she are as thick as thieves.'

'She'd better not come in here.'

Helen shook her head. 'I said *Leah*,' she repeated. 'Who did you think I was talking about?'

Abruptly Bertie's expression cleared. 'Nothing, I'm sorry. I'm a bit confused. Dreams, you know.'

Helen nodded and touched her hand. 'Of course. Do you want me to fetch a nurse for anything?'

'No, I'm all right. Has Xander been to visit?'

'Who?'

'Xander Nicholls. The motorcycle racer.'

'No, not as far as I'm aware.' Helen saw a frown crease Bertie's brow, and to save her the disappointment of waiting in vain, she wanted to point out that he was unlikely to visit now in any case, but how could she do that?

'I suppose I should have expected that,' Bertie said at last, saving her the trouble. 'After all it's not as if he's interested in me for his team now, is it?' There was an accusatory note in her voice, but she would understand one day, when she was in her right mind once more.

'You would have died,' Helen said calmly, yet again. 'You know what happened to Jowan's father.'

'That doesn't mean it would have happened to me.'

330

'The doctors seemed to think you were in danger of that very thing.'

'You should have waited.'

'Bertie, we could go around and around in circles for the rest of our lives,' Helen said, touching her daughter's face gently. 'I had to make the decision there and then.'

Bertie closed her eyes. 'Be sure to wake me when Ben and Aunt Leah come.'

When they arrived a little later, Bertie was still sleeping. Ben's face was troubled as he gazed down at her. 'She looks so small.'

Helen moved to let him sit down, and as he took Bertie's hand, he looked so much like Harry that it squeezed Helen's heart to look at him. The same tousled dark hair, the same clean, strong features, the same air of youth that Harry had retained until the day he'd died. That joyful innocence had been tempered, but never entirely disappeared, either in father or son, but Ben sat quietly watchful of his sister now, as if guarding her from fearful dreams.

Leah hugged Helen. 'How is she?'

'She asked me to wake her when you came in, but I don't really like to.'

'Leave her for a few minutes, at least.' Leah went in search of another chair, as Fiona had done, and returned to place it at the other side of the bed. She stroked Bertie's wrist. 'What have the doctors said about a prosthetic limb?'

Helen was briefly taken aback by the clinical nature of the question, then realised Leah was simply drawing on her nursing background. 'They've

331

tried to explain, but she won't talk about it. Not yet.'

'No, many don't. It's a sort of denial, I think.'

'Prosthetic,' Ben said. 'Is that what they call a false leg?' His gaze went to the lump in the bed. 'I can't imagine how awful it would be. She'll never ride a motorbike again.'

'That's the least of her worries,' Helen said, a little too sharply, then relented. 'I'm sorry, Ben, but really, it is.'

'Not to her, it isn't,' he said tightly. 'All her life, it's all she —'

'Hush,' Leah said quietly, 'she's waking.'

Bertie's lips were moving, though no sound was coming out, and her fingers twitched on the covers of the bed. Her breathing was becoming shallower and lighter.

'It's so good of you to come, Leah,' Helen whispered. Leah was not only a friend when she most desperately needed one, but also an effortlessly steadying influence on Bertie. 'She'll be so glad to see you.'

Bertie opened her eyes as Helen spoke, and Helen poured some water for her. 'Look who's here, as promised.'

'Hello,' Ben said, and Bertie smiled.

'Hello, Your Highness.'

Ben grinned. 'Spoken like the spoiled little princess you are.'

Helen watched the faces on her two eldest offspring during this exchange, and although she had known, in some distracted and relieved way, that they got on well, for the first time she really saw the deep affection they shared. It made her eyes

332

sting and her heart swell, and she let her hand rest on Ben's shoulder, squeezing gently and hoping the touch conveyed at least some of the love and gratitude she felt.

'Leah's here too,' she said. 'Isn't it good of her to come all this way?'

Bertie twisted her head on the pillow. 'Hello, Leah.'

'*Cariad.*' Leah leaned close and kissed her cheek. 'How are you feeling? Does it hurt much?'

'Did Mum tell you she let them cut my leg off?'

'Bertie!' Ben sounded shocked, and even though Helen was used to it now, she caught her breath.

Leah's lips tightened as she sat back again. 'Did anyone tell *you* that your mum was out all night in the rain, looking for you? Did they tell you your life was hanging by a thread when she, she,' she emphasised, 'found you by the river?'

'It's all right, Leah,' Helen began, 'she's just —'

'No, it isn't. Did anyone mention that your mother hasn't left your side in the three days you've been here? Not to bathe, nor eat properly, nor sleep in a proper bed?'

Bertie remained silent for a moment, and her eyes slid up to meet Helen's, but any hope of an apology was dashed as she looked back at Leah. 'How's the weather in Wales?'

Leah blinked. 'What?'

'Wales. Where you've spent the last week or so. How's the weather there?'

Leah threw a puzzled look towards Helen. 'Wet, just like here. Why do you ask?'

'Where did you get the wig? You should wear it all the time, it suited you.'

333

Helen stared at Leah, who had gone quite pale. 'Wig? What's she talking about?'

'Is she still delirious?' Ben asked worriedly, and he stood up. 'I'll fetch someone.'

'How's Uncle Adam?' Bertie persisted, as Ben went in search of help. 'You two seemed very close. Have you been with him ever since that telegram arrived from your *aunt*?' Her eyes grew bright with unshed tears, and Helen's throat went tight as she saw that, beyond the initial shock, none of this was coming as any surprise to Leah.

'Leah?' she stammered. 'What's this about?'

'Tell her,' Bertie said. 'Go on, *tell her*!' When Leah didn't speak, Bertie turned to Helen again. 'She's been seeing Uncle Adam. They were kissing, right out in the open, in front of everyone.'

Helen went very still. Leah had not made a sound. Bertie's fingers, holding the water glass, were turning white.

'Is that true?' Helen asked calmly. Inside she could feel the pressure building, and wondered, with a strange, detached curiosity, how it would find its release. 'Are you having an affair with Adam Coleridge?'

'No!' Leah stood up. 'Look, Helen, come outside a moment, let me —'

'Ask her who she was with at the race then!' Bertie shouted suddenly, and Helen was dimly aware of the sound of hurrying feet as nurses approached the bed. 'Why do you think I rode away in such a temper?'

'We ... we thought the fight between Jowan and that racer —'

'It had nothing to do with that! It was seeing

334

them!' Bertie was sobbing openly now, and she jerked back as Helen tried to embrace her, stabbing her finger towards the stunned-looking Leah.

'Who's she talking about?' Ben had returned along with the nurses, but Helen couldn't spare him an explanation now.

'Bertie, listen —'

'If they hadn't been there, if I hadn't been so shocked, I'd have ridden home with Jowan. She's the reason I'm here, the reason I've lost my leg!' Bertie sat upright and, before anyone realised what she was going to do, she hurled her water glass at Leah. Leah gasped and flung herself sideways onto the floor as the glass smashed against her chair, raising cries of alarm from all around.

'Fetch the doctor!'

'Fetch a policeman!'

'Hold her!'

'That could have killed someone!'

The ward sister took Bertie's hands and held them tightly, making quiet murmuring sounds while Bertie sobbed. She pulled away, but allowed Ben to put his arm around her shoulder, and turned to bury her face in his coat.

Two nurses crouched beside Leah, and made sure she hadn't been struck by flying glass, before helping her to her feet. Helen watched all this unfold with numb detachment, only Bertie's words penetrating the fog that shrouded her mind. Leah was the reason her daughter was here. Leah, who'd been lying to her for God knew how long, and had been courting Adam Coleridge. Leah, who had nearly cost Bertie her life.

'Helen?' Leah pleaded, looking back as the

335

nurses guided her, apparently more firmly than appearances would suggest, towards the door. 'Helen!'

Helen looked frantically at Bertie, but the young woman was inconsolable and once again becoming difficult to manage. Ben held her tightly, with her face pressed against his shoulder, and as one of the nurses left to fetch something to calm her, Helen accepted that she might as well not be there.

She followed Leah outside into the yard. Her friend was barely recognisable as the laughing blonde charmer who'd given them Millicent Scripps so long ago; she fumbled a cigarette from her silver case, and only when she'd lit it, did she look at Helen. She had used the time to gather herself and now seemed calmer, though her voice trembled.

'Whatever you're thinking, you're wrong.'

'Am I?'

'Unless, of course, you're thinking I took on the role of a widow from Scotland, and tried to swindle five hundred pounds out of your worst enemy.' When Helen didn't crack a smile, Leah sighed and drew deeply on her cigarette. 'Let's sit down over there,' she said quietly. 'I'll tell you about Susannah Paterson.'

Helen didn't want to sit anywhere; she'd been doing nothing else for three days, but she followed Leah to the small garden off to the side of the yard, deserted due to the weather and furnished with wooden seats that overlooked the river. Heedless of the puddles of rainwater on the slats, they sat down, and Leah offered Helen a cigarette. She declined. All she could think about was how distraught Bertie had been, and how no one had been able to properly comfort her, not even her own mother. Not even Ben. She sat on the very edge of the seat, ready to go back to her daughter the moment she'd heard all she needed to.

Leah spoke without emotion for a while, spinning some wild story about the war, and a child who was due to inherit an unimaginable sum of money, not to mention an estate in the Highlands. Distracted and only half-listening, Helen wondered how any of this could be connected to her family, or to Adam Coleridge, but she gradually grasped what Leah was saying.

'You invented all this, just to cheat Adam into embezzling money from Hartcliffe?'

'It was all I could think of.'

'And you didn't think to mention it to any of us?'

'Are *you* saying you'd have given your blessing? No.' Leah answered her own question, and shook her head. 'I know you too well.'

'Are you saying I'm weak? Too soft-hearted?'

'Far from it. I'm saying you're too emotionally tied to Adam. Not in that way,' she went on, before Helen could protest. 'I don't mean you're fond of him, but he represents a part of your past that goes back even further than Harry. You were friends once. Good ones, from what Fleur and the kids tell me.'

'We were. And you telling him your husband was killed in a gas attack is about the lowest lie you could have told.'

'Why?' Then Leah's expression reflected dismayed realisation. 'Oh, no.' She closed her eyes.

337

'Did he lose friends?'

'Friends, and nearly his own life.' Helen sat in silence for a minute, staring out over the fast-flowing river. 'You're saying I don't have the detachment I'd need to see a man I know brought to the same low point Harry was.'

'Anyone, I would think, but especially Adam. Hels, I *couldn't* tell you. To begin with it was to spare you knowing he was still hanging around after the party, and then it was because I knew you'd have become involved in it, and that wouldn't have been fair on you. You don't deserve to be dragged in.'

'I'm already in,' Helen pointed out. 'And so is Bertie. Why did you go to that race meet, knowing she might see you?'

'I tried everything I could to avoid that,' Leah said. She sounded subdued now. 'I told Adam I hated motorcycles, but he told me he was collecting the money from someone who lived nearby there. I stayed away from the start and finish point, and when the riders returned to the sheds, I went down to the track. I *tried*!'

'Not hard enough!' Helen rose and began to walk away. Bertie was all that mattered now.

'Wait, I'll come back in with you, I'm sure they'll —'

'Don't you dare!' Helen whirled, sure the anger must be burning white-hot in her eyes, and saw Leah shrink back. 'Don't you come anywhere near my family ever again, do you understand?'

Leah stared back at her, her mouth working as if she had a hundred things she wanted to say, but all Helen could think about was how Bertie must have felt, to see her idol locked in an embrace with the man who had destroyed her beloved father.

'Mum?'

She turned to see Ben in the entrance doorway, and went over to him. 'How is she?'

'Sleeping. The nurse gave her something.' Ben looked past her at Leah. 'Are you going to tell me what all this was about?'

Helen touched his arm. 'Later,' she promised. 'For now, I need to be with Bertie.'

'Is Leah ready to go back home?'

'Yes.' Helen's voice was firm, and as she looked at Leah, they both knew that home did not mean Fox Bay Hotel.

★ ★ ★

Leah remained silent on the drive home, despite the curious glances Ben kept giving her. She felt oddly calm despite all that had happened; telling Helen about Adam had been one thing but there was more she hadn't told her, and she wouldn't go home to Wales until she had. If ever. She tightened up again as she thought about what awaited her there —

'Are you staying this time?' Ben asked as he parked the car, cutting into her thoughts as if he could read them.

'For a day or two. Until I've had a chance to talk to your mother.'

'And will you talk to us too? I mean, it looks like something we ought to know. What did you do to upset Bertie so much? And Mum too.'

Leah sighed. 'Well you'll know soon enough, I

339

suppose, so you might as well hear it from me. Come up to my room and I'll explain.'

She sat on her bed and told the story yet again, and on this third time of telling it the words seemed to come more easily. When she'd finished, she waited for the explosion of betrayed outrage, but it never came.

'Why bother with a disguise if he didn't know you?' Ben wanted to know, ever the practical one.

'It's not so much him, it's the locals. I didn't go to the village much when Daniel and I visited his parents, but I didn't want to take any chances. Besides, dressing up always helps me become someone else. I even convince myself most of the time.'

'I can't believe you've been hiding this from us. That you've lied to us all.'

'And I can't believe I've turned into the kind of person who could.' She looked around the room, this same room where she and Daniel had planned to return every year. She had honoured that decision, but now, spilling this sordid little tale of deceit within these walls she couldn't help feeling she was poisoning the memory.

She got up and went to where her coat hung on the back of the door, and fished in the pocket. 'Here.' She tossed the wig to Ben, who balanced it on his fist so it hung more or less naturally. 'Bertie wanted to know where I got it, but I didn't get around to answering.'

'And where did you?'

Leah gave a half-smile. 'It was fate, really. I met these wonderful girls on the train. Actresses. They were part of a company on their way to Bude to perform in a play, perhaps you've seen it? *Diamond Lil*, it's called.' He shook his head. 'No matter. They were friendly, excitable, and we got on well. Then, when I realised I was going to need to hide this,' she caught up a fistful of her own curls and tugged them, 'they were the perfect solution. I asked you to run me over to Bude, so I could pick up Bertie's birthday cake, remember?'

'And the bakery was right by the theatre.' He gave a short, hollow laugh. 'Aren't you full of ideas?'

'Well here's another one. While I was there, I sent a telegram to myself here, claiming my Aunt Mary had dislocated her shoulder.'

Ben sat in silence for a minute, looking from her to the wig and back again. 'Who are you really, Leah Marshall?' he asked quietly. 'All this, the plan, the . . . the telegram . . . This isn't the type of thing someone normally *thinks* about, let alone puts into action so quickly.'

'If it had worked, you'd have all been thanking me instead of condemning me.' Leah picked up her cigarette case, just for something to do with her shaking hands. 'Goodness only knows why Adam should decide to play the knight in shining armour, instead of just handing over the cash.'

'I've known him all my life,' Ben said. 'He's reckless and thoughtless, and what he did to Dad was terrible, but he's not a monster. I always liked him, in fact, he was fun. Outrageous sometimes. And Mum's known him practically all her life, they'd always been good friends.'

'She's a rotten judge of character then.'

Ben looked at her shrewdly. 'Quite.'

341

Leah bit her lip; she'd deserved that. 'Well, fun or not, I don't for one moment regret trying to part him from his money.'

'He's still in Scotland, then?'

'Either that or he's gone back to Bristol.'

'Aren't you worried he'll come here looking for you, now he knows you tried to con him?'

'Why would he?' Leah touched the flame of her lighter to the tip of her cigarette. 'He won't connect me to your family, and he's got no reason to come here again, not now Bertie's made her feelings clear to him. Why do you suppose I asked *her* to tell him to leave?'

'He's not just her godfather you know, he's all of ours.'

'Oh? I didn't realise.' *Did he turn up with a big gift on your twenty-first?* But then, she remembered, he'd only recently regained part of his lost fortune or she was sure he would have. 'Anyway, I told Mrs Finch I was going back to Edinburgh, so this is actually the safest place for me to be.'

Ben handed back the wig and went to the door. 'You'll have to think of somewhere else to go though. Mum won't have you here, not now.'

'I'm going to ask your grandmother to plead my case with her,' Leah said, sounding more confident than she felt. 'If anyone can make her understand, Fleur can. In any case, Adam's lost nothing so I can stop feeling guilty about him. He'll get the money put back into the account he embezzled it from, and we're all back to square one. But at least I tried something.'

'I do hope you're not implying that you're the only one who's concerned?' Ben stopped

342

with his hand on the door handle, and his eyes were suddenly flint hard. 'Mum has been rather preoccupied of late.'

Leah nodded, a dull shame creeping through her. 'She's been through too much. Which is why I feel so wretched that my plan didn't work.'

He relented slightly. 'It might easily have done, and you're right, if it had, we'd have been thanking you.'

He gave her a little smile, banishing some of the tautness in his face. 'I miss the likes of Millicent Scripps,' he said. 'Why don't you bring her back for one last show before we close?'

Leah returned his smile, but her eyes were stinging. 'I think I've pushed my luck just once too often with those kinds of shenanigans, don't you?'

13

Bude Hospital

'I don't want to go home.' Bertie looked from her mother to the doctor. Her leg – the one that was no longer part of her – ached and burned, and she felt sick with fear at the thought of not being near these calm, competent nurses, and the medicines that helped her push the pain away long enough to sleep.

'We've curtained off half of the sitting room on the ground floor for you,' Mum said, as if that made any difference. 'You'll be able to call for anyone at any time, and you'll be part of the family too.'

'What family?' Bertie flung at her. 'Fiona down at the stupid lifeboat station, Ben either asleep or at work, and you the same. And Aunt Leah . . .' She stopped, too angry and frightened to go any further.

'Aunt Leah has told us why she did what she did,' Mum said quietly, though her voice was tight. 'She was trying to help.'

'You didn't see them.' Bertie shook her head. 'She might have started off wanting to trick him, but by the time I saw them at the race she was looking at him as if he were the answer to all her prayers. She's in *love* with him, Mum! You can't trust her.'

Her mother's face was pale, but she sounded

determined as she ignored Bertie's plea. 'You'll be better at home. The doctor will visit when you're ready, and talk to you about what can be done for . . .' She nodded at the empty leg of Bertie's pyjamas.

'I don't want anything. If I can't ride a motorbike, if I can't join Xander's racing team, what's the point?' Bertie's eyes flooded with tears. They seemed all too ready to do that at any moment, and although no one seemed surprised, or put out, she felt weak and stupid. Self-pitying. She swiped at her eyes furiously, ignoring the handkerchief her mother proffered. She hadn't even seen Jowan since that first day she had woken up, but Mum had said he'd been there when they'd taken her in to surgery . . . that told a story in itself, one which hurt too much to think about.

The porter brought a cane-backed wheelchair closer to the bed, and Bertie closed her eyes tightly as the nurse helped her into it. She had tried it yesterday afternoon, while Granny and Mum had been talking in the corridor, but then it had felt as if she had all the time in the world to get used to the idea. Now the feel of it under her made her whimper, knowing this was it; she wasn't going to be lifted back into her warm hospital bed, and cared for by these familiar nurses. She would be left alone for hours at a time, in her curtained-off section of the sitting room, listening to the world going on around her. Not needing her. Not wanting her. Not even thinking about her. The thought of the loneliness to come was crushing.

'Jowan will visit when he can,' Mum said. 'And someone can push you over to the farm to see him, too.'

'Someone can push me,' Bertie repeated dully. '*If* they're not too busy, and if Jowan still wants to know me.'

'Bertie!' She looked up, not recognising the voice at first, and was jolted to see a frothy spray of feathers and beads bobbing along behind the ward sister, and then the woman overtook the sister and hurried to Bertie's side. 'Devastating! I can't begin to tell you how shocked we all were.' Lynette kissed her on both cheeks. The feathers tickled, and Bertie jerked her head away.

'Why are you here?' she said. She knew it sounded rude, but she didn't care. 'I'm not going to be one of your crowd.'

Lynette drew back, her smile fading. 'Perhaps not, but I rather thought we'd hit it off. Didn't we? I mean, I admire you like mad.'

'And Xander?'

'Oh, I don't admire *him* at all.' Lynette grinned, immediately regaining her good humour. 'See? I knew I could perk you up!'

'I meant is Xander here?' Bertie said, rolling her eyes but unable to help smiling. There was something irrepressibly charming about Lynette, no matter how dark the world had become.

'He's having a meeting with some frightful sponsor-type, but he sends his absolute best. Aren't you going to introduce us?' Lynette held out her hand to Bertie's mother. 'Hello, I'm Lynette Nicholls.'

'Helen Fox.'

'Lovely to meet you. Bertie's a spunky one, isn't she?'

'Yes.' Mum looked at Bertie and her voice was

346

soft, making Bertie's eyes sting again. 'She is. We're enormously proud of her.'

'So you ought to be. It's a pity you couldn't come to see her race, she took the field by storm.'

Mum seemed to note the underlying criticism, and turned defensive. 'Unfortunately, it's the height of the season, and I had too much to do.'

'I expect you thought you'd have plenty of chances,' Lynette conceded. 'How cruel life can be.'

'Mum only went to see my father race once,' Bertie said. She'd intended it as a gentle reminder to Lynette that her mother had witnessed the shocking death of her husband at that one event, but it came out sounding accusatory, and she saw her mother's eyes darken in pain. 'I just meant to say —'

'We all think we'll have a next time,' Lynette said, 'but we never know what's around the corner, do we?'

'It was nice of you to come,' Bertie said, to change the subject. Lynette was beginning to wear her out already, as much as she liked her. 'Please tell Xander I'm sorry not to have had the chance to join his team after all.'

'He knows. He came and spoke to the doctors while you were still asleep, but they wouldn't let him in because your dishy farmer was sitting with you. They didn't want to risk another scrap.'

'Xander came here?' Bertie had thought nothing could surprise her anymore.

'As soon as we heard you'd hurt yourself, from your mechanic chap. What's he called?'

'Stan Houghton.'

'Yes, him. Xander went white, I don't mind telling you. Hared off the minute he could, to find out if you were all right. Then he brought the awful news back with him. You were in the newspapers, you know.'

'Well it's the last time I'll be famous for anything.' Bertie shifted slightly in the chair. It was already hard and uncomfortable, and she sent a look of longing towards the crumpled bed she'd been in just a few minutes before. It was odd – waking up in that bed, learning the shocking truth in it, lying for hours and hours in awful, contemplative silence, she'd longed to be back home and far away from this place. Now it felt as if this were her home, and the place to which she was going was some unknown prison, filled with strangers.

'I hope you'll come to the races when you're up and about,' Lynette said.

Bertie could think of nothing she would hate more. 'Of course.'

To her surprise, Lynette suddenly dropped into a crouch beside the wheelchair. 'I think you're absolutely magnificent,' she said, her breezy attitude vanished. 'I should think it an honour if we could remain friends. Brighton isn't too far on the train; I'll come back and visit you when you're up to having company.'

Bertie nodded, not trusting herself to speak, and Lynette stood up again, and this time when she kissed Bertie it was a warm press of her lips against Bertie's forehead. She stepped back to let the porter wheel the chair out to the ambulance, and it was only as the door closed that Bertie realised she wouldn't be living in the hotel for much longer, and that she had no idea where to write to Lynette to tell her.

The first obstacle to Bertie's homecoming was soon revealed: the wheelchair was narrow, and the porter experienced, but getting through the revolving door was tricky and frustrating. The porter jiggled and pushed, and finally they burst through the other side, hot and embarrassed. Mum followed and took over the pushing, then thanked the porter, who gazed around him for a moment in awe, before returning to the ambulance.

'Here we are, then,' Mum said. 'Home.'

'Home,' Bertie repeated. It still didn't feel like it. Granny bent and kissed her, and then she heard Fiona calling her name, and a moment later her sister had flung her arms about Bertie's neck.

Fiona had only been permitted to visit twice. Once Bertie hadn't even woken to see her, and the next time Fiona had left red-eyed, and looking so much more grown up than when she had arrived; it was something quite extraordinary to see, as if the hospital was some mysterious portal that had aged her beyond her years, and Bertie hated that she had been the cause of it. As Mum pushed the wheelchair towards the private sitting room at the far side of the lobby, Fiona explained the changes that had been made to accommodate Bertie in her new room.

'Of course, when the doctors give you a new leg, you'll be able to get around a lot more easily.'

'We have a lift,' Bertie pointed out as they

reached the sitting room. 'Why can't I have my old room?'

'Because it's not just about getting up to the third floor,' Granny said. 'It's about being nearby so we can come and talk to you, bring you what you need, and anything you'd like. So you can be part of things, and we can be with you too. Because, believe it or not, we do want to be.'

Fiona held open the door, and Bertie rolled slowly into the sitting room. A curtain rail was set up so that it bisected the huge picture window, and sectioned off almost half of the room, leaving only a slight rearrangement of the seating area, the fireplace, and the radio. In the private area was Bertie's own bed, brought down from her room, a generous expanse of window, and a small bedside cabinet.

'The curtains can go right back in the daytime, if you like, so they'll barely be noticeable. But you can close them when you want to, or need to. And once you've mastered getting in and out of this,' Mum tapped the side of the wheelchair, 'you'll only have to use it when you want to go somewhere. Otherwise you'll be able to sit on the sofa or the chairs, just like before.'

'And what about dressing? Washing? Using the . . . the toilet?' Bertie shook her head, trying not to give in to tears yet again. 'I need more than my family, I need a nurse. Can't we get a live-in one?' She looked up in time to see her mother and grandmother exchanging troubled glances. 'Is it that we can't afford one? We must be able to! Look at this place!'

'We have to save every penny we can now,

towards finding a new home,' Mum said gently. 'I'm sorry. Doctor Rowe will visit once a day for a while, and then we'll do everything we can for you. The nurses have told us all about your medication, and what to look out for when we're changing your dressings. There's nothing they can do for you that we can't, not at the moment.'

'But that's so stupid!' Bertie's curled fists struck the arms of her wheelchair. It hurt, and the pain drove the hopelessness and panic deeper. 'I've lost my *leg*!'

'Darling —'

'Shut up!' Bertie covered her eyes and let the tears flow. 'Take me back to the hospital.'

'You can't,' Granny said, and Bertie felt a slender hand on her shoulder. 'Sweetheart, they need to give your bed to someone who can't manage at home. You have people all around, who want to help.'

'What about Leah?' Fiona said suddenly.

Bertie lowered her hands and stared at her. 'Leah? Are you quite mad?' It only occurred to her as puzzlement crossed her sister's face, that Fiona had not heard about Leah's treachery. She looked up at her mother, expecting to see her own feelings reflected there, but Mum was looking at Granny again, and there seemed to be a silent conversation going on between them.

'Mum! Surely you're not —'

'What's wrong with Leah?' Fiona persisted, but was ignored.

'I told you, it wasn't like she said!' Bertie cried. 'She's in love with him. They've probably been plotting this together, all along. The farm, the

351

build, everything!'

'In love with who?' Fiona asked, wide-eyed.

'All that's over now,' Mum said wearily. 'We can't fight it anymore. The hotel has been sold, our life here is finished. All that matters now is getting you well again.'

Bertie could scarcely believe what she was hearing. Her eyes went to the plaque on the wall by the fireplace, the twin of one in the office: *Vulpes latebram suam defendit.*

'Does that mean nothing?' She nodded at it. 'Dad tried to protect his home. He might have failed, but he did at least try! What have you done? Rolled over and offered yourself to the first predator to cross your hearth!'

'You have no idea what you're talking about,' her mother said stiffly. 'I've protected all of you, all your lives, and this hotel is — '

'Helen, don't.' Granny crouched by the chair, bringing her face level with Bertie's. 'You do need someone, you're right. Leah doesn't have to be your best friend, or even to speak to you. But she *has* been a nurse during wartime, she's cared for men who've had limbs blown off. She knows how to help you, and what to look out for. Will you let her?'

Fiona was looking from her mother to her grandmother. 'What's going on?'

'Hush, darling,' Mum said. 'I'll talk to you later. Bertie?'

Bertie looked across at the bed and saw the chamber pot tucked beneath it, and pictured her family helping her to use it. She imagined them, tired and upset, talking together out of her earshot in the upstairs sitting room, or in the kitchen, telling each other what they'd had to do for her and how disgusting it was, or how harrowing. Or how terribly, terribly sad. She couldn't bear it.

'Yes,' she said quietly. 'All right.'

★ ★ ★

Leah had seen Bertie's arrival from midway down the stairs, and with the ache of the outcast she watched the women she'd considered her only friends disappear into the family sitting room. Fiona, who'd been holding the door open, caught sight of her and waved her over, but Leah shook her head and mouthed, 'Later.' Fiona looked exasperated; no doubt she was being told 'later' a lot at the moment.

Since Leah had told Helen the truth about Adam, their paths had not crossed again. But they would have to talk about it properly sometime, and Leah would have to tell her about Daniel too, when the time was right … if it ever was. The fact that Helen had not yet sent her away after all did not mean she had forgiven her, just that she had more important things to do and think about, and it was only a matter of time.

Guy had looked at her strangely once or twice since she'd returned, but not sought her out to ask any questions about this mysterious man Fiona had seen her with. He'd seemed preoccupied with his own thoughts and troubles, and done his job mechanically and efficiently, but without any of his usual breezy attitude. They'd always got along, and now it felt as if she was losing him as a friend, too.

Leah busied herself helping Martin Berry on reception; the Trethkellis train had brought the new influx of guests for the last week in August, and Leah worked steadily for an hour or more, summoning bell boys, chatting about the beach, about the church, and about the history of what was once Trethkellis Abbey, and was now Fox Bay Hotel. Soon to be, what? Pagett Towers? It was an unbearable thought, surely Helen must realise she had only been trying to stop that from happening?

As she worked, she kept one eye on the sitting room door. Fiona had left that room after only a few minutes, and on the way through the lobby she had thrown a curious, mistrusting glance at Leah. Leah's heart had sunk; her last ally was gone.

At last Helen emerged, and when she had pulled the door closed behind her, she leaned on it, her head resting back against the polished wood for a moment, her eyes closed. Then she came over towards reception and Leah's heart beat faster. She was about to discover how things stood between them; whether there was understanding yet, or even forgiveness. As Helen came behind the reception counter on her way to the office, Leah stopped her.

'Can we talk?'

'I was going to suggest that,' Helen said coolly. 'Come through.'

In the office, Helen gestured for Leah to sit down. A polite manager, not a friend. 'What did you want to talk to me about?'

'You know what.'

'Right then.' Helen took the seat behind the desk. 'Please begin.'

Conversely Leah could think of nothing to say that she hadn't already said. 'I wanted to help,' she managed at last. 'I thought I *could* help.'

Helen regarded her for a long moment, and Leah reflected with a kind of fear that the formerly bright, youthful-looking woman was now beginning to look tired and beaten.

At length Helen nodded. 'Yes, well, believe it or not I'm actually grateful.'

'Grateful?' Hope was a fragile thing, but Leah seized it with both hands. 'Do you mean you forgive me?'

'It was an elegant plan,' Helen said evasively, 'and a dangerous one. You were very brave.' But she didn't look impressed, nevertheless. 'I understand why you did it, and what you hoped to achieve. The thing is, Bertie tells me something different.'

'Different?' Leah frowned. 'She saw us at the race, yes, but only you, Fleur, and Ben know what that was about.'

'No, she knows everything now. There will be no more secrets in our family.' Helen's face took on a faraway look. 'When I was Bertie's age, I had been with the love of my life for two years. H and H, he called us. The Heavenly Twins.' She smiled, and it hurt Leah's heart. 'I thought the whole world should be in love, just like we were.'

'I remember that feeling,' Leah ventured, thinking of Daniel.

Helen looked sceptical. 'By that time, I was sure I could tell the true lovers from the casual,

355

just by watching them. If they didn't touch one another's hands, or faces, the way Harry and I did, or if their kisses seemed off in any way, hurried, embarrassed even ... whatever it was, I somehow *knew* they were putting on a show. Maybe for those around them, maybe for one another. Maybe even for themselves. But a show, nevertheless. Perhaps they themselves didn't even realise it until much later.'

'Helen —'

'That's what young love will do for you though, isn't it?' Helen looked at Leah sadly. 'Bertie and Jowan are probably almost as close now as Harry and I were by the time we married. I hope so, anyway.'

'He's a nice lad,' Leah said. The change in direction of this conversation was puzzling but she had no doubt it was leading somewhere, and she was right.

'Bertie is observant. You don't come second in a race against professionals without learning to read people, and their intentions. The thing is, she not only saw you and Adam in a clinch at the race, she saw you *together*. She understood what even you might not have understood yet.'

Leah's heart rolled over. 'She must have been quite a distance away, since I didn't see her,' she countered. 'She doesn't know what she saw.'

'Are you in love with Adam Coleridge, Leah?'

'No! Look, Bertie has got it wrong. It *was* all an act, to try and put things right.' She remembered the feel of his lips on hers, and pushed the memory away. She recalled the sense of despair as he'd driven off, leaving her standing outside Sandy

Cove, but that had been fuelled by the failure of the plan, not by the realisation that he would soon discover her deception and her true, duplicitous nature. The only love she could be sure of was that which she and Daniel had shared, and now it was time to acknowledge that for what it had been. And what it had not.

'I have something else to tell you,' she said in a low voice. 'Daniel and I were never married.'

As she talked, she watched Helen's face, trying to read her reaction, but for once she could not. Helen's bland, polite, hostess face was in place, and her usually transparent expression did not change, nor did she venture a comment, yet Leah was sure it was the first time she was hearing this sordid truth. When she'd finished, she was so relieved she almost told the rest of it too, but those words stuck in her throat and she couldn't force them out.

Helen rose to her feet, and she sounded strangely calm. 'I was so close to forgiving you, but you've lied from the very start, haven't you? Is *anything* you've told me true?'

'My love for Daniel—'

'And that's another thing! If you two weren't married your name isn't even Marshall. I know *his* was, because I've seen the memorial stone.' She held up a hand to forestall anything Leah tried to say. 'No, I don't want to know your real name. I don't care. Ever since the truth came out about you and Adam, I've meant to tell you to leave, but knowing you did it from the best of intentions made me reconsider. Now *this*?'

'I understand.' Leah felt sick at the thought,

but she couldn't blame her. This precious friendship was over, she couldn't expect to stay here now. She stood up and turned to leave, wondering where she would go now; she couldn't go back to Wales —

'You have made an utter fool out of me,' Helen said, and tears were standing out in her eyes now, making cold mirrors of the usually warm sherry brown. 'You must have laughed yourself sick all these years, watching me swallow your lies.'

'No! I place you and your family above everything. It was such a little lie to begin with, and by the time I realised how much you meant to me it was too late. I thought it was easier to keep things as you knew them. It made no difference to you, after all.'

Helen didn't answer for a while. Then she got up and stared out of the window. Just when Leah thought she might scream, if only to break the tension in the room, Helen turned back.

'Do you swear you're not having a relationship with Adam Coleridge?'

'How could I be? As far as he knows I've gone back to Scotland.'

'That means nothing. I can't have him brought back into our lives, Leah.'

'We're not having any kind of relationship, and nor will we ever.'

Helen regarded her steadily, then let her breath out. 'All right. Then I can offer you a job for a while. Will you sit down again, so we can discuss it?'

Astonished into silence, Leah did so, trying to suppress a sudden hope of rapprochement; if she were able to stay, she might yet convince Helen that she was still the same old Leah.

'Are you sure your Aunt Mary doesn't need you home?' Helen asked. 'As I recall you were only supposed to be here until Wednesday of last week. Or was that another of your lies?'

'I wrote to her and told her about Bertie. She's not as needful of me as Mother was.' Leah heard herself babbling, in her relief. 'In fact, I don't think she needs me at all —'

'Oh, she'll have you back soon enough,' Helen said. 'We won't be here for much longer ourselves, after all.'

Leah nodded, subsiding. 'Of course. What's the job?'

'I want you to become Bertie's nurse.'

Leah gave a short laugh, then she stared at Helen. 'You're quite serious! Helen, Bertie hates me! You heard her in the hospital, she blames me for what's happened to her!'

'So do I.' Helen's words tore through Leah like a blunted blade. 'Your part in her … her *situation*, is the best reason I can think of for you to stay and help her through it.'

'And what does she think?'

'She fought it at first, naturally, but she knows she needs professional help. Help that we can't afford.'

Leah twisted her fingers in her necklace. 'I'd give anything for her not to have seen us,' she said. 'It must have been such a dreadful shock.'

'Go and talk to her, before she changes her mind. Tell her what you can do for her, and start by changing her dressings and having the soiled ones

359

washed.' Helen gave her a steady look. 'Then you can move your things out of room eight, and up into one of the empty staff bedrooms on the third floor.' She busied herself with the ledger on her desk then, and Leah realised she was dismissed. An employee, no longer a friend. That was still better than the alternative, and Leah silently took her leave and went to see Bertie.

14

Of course she wasn't still here, stupid of him to think she would be. But then he was clearly a lot more stupid than he'd always believed himself to be. Adam muttered curse after curse as he threw his clothes into his case, his stomach churning with a mixture of humiliation and shredded nerves. He had to pay that money back into Hartcliffe's account, and before Simon returned from America, but how could he do that when he no longer had it? At least he hadn't given it to Susannah – or whatever her real name was. What a prize idiot he'd been …

★ ★ ★

Princes Street Gardens, Edinburgh

Waiting at the appointed meeting place, from three hours before the allotted time, until at least two hours after, he still hadn't worked it out. He'd left the railway station and completed the ten-minute walk in five, hurrying past the bandstand and up the path towards the ornate, forty-foot tall fountain. The park was overlooked by Edinburgh Castle, a familiar sight for Adam, but still it seemed to loom, imposing and dark, over him as

361

he found a spot near the railway bridge where he could watch through the trees.

At first, as the hands on his watch marched around, he'd assumed this Tommy character had been held up, or that he himself had got the meeting place wrong. Then he'd decided that Tommy had actually been and gone, that he'd turned up as arranged, somehow spotted Adam lurking in the distance, and melted away again. Every time a single male figure approached the fountain Adam had tensed, but they'd all moved on after a moment of staring up at the intricate ironwork, as if embarrassed to be caught gazing at the controversial piece of art.

It was only when he saw a groundsman watching him with narrow-eyed interest, that he accepted he'd been here for too long now, and that Tommy wasn't coming. The groundsman kept looking around, possibly for an authority figure to report to, and Adam had made a show of checking his watch and tapping his foot impatiently, then walked away across the bridge. At that point he'd still felt as if he'd let Susannah down; the memory of her trusting face, her tears, her determination to protect her son . . . Well, that much he *could* do for her, at least.

He'd planned to visit his cousin in Leith and beg a bed for the night, before returning to Bristol to collect his car, but instead he hurried back to Waverley and managed to catch the last Inverness train by the skin of his teeth. He sat watching the gentle lowland hills turn into mountains with angry stone faces, wishing he'd had chance to telephone Susannah and tell her what he was doing.

He would do so when he arrived in Inverness, and by then she would be glad to tell him the name of the Patersons' estate so he could warn Gregory he was in danger. But Mrs Finch had had no news for him about Mrs Paterson's whereabouts. She had tightly informed him he had overstayed his booking, and he'd apologised and asked to extend it further; crossing his fingers that it was the truth, he promised to pay extra upon his return, and hung up, relieved his belongings wouldn't be put out into the street, at least.

Without a car to travel beyond the city, he had booked into a hotel and spent the next few days fruitlessly searching maps and asking questions, sure a family as wealthy as the Patersons would have been easy to trace. But his questions were met with blank stares and shrugs, until finally, on Friday afternoon, one of his fellow guests asked if he'd tried the library.

'I doubt if anyone's written about them.' Adam frowned. 'But I'll try anything.'

'Well no, but if you're looking for an aristocratic family, *Burke's Peerage* ought to be of some help.'

Feeling foolish for not thinking of it himself, Adam went to the library first thing on Saturday morning, where a skim through their copy of *Burke's Peerage* also yielded nothing. It was only then that he sat back, a horrible feeling clawing at his gut. He thought carefully over everything Susannah had told him, and resolutely pushed away the image of her tear-streaked face every time it distracted him.

Without that, the story began to sound suspiciously overblown. Had he really been taken in by

363

a few manufactured tears and a pretty face? Adam thumped the library table, and was answered with glares and hushing noises. He left, not bothering to replace the book, and found himself out on the road and finally accepting the truth, determined to find out exactly who Susannah Paterson really was, and why she had targeted him with her vicious scheme. As for what he'd do when he found her, that would be something to occupy him on the long train ride back to Bristol to collect his car.

★ ★ ★

Sandy Cove

A knock at his door broke into his thoughts, and he snatched it open. '*What?*'

Mrs Finch shrank back. 'Sorry to disturb you, Mr Coleridge.'

'No, I'm sorry.' Adam took a deep breath. 'Do you happen to know yet, where Mrs Paterson went?'

'Back to Edinburgh, so she said.' She peered past him at the open suitcase. 'Are you definitely checking out this time?'

Edinburgh indeed! 'I have to return to Bristol,' he said regretfully. 'I've enjoyed my stay very much. Thank you for accommodating the extra days.'

'Dreadful business about your goddaughter. Do pass on my sympathies, and I hope she gets well soon.'

'My ...' Adam's heart slipped. 'Fiona or Bertie?' Had Fiona been hurt at the lifeboat station?

'Miss Roberta. Of course, you went off last Sunday, didn't you? Well that was when it happened. It was in all the local papers, but I reckon you've not —'

'When *what* happened?' She'd only been in that one race, he was sure of it. 'Mrs Finch?'

'I thought someone would have told you. She had a nasty accident on her way home Sunday night. They do say she had to have one of her legs taken off.'

Adam's vision darkened and he had to force himself to breathe slowly. 'Thank you,' he managed. 'Is she in the hospital at Bude?'

'She was, but I believe she went home yesterday. I met that nice farm boy she's courting, one of the Nancarrow boys. I can never work out which one it is. He told me.'

Adam looked back at his half-packed case. 'I might need to stay awhile, after all, if that's all right. I must go and see her.'

Mrs Finch nodded. 'I'll keep your room for you, just in case.'

Adam pulled his car to a slithering halt outside the doors of Fox Bay Hotel. It was a peculiar feeling to be here; warm memories mixed with something entirely new, something he wasn't yet ready to think about. He knew he should find Helen and try to explain everything, but Bertie was all that mattered for now — if he were even allowed to see her. He passed through the revolving doors, and was immediately assailed by the smells he recognised so well; polish, flowers, cigar smoke ... and the sounds too: talk and laughter, the occasional bark of an order to a bell boy, the metallic ding of the bell summoning the receptionist. It was Sunday again, a whole week since he'd left for Scotland, and he'd returned with more questions than answers, but they could wait.

He crossed to the desk, glad to see a familiar face. 'Martin! You're still here. And in charge now, I see.'

Martin Berry looked up, and his face split into a smile. 'Good lord, Mr Coleridge! It's been a long time.'

'Certainly has. Look, I've only just heard about young Bertie. Would I be able to see her?'

Helen had clearly not been trumpeting the family's private business around the staff, thank goodness, because Martin nodded.

'I'm sure she'd like that; she doesn't get many visitors. She's in the private sitting room. You remember where that is, I take it?'

'Of course. Thank you.'

It felt strange, and sad, to be walking towards that room. The last time he'd been in there Harry had still been alive, and they had sat there with their drinks, companionably discussing Blue Ensign and how Harry had worked out, over the past few days, that he could afford to invest after all. Adam remembered their self-congratulations and the way they'd toasted their success. It was a blessing there'd been no way of knowing what would come of it.

He was halfway across the lobby when the sitting room door opened and a blonde woman with a head full of curls escaping their pins came out, pulling the door gently closed behind her. From the way she did it, it was obvious the occupant of the room was sleeping, and Adam stopped. Perhaps he should go and find Helen first, after all. The woman, perhaps a nurse, although she wasn't wearing a uniform, was going towards the stairs, but had met someone coming down; Adam barely recognised little Fiona, so grown up now, older than Bertie had been when they'd all moved down from Bristol, and his heart turned over. They'd all been so close, once.

Fiona continued down after a short conversation, and the nurse turned to call something after her. Adam's forehead tightened, and he stared harder. Susannah? He instinctively shied back so he was masked by a group of new arrivals clustered around their luggage, and watched the nurse run lightly up the stairs. There was no doubt, even at this distance, that it was her; her hand drifted just above the stair rail without touching it, and she shook her hair back from her face as she rounded the corner at a walk, as if bracing herself for the next set of stairs.

Adam returned to the reception desk, on legs that felt like wooden stakes. 'Martin?'

Martin held up one finger, without looking at him, and finished serving his guest, while Adam fidgeted with impatience and increasing nervousness. He kept looking around, certain someone would see and recognise him. Finally, Martin came over. 'Sorry about that. What can I do for you?'

'That woman who's helping Bertie. The nurse, I assume?'

'Mrs Marshall, you mean?'

Another lie to add to the list, whether it was

367

himself or the Foxes she was lying to. 'That'll be her. I'm sure I've seen her before, is she local?'

'No, but she's been coming here as a guest for years. You might be remembering her from when you came here before.'

'Perhaps. Where is she from?'

'Somewhere in Wales.' Martin pulled his ledger closer and flipped back several pages. 'Here we are, look. Yes, Mountain Ash.'

'Oh, of course! I remember her accent now.' His own lie came smoothly. 'I didn't know she was a nurse, though.'

'Used to be, in the war.' Martin replaced the book. 'She's such a good friend of the Foxes, I tend to forget she's not family. She helps out whenever she can too, so she's the perfect choice to care for young Miss Fox.'

'She sounds like a charming lady.'

'Oh, yes. Leah's lovely.' Martin smiled. 'And pretty too.' He winked. Adam winked back, feeling like a bad actor overplaying his moment on the stage. His grin, he felt, was equally foolish.

'Right, well I think Bertie's actually sleeping,' he said, 'so I'll come back later.'

'Would you like me to tell Mrs Fox you called?'

Adam pretended to think. 'No, let's leave it as a surprise for now.'

Outside, he took a deep breath of the damp air and closed his eyes. *Leah Marshall. Mountain Ash.* At least he had somewhere to start.

His discussion with Helen could wait one more day.

★ ★ ★

368

Late on Sunday evening Bertie eyed the curtain that separated her bed from the rest of the sitting room, with a certain resignation. There seemed no point in staying up, everyone had their own business to see to; summertime at Fox Bay meant long warm nights, though the rain had driven people indoors, and there were gatherings and small parties, and dancing in the lounge until the small hours.

Listening hard, Bertie picked out the familiar riffs favoured by Billy Lang and the Pure Blues, and was instantly taken back to her birthday party, when everything had been wonderful and simple, and she had been able to dance . . . when her friends and family had looked at her with affection and admiration instead of pity and uncertainty. Her breath caught, and she bit the back of her hand to stop the sob breaking free. If it did she might never stop.

After a few minutes she was able to think clearly again. She looked out of the window to see the light rain had stopped, and the pills Leah had given her for the pain were taking effect; why should she shut the world away and crawl beneath the sheets, only to make another hopeless day come all the more quickly? Her mind made up, she shuffled forward on the sofa and grasped the arms of her wheelchair. Where was Leah? She was supposed to be here to help, not run away the moment she thought she wasn't needed.

She checked the brake was engaged on the chair, and, with some effort, she managed to half hop, half drag herself across until she was once more sitting in the cane-backed monstrosity. She wheeled herself towards the door, only for it to open when she was halfway there.

'Bertie! Where are you going?' Leah put down the freshly laundered pyjamas she was carrying and came over to her. 'I was about to help you get ready for bed.'

'Why?' Bertie demanded. 'I didn't say I wanted to go to bed, did I?'

'Well no, but —'

'But what else is there for me to do?' Bertie finished for her, her voice bitter.

'I was going to say you look tired,' Leah said gently. 'It's been a difficult time, your first full day back at home.'

'And I want to enjoy it.'

'Of course.' Leah raised her hands. 'Where will you go? Just so I can tell your mum if she asks,' she hurried on, as if braced for a barrage of abuse. Bertie's throat thickened; was she really behaving so terribly? Even if she was, she reminded herself, Leah had behaved much worse.

'Just out for a breath of fresh air,' she said. 'I don't need help, thank you.'

'Bertie, listen to me,' Leah said, perching on the arm of the sofa 'I don't want to make you feel as if you're not capable, but your mother has hired me as your nurse, and it's my job to make sure you're comfortable and not overdoing things.'

'Where's the Squirrel?'

Leah looked blank. 'The squirrel?'

'My bike.'

'Oh. Alfie Nancarrow put it back in the shed, I think.'

'Is it badly damaged?' Bertie watched Leah's

370

face, and saw the obvious question. 'I know I won't be riding it again,' she said patiently, 'I just want to see it.'

Leah nodded. 'I don't know if it's damaged or not. Let me come with you and help you with the shed door.'

'I can manage. I managed to get into this by myself, didn't I?' She smacked the arms of her wheelchair. 'No nurse required for that, apparently.'

'Hopefully no nurse required for anything, before too long,' Leah said, but the bright words didn't disguise the hurt in her eyes. 'Would you like me to ask Ben to come with you instead?'

Bertie hesitated, wanting it very much. 'He's working,' she said at length. 'He's not due a break for hours yet.'

'I'm sure he won't mind, not for you.'

'I said no!' Leah's face tightened, and she went on, more quietly, 'Look, the last thing I want is for people to feel they have to drop everything at my whim. I'm quite capable of doing this alone, thank you.'

She wheeled herself through the lobby, her face set into what she hoped was an unapproachable, expressionless mask; if anyone came over to speak to her she knew she'd disgrace herself, either by screaming at them or bursting into tears. Thankfully the door to the cloisters wasn't one of those awful revolving doors she'd struggled with yesterday, and before long she was rolling along beneath the deserted stone arches towards the shed.

It took a few minutes of reversing and careful positioning, but eventually she was able to pull open the huge door and push it wide, so the evening light spilled inside. It illuminated garden tools, a circular saw, an enormous refrigerator hooked up to a generator . . . And there, in the corner, a tarpaulin-shrouded shape that could only be the Scott Squirrel.

Bertie's hands trembled as they found the wheels of her chair again, and she rolled herself slowly across the floor. She grasped the edge of the tarpaulin and lifted it, and her breath stuck in her throat. Suddenly, from something that had previously given her heart-stopping joy, the motorcycle loomed like a hungry red animal, battle-scarred and vengeful.

She dropped the canvas, hiding its single dark eye, and spun her chair away, only to utter a breathless shriek as she saw the outline of a man in the doorway.

'Bertie?' Jowan stepped into the shed, his hands held up in a peace gesture. 'It's me. Mrs Marshall told me you were out here.'

'What do you want?'

'Just to talk. Can we? Not in here though.' He gestured to the crouching animal in the corner. 'That's not going to make you feel any better.'

'It's just a bike,' Bertie managed, but she heard the tremble in her own voice. 'It's not the first time I've fallen off one.'

'But it's the first time you've been ... altered by it,' Jowan said softly. 'Come on.'

She followed him outside, not wanting to admit, even to herself, the relief she felt when he closed and bolted the door behind them. They took the path back to the cloisters, and Bertie stopped

372

beneath one of the arches so she could look out across the grounds, and not at Jowan.

'You didn't visit once. After.'

'I know. I'm sorry.'

'Sorry?' Bertie had lashed out before she could stop herself, and punched Jowan's arm. Somewhere in the back of her mind she was thinking ahead, to when they would be falling into one another's arms, and Jowan would be calling her all those choice insults that somehow still burst with affection. But instead he moved away, massaging his forearm.

'I couldn't,' he began. 'When you woke, I was so relieved, and so happy, but then your mother had to make that decision—'

'It shouldn't have made a difference to how you felt!' Bertie's anger and dismay made it difficult to speak. 'I'm still me, Jowan!'

'I know.'

'Then why?'

'Because I thought I'd killed you!' Jowan burst out. She could hear the tears that choked him, but she couldn't think of anything to say. 'I thought, when they wheeled you away into that operating theatre, that it would be the last time I ever saw you.'

'But it —'

'And it would have been my fault. Just like Dad.' His voice was steadier now, but when she looked at his hands they were curled into fists. 'I killed my father, Bertie, and because of that stupid fight with Nicholls I could have killed you too.'

'Oh, Jo …' Bertie took his nearest hand in hers and tried to uncurl his fingers. 'You didn't kill

373

either of us. They were two stupid accidents that might have happened to anyone.'

'You rode away angry,' he said, pulling away from her, 'and that was my fault.'

'It wasn't, it was something else entirely.' Bertie closed her eyes. 'Yes, I admit I was a little bit annoyed that you were behaving like a jealous idiot, but that's not what made me leave the race-track like that.'

Jowan was silent for a long moment, then he looked down at her, and some of the strain had left his eyes. His voice was hesitant. 'Is that the truth?'

'It is.' She took his hand again, and he didn't resist. 'Is that truly why you stayed away?'

He nodded. 'I broke down into a complete mess. Mum and Uncle Alfie tried to talk to me, but I didn't listen. In my head you were already gone, and I couldn't bear it. Even when I learned you'd come through the operation, I still knew your life was changed forever, and that it was because of me.'

This time she was the one to pull away. 'Is that why you've come here tonight? Because you felt guilty?'

'Of course I felt guilty! But that's not why —'

'Did you want me to absolve you of that guilt?'

'No, I wanted you to have the chance to tell me what you thought. To throw me over if you wanted to.'

'I suppose that would let you off the hook,' Bertie agreed. 'Me giving you the push instead of you abandoning me, that's much easier on the conscience, isn't it? No one would think you were the cruel one then.'

'I wasn't thinking of my conscience!'

'And it's inevitable that we should break up. I mean, who wants a girlfriend who can't go walking or dancing with you? Who can't ride out anymore, or even climb over a fence and go for a swim?'

'Now you're being an idiot,' he said tightly. 'None of that matters to me. You're not one ounce less than what you've always been.'

'Except I am,' she snapped back. 'I can't do those things, or help you on the farm, because I'm quite a lot less than I was. I don't need anyone around me who's going to pretend everything's the same, because it's not.'

'I didn't say it would be the same,' he protested, 'but it doesn't have to be worse.'

'So says the man with two legs, and a home he can call his own!'

'Bertie —'

'Go home, Jo.' But her voice came out sad and tired, instead of angry.

When he didn't answer she looked up at him, expecting to see him staring at her in astonishment, and ready to say it again if she had to. But he was gazing out towards the deserted tennis courts, his arms folded, his face carved from stone, and she knew nothing would be resolved tonight, there was too much to talk about, too much to think about, both alone and together.

Their road had been smooth and bump-free until now; untested, they had barrelled happily along it and called it good. He had finally told her he loved her, and she believed he'd meant it, at the height of a deeply emotional time, and in

375

relief and joy that she'd woken at last.

But what about now? Would she be enough for him? Her own love for him had not lessened, it had taken so long to build that she was certain it never would, but it would change. It would have to. Her heart squeezed as she remembered last Christmas, how she'd scrambled up the ladder into the hay loft with unthinking ease; how she'd seized a handful of hay to throw over him as he followed, and how it had fallen from his hair to hers as he'd lain over her ...

'We'll talk again.' His voice broke into her vivid memories as if it were part of them, and for a moment she didn't respond.

Then, when he crouched beside her chair and took her face in his hands, she blinked her way back to the present and all its awful uncertainties.

'We'll talk,' he repeated. 'I want you to know that I love you. Truly. How you feel about me, about our future, is something only you can decide. And it's too soon yet, I know that now.'

That he had voiced her thoughts almost exactly made her want to throw her arms around him and tell him it was going to be all right, but in the back of her mind was the knowledge that, sooner or later, he was going to see her as a burden. And sooner rather than later there was also the issue of where she would be living, and that it might be miles and miles away. How would they manage then? It felt as if everything she'd known and accepted was slipping through her fingers, and it was going to take more than a hug on a summer evening to put it all right.

'We'll talk,' she agreed in a low voice. 'I promise.'

He leaned closer and pressed his lips to her forehead, and it took all her strength not to slip her fingers into his hair and draw his mouth down to hers. She settled for squeezing his fingers as he rose. 'I do love you, Jo, you know that. But —'

'Don't spoil it,' he said, and gave her the ghost of a grin. 'I'll come back in a few days, and you can tell me until you're blue in the face how you don't want me to pity you, or help you, or become your nursemaid. Then I'll tell you you're still being an idiot, that I love you, that we're definitely going to get through this, and in the end you'll agree. All right? Now get yourself indoors before you catch a chill.'

Before Bertie could respond, he pointed at her chair, then at the door, and with a smile he turned away and melted into the gathering shadows.

15

Monday morning. A full week after the verbal agreement was made, and the deposit paid, the paperwork had been drawn up; it seemed Ronald Gardner was keen to complete the transaction as soon as possible, before Mr Pagett could change his mind. Seated at her desk in the small office, Helen looked once more at the letter that had been waiting for her two days ago, when Bertie had arrived home from hospital.

Re: Fox Bay Hotel, Trethkellis, Cornwall.
Dear Mrs Fox
With reference to the agreed sale of the above-named business, the managing director of CP Holdings (the Transferee) will sign the transfer deed on the premises, on Monday 26 August 1929 at 11 am precisely.
Also present will be Mr Ronald Gardner (the Transferor) and witness James Newton LLB of Newton and Vibert Solicitors, Bude.
Signed,
J Hill, on behalf of
CP Holdings.

Helen tossed the letter back onto the desk and sat back, staring at the ceiling as if it held the answer to all her problems. Fleur would have to sign a separate document, accepting the termination of her right to remain at Fox Bay, but the rest of the family were owed nothing more than notice to quit their jobs and associated accommodation. It hurt so deeply to think about, that Helen could only skim across the surface of it: Harry's childhood home, the business Ben should have inherited, the place where they should all have been able to live out their days if they wished . . . all to be signed away in the space of a minute. And then, somehow, life would have to go on in the hotel as if nothing had changed, right up until their notice expired.

Fleur's solicitor had reassured her that they would be granted a generous length of time in which to find alternative accommodation, but she had no idea how long that would be; Pagett wouldn't wait forever, he'd want to start building soon. What if it wasn't long enough? And where would all their belongings go? With everything that had happened in the past week she hadn't been able to think about it properly, but now it was all too real, and while Ben was likely to find himself set up quite quickly, Fiona and Bertie still depended on her.

A knock at the door made her heart skitter, and she glanced at the clock, but it was too early yet for Pagett or Gardner. 'Come in.'

Martin Berry poked his head into the room. 'Mrs Fox, Mrs Marlowe is here and wishes to speak to you.'

Helen stifled a groan. Of all the times to get a visit from her sister-in-law. Their relationship had improved in the past ten years, but Kay was still Kay: judgemental, unable to resist poking her nose in, and certain she could have done everything better than Helen. This final sale would have lit a fire under her for certain, but how on earth had she found out about it?

'Thank you, Martin. Ask her to wait in the lobby.'

She closed her eyes for a minute, bracing herself for the pitying look she knew so well, and the thinly veiled assumption that it was some failure of Helen's that had led to her losing Fox Bay. But when she went into the lobby she found Kay looking anything but patronising.

'How is the poor girl?'

Helen felt shame wash over her; of course, Kay was here for Bertie. 'She's still confused some of the time,' she said, accepting the stiff embrace. 'Her pills, you know.'

'Of course.'

'Is David with you?'

'He's coming down on the later train. Can I see her?'

'In a little while. Leah, that's her nurse, said she didn't sleep much last night, so she's given her something to soothe her now. I'd rather let her sleep a little while longer.' She checked the time again. 'I have a meeting in twenty minutes, but I'll come and find you a little after that, and we'll go in together.'

Kay nodded. 'I've checked in to my usual room. I didn't expect it to be free at this time of the year.'

'Ah, yes. Room eight was recently . . . unexpectedly vacated.'

'Lucky for me,' Kay said, more brightly. 'I'll see you in a little while, then.'

She clicked her fingers for the nearest bell boy

to bring her bags, and stepped into the lift. Helen was about to return to the office when she saw Leah coming in through the door that led out to the cloisters. Perhaps she'd been sitting out there thinking about what she'd done, and how it had made everyone feel. Leah caught her gaze, and the look of unguarded regret on her face struck something in Helen. Today was momentous for all the wrong reasons, and in the deepest part of her Helen knew she did not truly believe Leah was responsible for Bertie's accident. Nor, she suspected, did Bertie herself.

'Leah, I think we should talk.'

Leah looked at her searchingly, the eyebrows above her clear grey eyes raised. Hopeful. 'All right. Where?'

'In the office would be best.'

'Let me check on Bertie, then I'll be in.'

'Good.' Helen's eyes met Leah's again, and she offered a faint smile. 'I hate that we've come to this.'

'So do I,' Leah whispered. Helen touched her arm, and then turned away, her heart growing a little lighter. Perhaps they would end this terrible day with something intact, at least. A few minutes later Martin announced another visitor, but it wasn't Leah.

'Mr Coleridge to see you, Mrs Fox. Shall I send him in?'

Helen stared at him in wordless astonishment. So many questions sprang to her lips that she couldn't utter a single one. Instead she just nodded, and stood up, pulling her blouse straight and deliberately bringing her shoulders up. She was ready, even if she didn't know what for. But the shock of discovering he'd had the audacity to come to Fox Bay was eclipsed by the actual sight of him, as he came into the office; one side of his face was puffed and purple, and there was a livid bruise across his chin, below a split and swollen lip.

'My God! What happened to you?'

'I met someone who was about as pleased to see me as you are.' He sat down, moving stiffly, lowering himself into the chair slowly and with a little grunt as he loosened his jacket buttons. Helen recognised the signs of a fight rather than an accident, but her instinctive concern still leapt to the fore and she didn't know whether to scold herself for her weakness, or be glad he hadn't managed to turn her into unfeeling stone.

'Do you need to see a doctor?'

He shook his head. 'I need to talk to you, Hels. I've got so much to tell you.'

'I've heard most of it,' she said. 'You told Simon Hill to buy up Higher Valley—'

'Not just that,' he broke in. 'Your friend, Leah.'

'Never mind, "not just that"!' Helen said, growing angry again. 'Just that, is what's lost us our home!'

'Helen, please—'

'Come in!' Helen gestured to Leah, who had appeared in the doorway and was staring at Adam in dismay. Then he twisted in his chair, and the dismay turned to horror.

'Who did this?' she breathed.

'I'll tell you, if you'll tell me why you did what you did.' Adam's eyes were hard, and a muscle

382

was jumping in his jaw. 'By the way, I liked your Scottish accent better.'

'Adam, I'm —'

'Is that your real one?'

'Yes.'

'And your own hair? God, no wonder you kept fussing with that wig, flattening it, pulling away and not letting me touch it—'

'Why does that matter?' Leah demanded, sounding defensive now. 'Just tell me what happened.'

'It matters because I want to be sure I'm finally talking to a real person. So, Leah Marshall, am I?'

'Yes.'

'But your name isn't Marshall,' Helen put in.

'Yes, it is.' Leah turned back to Adam. 'I'm so sorry about what I did. Or rather tried to do.'

'Why did you, then?'

Leah looked helplessly at Helen, who gestured impatiently for her to continue.

'We know what you're up to, see? With the farmland and all. I just wanted to . . . to tie up your company's money, to give Helen a bit of breathing space. And maybe the chance to find herself a home once they're turned out of here.'

He gave a soft, derisive laugh. 'Did you really think five hundred pounds would put a stop to a company like Hartcliffe?'

'Of course not,' Leah snapped. 'But it would have made your partners stop and think about how much of an asset you are, that you could lose the company so much money overnight.' It was her turn to laugh, but it was brittle and short. 'They would have brought things to a halt while they worked it out, questioned your motives behind recommending Higher Valley, and then you'd have been out on your ear.'

Judging from the look on Adam's battered face he hadn't even thought of that. He stared at her, then at Helen, and it seemed there was a new hurt in his eyes. 'Were you both in this together?'

'Helen knew nothing about it,' Leah said. 'If it's any consolation, she's furious with me too.'

Helen watched Adam carefully, and he did seem to relax just a tiny bit at that. Then he turned back to Leah. 'You'd ruin my life for revenge?'

'No, to earn Fox Bay a reprieve, however short. Destroying your career would have been an added incentive though.'

'But ...' Adam shook his head. 'You don't even know me.'

'Nor do I want to. I know what you did to Helen, and what you're still doing.'

'No, you don't!'

'And I'd still like to know who did that to you.' She pointed at his face.

'Why?'

'So I can write him a thank you letter,' Leah said, but Helen didn't believe that for one minute; Leah kept lifting a hand as if she wanted to touch him, then finding something else to do with it instead.

'I went to your home village,' Adam said at length. 'It's quite pretty actually, and thankfully small. I met some people who know you. The real you.'

Leah threw a quick glance at Helen, and swallowed with visible difficulty. 'And?'

384

'The nice lady cleaning up in the church after evensong told me where you lived. I met your Aunt Mary first, and then, just when I was about to leave, I met your husband.'

Helen snatched a quick breath, but Leah didn't look surprised. She just looked ill.

'That was a good story you made up,' Adam went on. 'About the posh family and the inheritance, I mean. Glynn recognised it when I told him.'

'He would,' Leah said quietly. 'It was his plan.'

'Is this Glynn your husband?' Helen demanded, but the two of them were locked in their own world now, and neither answered her.

'Yes, a good plan,' Adam said. 'Sorry it didn't work, but then it didn't work when you ran it together either, did it? Which was why he was in prison up until last week.' His smile was cold. 'So I suppose that part of your tale of woe was true, after all. Was he the one who'd collect the money, if anyone else was stupid enough to do what I did? Was he your Tommy?'

'I knew I could do it better alone!' Leah fired back. 'And if you hadn't been so . . . so gung-ho about everything, I would have been right!'

'Gung-ho, is it? To want to protect someone I cared about, from a potentially dangerous situation?'

There was a long pause.

'You cared?' Leah's voice had lost its stridency, and she touched his arm, but he shook her off.

'I didn't want you to face this Tommy person, Sus ... Leah. I was trying to help you.'

'At least you saved yourself from paying out all

385

that money,' she pointed out. 'Your partners need never know now, so your job is safe.'

'God, you have no idea —'

'So presumably Glynn did that to you then?'

'He did. But don't be too sorry for me,' he added, 'I left him with a matching set.'

'I don't doubt it. Two of a kind.' Her voice was hard. 'Why did you fight?'

'Because he's a jealous lunatic, and I wouldn't stand for being fobbed off.'

'What's your real name, Leah?' Helen asked quietly.

'It's Marshall. That's the truth.' Leah sighed, and her breath caught. 'Glynn is Daniel's brother.' Helen stared, still not sure what to believe, but Leah's expression said she was finally telling it all. 'He was arrested when we tried this same con up in Wales.'

'But you weren't?'

'No. Glynn kept my name out of it, at least. I met Daniel when he came up for the trial.' She pressed the heels of her hands to her eyes. 'We fell in love, I never lied about that, but we couldn't marry. So we told everyone we had. It was easy enough, since I had his name legally anyway.'

'You didn't meet in France, then.'

Leah shook her head. 'It was in Wales, before the war, and we went out there together. I'm so sorry I lied to you, Helen.'

'Again. Does Fleur know?'

'She knows we weren't married, because of this war memorial thing, but she doesn't know it's because I was already married to someone else. Like you, she just thought I'd lied about my

386

name. She found out that Daniel had a brother who moved away from here when he was fourteen, but never realised he was the one I was really married to. Once Glynn left Trethkellis he never came back.'

'Not even to tell his family about you?'

'They didn't part on good terms, his father was the reason he left. No one knew he was married, except Daniel, he was the only one Glynn kept in touch with. I'll tell you the whole story someday, if you'll let me.'

Helen lowered her head briefly into her hands. 'How can I trust you when you just keep on lying like this?'

'That's all of it,' Leah said. 'Except that the real reason I came here this time wasn't because of Bertie's birthday. It was because of a letter Glynn sent, telling me he was being let out of prison early. I was so scared, knowing he'd find out from Aunt Mary that Daniel and I had been together while he was in prison, I came down here the day I got the letter.'

Helen frowned. 'He's only just getting out? That's a very long sentence, for someone running a con trick. At least sixteen years.'

Leah nodded. 'Eighteen. He was sentenced to twenty. During the arrest he pushed a police officer over, and the man hit his head on a wall and died.'

Helen felt sick. 'And you worked these cons with him?'

'Sometimes. When he needed my particular talents.'

Adam made a derisive sound. 'Susannah said

she married her Glynn because he was 'exciting, and a bit dangerous', if I remember correctly. I assume you were basing that on the real thing too?'

'It wasn't nearly as awful as you think,' Leah said quietly. 'He was all those things, and yes, he was a bad influence, but . . . Oh, there's no sense trying to explain.'

'Mrs Fox?' Martin pushed open the door without knocking this time, and he flinched as all three of them jumped and turned to him with thunderous faces. 'I'm . . . I'm sorry to disturb you. Mr Gardner is here.'

Helen's heart tightened. For these few fraught minutes she'd put the sale to the back of her mind, but this was it now. The end. 'Leah, go and see if Bertie's awake and dressed, I want this meeting to take place in the sitting room, so we can all be there. Martin, please ask Mr Gardner to wait in the lounge while I find Fleur and Ben. Is Mr Pagett here yet?'

'Not yet.' Martin vanished, and Leah looked beseechingly at Helen.

'Do you forgive me?'

'Now isn't the time,' Helen said. 'Go and see to Bertie please.'

Leah looked as if she wanted to say more, but after a moment she followed Martin out into reception.

'Why's Mr Pagett coming?' Adam asked, frowning.

'Why don't you just go away? You've caused enough upset for one day. Besides, I need to lock the office while I go and look for the others.' She gestured towards the door and Adam went, but

388

as they drew close to it together, he stopped and turned, taking her gently by the shoulders.

'I can see you feel responsible for what's happened, but you shouldn't. You've held this family together despite—'

'Despite all your attempts to ruin us? How dare you patronise me!' Helen couldn't look at him. After all those years being childhood playmates, and then real friends, how could he have brought them to this low point? She sighed, too tired and distracted to continue the fight now. 'Bertie's a grown woman and I can't stop her seeing you if she wants to. But *only* if she does. I want her to be happy, but I don't want to see you here anymore after that. I wish to God Leah's plan had worked, I really do.' She stepped back and his hands dropped away. 'She's in love with you, you know. She denies it, but it's true.'

Adam looked shaken. 'I thought I loved her too,' he confessed in a low voice, 'but the lies . . .' He left the sentence unfinished, and Helen nodded.

'Then you'll understand.' She waited until he'd moved away, then locked the office door and went to bring her family together for the beginning of the end.

★ ★ ★

Leah helped Bertie into her chair. There was still a tension between them that Leah would have given anything to ease, but their friendship was as fractured as that between her and Helen. No matter what her motives had been, she had lied for years to a family that had already had its fill

389

of deceit. And those motives hadn't always been born of a desire to help either, she reminded herself; the truth about Daniel had stayed hidden because of embarrassment and shame, unworthy of a love that had been so complete and so pure. Would Helen ever have lied like that about Harry? She couldn't imagine it.

'Are you comfortable?' she asked Bertie, keeping her eyes averted so the girl would not see the redness in them.

'I'm never comfortable,' Bertie said dully. 'But it's tolerable for now, thank you.'

'Your mother is fetching the others.' Leah straightened the cushions on the chairs dotted around the room. 'Mr Gardner will be called in when Mr Pagett arrives, and the documents will be signed.'

'And our home will be gone.'

'Yes.' Leah stopped fussing. 'I tried to help, Bertie, I honestly did.'

Before Bertie could reply the door opened. Everyone knew to knock before entering, since Bertie had moved in, so they both turned in some surprise. Adam stood there, rightly looking uncertain of his welcome, and Bertie twisted back to face Leah. 'Did you invite him here?'

'No.'

'Well it looks like someone finally gave him what he's been asking for.'

'Bertie!' Leah was less shocked than saddened. 'He's your godfather, and he loves you.'

'It's because of the two of you that I'm—'

'No, it isn't,' Adam broke in mildly. 'This happened close to home, I gather, not at the track.

You and Harry both knew better than to hold on to your anger while you're riding.'

'How do you know what I know?' Bertie flared. 'You've not been part of my life!'

'Because you're just like Harry, always have been. Ben got the looks, Fi got the independence, you got everything else.' He sat on the arm of the nearest chair and his voice gentled. 'What was it, really? What caused the accident?'

Bertie's eyes swam as she looked from him to Leah. 'Jowan's dog,' she said at last. 'But if I hadn't seen the two of you I wouldn't have raced away from Bude like I did.'

'I understand that, and I'm sorry. But you can't blame Leah for this.'

There was a long silence. 'It's just . . . easier,' Bertie said at last. 'To have someone to push it onto other than myself.'

'Or the dog,' Adam said, with the hint of a smile.

Startled by his levity, Leah almost told him to hush, until she saw Bertie's lips twitch too. 'Or the dog.' Bertie dabbed at her eyes with her sleeve. 'Look, perhaps you can stay, and we'll talk later. I just want to take a quick turn around the lobby before everyone gets here. Just for a change of scenery, you know.'

Leah understood what she was doing, and she gave her a grateful look and opened the door. 'Don't be too long, everyone will be here for the meeting in a few minutes.'

Bertie nodded, and wheeled herself to the door. When the chair became wedged at an angle in the doorway Leah almost leapt to help, but Adam caught her arm and stopped her. Bertie jiggled, and freed herself, and a moment later she was gone, and Leah pushed the door closed, stopping just short of letting it latch.

'I don't want it to be difficult for her when she comes back,' she explained, seeing Adam's questioning look. 'This way she can just bump it open. Look, can we talk?'

'There's nothing to discuss,' he said curtly. All his tenderness was reserved for Bertie, it seemed, and Leah felt hopelessness welling up again.

'I'm so sorry for what Glynn did to you,' she said in a low voice.

'I told you, it was fairly even as far as fights go. Though he's learned a few nasty tricks,' he added, pressing at his jaw.

'And ... and I'm particularly sorry for telling you it was a gas attack that killed Susannah's husband.'

Adam's expression darkened, but he didn't respond and Leah bit back another useless plea. 'Well, I'd better go,' she said, her voice breaking a little. 'So should you. This is family business.'

'And we're not family, you and me, are we?'

Leah recognised the sadness in his voice. 'No. Not when it comes down to it.'

'We're a couple of lame ducks,' Adam went on. 'They've welcomed us like their own, in our different times, so when they close rank against us it's a horrible feeling.'

'It's not their fault,' Leah pointed out. 'I mean, they're far from perfect, but in both our cases we only have ourselves to blame.'

'I know. But that doesn't stop it from hurting.'

Leah nodded. 'Look, Adam, about what I did

392

to you, or tried to do.' She took a deep breath. 'It was wrong and I'm sorry.' She crossed to stand beside him and put a tentative hand on his arm, her voice softening. 'I hope they welcome you back one day.'

A faint, rueful smile crossed his face. 'You too. Perhaps when this is all over, they will. Your sins were much less than mine after all.'

'Does that mean you forgive me?'

He studied her for a long moment, and she watched his blue eyes searching her face. She saw none of the interest and attraction she'd seen in them for Susannah Paterson, so when he bent to kiss her, she was so surprised she stiffened for a moment. Then she leaned against him, responding to his kiss with relief and enthusiasm as his arms came around her. His kiss was more urgent than loving, but it awoke long-buried feelings, even more so than when he had kissed her at the racetrack. Her breathing quickened, but a second later he had pushed her away and turned to face the open doorway.

A woman stood there, and in her blurry, bemused state, Leah vaguely recognised her. Tall, quite thin, and wearing very heavy make-up . . . Of course: Helen's sister-in-law. Kay was looking at her too, but it didn't seem as if she recalled having met her before. She had a disapproving look on her face, but her tone was polite.

'Hello, Adam.'

He nodded. 'Kay.'

'Sorry if I'm disturbing you,' Kay said, sounding anything but.

Leah moved away and picked up Bertie's

sweater from the back of the chair. 'Not at all. I'm just, I'm going to . . .'

She didn't finish, instead she moved back to draw the curtain around Bertie's sleeping area, her heart still beating fast. Adam knew the whole truth now, and still he had kissed her. It had felt more like a victory than a gentle question, but still he had kissed her. And he'd have gone on doing so if that wretched woman hadn't interrupted.

A commotion in the doorway signalled Helen's arrival, along with Fleur, and then Ben pushing Bertie's chair.

'Fiona's finishing a room, she'll be down in a few minutes.' Helen belatedly saw Adam, and frowned. 'Why are you in here? I thought you only came to see Bertie.'

Kay stifled a snort, but not very successfully, and Helen turned to her. 'I'm sorry to be short with you, but this is a business meeting. We'll talk later.' She waited while Kay left, shooting a glance over her shoulder at Adam and Leah, and then she looked questioningly at Adam. 'Well?'

'I need to be here for this.'

Helen stared at him, and Leah read exasperation on her face and was expecting her own curt dismissal, but the arrival of Ronald Gardner and James Newton, his smiling solicitor who was blissfully ignorant of the tension, put a stop to any argument.

'Now,' Gardner said, 'let's get this over with, shall we?' He proffered the pen to Fleur. 'Mrs Fox, if you wouldn't mind?' He pointed to one of the documents Newton had laid out on the table. 'This is to certify you are no longer a protected

394

tenant of Fox Bay Hotel.'

Fleur snatched the pen from him, though Leah could see her hand was shaking. 'There's no need to spell it out so cruelly.' She bit her lip and looked at Helen, who shook her head in mute apology. Then she signed the document, and the solicitor witnessed it before waving it to dry the ink and sliding it into his case.

'Now for the main event,' Newton said. 'The transfer of Fox Bay Hotel from Mr Gardner to CP Holdings.'

'Mr Pagett's not here yet,' Helen said, and her voice held a note of almost desperate hope that this sale wouldn't go ahead after all.

'Pagett?' Gardner looked from her to Newton, clearly puzzled.

'What's Mr Pagett got to do with this?' He affixed his signature to the document, then passed the pen to Adam. 'Here, you may read it again if you wish, but I can assure you nothing's changed since you paid the balance this morning.'

Adam ran his eyes down the document and then bent to sign it. When he straightened again his gaze went to Helen, who was staring at him in disbelief.

'CP is Hartcliffe?' she stammered. 'You're the ones turning this place into holiday flats?'

'Not Hartcliffe, just me. And I'm —'

'Bastard!' Helen whispered the word, her face white. 'How could you?' She stepped forward, her hand drawn back, and swung it, hard.

'Wait, Helen! Please!' Adam caught her wrist, stopping her just in time from adding to his bruises. 'Let's finish everything here, and then I'll

395

explain. All right?'

Leah spared a quick look around the room: Ben's face matched Fleur's as a study in shocked bemusement, and Bertie's eyes were wide and horrified. Helen's were flashing dangerously and Ronald Gardner and his solicitor were both watching, clearly fascinated as the family drama erupted around them. Seeing Adam still holding the pen as the transfer was taken gingerly and put into Newton's briefcase, it took all Leah's self-restraint not to follow Helen's example and launch herself at him. Instead she marched to the door and pulled it open. 'Goodbye, Mr Gardner. Mr Newton.'

'Mr Newton,' Adam called after them, 'if you'd be so kind as to wait in the lounge, I might need to consult you on something else before you leave. Drinks on the house, of course.'

As soon as Leah shut the door behind them the room took on a very different air. Adam had a strange look on his face, part triumphant and part scared, and Helen still looked stunned and heartsick.

'To think I was on the verge of letting bygones be bygones,' she said in a low, furious voice. 'Did you put him up to it?' she shot at Leah.

'Of course not!'

'*I'd* started to wonder if Leah was secretly jealous of you having this place,' Bertie put in. 'Her home in Wales is tiny, she always said so.'

'I didn't put anyone up to anything,' Leah snapped. 'Tell them, Adam!'

Adam poured himself a drink from the decanter on the table, and drank it down in one gulp, pulling a face as he replaced the glass. He still looked worried about what he'd done. 'I need you all to listen, and not interrupt.' He glared at Helen as he said this, and Helen opened her mouth to retort, but Ben stopped her with a raised hand. He was looking at Adam with a frown, but with curiosity too, and he folded his arms and leaned against the desk.

'Let's hear what he has to say first.'

Helen subsided. 'Go on then.'

Adam took a deep breath and rubbed his hands together slowly; Leah recognised it as something he did when he was trying to straighten his thoughts before speaking. Her anger at Bertie's assumption of jealousy faded, as she saw how it must look to everyone, but the accusation still hurt.

'From the very beginning then,' Adam said. 'You probably already know I work for Simon Hill, at Hartcliffe. I joined as a broker back in '22, but I was accepted onto the board of directors as a junior partner a couple of years ago.'

'Good for you,' Helen said.

He gave her an exasperated look. 'Well you might not know that Guy Bannacott is a close friend of Philip Rose, who's —'

'Pagett's architect,' Helen said. 'Yes, we know. Get to the point. How long have we got?'

'I said don't interrupt,' Adam reminded her quietly. 'You have to hear how it all happened or you won't understand.' He poured himself another drink, and after a quick look at Helen he seemed to decide she needed one as well. She took it wordlessly and gestured for him to go on.

'I heard through the grapevine that Nor-

397

man Pagett was planning to buy Fox Bay, and I couldn't think of any way to stop him other than to put in a counter-offer. But I couldn't afford to better his.' He took a swig of his brandy. 'So, I told Simon that the hundred acres or so of the northernmost part of Higher Valley Farm was prime building land, that Hartcliffe should snap it up before Pagett heard about it and went after it himself. I told him to make sure Gardner knew what Hartcliffe planned to do with the land.'

'So that lowered the value of the hotel right away,' Ben mused, his eyes narrowing as he worked it all out. 'But surely Pagett would have found this out too, so he'd have pulled out anyway.'

'That's what I'd hoped, certainly, but what we didn't know yet, was that Pagett planned to convert the hotel into seaside flats for holiday makers, so a development wouldn't have hurt him in the slightest. He'd still consider it a bargain.' He looked over at Leah then, his eyes cool. 'It wasn't until I thought I might have a good return on a five-hundred-pound investment, that I had the idea of setting up a holding company within Hartcliffe, and topping Pagett's offer.'

'You suggested it first!' Leah snapped. 'I didn't ask you for a single penny!'

'You manipulated me,' he reminded her softly, and she could see real hurt in his expression. 'Oh, I'm not proud of the fact that I was taken in by you, but when I first tried to help it was genuine. I just didn't know how I could. But then you implied there would be so much more reward money, and that's when CP Holdings was born up here.' He tapped his temple. 'I got the idea from an extremely dull book I was reading at the time. I used the blackmail money as a deposit, instead of giving it to you.'

'So there was no friend in Bude.'

'No. I called in to see my business partner in Bristol, before I caught the train to Edinburgh, and made the arrangements then.'

'And what would you have done if there really had been a Tommy, and he'd turned up?' Leah wanted to know. 'Surely it would have been better to hold on to the money, just in case?'

'I had to get the offer in, and the deposit paid, while Pagett and Simon were both away. Which meant getting the money to my partner before Monday when Gardner accepted my offer. As for what I'd have done if Tommy had been there,' Adam gave her a wry smile, 'I've always been quite nifty on my feet, I'm fairly sure I'd have led him quite a dance before turning him in to the police for harassment.'

'And if he'd been armed? Adam, I told you he was a desperate man! As far as you were concerned, he might have been prepared to do anything to get that money.'

'That's neither here nor there now, is it?' Adam said mildly. 'He doesn't exist.'

'How did you set up a company so quickly?' Helen demanded, bringing the conversation back to the subject at hand. 'This all happened over a few days at the most!'

'There's no such company, not officially. Only a name on paper.

I worked with Jean . . . You'll remember her as Jeanette, Helen. Simon's sister. She was keen enough to help.'

'She always dismissed me as a hanger-on,' Helen said. 'Not one of your set, at all.'

'To be fair, you always dismissed her as a bit of a clot-head,' Adam pointed out, 'as did I. It seems she's actually an astute businesswoman underneath all that social mountaineering. Anyway, she's sent Simon off on a business trip to America, and since she's a director of Hartcliffe too, we were able to set up the company with our majority of two signatures.'

Leah's whirring mind made the connection with the telephone call Mrs Finch had overheard. 'Why would she do that though?' she asked. 'And against her own brother? What's in it for her?'

'I can answer that,' Helen said. She gave Leah a tight little smile. 'You're not the only one to have fallen for Mr Coleridge's charms, and Jeanette has known him a lot longer.' She looked back at Adam. 'This must be the longest engagement in history.'

Leah's heart tightened, then relaxed as he shook his head. 'That was over a long time ago. But we're still friends.'

'You mean she'll still do anything in the hope of earning your favour.'

'She wasn't doing it for me, Hels,' Adam said. 'She's got an eye for a good deal just the same as any of us. I promised her a cut of the reward money, to put towards setting up her own business.'

'So now the two of you have defrauded her brother.' Helen looked disgusted.

'We'd have put it back, that was always the

400

intention.'

'How?'

'I was due this lovely big pay-out, remember?' Adam shot Leah another wounded look. 'By the time I realised it was all a con trick, Jean and I had set up CPH, paid Gardner the deposit, and set this whole thing trundling along the track to where we find ourselves today.'

'With you facing prison for fraud.' Helen sighed, but her anger had clearly dissipated.

'As Mr Gardner said, I paid the balance just this morning, using Hartcliffe's money.'

'So now what happens? You'll sell to Pagett after all, I assume, to recoup your losses?'

'No. I'm not selling to anyone.'

'But if you don't pay Hartcliffe back, you'll be arrested!'

Adam put down his drink and took hold of Helen's hand, and Leah bit her lip, disturbed by the leap of jealousy she felt at the look on his face.

'All I ever wanted was to make amends,' he said softly, 'and this ... disaster, as it's turned out, was the only way I could do it. I'm giving you half of the hotel, Helen. In memory of Harry, and of the friendship the three of us shared.'

'Giving it?' Helen looked stunned. 'I . . . don't understand. How can you give me this?'

'I don't believe you.' Bertie shook her head. 'You can't have intended to do this for us, not all along. You're lying again.'

'She's right,' Ben added. 'You're only saying that now because it's all gone wrong.' But he looked both hopeful and sad at the same time and Leah recalled his high opinion of the old Adam Coleridge, the one he'd known all his life.

'Not so.' Adam's eyes were still on Helen's. 'Shall I tell you what the C and the P stand for?'

'We thought the P was Pagett, until now.'

'It's Castor and Pollux.'

The family looked at him blankly, and then at each other, and after a silent moment Leah understood. 'The Heavenly Twins,' she breathed, tears prickling at the back of her eyes. *Oh, Helen, he meant it ...*

'So, Fox Bay is half yours now,' Adam said to Helen. 'I'll get Mr Newton to draw up the paperwork as soon as you accept.' He shrugged. 'At least that means that, when the courts strip me of my assets, whoever ends up with my share can't sell it on again. Not without consulting you.'

'Can they do that to you?'

'As soon as Simon realises what I've done, he'll have the police onto me. I can't exactly blame him, but in the meantime I'll need somewhere to live. If you could bear to have me so close again,' he added.

'And you don't want anything in return for this ... gift?'

'Not a thing. Except a room. Preferably on the first floor.' He gave Helen a quick, hopeful smile. 'Does this help you to forgive me, at least?'

Helen didn't answer right away. She released her hand from his grasp and went to sit next to her mother, plucking absently at the fringe on the arm of the sofa. Leah felt the silence stretch to a point where it was just about unbearable for her, so goodness knows how it felt to Adam, awaiting absolution for a decade's worth of mistrust

402

and blame. She wanted to remind him that she had been acting from the same desire to help, and deserved the same hope of forgiveness, but she couldn't bear it if he snubbed her now.

Ben, Bertie and Fleur all remained silent, and the distant sounds of bells summoning porters, and people laughing and chattering on the other side of the door, mingled with the smell of lunch being prepared, almost drowned Leah in a wave of desperate familiarity. If she had to leave now, she would never find such friends or such a home again.

'You never answered properly, when I asked all those years ago,' Helen said at last. 'Who told the directors at Blue Ensign that the insurance was valid for the date it sailed? Have I been blaming the wrong person all this time, or was it . . . was it Harry?'

Adam sighed. 'No, it was me.'

'You do have a streak of honesty in you, then.'

'My honesty was never in question,' he said. 'Not when it comes to those I love, and I've never lied to you, Helen. Not once. I never lied to Harry, either.'

You've lied to me though, Leah thought, with a little sting of bitter realisation. But she was hardly one to complain about being deceived.

Bertie spoke up. 'What's the use in giving us this hotel, when we're going to lose it in a few months? It's worthless now, thanks to the development you set in motion.'

Helen turned to her. 'Once we sell our share it will still give us enough money to help Adam pay back Hart —'

403

'No!' Adam shook his head. 'You can't. And you won't have to sell.'

'We'd be fools to hold on to it until that build gets under way,' Helen pointed out. 'Ronald Gardner worked that out, but you don't have to be a business expert.'

'Ah, yes. The build.' Adam smiled, and this time it was his most disarming smile. The real one. His blue eyes glinted, and the dimple showed high in his cheek, and it made Leah's heart speed up just to see it. 'The thing about the land at Higher Valley is that, as it turns out, it's absolutely no good for building on at all.'

There was a stunned silence.

'What?' Helen looked as if she could barely take in any more surprises. 'No good?'

'Sadly, no.' Adam's widening smile contradicted the words. 'My fault entirely; I should have had the report drawn up first, instead of taking the farmer's word for it. Apparently only about five thousand square feet is suitable, the rest is too rocky to dig down for foundations or drainage.'

Leah shook her head. 'Who in their right mind would authorise the purchase of land if they hadn't seen the survey report?'

'Someone who trusts their partner,' Adam said, having the grace to at least look faintly guilty. 'It must have, um, slipped my mind since I enquired about it around twenty years ago. Silly, silly me.'

'You did what?'

'Harry and I were interested, in a vague way. Remember when we all went to the White City Stadium for the Olympics in the summer of '08? You were about to pop with young Bertie here.'

He shot Bertie a half-smile. 'So you might not have been paying attention, but we got, sort of, caught up in it all, Harry and I, and we looked into it back then with the half-baked idea of some kind of sports venue. Running tracks and a pool, that sort of thing. No, I confess I've always known you can't build on that land, but Simon doesn't have to know that. He's been in the business long enough to know the ups and downs. The risks. He'll sack me for incompetence, and then he'll just have to sell it on, at a loss.'

'But not as much of a loss as it appears in your books,' Helen guessed.

He nodded. 'Precisely. It's just ink on paper, Jean will be able to make it look right, across several transactions over the coming months, before our next audit.'

'But what about what you paid for the hotel? Even Jean's remarkable book-cooking skills won't cover that.' She looked at Ben and Bertie. 'I'm sorry, but if we don't want Adam to be arrested, we'll still have to move.'

'I don't mind if he's arrested,' Bertie said bluntly, and Leah saw the pain flash across Adam's face before he shook his head.

'I said no.'

Helen stood up and went to the door. 'I'll be back in just a moment.' She sounded distant, and didn't elaborate before she vanished, and those remaining turned to one another with questioning looks.

'She's had an idea,' Adam said, his eyes narrowed. 'I'd know that look anywhere.' He smiled, a crooked little smile of remembrance. 'She got that

405

same look on her face when she suggested David and I should stand guard while she scrumped apples from the Bathursts' orchard. Guess who got caught by the gardener, while she got clean away?'

Leah found herself smiling, despite everything, and Ben and Bertie were doing the same as they all no doubt pictured a grinning Helen scampering away with her dress pockets full of apples, while Adam and David were pulled up to the Bathurst house by their ears.

'I'm sorry, Uncle Adam,' Bertie said quietly, 'I shouldn't have said what I did, and I didn't mean it.'

Adam blinked, and Leah wondered if she were the only one close enough to see the brightness in his eyes. 'I understand why you did,' he said gruffly. 'I'd feel the same.'

'But I don't,' she said. 'It's just . . . we've missed you so much, and we all thought Mum was being horrible about you. Then to discover it wasn't Mum's fault at all, that she had a reason to hate you. Now I feel bad all over again for not trusting you.'

'You weren't to know all this was going on,' Leah said. 'You've had your own struggle.'

'Still.'

'I hope we can put all this behind us some day,' Adam said. His gaze slipped to Leah as he spoke, and her heart lifted. She gave a tiny nod, and was about to say something when Helen came back in, followed by a bemused-looking Guy. Fiona trailed them, hot and bothered from rushing to finish her room, and clearly upset that she'd missed everything after all.

'Right,' Helen said, and the effect of her return to her old briskness had a visible effect on them all. Ben and Bertie sat upright, Fleur too squared her shoulders, and Adam and Leah glanced at one another once more, eyebrows raised; it had the exciting and suddenly intimate feeling of a shared secret, and now Leah felt safe wrapping her fingers around his. After a moment he returned the pressure, and she allowed herself to hope that, whatever happened to Fox Bay Hotel, she and Adam might have a chance.

'Guy. I know you and Mr Rose are no longer friends,' Helen said, 'but I want you to tell me, if you can, how upset Mr Pagett was to lose the sale of Fox Bay.'

'He was angry,' Guy ventured, 'Trethkellis is growing more popular, and he wanted to be part of that. But I wouldn't say upset, exactly.'

'Good.'

Adam sighed. 'You're not going to sell it to him after—'

'No, I'm not. Guy, do you have the number for Mr Rose?'

Guy took his notebook from his pocket and found the page before passing it to her. 'Might I ask why you wish to speak to him?'

'No, you may not.' Helen turned and flashed him a grin that took the edge off her words. 'But all of you, be back here this afternoon at two o'clock. Adam, go and do what you need to do with Mr Gardner's solicitor.' She looked around at them all as no one moved. 'Chop chop, it's time for lunch.'

When everyone but the three Fox siblings had left, Bertie levered herself onto the sofa, then held out her hand to Fiona and drew her down to sit beside her.

Ben sprawled in the chair opposite; one long leg crossed over the other. 'How do you both feel about it?' he asked.

'I believe him,' Bertie said. 'You?'

'Yes.'

'What about Mum?'

Bertie considered. 'I think she's starting to forgive him.'

Fiona flung herself back against the cushions. 'Will someone please tell me what's going on? Bertie? What's Uncle Adam done? Are we moving, or not?'

'I don't know.' Bertie shook her head. 'I'm sure something good's happening, but it's turning pretty complicated!'

'Not really,' Ben said. 'Not if you think about it.'

'Go on then,' Bertie challenged him. 'You tell her.'

He cleared his throat and sat forward, linking his hands between his knees. 'Norman Pagett was buying the hotel, right?'

'I know that bit.'

'Uncle Adam heard about it, and wanted to stop it. So he got his boss to buy the farmland and *pretended* they were going to build on it. With me so far, Queen Roberta?'

'It's Fi who wants to know, Prince Charming, not me.'

'Perhaps you could take over the explanation

408

then?'

'Just get on with it.' She pretended boredom, and Ben grinned.

'He borrowed the money from —'

'Stole it,' Bertie corrected. 'From the company he works for. And now he owns the hotel, but he's giving half of it back to us.'

Fiona shook her head. 'But if he stole the money to buy it, it's not really his. He can't give it to anyone.'

'That's what Mum's gone off to sort out, I think,' Bertie said, her certainty drifting again. 'That's the bit I don't understand.' She looked over at Ben. 'Do you?'

Ben sighed and flopped back in his chair again. 'Not one bit.'

He looked so much like their father that Bertie's triumphant grin faded, and a pain rose in her heart. But at the same time it felt as if Harry Fox had melted into all three of them today: Ben's humour, and mock pomposity; Fiona's impatience to know everything, right now, and as for herself . . . She looked down at the folded and pinned trouser leg, and just for a moment she remembered only the thrill of the triumph in the race, and felt the tiny smile that finally touched her lips. Dad was still here, in this hotel, as Mum had always claimed, but he wasn't in the walls or drifting down the halls, he was in his children. And now, if Mum's plan worked, they would be able to keep him here.

16

The afternoon had cleared, leaving the leaves overhanging the southern end of the churchyard at St 'Dwinn's dripping onto the stones. Helen leaned on the wall beside the kissing gate, her chin propped on her hands, and watched them for a while, hypnotised by the steady sound. The westerly wind brushed her face, leaving it chilled and feeling fresh. *The Cornish wind favours the fisherman* ... it was a wind that had been blowing strongly for a while, and at last there was hope that she had used the buffeting to help her to grow stronger. And if Mr Pagett accepted her invitation, they'd all know for sure in just over twenty minutes.

'Helen?'

She turned to see Adam approaching, and for an instinctive second her heart skidded in her chest at the thought of confrontation, then she relaxed; he was no longer the enemy. It was a peaceful thought.

'Hello, Adam.'

'Are you going to tell me what you're hoping to do in a few minutes, about Mr Pagett?'

She shook her head. 'I'm a little bit superstitious.'

'I remember.' He smiled and leaned beside her. 'I also remember teasing you about it. Crossed knives, opened umbrellas, saluting magpies ... The list went on.'

'I stopped saluting magpies for a while,' Helen mused, 'but I've recently begun again.'

'Why the change?'

Helen shook her head and smiled. 'It doesn't matter.'

'You turned me into a magpie-greeter, you know,' he said. 'I still feel pretty stupid doing it, I usually just mumble and pretend I'm scratching my head.'

She laughed and plucked at a bit of ivy in the wall. 'Where's Leah? Have you spoken to her since our meeting this morning?'

'Yes.' He turned around, so that when he leaned back he could look at her directly. 'You've forgiven her, haven't you?'

'I think so.'

'She truly loved Daniel, you know. She was just conscious that other people might not understand. By the time she knew you well enough to come clean it didn't seem important anymore. Daniel was gone.'

'So she said. Did she ask you to put her case for her?' Helen was aware she sounded sharp, and modified her tone. 'Because I would never have judged her anyway. I just hated the lies.'

'I know,' he said softly. 'But no, she didn't ask me to speak on her behalf. Come on, you know Leah better than I do.' He shoved his hands into his pockets and squinted up at the sky. 'It's going to rain again.'

'We have to go inside now anyway,' Helen said. She straightened, ready to begin walking back, but Adam caught her arm.

'You never told me if you forgive me, either,' he

411

reminded her.

'Why do you need my forgiveness?'

'Because of what I did to you,' he said quietly. 'And at Harry's funeral, when I said you were as much to blame as me —'

'I was.'

'No. You weren't.' Adam let go of her arm. 'I was trying to shift it all onto you. It's what I always do, and I'm sorry.'

'But you were right, both of us dismissed what he was going through.'

'He fooled us both,' Adam reminded her. 'That was Harry all over.'

'I used to say he could make anyone believe anything,' Helen agreed with a sad smile. 'And that's what killed him in the end.' She drew a heavy sigh. 'I said, that same day, that I was glad you'd lost everything too.'

'And I didn't blame you for saying that.'

'The thing is, I couldn't forgive you back then, because you'd lost everything too.'

His faint smile faltered. 'I don't understand.'

'You lost it all, but you lived. You raced, and you lived. I couldn't bear to look at you, and wonder what would have happened if it had been you who'd died instead.'

Adam looked away, and she saw how taut his frame had become. Was he fighting anger, or memories? 'I would hope you'd have been a bit sad,' he said in a low, tight voice, 'even knowing it was my fault Blue Ensign took everything when it folded.'

'A bit sad?' Helen reached out to touch his shoulder, bringing him around to face her. 'Adam,

I'd have been devastated. And so would Harry.'

'But you'd have had each other. Which is how it should have been.' His eyes rested on hers, and she read old pain in the set of his brow.

'That's what I couldn't bear to wonder about.' Helen found herself voicing the realisation she'd suppressed, hiding it from everyone, including herself. 'I'd started to think that perhaps his recklessness would have eventually driven us apart, that our relationship wouldn't have been strong enough to survive losing everything, after all. And I hated myself for thinking like that, so I shut you, and those questions, away.'

'So now you have the memory of a perfect love,' he said softly. 'Would you swap that, to have Harry back again?'

Helen didn't hesitate. 'For the sake of the children, yes.'

'And for your own?'

'I can't answer that. But I don't need to, do I?'

He shook his head. 'And you truly want me back in your family again?'

'You'll do.' She smiled then, and saw him relax. 'But you have to remember we're not some magical little unit that's going to solve all your problems. We fight, we lose patience with one another, we get on each other's nerves . . .' She gave a little laugh. 'Oh yes, we certainly do that. But if you and Leah can bear to be so close to us, then by all means move in.'

'Why do you put Leah and me together like this? It was Susannah I fell for.'

'Because you're such a couple of scoundrels, you were made for each other.' She laughed as

413

he rolled his eyes. 'I'm glad we're friends again, Adam. I've missed you.'

'And I you.' Adam's own smile was back; the sweet, natural one, the one she remembered from the old days, before all this. 'I'll do my best to make sure I don't give you an excuse to hate me all over again.'

'Then stop scratching at Leah, hoping to find Susannah,' Helen said. 'Accept her for what she is, and you can keep each other from straying down any more crooked paths.'

'And what about now that Glynn is out? They're still legally married.'

Helen looked at him with sympathy. 'At least now you know about him. You'll just have to see to it that she has no reason to go back to him.'

'Or that he has no reason to come looking for her.' Adam pulled a face and touched his jaw. 'I might have fibbed about giving as good as I got.'

'I know.' Helen took his hand. 'Come on, let's see if Mr Pagett is here.'

He had arrived, and Helen showed him into the sitting room. The others had already re-assembled, and Guy took up a position by the door, chewing his knuckles and eyeing Pagett with a mixture of nervousness and dislike.

Helen nodded. 'Mr Pagett, I understand it was your intention to buy this hotel from Ronald Gardner.'

Pagett drew himself up to his full height, every inch the seasoned businessman, and took a cigar

414

from his pocket. 'It was indeed. And I feel CP Holdings acted in a very underhand manner throughout the entire proceedings.'

'It was Mr Gardner who did that,' Helen said smoothly, before Adam could snap a response. 'He was the one who accepted the higher offer without coming back to you. You can hardly blame Mr Coleridge here for showing an interest.'

'Agreed,' Pagett conceded. He flicked his lighter and played it over the end of his cigar, toasting it. 'The thing is I made the initial offer on the proviso that Mr Gardner told no one else of it, and I'm still convinced he didn't.'

'So someone else spread the word.'

'My architect, Philip Rose.' Pagett plugged the cigar into his mouth, and sent clouds of fragrant smoke drifting across the room. 'I was away on business from Friday until yesterday, and Mr Gardner knew I'd withdraw my offer if I found out, so he accepted the new one.'

'You're sure it was Mr Rose?' Helen glanced over at Guy, who in turn looked at Adam. Another piece of the puzzle slotted into place: Mr Rose had told Guy about the sale, and he was the one who'd told Adam.

'Sure enough to fire him.' Pagett waved his cigar to dismiss the subject. 'Well? I take it you have business to discuss, pertaining to the sale? Are you prepared to sell it on? Because I can tell you, much as I would like to be part of the Trethkellis landscape I won't be offering —'

'I was thinking about another transaction actually.' Helen took a deep breath. 'Have you ever thought about branching out into the leisure

415

industry, Mr Pagett?'

'Leisure?' For a moment she thought he was going to dismiss it and walk out, but his curiosity got the better of him. 'What aspect of it?'

'Specifically, golf.'

Pagett raised an eyebrow, then looked for somewhere to sit. Fiona jumped up and offered her seat and he inserted himself between Fleur and Ben. 'Go on.'

'This hotel plans to go from strength to strength under its new management,' Helen said, slipping into her smoothest hostess voice; enthusiastic but restrained. She could feel her heart skipping unevenly and hoped her desperation didn't show in her face. 'I'm sure you carried out some research before you put in your offer, and discovered that Fox Bay is well known for its . . . discerning guests. People expect the best here, and they're prepared to pay for it.'

'Yes, yes,' Pagett broke in testily. 'If you're not selling, then spare me the sales pitch!'

Helen refused to be rattled. She cast a quick glance at Adam and saw realisation cross his face. Then she looked back at Pagett, who was still puffing out clouds of smoke that Fleur had averted her face to avoid. 'The guests have access to the cliffs and the beaches, tennis courts, of course, and a rich programme of entertainment at night. What they don't have is easy access to a golf course.'

'What are you blathering about, woman? I don't build golf courses!'

'I'm not just talking about a course, I'm suggesting the development of a luxury golf retreat, just a short distance from the hotel. An exclusive

416

club, where you could charge what you liked, and most of our guests would pay it without blinking. The local residents would also be invited to use the course, naturally, but perhaps the rates could be lower for them.' Helen realised she was musing aloud, and hurried on, 'That would be up to the owner of the club of course.'

Pagett was chewing the inside of his lip, and frowning, but there was a dull flush of what might be interest spreading across his cheeks. 'And where would one find the land for this resort?'

'I know of roughly one hundred acres, close by and about to come onto the market, that would be perfect. Almost flat, but with enough dips and hollows for some fiendish natural sand bunkers, and room for a top-notch clubhouse to boot.' Helen smiled her widest smile, and hoped it looked sincere. 'No matter who buys it, we'd be doing each other a favour, and imagine if that were you, Mr Pagett? You'd still have your slice of Trethkellis, and we'd have an additional entertainment to offer our guests.'

'How close is 'close by'?'

'Part of Higher Valley Farm, recently bought for development it's true, but the new owner is prepared to sell it on to the right buyer, for the right price. You won't find a better site, *if* you were considering this growing market.'

'You can stop the salesman talk,' Pagett grunted. 'If I'm interested, I'll say so.' He fell into silence again and went back to chewing his lip. The tension in the room was creeping higher, and Helen was having trouble curbing the impulse to say something, when Pagett stood up and straightened his waistcoat. He stubbed out his cigar in the ashtray on the occasional table, and although he didn't nod, or smile, the small tilt to his head betrayed his interest.

'Who's the owner?'

'Hartcliffe Developments. Based in Bristol.'

'I know them. And I know he's on the board.' Pagett looked at Adam. 'Send the plans over, Coleridge. I'll get the land inspected, and if it suits, I'll be in touch. Send a guide price while you're at it. A sensible one. If *that* suits, well, then we'll have something to discuss.'

He offered his hand first to Adam, and then to Helen. 'Mrs Fox. I think we can work together if this pans out.'

'There's one thing,' Helen blurted, not realising she was going to do it until the words were out. 'If you go ahead with this, and if you retain ownership once the project is completed, I should very much like the clubhouse to be named for my late husband, Harry Fox. It was always his dream to build his own golf course, you see, and —'

'I don't need the details,' Pagett said brusquely. 'I'll name it as I see fit. *If* I choose to go ahead.' He stared at the ceiling for a moment. 'I'll need a new architect,' he mused. 'Know just the chap. James Fry. Heard of him?'

'Of course,' Adam said. 'He helped build the Cliffside Fort Hotel, didn't he?'

'That's the one. Reliable, if a little nit-picky.' Pagett looked around once more at the simple, elegant décor of the sitting room, and nodded his approval. 'I'd be interested in forming an alliance with Fox Bay. The reputation's a good start.' He held out his hand to Helen again. 'Good afternoon, Mrs Fox, I'll be in touch when I've seen the plans and the survey report.'

Fleur saw him to the door, and when she'd closed it behind him, she leaned on it and burst into tears. Dismayed, Helen hurried to her side, but Fleur was smiling.

'I've never been prouder,' she said, wiping her eyes on her sleeve. 'You've saved us. Harry will be beaming down at you wider than ever.'

Helen's own eyes prickled, and she hugged Fleur tightly. 'Thank you,' she murmured, drawing back. 'I was terrified I'd ruin everything.' She went to pour a drink, and on her way past Ben he caught her up in a hug of his own.

'That was brilliant, Mum.'

'You had his attention right from the words, 'pay it without blinking', I think,' Leah said. 'That was a marvellous idea, Hels.'

'And if we push the price we quote to the very limit of what Pagett will pay, it might just keep Simon off my back,' Adam added. He sat down suddenly on the sofa, as if all the strength had run out of his legs, and let his head drop into his hands. Instinct propelled Helen forwards, but Leah reached him first, and sat beside him.

'I can't believe it,' he murmured. 'Helen, you've worked a miracle.'

'It's not a certainty,' Helen cautioned, but relief was stealing through her at last. Whatever happened with the land, Fox Bay itself was safe. Adam looked up again, and held out a hand to her, and she took it and squeezed.

'I'm glad to have you back in our lives, Adam.' She looked at Leah. 'You too.' She smiled ruefully. 'Though I wouldn't blame you if you'd had enough of us.'

'More than enough,' Leah said, her own relieved smile belying her words. 'But someone's got to keep you reckless Foxes in line.'

'This calls for a celebration,' Adam declared. He picked up the decanter and pulled a face. 'This stuff is revolting. I'm sure you . . . we,' he amended, 'have something much better in the bar.'

'This is Fox Bay Hotel, Adam.' Helen smiled. 'We still have champagne! The cold bottles are in the kitchen.'

'I'll fetch it,' Leah offered, and on her way past Bertie's chair she dropped a hand onto the girl's shoulder. Helen watched Bertie's face hopefully, but it remained expressionless. Leah still had work to do there.

Soon after Leah had left, the door opened again and this time admitted Kay, who looked surprised to see everyone gathered. Helen briefly explained, and Kay beamed. 'I'm so relieved for you!' She embraced Helen, and although it was as stiff and awkward as ever, Helen felt it was at least genuine.

'Mind you,' Kay said, 'I'm not at all surprised Mr Gardner sold to Adam instead of Mr Pagett.'

'Why not?'

'Well, it will have been his wife who put him up to it. Helped him decide which way to go.'

'His wife?' Helen frowned. She looked at Adam, wondering what he'd been up to now, but he looked equally puzzled.

420

'Grace, wasn't it?' Kay said patiently. 'Remember her? Frightful blonde woman. It was a long time ago, mind. When you first moved back down.'

Helen's memory flashed back to Leah's little bit of playacting. 'Grace Gardner . . . Oh, of course! Yes, I remember her. But why would it matter to her, who her husband sold the hotel to? Why should she tell him to favour Adam, of all people?'

'Because she's clearly having an affair with him. Isn't she, Adam?' She smiled, somewhat tightly. 'A little bit risky getting into a clinch, with her husband hovering around. You separated quickly enough, but I'm not an idiot. I knew I recognised her when I saw her, but I couldn't place her at first.'

Adam still looked flummoxed, but of course he had no idea about Grace Gardner, and Helen decided it was more fun not to explain; one didn't often see Adam Coleridge lost for words.

'The thing is,' Kay went on, 'she's doomed to disappointment. Isn't she?' She directed this at Adam, who returned her gaze, unblinking.

'And why is that?' Bertie asked, sitting forward now, and looking from Kay to Adam with great interest.

Kay only smiled at her 'Never mind, it's none of my business, or yours.'

Helen sighed. Her sister-in-law was becoming tiresome now, and this was a day for celebration. 'Kay, the woman you saw nine years ago, and again today, isn't Grace Gardner,' she said. 'In fact, I don't believe Mr Gardner is even married. I've certainly never met his wife if he is. That woman

421

is my friend Leah, who was just a bit fed up with the way you were treating the young man who is now my reception supervisor. She was playing a little joke, that's all.'

'A joke?' Kay's mouth formed a thin, hard line. 'I see. Oh, *how* you must have laughed.'

'It wasn't like that —'

'Is *she* married?'

'She's a widow.' Helen didn't see any point in explaining Leah's situation, and certainly none in giving Kay any ammunition against her. Besides, Kay had little room to talk when it came to extra-marital affairs.

'Adam is single, now he's seen sense and dropped that silly little socialite.' Kay shrugged. 'So why the secrecy, Adam? You were very quick to push your friend away when I caught you, that doesn't look like the act of a man in love.'

'No one wishes to be caught embracing in public,' Adam said blandly. 'Of course I wouldn't want Leah to have been embarrassed in that way.'

'Quite!' Helen glared at her sister-in-law. 'If Adam and Leah want to be together, I'm very happy for them. Now, are you going to join the celebration, or just stand there trying to drive a wedge between us?'

The way Kay looked at Adam, and his casual refusal to rise to her accusations, made Helen wonder how close the two of them had been in the past. There was something there . . . Abruptly she recalled Kay's declaration that one of her lovers had been at home convalescing before returning to the Front, and her eyes widened a fraction. She might have to ask Adam about that, when all this was over.

'Are you staying?' she asked Kay now. 'You came to see Bertie, after all.'

'I'll certainly spend some time with her, but I'll be leaving first thing.'

'Oh, do stay, whoever you are,' Leah said, appearing in the doorway with Guy, who carried a champagne bucket and two bottles. She gave Kay a wicked grin. 'Hello again, Mrs Marlowe. I understand it's your turn for room eight. I do hope you find it prepared to your liking.'

'I've heard the good news,' Guy said, cutting across Kay's biting reply, and he offered his hand to Adam. 'I'm very glad to be working for you, Mr Coleridge.'

'Likewise. And let's not forget it's largely down to you and Philip Rose.'

'A toast, to us all,' Fleur said, pressing Guy's arm and giving him a sympathetic smile. 'Adam, you should propose it.'

'I'll be happy to.'

A few minutes later they all stood with a glass of champagne in their hands ready to toast the new era of management and ownership at Fox Bay Hotel. Leah had moved to stand next to Adam and now he put one arm around her and drew her close against his side. Helen was glad for her two closest friends, though she felt a little empty as she recalled the warmth of Harry's hand at her own waist. She fleetingly wondered if she would ever know such a love again. Then she lifted her gaze to see Adam looking directly at her, a half-smile on his face.

He raised his glass. '*Vulpes latebram suam defendit*,' he said softly, deliberately, his eyes steady on hers. 'To Helen.'

Acknowledgements

I would very much like to give my particular thanks to those wonderful people who have generously given me their time and their help.

The RNLI, for their offer of help with research, as well as for their tireless and selfless devotion to *Saving Lives at Sea*. They will be called upon much more for book two, and I look forward to learning all they have to share about the service in the 1930s.

The management and staff at Burgh Island Hotel, Bigbury-on-Sea, Devon, for allowing me to take my notebook into their beautiful establishment and make copious notes on the furnishings and facilities there. They were kindness itself, and the hotel is a stunning example of Art Deco glamour.

Alison Morton, author of *The Roma Nova* series of Historical thrillers, for the Latin translation I have used for the Fox family's motto; and Rebecca Colley-Jones by way of Louise Mutley, for the Welsh translation of the traditional Magpie salute.

Professor Angela Smith, lecturer at the University of Sunderland, for her information on the workings and the legalities of First World War widows' pensions. And for her offer of further help should it be needed – I suspect it will!

As always, my thanks to my agent Kate Nash, and to Eleanor Russell, my editor at Piatkus, for their patience when I've been the needy little writer, and their skills and advice during the creation of this brand new series.

Finally, my thanks to my amazingly supportive readers, who are always at the heart of everything I do.

We do hope that you have enjoyed
reading this large print book.

Did you know that all of our titles
are available for purchase?

We publish a wide range of high
quality large print books including:
Romances, Mysteries, Classics
General Fiction
Non Fiction and Westerns

Special interest titles available in
large print are:
The Little Oxford Dictionary
Music Book, Song Book
Hymn Book, Service Book

Also available from us courtesy of
Oxford University Press:
Young Readers' Dictionary
(large print edition)
Young Readers' Thesaurus
(large print edition)

For further information or a free
brochure, please contact us at:
Ulverscroft Large Print Books Ltd.,
The Green, Bradgate Road, Anstey,
Leicester, LE7 7FU, England.
Tel: (00 44) 0116 236 4325
Fax: (00 44) 0116 234 0205

Other titles published by Ulverscroft:

PENHALIGON'S GIFT

Terri Nixon

Cornwall, 1911. Freya Penhaligon is eagerly awaiting the return of her beau, the historian Tristan MacKenzie, but the surprise arrival of her mother on the same coach brings uneasiness and suspicion to more than the Penhaligon family. When Tristan proposes to Freya it feels like the beginning of a new life, but not all his family are pleased with the news, and Freya finds herself viewed with hostility and mistrust.

When Freya finally discovers the truth behind Isabel's return, it shakes her to the core. Life in Caernoweth is on the cusp of change, but can she embrace what lies in store?